FATALIS

Also by Jeff Rovin

Vespers

FATALIS

Jeff Rovin

ST. MARTIN'S PRESS
NEW YORK

 For information address St. Martin's Press, 175 Fifth Avenue, New York, N.Y. 10010.

www.stmartins.com

Design by Nancy Resnick

Library of Congress Cataloging-in-Publication Data

Rovin, Jeff.
Fatalis/Jeff Rovin.—1st ed.
p. cm.
ISBN 0-312-24103-8
1. Animals, Mythical—Fiction. 2. Los Angeles (Calif.)—Fiction. I. Title.
PS3568. O8894 F3 2000
813'.54—dc21 00-025474

First Edition: May 2000

10 9 8 7 6 5 4 3 2 1

Acknowledgments

Thanks to the following facilities and individuals who unselfishly gave their time, knowledge, and experiences:

Maria Tello, an expert on all things Chumash;
Steven Michaelson, mountaineer and guide;
Lt. Nick Katzenstein of the Santa Barbara Police Department;
Pam Christian at the State Department of Fish and Game;
The Santa Barbara Department of Water Resources;
The West Hollywood District Sheriff's Station;
The City of Beverly Hills Police Department; and
The staff of the George C. Page Museum.

FATALIS

1

The bobcat moved slowly through the cool, shallow mountain stream. His stocky torso swayed easily between four heavily muscled limbs, his head slung low between powerful shoulders. The cat's large paws didn't so much rise as slide forward as he followed the westward flow of the stream.

The cat liked moving through water. Unlike the boulders and trees on either bank, water did not retain traces of the cat, odors that another predator could track to his den. Far more important than his own safety were the lives of the cats he had left behind.

When the stream finally disappeared beneath the large rocks and mossy, fallen trees of a wide ravine, the cat vaulted to the largest of the boulders. He took a moment to sniff the air. Then, with a great, surefooted leap, he set out for the hills and valleys below.

The muddy earth was cool beneath the cat's thick footpads. A stiff wind blew up along the weatherworn crags and tangled scrub of the steep mountaintop. The wind ruffled the cat's reddish-brown coat and carried smells from the distant foothills. His flesh-colored nose wrinkled from left to right as it searched for the familiar scent of a cottontail or wild turkey. Since leaving its small cave the cat had smelled nothing but damp earth, vegetation, and the distant sea.

The cat's short, black-tipped tail swayed stiffly behind it, a sign to other cats that he was hunting. Ordinarily, a rigid tail would have been sufficient to drive rival predators from the territory, both bobcats and coyotes. But tonight was different. Tonight there was hunger in the mountains. If it met another predator it might have to fight for the mountain pass.

The cat's large, rigid ears resembled tawny rose petals. Topped with short black tufts, the ears moved independently of one another as the cat listened for blats from a litter, the crack of a twig, a stone clattering down the slope—anything that might indicate the presence of prey.

But there was no sound. Since the coming of the rains, many of the smaller animals had been washed from their burrows and nests. Even the field mice were gone. Two or three would have been enough to calm his raging belly and a few more would have fed his mate and her litter.

The flooding had forced the cat to venture farther down the mountain each night, closer to bright lights and to strident, unfamiliar sounds. But at least the grass was higher here and there were deep ditches and gullies, both caused by heavy runoff from the peaks. Ground fog was also thicker because of the rains. That made it easier for the cat to hide.

As he neared a long, level patch of stone, the cat suddenly smelled something musky. He stopped and crouched down on his lean, powerful legs. His white underbelly nearly touched the ground as he settled into a springing stance. The smell rose and fell, moved from side to side, grew weaker and stronger. But it always came from the same place on the mountainside. Pinpointing the scent, the cat turned his ears in the direction of the spoor. His luminous golden eyes peered through the mist. Silently he crept forward.

And then he saw it. His prey was a shaggy creature moving at a slow, uncaring pace. The animal was slightly smaller than himself though not close enough to attack with a leap. Not yet. It would have to be stalked.

The cat ignored the loud sound coming from somewhere beyond the prey. Still crouched low, the hunter moved forward swiftly and confidently.

"Here, Ruthie!"

Heather Jackson stood in the open doorway of the small foyer shaking a half-empty box of dog biscuits. Dressed in jeans and a University of California, Santa Barbara, sweatshirt, she shivered as the uncommonly cold fall night wind stirred her long, black hair and brushed her cheek.

"Ruthie, Please! Don't make me have to come and get you!"

The tall, twenty-seven-year-old actress and her six-year-old springer spaniel shared a large, storybook log cabin three thousand feet up in the rugged Santa Ynez Mountains north of Santa Barbara. Except for the security bars on the windows, rooftop satellite dish, electric wires strung to a pole high up the hill, and an attached garage—some mornings it was just too cold to go outside, and lately it had rained every damn day—except for all that, the cabin was straight from a fairy tale. There was a glorious vegetable garden, hardwood floors nearly half-a-century old, a stone fireplace in every room, and an epic view of cliffs, valleys, and ocean that stretched clear out to the Channel Islands. Even on dreary La Niña–bad nights like this, the thick rolling clouds that covered the mountaintops were spectacular.

Heather stopped shaking the box and listened. The only sounds were the rustling of the two-foot-high blackberry hedges that lined the short stone walkway and the muted *ruff*s and *snort*s of the spaniel. The little barks were coming from somewhere beyond the driveway, past the white glow of a spotlight mounted above the front door.

Ruthie never went far but Heather didn't want to go out looking for the dog. She was exhausted. And since La Niña had spent the last week slamming the Southern California coast, dog-fetching meant getting a flashlight to pick through the heavy fog, pulling on boots to slog through the mud, and wearing a heavy coat and gloves to deal with the wind-whipped cold.

Not that Heather blamed Ruthie for blowing her off. They'd moved here three months before, from a tiny Tarzana rental. A hit series and a mortgage were wonderful new experiences for the young woman. And for Ruthie, instead of the same old same old—running back and forth on a fenced-in sixth-of-an-acre, barking at dogs she never got to see, napping, and napping some more—the dog now spent the day chasing scavengers from the compost heap and exploring her little corner of several thousand wild acres.

"Ruthie, *please!*" Heather implored. "I can't let you stay outside, it's too cold!"

Something crunched at the end of the long gravel driveway, just beyond the edge of the spotlight. Heather's spirits perked.

"Come on, Ruthie! Come on, girl!"

The crunching stopped.

Heather gave the box of biscuits another shake. "Come on, La Roo, be nice to Mommy. She's got an early call tomorrow."

A moment later the crunching started again. Heather watched for the familiar hangdog eyes, the droopy smile, and the white-and-brown coat which often came home tangled with burrs.

After a few seconds Ruthie strutted into the spotlight as if she were the star. Her tail wagged in big, sweeping strokes and her license jangled like a diamond from her flea-and-tick collar.

"There's my girl!" Heather said sweetly.

Ruthie didn't hurry and Heather didn't take that personally. The days of being greeted with puppylike leaps and yips were long gone. They'd been replaced with a dignified saunter and a perfunctory kiss-before-biscuiting.

But that was okay. Ruthie still cuddled close to her at night and was more honestly affectionate than any man Heather had ever known.

Ruthie was on the walkway, just a few feet from the door, when the tan streak shot over the hedges. The bobcat landed less than a yard behind her, turned ninety degrees without stopping, and charged the dog.

Heather screamed when she saw the animal. As Ruthie turned to see what was behind her, Heather threw the box of biscuits at the predator. The carton struck his head and caused him to break his stride. Taking a long step out, Heather grabbed the spaniel by the tail and pulled her back. Ruthie barked but Heather got the dog inside and threw her shoulder against the door.

The bobcat hit the door before the latch caught. The impact bumped Heather back and opened the door a crack. The bobcat pushed its muzzle and right forefoot through the opening before Heather could close it. Releasing the dog, she threw both hands and her full weight against the door. Growling and turning her head this way and that, the spaniel tried to bite the bobcat.

"No, Ruthie!" Heather cried.

The door jumped and shuddered as the cat clawed at the spaniel. Heather kicked awkwardly at Ruthie, who continued to snap at the attacker.

"Ruthie, go away! Now!"

Suddenly, the bobcat's leg and muzzle pulled back so quickly they seemed to vanish. The door slammed shut and Heather stumbled against it. The latch clicked. Acting quickly, the young woman threw the deadbolt, pushed herself off the door, and stood back. She was panting, her heart slapping against her ribs.

"We did it," she muttered breathlessly.

Ruthie continued to bark.

"It's okay, Roo," Heather said, only half believing it.

Ruthie stopped barking and Heather listened. The silence seemed thicker than before, perhaps because of all the snarling and hissing that had just gone on. Heather didn't know and she didn't care. She stepped over to the window on the side of the foyer, looked out, saw nothing.

As soon as Heather calmed down a little she'd call the Santa Barbara sheriff's department, ask someone to come up and have a look around. Heather had never even seen a bobcat in the hills and was afraid that this one might be rabid. She had visions of being told that she'd have to ring her mountain retreat with leghold traps, poisoned meat, and barbed wire.

End of fairy tale. Next stop: Brentwood.

Heather walked over to where Ruthie was standing, sniffing the air. The dog's tail had drooped and she was shaking. The young woman picked Ruthie up and kissed her nose.

"You can stop now," Heather said. "You won. The cat's gone. Let's just call the sheriff and go to bed."

Cradling the dog under her chin, Heather shut the outside light and headed up the dark staircase to the bedroom. She put the dog on the bed while she went to the phone on the nightstand.

Ruthie hopped off the covers and slid beneath the bed.

She was still trembling.

It was as though the fast-moving clouds had snagged and torn on the sharp mountaintops. Thick beads of rain fell suddenly, pelting the sandstone crags and beating down the wildflowers and ferns that covered the higher slopes. Rushing water cut deeper into the gullies, washing dirt from the underlying shale and spilling it onto the ridges below.

The rain also pounded the homes scattered through the high foothills. It drummed on rooftops, windows, and decks. It flooded storm drains and garages and uprooted plants.

At one house the rain slashed through the low hedges and dissolved a small, discarded cardboard box that lay beside them. The downpour ate away dog biscuits that were inside the box and washed them toward the house. There, the crumbs mixed with ruddy streams that were swirling off the stone walk, running down the front door, and dripping from the windowsill.

Streams of blood, all that remained of a bobcat on its final hunt.

2

Jim Grand was having trouble sleeping. Again.

Wearing white boxer shorts and lying on a twin bed tucked in a corner of the bedroom, Grand stared up with his arm thrown behind his head. Rain pelted the roof and a streetlight threw gray, watery shadows on the ceiling.

Grand's black Labrador retriever, Fluffy—Rebecca's joke name for the sleek-haired monster—was flopped across the foot of the bed. The dog's legs were pointed toward Grand, his head half off the far corner of the bed. The Chumash had always said that animals were better suited to this world than we were. Fluffy was certainly evidence of that. He was breathing easily, occasionally *woofing* softly from somewhere in dog dreamland.

As Grand watched patterns on the ceiling melt one into the other, he couldn't help but think of happier shadows. The ones he lost when Rebecca died nine months before. Those were the reason he was still awake. He thought of Rebecca at their small home, where they hardly ever were because they were always doing things and going places. On her boat, in their plane, across a restaurant table at the god-awful Chris's Crinkles—she loved the fries, the more burnt the better—at the movies, or beside him in the car on a long weekend, a map in her lap and no destination in mind. Whatever they were doing she was as curious and outgoing and *fun* as the day he met her.

This isn't good, he told himself. Grand's eyes grew damp. He had to stop this and get to sleep.

The ancient Thules of Alaska believed that spirits existed by feeding on belief and that turning away made them go away. Grand forced himself to think about something else. Like the newly uncovered cave he was going to explore above Arrowhead Springs. Or a student he hadn't thought of in years.

Anything.

But it was night, and because it was dark and quiet his mind went where it wanted to go. Whichever way Grand tried to go his thoughts always cycled back to Rebecca. How the *hell* could he not? The first time Grand spoke to her, that cold day on the beach near Stearns Wharf—when he was gathering shells to make prehistoric utensils and she was bagging kelp for research—he knew they'd be together forever. She was just so happy, bright, and self-effacing.

Except when someone screwed with her fish, he thought with a smile.

Like the evening she confronted the oceanographer whose deep-sea research with bright lights was blinding shrimp. She threatened to burn his house down if she found one more shrimp with chalky-white eyes and degraded photopigments. Grand was the one with the massive rock-climbing biceps and chest but Rebecca was the scary one when enraged.

And then the smile vanished as quickly as it had appeared, and the emptiness and tears returned.

Grand turned to his left and looked at the clock on the nightstand. It was nearly one-thirty. He had spent over two hours jumping from one thought to the next. This was going nowhere.

Throwing off the top sheet, the thirty-five-year-old paleoanthropologist sat on the edge of the bed and stared at nothing. Fluffy lifted his large head and looked back.

"It's okay," Grand said softly.

Fluffy continued to look at him.

"Go back to sleep."

At the word "sleep," Fluffy put his head down. He knew the drill.

Grand had hoped that things would start changing when he brought this house on Kent Place nearly six months before. A quiet, dead-end street in Goleta, west of Santa Barbara. A different environment. That should have created new dynamics, helped keep Rebecca in his heart and memory.

He was wrong. Grand desperately missed the house on Shoreline

Drive, a sunny Mediterranean his wife had picked out for them and decorated. He'd never had trouble sleeping with her beside him. Though he and Rebecca had a king-size bed, they always ended up in a less-than-twin-size space somewhere around the middle. She loved being rocked by him and lullabied by the nearby sound of the surf. If anything, moving here had left him feeling another degree removed from her and he missed her even more strongly. He could still feel her nakedness and warmth in his empty arms—

Stop it.

He put his strong, calloused hands on his scarred knees. He needed to be rested and clearheaded when he went back into the cave, and sitting here thinking wasn't going to help. Maybe if he weren't in bed where Rebecca's absence was so keenly felt. Maybe then he could sleep.

You weren't there for her—

Grand pushed himself up and walked into the short corridor with its framed degrees and photographs on the wall, all of them crooked and dusty. The hall ended in a small living room where there were three walls of bookcases, their shelves overstuffed with books, research videos, and artifacts from thirteen years of digs. The front door and windows were behind two of the bookcases. Against the fourth wall was a gunmetal desk he'd taken from the university, a stationary bicycle, a brass floor lamp, a nineteen-inch television, and a secondhand sofa. Everything but the bicycle and lamp was stacked with folders and cardboard boxes. Between the desk and the TV was the door to the kitchen. Beyond the kitchen was the bathroom and his den workshop.

Grand turned on the lamp. He wasn't hungry and he didn't feel like going into the workshop or drawing a bath and reading. That left the desk, so he walked over and sat down. But he also didn't feel like editing his paper on the Ice Age caves he'd explored three months before in Greenland or logging on and debating human origins with some armchair academic. So he just stared at his dour reflection in the dark computer screen.

Grand's deepset blue eyes were dark and his wavy black hair could use a trim. He also hadn't shaved in two days. He used to shave every day. The chin was still strong but the long jawline had no meat on it. His face looked thin. Or maybe it only seemed thin because the rest of him was so healthy-looking from all the hiking, climbing, and spelunking he did. It was strange. Hammer the body and it became stronger. Hammer the soul and it grew numb.

Grand shook his head as his eyes drifted from the monitor to the small framed photo on the left, beside the phone.

The picture was of Grand and Rebecca on her sailboat *Kipper Skipper.* He smiled broadly. That had been a perfect day. Great wind but smooth seas, a lot of laughs, and a total surprise when he went into the cooler and came back with tuna sandwiches, iced tea, and a diamond engagement ring. It was one of two occasions he'd seen his stoic little New England Yankee cry with happiness. The second time was when he got a three-year grant from the National Science Foundation to explore and map the more remote Chumash caves in the high Santa Ynez Mountains. Even though Rebecca's own funding at the National Oceanic and Atmospheric Administration had been gutted and her own job was in jeopardy, she couldn't stop hugging him when he got the news. She knew how desperately he wanted to get out of the classroom more and into the field.

Grand felt tears behind his eyes and looked away from the photograph. It was strange. Part of him didn't want to lose the pain, as though by losing it he would also lose the love he still felt for Rebecca. It was a passion he continued to feel, the only one he could express. But he also knew that he needed to let it go. Tears were draining enough during the day. At night they kept him awake, filled his dreams, and left him unrested in the morning.

Grand slid the computer keyboard to the right, then folded his arms on the desk beside the photograph. He lay his head down, shut his eyes, and listened to the rain.

"I'm sorry that you have to see me like this," he said softly, thinking of the photograph. If Rebecca *were* spirit, he wondered what she thought about his suffering. Probably sadness. And what about the little things she'd never have seen when she was alive? Everything from buying products from companies she was boycotting to letting fingernail clippings fly across the room and stay there.

That last, at least, brought him a little smile. If spirits could go *ecch,* she did that for certain.

The downpour caused him to think about the cave and the conditions he'd find in the morning. The mossy rocks on the cliff would be slippery, there might be flash floods from captured rainwater, and rock slides both inside and out were a real possibility. But Grand wasn't worried about that. The danger had always been part of the appeal.

Besides, what was the worst that could happen? He'd be trapped down there and preserved and discovered by some other anthropologist in a few thousand years.

Big deal, he thought. He'd end his own suffering and he'd make headlines as the Brooding Mountain Man. They'd try to figure out his life and habits from the clothes he wore and the tools he carried. They'd open his stomach and pick between his teeth and try to learn something about his diet. They'd study the fillings in those teeth and the scars on his arms and legs and marvel on how primitive medicine was. But when they found the faded photo slipped into his shirt pocket they'd feel a kinship that spanned every age of human endeavor. They'd know that his ancient man had the capacity to love, and that he'd loved a woman named Rebecca Schuman-Grand.

Grand's tired mind was cycling again but he kept his eyes shut. And as he returned to Rebecca and thought of the picture standing beside him, he no longer felt so terribly alone. The rain turned to sea spray, the desk became a deck, and in a few minutes he was finally able to sleep. . . .

3

On most days, senior structural engineer Stan Greene and his junior partner William Roche of the California Department of Transportation, Office of Structure Maintenance and Investigations, District 7, would have enjoyed this morning's TroDA—Tertiary Road Degradation Assessment duty. Though the partners had only a rudimentary knowledge of geology, they were already on the payroll. Sending them up for preliminary analysis was less expensive than bringing in a three-hundred-dollar-an-hour UCSB geologist for an opinion. Ordinarily, walking around with a hand in his pocket, sipping coffee and poking dirt roads with toe, heel, or pick, was more fun than being suspended from a windy bridge and taking vertical angle measurements with a Laser Theodolite.

Ordinarily.

Mucking around in thirty-degree temperature at five in the morning on the top of a mountain with a cool drizzle still falling—that wasn't the forty-two-year-old Greene's idea of a fun start to the day. But hundreds of people lived high in the Santa Ynez Mountains. One of them had called the sheriff about a prowling bobcat. After investigating, the deputy had spotted a sinkhole. Greene and Roche were on call; if the only road in and out of the mountains was collapsing, they had to find out where and why and figure out how to fix it.

After getting the call from the assistant deputy district chief, Greene hurriedly dressed and went to pick up the thirty-four-year-old Roche at his foothills condominium. Greene had forgotten to bring his doxepin, the antidepressant he'd been taking since hitting forty, but he'd been feeling better the last few weeks and hoped he'd be okay. The men had driven along rain-slippery roads from Santa Barbara. They headed up Camino Cielo, the eastern approach to Painted Cave Road, following the snaking dirt road into the mountains. Painted Cave Road itself was little more than a one-vehicle path and Greene took it slowly. During storms, in the dark, branches fell from the overhanging trees and rocks dropped from the ledges, making it especially treacherous.

The men parked their Caltrans van beside the tree-lined ravine. Below them, to the north, the Ygnacio Creek went underground. Up ahead was where the sheriff's deputy had spotted the small sinkhole. They pulled on their orange ponchos, took flashlights from holders on the door, and got out. Then they went to the side of the van and retrieved their large field backpacks. The packs weighed twenty pounds each and contained a small collapsible pick/shovel combination, a digital camera, a hammer, various size pitons, flares, waterproof portable radios, a ten-foot rope ladder, and a first-aid kit.

The men turned on their flashlights and started up the steep, dark hill. To their right was the tree-lined ravine, which disappeared into the darkness. To their left was a narrow ditch at the foot of sandstone bedrock that rose almost vertically. Greene walked a few steps in front of Roche. The only sounds were the rippling creek below, the rain tapping on leaves, and their boots crunching on the wet dirt. The only living things they saw were three-to-five-inch lemony-gray banana slugs inching along the rocks and mulchy sides of the roadway.

"I was just telling the kids that when I was their age I used to play soldier up here," Roche said. "Y'know, we took away a lot of the enchantment up here with all the paving we've been doing. When we were kids it was all manly dirt. You felt like a pioneer or a soldier behind enemy lines."

"*You* did, Bill. I was busy bringing girls up here to make out."

"When you were eight?"

"When I was eight."

"Man. No wonder you're burned out now. Gave the Chumash spirits all your life essence. Me? I used to borrow my older brother's dog tags, grab my Daisy rifle and a backpack full of provisions like jerky and Twinkies, and I'd be on a mission in Europe. I had this Clint Eastwood, *Where Eagles Dare,* thing going. Storm the mountain fortress. The scuzzier the weather, the happier—"

"Shit!" Greene stopped and shined his flashlight ahead.

Roche stopped abruptly beside him and echoed the remark. Both engineers stood staring for a long moment.

About fifteen feet in front of them the left side of the road seemed to sag in. The sides of the depression were smooth and mushy. They reminded Greene of paper towels that had been run under a faucet in a TV commercial. Torn and ragged in the center and sagging around the edges. Mist swirled from the sides as damp, cool air mixed with the warming air.

"That's a big goddamned sinkhole," Roche said. "Either that or a small volcano. You sure the deputy said it was a one-footer?"

"Yeah," Greene replied.

Greene picked up a long tree branch that was lying in the shallow ditch between the mountain and the road. He didn't take a step without first jabbing the fat end of the branch straight down into the road. Earth around a sinkhole could be like quicksand, especially if the underlying rock had collapsed. That was a definite possibility in this area. On the drive up Roche had checked California Institute of Technology geological charts using the van computer. This section of the mountains sat on a confluence of fault zones: the Mesa-Rincon Creek, Santa Ynez, Mission Ridge, Arroyo Parida, and Santa Ana. The region could be laced with fissures large and small and it wouldn't surprise Greene if the weeks of rain had tapped into one. The potential volatility of the region was one reason the United States Geological Survey and the National Science Foundation were spending millions of dollars to study it, both on the ground and by satellite. What worried Greene was how much of the road might be in danger of falling in.

The ground approaching the sinkhole was stable and it took the men less than a minute to reach the rim. The opening was about six feet across, half of it on the road and half of it in the ditch. Dirt from the road was washing in with the rain and the smell that hung above the pit was awful, like a freshly opened cesspool. Exposed roots and the edges of slablike rocks jutted from the mountain and ravine sides. The stratum beneath had obviously collapsed and the dirt had been washed into the hole. There were about four feet of road to the right where the treadmarks of the black-and-white patrol car were still visible.

"The treads are right at the edge but the driver didn't have to swerve to avoid it," Greene pointed out.

"The sinkhole's getting bigger fast," Roche said.

Greene nodded.

"I'd better set out flares," Roche said. He turned and walked up the road, to the west. There would be more traffic coming down the mountain than going up at this time of day.

Cautiously, Greene moved closer to the sinkhole. As he neared the edge the ground felt like foam rubber; it was that saturated. The engineer could hear rocks coming loose underneath, possibly pieces from other cracked sections of bedrock. With nowhere to go, rainwater would have been pushed into existing fractures of the natural roadbed, stressing and expanding them. Daily traffic destroyed the remaining structural integrity. What Greene needed to know was how much of the road was in danger of collapsing. The hole beneath the bedrock might have been an isolated one caused by centuries of runoff from the mountain to the ravine.

Greene carefully knelt and leaned over the rim. The rocks of the roadbed had cracked and fallen about three feet. They were covered with dirt that was still washing in from all four sides. Greene ran his light across the edges of fallen rock. Each slab was about four inches thick.

As he knelt there more tiny pieces became dislodged and fell. Greene lay on his belly to distribute his weight over a wider area. He poked his head and the flashlight into the sinkhole and looked at the sides. The hole continued to the east and west, directly under the road.

"That's just great," he said.

Roche's workboots slapped on the mud behind him. "What's wrong?"

"Don't come over," Greene said. He looked back. Light from the flares had turned the world around them a dull, flickering red. "We've got a fissure."

"A big one?"

"I can't tell," Greene said. "Set out the rest of the flares, then call

Chelmow and let her know what we've found. Tell her that until we know how far the fissure follows the road, this section should be closed. I also suggest that she get a geologist up here."

"Right," Roche said. He circled the sinkhole wide, walking along the ravine among the ferns and ivy. Then he jogged back to the van.

Greene lay down again and stuck his head back in the opening. He turned to the side to try and see deeper along the fissure. As he ran his flashlight along the mountainside wall, he heard a faint echoing cry from the fissure.

"What the hell?"

Roche stopped and looked back. "Did you say something?"

Greene shushed him with his hand and listened. After a few seconds he heard the cry again, louder than before.

"Christ," Greene muttered. He sat up on his knees and quickly slipped off his backpack.

"What's wrong?" Roche shouted.

"I hear crying down there."

"You hear what?"

"Crying!"

"Like a baby?"

"No," Greene said. "Like someone might be hurt."

The engineer hoped that an early-morning jogger or a dog-walker or teenagers who'd camped out in a cave hadn't taken a tumble into the sinkhole. He hadn't seen any footprints around it, but then they wouldn't have been as deep as the tire treads. The rain might have erased them.

Greene slid his legs around so that he was sitting on the soft edge of the sinkhole.

"Whoa there! What are you doing?" Roche asked.

"Going down," Greene said.

"Stan, no."

"It's okay," Greene told him.

"Stan—"

"Listen to me," Greene said. "I don't think any more of the road is about to fall in—"

"But you don't know that."

"It'll be okay."

"Famous second-to-last words," Roche said. "They're the ones that come right before, 'Oh, fuck!' Anyway, whatever's down there may not be a 'someone.' It could be a dog or that bobcat the deputy never found."

"It could be," Greene admitted. "So?"

"If it is an animal and it's hurt—"

"I know," Greene said. "It'll be really pissed off. But it could also be somebody's kid."

"Yeah. There's that."

"I'll be careful. Give me a radio check, then set out the damn flares and call Chelmow. Stay there in case I need you to tell her anything."

"Stan—"

"Just do it, okay?"

Greene removed the two-way radio from his backpack. He slipped his hand through the strap on the waterproof carrying case, then switched it on.

"Roche to Greene."

"I read you," Greene replied. "Stay tuned."

"I'm not going anywhere," Roche said. "But I want to say one more time that I think this is a stupid idea."

"Noted," Greene said.

Armed with the radio and flashlight, he saluted his partner back at the van and slid over the side. Landing on the rocks below, Greene lost his footings as well as the flashlight.

"Stan?" Roche cried. "Are you okay?"

"I'm fine," Greene said. "I tripped."

"Damn it, this isn't what we came out here for—"

"I said I'm fine," Greene insisted. "Just give me a second to get back on my feet."

As he was pushing himself off the rocks he heard the cry again.

"Bill, did the radio pick that up?"

"Yes," Roche said. "But it sounded like the wind."

"It wasn't," Greene said. "It definitely wasn't." He wiped his hand on his pants and retrieved the flashlight. "It came from the western side of the fissure. I'm going to check it out."

The engineer turned slowly. Behind him, the roof of the fissure was only five feet high. He had to stoop in order to move inside. He was glad he wasn't claustrophobic. The mountain was just a foot to his left. It sloped toward him, forming the floor of the fissure. Two feet to the right was the inside of the ravine, with its snarl of roots, rocks, and worms.

He shined his light around. There was about seven feet of tunnel in front of him. After that it turned to the south, into the mountainside.

"Shit."

"What's wrong?" Roche asked.

"There's no one here."

"I told you," Roche said. "Now come on out. I just talked to Chelmow. She's sending a repair crew and a rock hound. They should be here in forty-five minutes."

"But I don't understand," Greene said. "I heard it."

"It was the goddamn wind—"

"And I'm telling you it wasn't!" Greene barked. He winced as bits of dirt and stone fell from the roof of the fissure, pelting his cap. He had to remember not to yell like that. Loud noises could bring down weakened pieces of roadway.

Just then, he heard the sound again.

"There it is," Greene said quietly. "It's definitely a cry. It's coming from around the turn in the fissure, just a few feet away." Crouching, Greene took small, shuffling steps toward the dark curve ahead.

"Stan, please," Roche said. "You're an engineer, not a spelunker. Wait for the damn rock hound!"

"No," Greene whispered. "I'm already down here. I'm just going in a little deeper."

It was surprisingly muggy as he moved further from the sinkhole, especially since the opening had been relatively cool. And it smelled exponentially worse inside than it did outside. On top of that, Greene's pants were wet and uncomfortable, his backside was sore from the fall, and rainwater was dripping from his poncho into the tops of his boots and soaking his socks. Windy bridges and prickling sea spray were starting to glow brighter in his memory. But there was no way he could turn his back on someone who might be injured.

Greene had the flashlight in his right hand and the silent radio in his left. He reached the opening in the mountainside and rounded the corner. He shined the light inside.

"I'll be fucked," he whispered.

"What?" Roche said.

Before Greene could answer he felt a sharp, merciless pain along his upper torso. It shot from shoulder to shoulder and from the base of his skull to the small of his back. He screamed but he couldn't breathe, so there was no sound. His hands opened up and then his arms went limp. For an instant he felt extremely heavy and then he felt nothing at all.

He was dead before the flashlight hit the floor.

Roche heard the *clunk* of the radio followed by silence. It wasn't the open silence of someone being quiet but the solid silence of a radio that was no longer broadcasting.

"Aw hell, Stan," he said to himself. "What'd you do?"

Roche was standing by the driver's seat of the van. The engine was running, the door was open, and the radio was on. Roche had poured himself coffee from a thermos and was sipping it as he stood tapping his foot anxiously and listening to his partner.

Roche informed Marcy Chelmow that Greene's portable radio had died and that he was leaving the van to investigate. He kept the portable radio in case it came back on. Then, snatching his flashlight from the passenger's seat, he jogged up the road. The hard drizzle was more relentless than before, making the road even muddier. At least it was brighter now as the sun rose behind the clouds, turning the black hills deep brown.

The engineer slowed when he neared the weakened area of the sinkhole. He called Stan's name.

There was no answer. He moved closer.

"Stan!"

He listened. There was silence. He was willing to bet that Stan had been so anxious to reach whatever was down there that he'd hit his head or else slipped and fell.

"Stan, if you can hear me, moan or bang a rock or do something," Roche shouted down.

He listened hopefully but Greene didn't respond. He was going to have to go down.

Something cracked to his left. He turned as several large rocks tumbled down the side of the mountain. He shined the beam up the mottled, moss-covered rock. He thought he saw something move on a ledge about twenty-five feet up, behind a row of ferns. Still holding the radio in case Greene tried to reach him, Roche used the back of his left hand as an extension of his baseball cap. He shielded his eyes from the rain.

Almost at once, Roche felt something strike his right side, just above the waist. It was a hard, solid blow, as though he'd been whacked with a baseball bat. The engineer lost his radio and his breath as he staggered to the left. His right arm went numb and the flashlight seemed to vanish. When he tried to breathe pain ripped through his side, as though every rib were shattered. Wincing and gasping through his teeth, he turned to the right.

In the early morning darkness all Roche could see were two pale white lights, like twin moons glowing behind a thick haze. The lights were hip-high and about two feet away. He tried to reach out to them but while he could feel his right arm he couldn't move it. His first thought was that whatever hit him had broken it. Then he looked down. He saw blood pumping onto the road. He reached over with his left hand.

The blood was coming from his shoulder. Roche's fingers moved up his side.

"Oh, no. No."

Roche couldn't find his arm. It was gone. His torso began shivering violently and his vision started to swim. Then something struck the engineer from the left. It came from above, hitting his head and snapping his neck. The back of his head hit his right shoulder blade. He died instantly.

Two glowing orbs hung above the body in the fine rain. They moved down and then away.

A moment later there was only the rain.

4

Hannah Hughes stepped from the stall shower. She was headachy and tired as she cracked the bathroom door to let out the steam. Her eyes felt bloated, her round cheeks hurt, and her temples were making a chugging sound.

The rain didn't help. Gray weather, gray mood had always been a mathematical certainty in her life, along with other certainties like super-well-groomed guy, self-absorbed guy. Jocky guy, self-absorbed guy. Guy who drank, guy who overdrank. One day she'd write a book of certainties.

The petite young woman slipped a big towel from the hook behind the door and began drying off. The founder, editor, and publisher of *The Coastal Freeway*, Hannah was tired because she'd only slept for four hours after working eighteen hours straight. Senior reporter Jimmy Taubman had been trying to finish his feature on La Niña for today's edition and junior reporter Susan Crab had spent the previous day bopping between the drizzle-soaked Montecito Trails Foundation San Ysidro Saddleback Loop Trail Run and the Semana Nautica 15K at San Marcos High School. That left only Hannah to write and edit the page-one stories and come up with the editorial. She always saved that for last; opinion pieces always had more teeth when she was tired and less inhibited.

But while Hannah wasn't quite ready to rumba, she had faith in what one of her journalism professors at Brown University used to call "the adrenaline rush of the world, the flesh, and the devil." Something would always come along to get her engine going.

Pulling on a white terrycloth robe, Hannah rubbed the steamy mirror with her sleeve, and began blow-drying her short, brown hair. As she did, she looked unhappily in the mirror.

She looked wan and tired, like the sober, tiny black-and-white photo on the "Hughes Views" editorial column. Even when she didn't look pale, Hannah hated what another college "mentor"—her then-boyfriend Jean-Michel—used to lovingly call her "angelic" look. Hannah would gladly surrender her inheritance to be a few inches taller. Nothing Amazonian, maybe five-foot-seven with strong cheekbones and dark, compelling Asiatic eyes. Instead, she had large, pure-blue, Lithuanian eyes and a round youthful face that made her seem even younger than her twenty-five years. Younger and more innocent. Whenever she interviewed men they tended to talk distractedly or with polite condescension, as though neither she nor the piece had any weight. A handful, like Sheriff Malcolm Gearhart, barely talked to her at all. What was *The Coastal Freeway,* after all, but a liberal-leaning daily giveaway, fighting for attention in a TV-and-Internet dominated world and earning over half its income from personals placed by lonely women in Ojai and horny men everywhere else. Sheriff Gearhart once said that more people picked up the paper to catch grease during lube jobs and scoop up dog poop in the street than to catch the news. He wasn't right about that, though Hannah knew that if she weren't the daughter of billionaire transportation giant Arthur Curry Hughes, many of the politicians, CEOs, and local movie bigs probably wouldn't talk to her at all. Many were closeted and not-so-closeted woman-haters.

Powerful men, closet misogynists, Hannah thought. That was another certainty.

Other members of the Santa Barbara County Women's Business Association said the same thing. Samantha Patrick bought Kevin Gold's computer store, didn't change a thing, and watched business fall off thirty percent. Caroline Bennett, owner of Bennett's Surf, said she actually lost customers when she inherited the place from her father. Same fish, same trucks but until she lowered her prices, they went elsewhere.

Interviews with women tended to go better for Hannah, not only because it was us-against-them in many cases but because it was often like talking to her mom or sister. They trusted Hannah and usually gave her terrific quotes wrapped around bare-soul confessions.

Unfortunately, not enough women were part of the Ventura–to–Santa Barbara political and business networks that made decisions—and news. Power was still a boy's club.

Hannah thought she heard her cell phone. She shut off the hair dryer. She couldn't understand why manufacturers didn't make these things quieter. Maybe they were afraid we'd think they weren't working. She'd mention it to her Friday at Home editor. Hair dryers, vacuums, and other things we didn't have to hear were too loud. Phones, car ignitions, and things we had to hear weren't loud enough. There had to be a reason why.

The phone beeped again. Hannah put the dryer down and walked into the bedroom of her beachfront condo. The glass sliders, crawling with rain, looked out onto a choppy, overcast sea. What was that, twelve gray days in a row?

Hannah looked away. Ever since she was a kid in Newport, Rhode Island, she suspected that she was the next stage in evolution. A human solar battery. That was why she'd moved to Southern California after graduating from school. Bake her with sunshine and she could run happily and productively forever. Even when she was tired. But darken the day, cool the air, force her to cover her arms and legs with fabric and she was ready to take hostages.

Hannah plucked the cell phone from the antique secretary beside the door. It was either her mother or her managing editor. She glanced at the digital clock on top of the dresser. It was nearly 7:00 A.M.; ten o'clock in Rhode Island. It couldn't be her mother. Evangeline Benn Hughes would be out on the tennis court at this hour.

"Good morning, Karen," Hannah said as she picked up a pen and pulled over a notepad from the state legislature.

"Good morning, Chief," Karen Orlando said. "Got what might be a hot one for you."

"Shoot."

"I just picked up a call from a Caltrans emergency road crew," Karen said. "A couple of engineers disappeared about an hour ago while they were checking a sinkhole up near Painted Cave. One of the crew members said he found blood on the road."

Hannah made notes. "But no trace of the engineers?"

"Zippo," Karen told her.

"What else?" Hannah asked.

"The crew guy said the sinkhole was 'fatiguing,' whatever that means," Karen went on. "Falling in, I guess. So they're going to have to dig. A second emergency crew is on the way. So is Sheriff Gearhart."

Hannah was waking up fast. With the possible exception of Caltrans, no one hated her more than Sheriff Gearhart. The prospect of getting them both to talk to her was the kind of masochistic challenge Hannah loved.

"I would've sent Jimmy to cover this," Karen said, "but he's rushing to make deadline and before calling in any stringers I figured you—"

"Absolutely," Hannah said. "Caltrans is mine." The headache, lethargy, and exhaustion were gone. "Where's the sinkhole?" Hannah asked.

"It's just east of the cave itself," Karen told her.

"Did they say what shape the road's in?"

"Route 154 and East Camino Cielo are open," Karen said, "though the area around the sinkhole is closed off for two hundred yards in both directions. You'll have to park and walk."

Hannah thought for a second. It was less than three hours before today's edition went to press. She also liked to push herself with breaking news. This was doable.

"I should be there in about a half hour," Hannah said. "Have Walter meet me at the site and tell Weezie I'll E-mail the story in. Save me two columns above the fold."

"You got it."

Hannah thanked her and hung up. She didn't bother finishing her hair. The dampness on the hill would cause it to frizz anyway. Pulling on black jeans and a *Coastal Freeway* sweatshirt, she slipped on her dog tags and then grabbed her red leather shoulder bag and dropped the cell phone inside. Her office-on-the-hoof, she called it. A high school graduation present from her mother, the bag contained two audio microcassette recorders, her nearly indispensable Palm VII electronic organizer, a no-tech notepad and pens in the event of Palm VII battery crash, and a digital camera in case Walter got a flat.

Within five minutes Hannah was in her red Blazer, listening to the radio talk between Caltrans headquarters and the crew as she tore along the damp, deserted side streets toward the mountains.

5

Thanks to three cups of coffee, two hundred pushups—using just the first three fingers of each hand to strengthen them—and eagerness to get out of the house, Jim Grand was alert as he drove to the office. *His* office. The mountains.

The terrain of the peaks in the upper Santa Ynez Mountains was extremely steep and unstable, with loose boulders, muddy slopes, and ledges made of leaf-thin layers of rock. Eroded by millennia of wind, water, and tectonic activity, the ledges crumbled easily underfoot. Caves here were often the home to bobcats and brown bears while tumbleweeds and scrub frequently concealed deep pits and crevasses. On days when the clouds were low and covered the peaks, visibility was no more than three or four feet. At night, temperatures typically fell to well below freezing. During the winter, snow and fine, clear ice made the mountains as deadly as higher, more infamous ranges. During the warmer seasons, unwary climbers often rappelled into fields that were used for turkey shoots. Smug mountaineers who saw the peaks as a warm-up for tougher challenges frequently had to be hauled out by the highly skilled members of Los Padres division of the Santa Barbara County Sheriff's Search and Rescue Team.

Jim Grand had climbed, fought, and studied the Santa Ynez Mountains for nearly seven years, ever since he'd returned to UCSB to take over the classes of his former professor Joseph Stroud Tumamait. Tumamait had abruptly left his post to found the environmental group *Hutash,* the Chumash word for earth. Grand knew the mountains well, he respected their moods, and above all he enjoyed the challenge of what Tumamait—when he still had a sense of humor—once referred to as "one of earth's most seductive and temperamental orogenous zones."

But then, the world of mountains, canyons, caves, cave paintings, and especially prehistoric civilization like the Chumash was one that Grand had loved for nearly thirty years.

Crouched on a narrow ledge in a dark, dome-topped cave, Grand was surprisingly rested. For someone who once called petrified wood a pillow, the desk hadn't been half-bad. When the alarm went off in the bedroom five hours later he was alert and ready to focus on the job at hand. He had no classes to teach until the following afternoon and, for the time being, the only ghosts he had to deal with were those of the ancients.

Grand was dressed in warm, light blue, waterproof microfleece pants and a yellow wool jacket. The jacket was cut long to keep his backside and upper legs warm, though he had removed the large, zip-away peaked hood. Grand had always preferred to go bareheaded when he was exploring a cave. If something came loose from above he wanted to hear it; small stones often fell before larger ones. And if one of those bobcats or bears came along, or if he went someplace where there were rattlesnakes, he wanted to be able to hear them too. Right now, all he heard was the hollow but delicate trickle of water spilling in from the swallow hole and dripping down the sides of the ledge.

Grand finished checking the pulley rig. It was attached to the rock at the very edge of the cave ledge, held there by a widely set series of short pitons. Grand had designed the array himself to cause as little damage as possible to a site. Slipping the lightweight harness from his duffel bag, he fastened the thick waist-wrap tightly above his slender hipbones and slid his legs through the two, two-inch-wide nylon bands. He adjusted the slider buckles, leaving the leg loops relatively loose. This would give him extra mobility and also help to avoid "rug burn." Once the harness was on, Grand attached two slender climbing ropes to the belay loop. The other ends of the two-hundred-foot nylon lines were coiled through the pulley system. He would hold one rope in each hand, using the one on the left to lower himself and the one on the right to pull himself up.

After making sure that the lines were secure and untangled, Grand lay them on the ledge and reached back into the bag. He slipped on his night-vision goggles. The four-inch-long cylindrical eyepieces amplified existing light from the visible through the infrared spectra and presented them in different intensities of green, shades to which the human eye was most sensitive. Then he hooked a compact 8-mm videocassette recorder to his belt. There was a lightweight headset and microphone built into the goggles and a small, silver tube attached to the right side of the frame. The tube contained a fiber-optic night-vision video camera, which was jacked into the tape machine. Everything Grand saw and described would be recorded. The tape was not only a useful study tool, it was a valuable precaution. Chumash cave art had been painted with brushes made of animal tails that had been dipped into bowls of powdered minerals such as hematite, diatomaceous earth, and manganese mixed for red, white, and black—the primary Chumash colors. Held together with a binder of animal fat, these pigments could be extremely volatile when exposed to air or light. Significant details, if not entire murals, could be lost within days of a cave being opened. In a geologically active zone, rock slides and earthquakes could also compromise or destroy the art. If anything like that happened here, at least there would be a record of the work.

Grand touched a button on the videocassette recorder. The machine began to hum.

"This is Jim Grand," he whispered. He was speaking softly so his voice wouldn't echo and cause dangerous vibrations. "I'm in a cave that's about fifty feet from the summit of La Cumbre Peak and about twenty-four-hundred feet above sea level. The opening of the cave is roughly a one-hundred-foot climb from East Camino Cielo Road. I came here after finding what seemed to be a reference to the mountain in the Chumash map painted in a cave on Figueroa Mountain. I found the entrance yesterday, on September thirteen, after it was exposed by a rockslide. There's a slide-path directly from the cave opening to a pile of boulders scattered thirty to fifty feet down. In size and composition the boulders match the sandstone on the summit. Their presence in the cave mouth could have been the result of tectonic activity or they may have been placed there by design."

Grand turned toward the dim light coming through the narrow roof entrance.

"What you're looking at is the cave ingress," he said. "It's a swallow hole and it's about seven feet behind me. The hole itself is about three feet across and five to six feet deep. Water from the higher peaks and from ongoing rainfall is continuing to pour into the swallow hole and spill over the sides of the ledge I'm on. The slope of the ledge is approximately twenty degrees from the bottom of the hole to the edge, which is consistent with long-term erosion from running water. However, until the La Niña effect there probably hasn't been any runoff in here since the late Pleistocene flooding. That's very promising. A dry interior would have suited a Chumash artist. The height and also the inaccessibility of the site also would have been appealing to a shaman looking for solitude. The cave elevation is approximately one hundred and fifty feet higher than any I've found in this region."

Grand turned back toward the heart of the cave.

"From where I'm standing, the size of the cave is deceptive," Grand continued. "It's only about thirty-five feet to the other side of the cave but it goes down quite a way." The scientist stepped to the edge and looked over. "It's a little over two hundred feet to the floor of the cave. And as soon as I finish gearing up I'll start my descent."

Grand paused the video camera. He squatted and removed a tiny flashlight and a packet of thick, white chalk from the duffel bag. The chalk was to make temporary notations on the rock, if need be, from water-flow patterns to a record of his own travels. He put both in his jacket pocket, then put his research pouch in another pocket. This was an oblong leather case that contained a scalpel for scraping off paint samples, tiny plastic bags for storing them, and a magnifying glass. Then he pulled out a pair of work gloves. After slipping them on, Grand stood and looked out at the cave.

Before returning to the UCSB, Grand had spent two years working as a field researcher for the anthropology department of the Smithsonian Institution. During that time, and before that when he was in grad school, he had explored caves in Russia, Spain, France, Turkey, Australia, and the United States. Wherever Grand was, when he was alone in a cave, searching for prehistoric art and artifacts, he felt as though he'd come home. Yet he had always felt a special closeness to the Chumash. The early inhabitants of the American West Coast had a singular view of nature and their place in it.

Though Chumash meant "bead maker" in their native tongue, these ancient people were much more than that. Migratory bands of Chumash had apparently come to Southern California as far back as thousand years ago, drawn by the warmer and drier climate that followed the Ice Age. Unlike most hunter-gatherers of the time, who followed the seasonal movement of animals, the Chumash made permanent homes in the mountains and ravines. They harvested food from the sea and rivers, collected nuts and berries from the Lower Santa Ynez River Canyon, and trained themselves to be exceptional predators, because those who were not were *chotaw*—prey. Grand had found the remains of many of their weapons in the caves and along the riverbeds. He marveled at their precision, at the aerodynamic arrows made of hollow bird-bone and the rocks that had been split so carefully that their edges were sharper than modern razor blades. The Chumash also left paintings on cave walls. Grand had personally studied and interpreted more than a dozen of these, adding to the handful that anthropologists had already found.

The paintings were fascinating because they didn't only depict daily activities. The Chumash were deeply religious and used small, hidden places like this to document their beliefs with art. They believed that life was a game called *Peon,* in which the benign and destructive gods collected knowledge and experience. When the game was over, it would start again. If the benign gods had won, all living things would benefit. If they had lost, the world would suffer.

All gods, good and bad, were pictured as animals. The Chumash did not hold humankind in high regard. They considered them awkward and vulnerable, which was why they worked so hard to hunt and to live in packs and to become more like the wolf or the bat or the insect.

The Chumash believed that the chief of the gods, the Great Eagle, carried the sun, moon, and stars in its beak and talons. During the day the sun prevented the Great Eagle from being seen; at night it was hidden by the darkness. The Great Eagle was served by the Sky Coyote, who dwelt in the clouds above the earth. The Sky Coyote nourished the inhabitants of our world by making it rain. Meanwhile, roaming the earth itself in spirit, the Bear Mother protected the Chumash by keeping the monstrous denizens of the lower world at bay. The Chumash believed that this underground realm was ruled by the chief of the evil gods, a pair of giant serpents, on whose backs the world rested. Sometimes the snakes stirred, causing a great shaking. Only the diligence of the Bear Mother kept them from emerging. But sometimes the shaking woke the evil *Nunashush,* monstrous creatures that lived in the foot of the mountain peaks and came out at night to eat all living things.

Curiously, though the Chumash had left behind paintings of the other spirits as well as many animals of the late Ice Age, Grand had never found a rendering of the *Nunashush.* Most students of Chumash mythology believed that was because evil was a personal thing, different to every member of the tribe. To some it might be a wasp or a shark, to others a hurricane or a rival tribe member.

Grand disagreed. The Chumash were extremely articulate, art-wise. The shamans who created the bulk of the artwork had ascribed symbolic meaning to everything. Spiders and their webs were life and its changing nature, snowflakes were death, fish were the young, and wolves were the old. Grand believed that the shamans knew exactly what the *Nanashush* looked like. He felt that the holy men didn't paint them because they had found a different way to portray them. Perhaps they painted them beneath a rock from which they couldn't escape or on tree bark, which they burned in effigy.

Standing here and thinking that the last humans to see this place may have been the Chumash reminded the scientist of when his parents had taken an unhappy six-year-old to Arizona to see the Grand Canyon. Now, as then, he felt immortal and humble at the same time.

After checking to make sure there were no paintings directly below the ledge, Grand was ready. Stepping over the double ropes so they were between his legs, he turned his back to the ledge, knelt, and took one rope in each hand.

"I'm going over," he said as he stepped off the side.

Grand descended at a forty-five-degree angle. The pulleys kept the ropes from rubbing on the rock ledge as he literally walked down the face of the cliff, his strong arms constantly working the lines. Releasing the down-rope not only allowed him to descend but gave him the ability to walk from side to side. Tightening on the up-rope brought him back to center. The combination of his angle and the horizontal play enabled Grand to read the entire escarpment as he descended.

It took nearly an hour to crisscross the top half of the cave wall. Grand moved slowly so he wouldn't miss anything; Chumash paintings were sometimes just single icons that could easily be mistaken for moss, seepage stains, or a mineral embedded in the wall. As he knit his way back and forth along the cave wall, Grand occasionally recorded a note about something that wouldn't be apparent to the fiber-optic lens: the length of the escarpment, which was about thirty feet; the degree of declination, which was about ten degrees off-plumb, the wall sloping in toward the base; the dampness of the air the lower to the ground he got; and the fact that there appeared to be large, vertical cracks on both sides of the cave at ground level. Grand wouldn't know for sure whether it was an opening or a shadow until he got to the bottom, which would be soon. Typically, Grand's time limit in the harness was about ninety minutes. There was the strain on his arms, chafing from the leg loops, and exhaustion from the intense, careful concentration. The air was also thin in these high caves, adding to the strain. It wasn't that he couldn't push himself; but he was afraid he might miss something if he did. He would go back up in a few minutes, rest and change the tape, then come back down.

Just below the halfway point, on the right side of the cave, Grand suddenly stopped.

"Hold on," Grand said into the microphone. "There's something here."

Grand straightened his knees so that he could step back slightly from the escarpment. He stared at the relatively smooth expanse of rock. There were definitely images there, large shapes that appeared to cover nearly the entire bottom right-hand quarter of the cave wall. From the corner of his eye Grand saw something on the opposite wall. He turned to look across the chasm. The same images had been rendered there as well.

Grand didn't know exactly what he was looking at. He was certain of only one thing.

He'd never seen anything like them.

6

Forty-seven-year-old Malcolm Gearhart hung up the phone. After quickly finishing his second cup of coffee, the former Marine took his portable radio from the desk drawer. He slipped the radio in its belt loop, grabbed his freshly blocked cap from the hook behind the door, and left his office in the back of the Santa Barbara County Sheriff's office station in Goleta.

Gearhart made two stops on his way through the quiet administration center. The first was at the office of Chief Deputy Mike Valentine. Gearhart briefed the veteran law officer about the call he'd just received from the Caltrans District 7 Division Chief, Maintenance, regarding a 3611-10—two missing engineers. The only clue a repair crew had found was a portable radio lying in the road. The sheriff asked Valentine for four deputies from his LEO—Law Enforcement Operations, Investigations Division. He wanted two of them to meet him at Painted Cave and the other two to have files on the missing workers E-mailed from Caltrans. He wanted a complete breakdown: telephone records, bank transactions, credit card charges, and anything else that might point to a debt, extortion, or a potentially hostile contact—a mistress, a bookie, a bar or restaurant or gas station where angry words might have been swapped.

Valentine wrote down each of the requests because that was how Gearhart liked things done. Thorough, accurate, and carefully documented. No confusion, no repetition.

Next, Sheriff Gearhart stopped at the dispatcher's cubicle in the communications center, which was also where the 911 calls were received. It was Deputy Felice Washington who had taken the call from Caltrans. Gearhart informed the young woman that he wanted an immediate update of any news from the site or from Caltrans and that Chief Deputy Valentine should be copied on any of the updates. He wanted the data sent digitally, to the patrol car's mobile data computer, with an audio backup to the car radio to make sure the information had been received. The dispatcher entered the instructions on her keyboard and sent them to the other stations. If she were on a call or away from her post, one of the other communications officers would know exactly what to do.

The procedure having been established and executed, Gearhart continued toward the door.

Without breaking his stride, the tall, broad African-American set his cap squarely on his head and made sure that his black tie was tightly knotted before stepping outside. The sheriff's black-and-white was parked directly in front of the recently remodeled two-story building. Ignoring the cold drizzle, he walked to the car and eased in.

Ordinarily, Gearhart would not be investigating a routine 3611-10—a Santa Barbara County noncriminal missing-persons report. Nor would he have involved Chief Deputy Valentine or the LEO. More often than not, missing persons in Santa Barbara County were boaters who'd been knocked around in a storm, a child who'd wandered away from the beach, or a hang glider who'd become disoriented in a cloud and smacked into a tree. But the Caltrans DCM said that there was blood at the site—a great deal of it. When a 3611-10 became a possible 187—which referred to the homicide section of the California Penal Code—Gearhart became involved.

The sheriff started the engine, turned on the windshield wipers, and adjusted the rearview mirror. He caught sight of his dark eyes. They said, *God help anyone who fucked with his county.*

They were right.

There was violent crime in Santa Barbara County. The sheriff's office had a most-wanted list of murderers, rapists, kidnappers, child molesters, bank robbers, and even a terrorist who had posed as one of Santa Barbara's over one hundred homeless people in order to hide explosives at the shelter in the center of town. However, most of those crimes predated Gearhart's term. Since being elected sheriff of the

SBSO two years before, the popular officer had turned crime fighting into a team sport. He'd expanded the Reserve Deputy Program, enlarged the Aero Squadron to patrol the mountains and coast, set higher fund-raising goals for the civilian Sheriff's Council, and beefed up the youth-oriented sheriff's Explorer Post—which an editorial in the radical *Coastal Freeway* dubbed the "Gearhart Youth," a nasty allusion to the Hitler Youth. That had earned the paper and its editor a permanent place on Gearhart's personal shit list. Not that he'd ever had any love for the press. They'd helped cost him and his fellow soldiers a victory in Vietnam with their endless coverage of protests, sit-ins, and fashionable antiestablishment bullshit. Now the press was simply hooked on the public's right to know. Which was fine, except that reporters usually took that to mean they had the right to pry, insinuate, slant, and panic.

Since Gearhart's election, the SBSO had enjoyed a sense of purpose and community. The number of names on and below the most-wanted top twelve had dwindled. Directly across the street, the county jail was half as full as it had been when Gearhart took office. The minimum security Honor Farm was nearly empty. Murders were primarily crimes of passion and the county still had them. But people who wanted to rob, rape, kidnap, and molest tended to stay clear of Gearhart's beloved hills and shoreline.

The sheriff activated his red-and-blue flashing lights though he didn't turn on the siren. There was no need to disturb the community while it was still so early. Swinging from the parking lot onto Calle Real, he followed it east for nearly two miles before turning left onto Route 154, the only western approach to Painted Cave Road. He would stay on the twisting road straight into the mountains, through Los Padres National Forest. Just over five miles up, a winding right turn would put him near the sinkhole.

As he drove through the light morning traffic, Gearhart was proud of the fact that the people of the county and its three hundred Sworn Deputy Sheriffs hadn't been the only ones to benefit during the past two years. Perhaps the greatest winner had been someone who had survived almost daily belt-whippings as a kid, two tours of duty in a losing war, and eighteen years of fighting not only Los Angeles street gangs but judges and politicians who believed that the answer to crime wasn't hard time but compassion and gentle rehabilitation. Until one of those pundits had his car jacked or his wife mugged, they weren't going to believe that they were wrong. But they were.

After a lifetime of losing, Malcolm Gearhart had no intention of ever losing again.

7

Jim Grand always carried a small, slender penlight. He fished it from his pocket. Then he slid the night-vision goggles to his forehead so he could turn on his light without being blinded. He thumbed on the switch and a thin cone of white light spread across the cave wall.

Grand stared at the image.

Painted on the western wall of the cave was a volcano. The nearly pyramidal peak was massive and black and covered in a long, flat red cloud. Coiled in the base of the volcano was a serpent, its red tongue rising through the center to the top. There the tongue forked in two directions, becoming streams of red that ran down the mountain's smooth sides. The lava collected in flat, spidery pools along both sides of the volcano. On the far side of the wall, one leg of lava stretched all the way to what looked like a fissure and stopped, though the art did not. Grand twisted slightly and swung the light around. What he saw on the opposite wall was even more remarkable.

On the southern wall was another painting, different, yet not. It was virtually a mirror image of the first, with a black mountain at the center. Only instead of red flows the lava was white. And instead of a serpent there was a dolphin inside the mountain, spraying two streams of water.

Whatever it was, Grand had never seen Chumash renderings so large. And while the northern painting seemed to suggest that the Chumash had witnessed a volcanic eruption—either here or in the north, before their migration to Southern California—the white mountain puzzled him. Could it be an underwater volcano? Or maybe a geyser of some kind.

He snapped off the penlight, tucked it away, and slipped the night-vision goggles back on. Relaxing his legs, he lowered himself the rest of the way to the ground. The surface of the cave was lumpy granite softened by ancient water flows. He removed the ropes and tied them together so they wouldn't slip from the pulleys. Then he stepped back from the wall. He studied the red volcano for a moment, then turned to look at the opposite wall.

Grand's initial reaction was that he was looking at some kind of geological yin and yang, the polarity of fire and water. Why it was painted and what it meant he had no idea; not yet, anyway. But he would. This was the kind of puzzle Jim Grand lived for.

He took a moment to describe the art on tape and then turned to the right. Though he wanted to spend more time with the paintings, just to examine the artistry, he also wanted to examine the rest of the cave. The particular cavern might have been sacred, but Chumash may have lived in other sections. If so, there might be other artifacts, from weapons to tools to clothing, in which case he would need to get graduate students up here before hikers and treasure hunters found the site.

Grand walked forward.

"Now that I'm on the ground I can also see the bottom of the cave more clearly. There are definitely fissures on both the northern and southern sides. There's also runoff from the rains spilling into both. I'm going to take a look."

The lingering pain of the previous night faded. His tired mind was alert. Feeling sinfully rich, Grand started walking to the nearer of the two openings, which was about fifteen feet away. His echoing footsteps were like gentle drumbeats on the smooth rock.

"The opening on the northern side is seven or eight feet high," he said. "It's about five feet wide at the bottom, three feet at the top, and surprisingly symmetrical. I don't see any of the jagged breaks that indicate a stress fracture. I also don't see any scoring outside, so it wasn't hand-cut."

Grand was just a few feet from the mouth of the cave. The light from swallow hole was blocked by the ledge, even with the night-vision goggles it was difficult to see.

"I'm looking inside the fissure now," he said. "It's dark, but from what I can see, the walls look blistered. They remind me of the collapsed lava tube at Bandera Volcano in New Mexico."

He wondered if the volcanic art on the wall represented something that had happened here instead of to the north. This was going to cause some eruptions of a much different sort among the conservative old guard in the UCSB geology department. Elma Thorpe would have two reasons to be angry at him.

Volcanism in Southern California was a contentious subject. There were volcanoes well north of this region up through Canada—in Black Butte, Clear Lake, Gorda Ridge, and over a dozen others. But volcanism in the north was due to subduction zones, crustal plates moving together from opposite directions. That convergence caused earthquakes as well as huge gaps that released magma. Tectonics in the south were mostly transform faults, with one plate sliding past another like grinding teeth. The horizontal scraping caused earthquakes but it did not cause lava to vent.

Or so many geologists had always assumed. Armed with computer simulations, a few scientists believed that millennia of heavier earthquake activity had simply obliterated calderas and other signs of ancient eruptions in Southern California. They suspected that smaller subduction zones were hidden deep in the crust of the southlands, beneath strata that distorted or swallowed sound waves from acoustic mapping instruments.

Grand stopped just outside the opening; he thought he heard something under the trickling water. He listened. After a few seconds he heard it again. The sound was coming from deep inside the tunnel.

"I don't know if the mike is picking this up," he whispered, "but there's a noise in the fissure."

The runoff from the swallow hole was washing slowly down the center of the tunnel Grand stepped inside. He was careful to place his feet on either side of the flow, which ran along a shallow, foot-wide trench in the center. Sinkholes often formed beneath these trenches. The rock underfoot was brittle, eroded. He stood still and listened.

"There it is again," he said. "A deep, intermittent gurgling. I can't tell what it is or exactly where it's coming from because of the echo. Maybe it's a Chumash spirit," he joked. "I'm going to see if I can find the source of the sound."

The scientist began walking slowly along the fissure. It was almost completely dark and he proceeded cautiously, looking around with each step. There were wide cracks in the tunnel floor where sinkholes were forming—probably leading to a network of similar tunnels—and there were occasional stalactites like those at the Bandera site. In some places the walls closed in suddenly and he had to move sideways to get through. The walls themselves were thickly pocked and bubbled. Grand didn't think he'd be finding any art in here.

After he had taken less than a dozen steps the light vanished completely. Removing his goggles, Grand snapped on the penlight and continued ahead. The gentle step of his boots and the rubbing of the harness against his pants echoed locally. They blended with the distant, hollow groan that he still couldn't identify while everything around him was solid and soundless. It was a strange combination, a hip-hop underbeat in a tomb.

But Grand didn't stop. He was driven by more than just curiosity. For most of his life Grand had worked on skills that most people never got to use. His senses had been refined and heightened by years spent reproducing prehistoric tools and using them to hunt small game for food on remote savannas and chaparrals. His endurance, his balance, his instincts had been pushed and enhanced by moving through dozens of caves and tunnels, by climbing mountains and hacking his way through unmapped jungle.

Something about this place had turned those senses on. The penlight roamed the walls like an eye looking back at him. It illuminated dark, narrow fissures on both sides. The rents were jagged, vertical cracks about five feet high and glistening with water seepage from the surface of the mountain. They were classic earthquake fractures; each successive split had relieved some of the stress caused by the shifting earth. By measuring the angles at which they had cracked, geologists could plot the direction of the underlying tremor.

But Grand also felt things that scientists couldn't plot. He knew that non-Chumash were not welcome in the caves. Not welcome by surviving Chumash and not welcome by the spirits that were said to dwell in the mountains. There were times in some of these caves when Grand knew that he wasn't alone. Reason told him that it was an animal hiding in the shadows. But isolation, eerie noises in the dark, and tunnels that were often the size and smell of a grave had a way of convincing one otherwise. There were times Grand could swear that it was not cold he felt but the delicate tail of an animal spirit brushing the small of his back.

Maybe you shouldn't have made that crack about it being a Chumash spirit, he reprimanded himself. He wondered if the sound might be an underground geyser sputtering awake, perhaps the one pictured in the cave painting.

About twenty yards in the tunnel suddenly forked. On the left it continued as before. On the right the ground dropped away sharply and the ceiling was less than five feet high. The water went mostly to the right. Grand turned an ear toward that opening. The gurgling was coming from there.

"It figures," he murmured, looking at the steep, wet passageway.

The sound was much clearer now, with less echo. It couldn't be very far away. Grand also heard dripping water, which didn't surprise him. The antediluvian flows that carved caves and tunnels like these often created underground streams and lakes as well. Many of those became part of other subterranean water systems and survived.

Grand crouched and shined the light down the passage. The stone was very smooth here, definitely an ancient channel. It sloped down like a children's slide for about twenty feet and then leveled off. He ran his hand across the top of the tunnel; the rock seemed solid, not in danger of collapsing. Then he shut off the penlight. There was no other illumination. That meant this tunnel was the only immediate access to the lower level.

He switched the light back on. Jim Grand was not a reckless man, but he had never started an exploration he hadn't finished. Unhooking the videocassette recorder from his belt, he left it on the tunnel floor. He didn't want it damaged if he slipped or fell. And if anything did happen to him, at least the search-and-rescue personnel would know exactly where to look.

Holding the penlight in his mouth, Grand started creeping down. He kept his left hand on the ground and his right hand on the tunnel wall. There were small outcrops that helped him to steady himself.

The wall and its projections were warm and damp and a bit slippery. The warmth made sense. This section was located in the northeastern face of the mountain. Foliage was relatively low-lying here and the sun hammered it for a good part of the day. There was obviously enough water below to evaporate during the day and condense when it cooled at night.

The gurgling sound and the dripping water were much louder now. So was his own breathing, which echoed back at him in the tight passage. It took only a few minutes to crawl down the tunnel. Stopping when he reached the bottom, Grand took the penlight from his mouth and shined it around.

The scientist was in a small, rank, muggy cavern, about twenty feet high and perhaps forty feet across. He couldn't be sure since his light didn't quite reach the other side. Large, unusually tenacious gnats clouded around him but he ignored them. Waving them away was pointless. The roof of the cave was crowded with stalactites and the walls, as far across as he could see, were smooth. In the center of the cave was an underground lake, about thirty feet across. Water from his tunnel and from a tunnel on the opposite side fed the lake. Overflow from the lake formed a gentle waterfall that vanished in the darkness of another tunnel.

Close to his boots, lying half in the water and half on the stone ledge, he also saw what was making the gurgling sound. It was neither a spirit nor a geyser.

It was a handheld radio.

8

Hannah Hughes was sitting in the front seat of her muddy red Blazer. It was parked off-road on a rutted, ravine-side ledge one hundred yards east of the sinkhole. In front of her was the gray van the engineers had used to drive up. Angled behind her was the black Jeep belonging to her linebacker-big photographer Walter "The Wall" Jones. The Wall was over at the site, taking pictures. Despite his girth, which was formidable, the Wall was a self-admitted wuss who practiced photojournalism because that's what he'd studied in college, where he met Hannah. What he really wanted to do was open a photo-portrait studio in Santa Barbara. He was saving up for that now. Until then, he was busy taking pictures with both a Kodak DC 260 digital camera and an old 35mm Bolsey that had belonged to his grandfather. The former could be sent to the newspaper from his car uplink. The latter was for backup in case the pixels got temperamental, which sometimes happened in the rain. Or when he dropped the camera. Or when he got disgusted with his work or Hannah or digital technology and threw it.

The heat was roaring from the dashboard vents and the wipers flip-flopped loudly. Hannah's jeans and sweatshirt were flecked with mud and darkened here and there with rain, and her head was wetter than it had been forty minutes before. But the cold and discomfort didn't bother her. She only hoped that the water dripping from her hair onto her laptop didn't cause it to short. Not until she finished her copy and had E-mailed it from the car phone to production chief Weezie Hanson.

Though Hannah had only been on the mountain for fifteen minutes, she'd already framed the story. Just before she arrived the sinkhole had collapsed again. It now occupied most of the road from the mountainside to the ravine. The section where the blood had been found was gone. The area was ringed with five work lights on stainless-steel tripods. Hannah had watched as the three crew members dug dirt with their hands; they couldn't use shovels lest they accidentally spade one of the buried engineers. She'd offered to help but the short, muscular foreman Victor Singer told her that wouldn't be necessary. A second crew was due momentarily. Apart from sharing that information, Singer had no time to talk—he said—because he was busy using a portable radio they'd found in the road to try to raise Stan Greene or Bill Roche.

However, Hannah had managed to snare an interview with Dr. Elma Thorpe, the UCSB geologist. Dressed in gray sweatpants, a red windbreaker, and an Australian Outback hat, the tall, robust, silver-haired professor seemed very much at home here. Hannah had profiled the London-born scientist two years before, when she'd been campaigning for a U.S. Geological Survey grant to research blind thrust faults in the region. Instead, the money went to charting the caves in the Santa Ynez Mountains.

The two women stood in the rain for several minutes, talking about fissures and the rural road infrastructure.

The journalist's long fingers moved across the laptop keyboard like spiders on a hot plate, as the Oklahoma-born Weezie once described them. But even that wasn't fast enough for Hannah. She didn't want to miss today's edition. She *wouldn't* miss today's edition. The *Los Angeles Times* hadn't sent anyone up to cover the story. Either they hadn't heard about it or they didn't care because there wasn't a body. The local TV stations would wait a few hours before dispatching a team because the sinkhole was getting larger and the bigger the pit the better the image for dinnertime news. So for a few hours the story would be hers, and it could be a big one. Not just the two missing engineers but the potential danger to all the mountain roads of Southern California. According to Dr. Thorpe—Hannah loved this quote—"Fissures like this one could thread through the entire Santa Ynez range and pass under the roadway in innumerable places. Caltrans should look into it before there are other disasters."

Hannah was nearly finished with the draft when there was a back-of-the-knuckles rap on the window. It was the Wall, his bald head and face made ruddy by one of the dying flares on the road.

Hannah cranked down the window. "What's up?"

"He just arrived," said the photographer.

"Thanks," Hannah said.

The Wall didn't have to say who "he" was. It was the man who was unofficially dedicated to overthrowing the free press and overprotecting the rights and lives of the rich who had financed and helped to elect him. The chief Santa Barbarian himself, Sheriff Malcolm Gearhart.

"You cool, Chief?" the Wall asked protectively.

"Completely."

"You sure?"

"Yes!" Hannah snapped.

The Wall scowled at her. "Uh-huh."

"Go away," Hannah said. "You made your point."

The Wall returned to the sinkhole and Hannah took several deep breaths to calm herself. Saving the draft of her story, she set the laptop on the passenger's seat—amidst the crumbs of countless Wheat Thins, a box of which was always kept in the glove compartment—and grabbed her audiotape recorder. Then she touched her lucky dog tags and stepped out into the cold rain. She didn't take an umbrella on assignments like these because she didn't like to be encumbered. She also believed that if you were thinking about staying dry or warm you weren't thinking about the story.

Hannah slogged toward the sinkhole as Malcolm Gearhart approached from the west. The sheriff and Singer acknowledged one another with nods. Gearhart tipped his hat to Dr. Thorpe. He acknowledged Hannah and the Wall by ignoring them. He couldn't order them away because there was no clear and present danger and this wasn't a restricted crime scene.

"Where did you find the blood?" Gearhart asked Singer.

Singer pointed a gloved finger to the northeastern side of the pit. "It *was* right there."

"What do you mean 'was'?"

"We were setting up a little shelter there when the section of road where we found the blood just crumpled. It happened about two minutes after we got here. There was nothing we could do. The sinkhole just expanded outward and that was that."

Sheriff Gearhart didn't look happy. "What about the rest of the road? Is it safe?"

"I ran an ultrasound check. There's solid rock under the rest of the road for about two hundred yards in each direction. It's not going anywhere."

"Why didn't we know about the weakened condition of this section?" Gearhart asked.

"Because we just don't do routine surveys like that," Singer said. "Why don't you know about killers before they kill?"

"I do," Gearhart said. "The law just doesn't allow me to do anything about them."

Singer made a face then excused himself. He raised the radio to his mouth and pressed a button on the side. A small green light glowed above the mouthpiece grid. When there was an incoming call, a red light came on. During a two-way conversation, both were lit.

"This is Caltrans emergency crew calling Stan Greene and William Roche," Singer said. "Greene and Roche, if you're receiving, come in. If you're receiving, come in. Over."

The silence was disturbing.

The sheriff turned and walked slowly along the pit. He studied the ground, ignoring the Wall as he followed taking pictures. Then he stopped at the ravine and looked down. He used the toe of his boot to move the foliage around before walking back along the western rim of the pit.

"You found no footprints at all?" Gearhart asked Singer.

"Nothing," Singer said. "The rain washed away everything, even the footprints by Roche's van."

"Where did they park?"

Singer pointed the radio toward the van. The sheriff looked back at it. Rain was beaded on the sides and windows.

"Where did you find the radio?" Gearhart asked.

"About ten feet from the van, closer to us," Singer said.

"Then Mr. Roche left the van after his last communication with Caltrans," Gearhart said. "Perhaps because his partner called him."

"It's possible," Singer agreed.

"Was the van running?"

"Yes."

"So he obviously expected to come back," Gearhart said. "Then something happened. Something that made him drop the radio."

"Apparently," Singer said.

Sheriff Gearhart looked up along the side of the mountain. The face was smooth gray stone streaked here and there with a thin layer of green moss. Chalk-white rocks were piled around the base, having fallen from above or been deposited here by an ancient flood. Fat, lop-sided oaks and spindly alders grew along the base and on top.

"Dr. Thorpe, could a rockslide have done this?" Gearhart asked.

"Certainly," she said. "The same forces that undermine subterranean rock can undermine surface rock."

"Would a rockslide have registered on any of the regional seismographs?" Gearhart asked.

"A small impact like that—probably not," she said.

Gearhart was silent. Hannah took the opportunity to step toward him. She held out the tape recorder.

"Sheriff, there have been several recent reports of bobcats being forced from their upper mountain habitats by the rain," Hannah said. "Is it possible that the men were—"

"Ms. Hughes, I just got here. Right now I haven't ruled out anything," Gearhart said. He turned to Singer. "I looked along the ravine for signs of blood and didn't find any. I've got two deputies on the way up. When they arrive we'll start looking along the creek bed. If there were a rockslide, that could be where we'll find them."

"Sheriff Gearhart," Hannah pressed, "over the past few weeks the bobcats in this region have become increasingly aggressive. Those engineers were out here in the dark, which is when these animals hunt. Is it possible that the men were attacked?"

Gearhart looked at the young woman. "Have you ever tried pulling a man? Dead weight?"

"No, Sheriff."

"I have. A bobcat can attack a man but not drag him off. These men are missing."

Gearhart stepped around her and headed for the van.

Singer went back to the radio while Hannah stewed. She could deal with the sheriff being taciturn or even cooperative. But when he was dismissive and condescending—that was when she wanted to kick him.

"This is Caltrans emergency crew calling Stan Greene and William Roche," Singer said "Greene and Roche, if you're receiving, come—"

He fell silent, but only for a moment.

"Sheriff!" he cried.

Gearhart stopped and ran back. Hannah and the others looked down at the radio.

The light above the mouthpiece was flashing red.

9

Jim Grand bent carefully and carefully picked up the radio. He listened for a moment to the crackling voice coming from it. There was a great deal of interference because of the mountain walls, but he was able to make out most of what was being said.

Grand looked for a volume dial. He found it on the side of the radio, then turned it up and pressed the transmit button.

"Caltrans emergency, this is James Grand. Can you hear me? This is James Grand."

There was a momentary delay. Then the voice on the other end said, "We hear you, Mr. Grand." The sounds reverberated loudly through the upper reaches of the cave. "Where are you? Are our two engineers with you?"

"There's no one here," Grand said. "At least, not that I can see."

"Exactly where are you?" the caller asked.

The scientist described where he was in the mountain and how he'd gotten here. The man on the radio asked him to hold.

Grand used the time to take a slow look around the cavern. The illumination from the penlight spread across the center of the lake. The distant cave wall was a thick shadow and the water was dark and clean. There were no leaves, no flecks of wood, no detritus of any kind on the surface. Save for the gentle swells caused by the slow-running stream, the lake was unnaturally still. There were no fish moving underwater, no lizards crawling along the walls or ledge, no bats on the ceiling. Just the gnats, which was surprising; they usually weren't found in caves.

Grand began to feel uneasy again. Most caves had a personality he could feel when he entered. The geology-personality types tended to be craggy-and-hostile, tall-and-proud, sinuous-and-aloof, deep-and-dangerous. But this cave felt empty, like a corpse.

And the tunnel had reminded him of a tomb.

The cave had apparently unsettled the Chumash as well. Grand couldn't imagine that the shaman who worked in the outer cavern would not have come here. The cave couldn't have been submerged then. Stalactites can only form in a dry gallery, as water containing minute mineral particles drips to create stone "icicles." That process takes millennia. The Chumash would have had access to the cave. They obviously didn't want it.

"I assume this is Professor Grand?"

The voice coming from the radio was deeper, sharper than before. But familiar.

"This is Professor Grand," he said. "Who is this?"

"It's Sheriff Gearhart."

Grand felt as if he'd been drop-kicked a year into the past. He went from zero to angry before the echo of the radio had faded.

"How long have you been at that site?" Gearhart asked.

"About two hours." Just hearing the man's voice brought back the sheriff's stony face, his flat eyes, his intractable stand—

"And you saw and heard no one," Gearhart said.

"That's right."

"Do you see blood anywhere?"

"No," Grand told him. "Was there an accident somewhere?"

"Professor, is there another way into the cave?"

"Possibly," Grand said. So the sheriff was going to play alpha dog and not answer his questions. *Fine,* Grand thought. He could mark that territory if he wanted it so badly. "That's one of the things I'm doing up here," Grand said, "mapping the caverns and tunnels."

"Which means we've still got two missing persons," Gearhart said. "We're going to have to send a search team in there. Can you meet me at Painted Cave in fifteen minutes?"

"I've got some climbing to do to get out," Grand said. "I can meet you in half an hour."

"All right," Gearhart said. "Park down the road, we've got a major sinkhole here. Are you wearing gloves?"

Grand said that he was.

"Please put the radio down carefully so you don't rub off fingerprints or other markings."

"Sure," Grand said.

Grand clicked off the radio, put it down, then turned and walked back to the tunnel entrance. He'd signed off quickly, not only to end the conversation but to keep from taking his long-festering anger at Gearhart out on the radio. He would put what he was feeling into his ascent. Channel it from the heart to the arms and out the fingers, the same way he had always climbed or thrown spears he'd reconstructed or made love to Rebecca.

Grand hauled himself into the tunnel opening and began crawling back up to the main cavern. There was something back at the sinkhole he wanted to check, something that might help answer some questions. And at least there was one positive result of the conversation. He didn't feel uneasy anymore.

The cave was silent again and dark, save for the fast-fading glow of the flashlight. Soon the only movement was the river and the only light was two small, faint, iridescent globes on the far side of the cave, hovering just above the surface of the lake.

And then they too winked out.

10

Sheriff Gearhart went back to his patrol car. He arrived just as the team of deputies from LEO Investigations arrived. He sent deputies Scott and Bright down into the ravine then shut the door and radioed Chief Deputy Valentine. Gearhart told Valentine what Grand had found in the cave and asked him to have the town's director of social welfare check on the whereabouts of any homeless persons with a history of aggression. Gearhart also wanted the chief deputy to contact the police departments in Santa Paula, Santa Clarita, Thousand Oaks, and other communities in the mountains. He wanted to know if any kidnappings or violent crimes had been reported there. Perhaps some maniac was heading west through the hills. If so, this would be as far west as he got.

"I want this kept as quiet as possible," Gearhart instructed him. He looked at Hannah Hughes who was looking back at him. "This could still be an accident—a bobcat or a coyote could have carried that radio into the mountain. He looked back at Valentine. "If not, I want some thoughts on who we might be looking for."

Valentine said he'd get right on it.

Gearhart got back out of the car. In the distance he saw the ruins of Knapp's Castle. Begun in 1916 and completed in 1920, the sandstone edifice was destroyed by the Paradise Canyon fire in 1940. The owner did not rebuild. Some say it was because of nightmares she'd had, black dreams that the ancient gods had sent the fire to keep humans from settling in the mountains.

Perhaps the gods were pissed off again, Gearhart thought.

If they were, they'd have to fight for the hills this time. Malcolm Gearhart loved them. He loved all of his county—the air, the ocean, the sun, and the breeze. He loved the pace, the low white buildings in the center of Santa Barbara, the neat suburban streets and homes outside the incorporated town, and the overall quality of life. He loved the fact that people felt safe here and children could be raised with a sense of ethics and community pride. Sanity had to start somewhere and it might as well start here.

That was something he'd never had as a child.

Gearhart grew up in impoverished South Norwalk, Connecticut, where his father painted boats in the marina by day and got explosively pissed off at his wife and son at night. The boy's mother blamed it on the paint fumes, on having no money, on frustration. But that didn't make the screaming and the beatings any easier. The boy took so many belt whippings that today Gearhart felt self-conscious going to the beach in a bathing suit or shorts. His legs had been permanently marked in spots by the metal buckle.

The day after he graduated from Norwalk High School, Gearhart bicycled to the Selective Service office on East Avenue to find out how to get himself into the Marines. One of the neighbors had a son who was a Marine and Gearhart liked the way the man carried himself, with confidence and dignity.

A kind, soft-spoken woman named Mrs. Moriarty told Gearhart how to sign up. Four weeks later he was at Camp Pendleton, California.

Gearhart did two tours of Vietnam. He came home with a chestful of medals, the pride he'd been looking for, and the uncomfortable sense that he'd been beaten there too. They'd won skirmishes and destroyed villages and killed Vietcong. But now that he was back and heard the politicians and protesters and whining singers, he realized that what he and his brothers fought was a holding action, not a war. He had been beaten, this time not from without but from within.

With no idea what he wanted to do with his life, Gearhart bought a '63 Ford Galaxie—pink, because it cost him a couple hundred less than if it had been any other color—and drove cross-country to look at the nation he'd spent his early twenties defending. He saw Gettysburg, the Alamo, and the Little Big Horn. He felt close to those places and to the men who'd fought in them. He also saw armies of scraggly haired punks doing nothing, college kids avoiding the draft, shameless women, and—worst of all—many of his own people advocating violence. It was as if everyone had been sucking up paint fumes. By the time he made his way back to California, Gearhart knew what he wanted to do. He wanted to make sure that other good people didn't get beat. He wanted to protect the honest people who were working and trying to provide for themselves and their families.

Gearhart entered the Los Angeles Police Academy, where his Marine training helped him graduate at the top of his class. He was assigned to a foot beat, Wilshire Area, and, after countless commendations, had risen to Commanding Officer of the Organized Crime and Vice Division.

But he was beaten there too. Not by the ineffectiveness of his own units or by the enemy—the street gangs, the Mafiosi, or the ruthless new criminal families from Armenia, China, Colombia, and Russia. He was beaten by people outside the trenches, the judges and politicians who believed that the answer to crime wasn't hard time but compassion and rehabilitation.

Rather than sit back and wait for his pension to kick in, Gearhart packed up his résumé and campaigned for the position of sheriff in Santa Barbara. He wanted to be in a place where the war was still winnable, where the people and leaders had a community vision and would support him. Backed by well-to-do émigrés from Los Angeles, who had come an hour north to escape the crowds and crime, Gearhart got his chance. Some people, like Hannah Hughes, still believed that he was overzealous. But Gearhart viewed his job as no different from that of the forest rangers who looked after the local environment. Allow a single spark to go unattended and soon there would be nothing but flame, smoke, and ruin.

Nearly two years after the election, Gearhart had earned the trust of most of the locals who viewed him as a carpetbagger. He had addressed the state legislature several times on matters of law enforcement. He'd justified the faith of the people who had supported him. But most important, he had the one thing he had always wanted.

He was winning.

As he started back toward the sinkhole, he vowed that nothing—no act of God, no madman, and no displaced predator—was going to change that.

11

Grand had climbed down the first hundred feet of mountainside, after which the ground sloped sufficiently for him to walk. He weaved his way through the pines that broke the otherwise flat landscape. He was perspiring from the exertion and the cool drizzle felt good. He had parked his sports utility vehicle just past Snyder Trail. After placing his duffel bag in the back, Grand climbed behind the wheel, turned on the wipers and heat, and sat for a moment. It was ironic. Jim Grand spent most of his time in the distant past, trying to think like the ancient settlers of this region—figuring out where they would have lived, how they would have hunted or fished, what they would have done with their dead. He never had any trouble returning to the present—until now. Before he saw Gearhart he wanted to try and flush some of the bitterness and rage away.

It was difficult.

Rebecca Schuman-Grand had died in a boating accident off Sandy Point on nearby Santa Rosa Island. She had gone out to assist an elderly colleague who ran a tortoise farm. Grand was going to take the day off and go with her. But he got caught up studying DNA results that had come in early—thanks to one of his students being in charge of the equipment—of nineteen-thousand-year-old fossilized sloth dung that had been found in a cave in Las Vegas. Rebecca's last words to him were a teasing, "You're always giving me one shitty excuse or another."

That was it. Their good-bye. Just the one-liner, a kiss on the forehead, and she went smiling out the door.

On the way back, Rebecca's small jet boat was rammed by a motor yacht that just didn't see her. The Santa Barbara coroner later determined that Rebecca had died instantly.

The United States Coast Guard's Eleventh District Search and Rescue team—which was based on the Channel Islands Harbor in nearby Oxnard—and Sheriff Gearhart's own SAR team were both on-site in twenty minutes. However, after the Coast Guard's motor lifeboat carefully pried the jet boat from the prow of the much larger motor yacht, Gearhart insisted that they bring both vessels to Santa Barbara for impoundment. The ships remained at sea for nearly four hours until the SAR unit finally yielded control of the investigation. The sheriff used the accident to establish absolute jurisdiction over the coastline. Within two days he had also turned Rebecca into a poster child for fund-raising efforts to obtain a motor lifeboat for Santa Barbara County.

Gearhart called the scientist and asked him to assist in the effort. Grand declined. At the time, all the scientist could do was sit in front of the open door of the bedroom closet, staring at his wife's blouses and pants and stacks of shoeboxes and hats and scarves and remembering when they were full of her and alive. He didn't want to see or talk to anyone. Gearhart called him a disappointment, not just to the community but to the memory of Rebecca. Grand should have called the bastard out then and there, but didn't. He was too busy trying to hold onto his wife, the goodness that was in her. Until today, that phone call had been their only contact. Unfortunately, though the moment had passed, the anger never did. A big part of Grand still wanted to hurt him.

The sheriff eventually got his motor lifeboat. He also got an involuntary manslaughter conviction for the seventy-year-old skipper of the motor yacht, who had been kissing his young bride when he should have been watching the water. Grand had always wondered if the bastard expected his thanks.

The scientist set off along East Camino Cielo and followed the long, narrow U-shaped turn to Painted Cave Road. He turned south and was at the sinkhole five minutes later. Grand pulled around the flares. He had to park on the road itself since all the off-road space was taken by private cars and Caltrans emergency vehicles. As he approached, he saw two deputies walking along the creek some thirty feet below. Up ahead there were eight men digging in the sinkhole while his colleague Elma Thorpe, reporter Hannah Hughes, and a man-mountain of a photographer stood around the site. Gearhart was on the other side of the sinkhole, sitting in his patrol car and talking on the radio. As soon as the sheriff saw Grand he stopped what he was doing and came over.

Hannah Hughes followed but stayed several paces behind.

Gearhart exemplified the expression "Once a Marine, always a Marine." His posture was ramrod-straight and there was nothing lazy about his movements. The men met halfway between Stan Greene's van and the sinkhole. Neither man offered a hand or a word of greeting.

"Professor Grand," Gearhart said, "a couple of my Special Ops volunteers are going to enter the cave and retrieve the radio. I'll need precise instructions on how to get to the lower cave."

It wasn't a request but a command.

"Sheriff, I'm not good at giving directions, orders, that kind of thing," Grand said pointedly. "Why don't I just take them in myself?"

"I don't have a problem with that," Gearhart replied.

"They'll need harnesses to get down there," Grand told him. "They'll also need night vision capability until we get to the subterranean level."

"Why?"

"I discovered paintings in the outer cave," Grand said. "Bright lights may damage them."

"I'll let them know," Gearhart said.

The sheriff didn't make an issue of that. California state law required the "participation, guidance, and accommodation" of specialists whenever there was police activity in or around an historic site. In the absence of a clear and present danger, search-and-rescue operations or criminal investigations were obliged to follow the expert's advice to protect the integrity of the site.

"The men should be up here in about an hour," Gearhart went on. "Can you wait?"

Grand nodded. Gearhart nodded back, then strode over to the ravine.

Hannah wandered over. She watched Gearhart go. "You're welcome, Sheriff," she grumbled.

Grand looked at her.

"You know," she went on, "the movers and shakers are actually talking about running him for governor."

"Sounds like a good idea," Grand said.

"Oh, come on—"

"Hell, I'd vote for him," Grand went on. "Get him out of Santa Barbara."

Hannah smiled. "Professor, we could become great friends. I'm Hannah Hughes—"

"With the *Coastal Freeway,* I know." Grand took off his glove and offered the young woman his hand. "You wrote some very nice things about Rebecca. Thank you."

Hannah shook his hand. "She was a terrific lady, she did a lot of good work. But how did you know it was me?"

"From your photograph."

"Which photograph?"

"The one on the editorial page."

"That tiny one?"

Grand nodded.

"Wow, you *do* know how to interpret cave art."

Grand smiled. "It's not so bad."

"Not for high school circa nineteen seventy," Hannah said. "It was the Wall's idea of a glamour shot."

"The Wall?"

"My photographer." She pointed him out. "Walter. The big guy."

The Wall saw her and waved.

"I used the photo because I didn't want to hurt his feelings," Hannah said. "Anyway, speaking of what we do, I have a nasty-wicked deadline. I overheard your conversation with Gearhart and I was wondering if you could tell me more about what you found in that lower cave."

"The radio, I assume. Not the paintings."

"Correct."

"There isn't much more to tell," he said. "The only thing I found in the lower chamber was the radio. There's a lake, but I wasn't able to check it."

"Where exactly is the cave?"

"I'd rather not say," he told her. "People might go out there—"

"—and climb all over the paintings," Hannah said. "I understand."

They could also get hurt," Grand said. "Several of the caves have been opened because of rockslides. The ground is still pretty unsteady around the entrances."

"Say no more," Hannah said. "Professor, you were at that site roughly the same time as the men disappeared. Could anyone have snuck in or out without you knowing it?"

"Someone might have been able to get in through another entrance or fissure," he said, "but it would have been very difficult to *sneak* in. Even small sounds can carry for miles in those caves."

"There are miles of caves?" she said.

"Typically," he said. "The Chumash often used them to move under grazing herds in order to get upwind. And with all the flooding we've had, tunnels are probably being opened that have been blocked for tens of thousands of years."

"Bet you can't wait to have a look at them," Hannah smiled.

"I'd be camping there if it weren't for my classes," Grand said. "But there is something we can have a look at right now, if you'd care to join me."

"Something—?"

"A place that may tell us how the radio got underground."

"I'm there," she said, beaming.

Grand and Hannah walked down the road, away from the sinkhole. He stopped at a spot past the parked cars. It was only about fifteen feet to the bottom of the ravine here. Large boulders were piled most of the way up, with newly broken tree limbs and soft, rotted logs scattered about. Grand started down the jumble of rocks and debris and Hannah right behind him. It was an easy climb.

The rain-swollen creek coursed swiftly to the west. Grand picked his way across the jagged rocks along the bank. It was even cooler down here than up on the road, the thickly leafed branches preventing sunlight from getting through. They created a sense of quiet isolation that was actually enhanced by the rushing waters. As the Chumash described riverbeds, this was the home of the waters. Everything else dwelt here at its pleasure.

The two sheriff's deputies were walking along the ravine several hundred yards ahead. It was extremely dry there. Grand stopped as they neared the little cove where the waters slid under the creek bed and went underground. He remembered it being a small, natural depression in the center of the creek, covered by two flat rocks that were steepled one against the other.

He reached the spot and stopped. The depression was there but it wasn't small anymore.

"Score one for Professor Grand," Hannah said as she stared at the spot.

Rushing water wasn't the only thing in the opening.

12

Grand called to deputies Scott and Bright, who called up to Sheriff Gearhart. The sheriff and Victor Singer came down one of the steep walls near the sinkhole. Hannah shouted for Walter Jones to hurry over. The Wall was in his Jeep sending photos to the paper. He was closer than the sheriff, and though he had some trouble getting down the side of the ravine, he made it before Gearhart did. He looked where Hannah was pointing and began snapping digital photographs as he approached. He and Hannah had both been in situations where Gearhart declared a place a crime scene and threw them out before they had a chance to get pictures. Occasionally the sheriff did it to protect the integrity of a site; more often than not, Hannah suspected, it was to minimize the space in which she could give bad news. *"Photos rock,"* as the Wall was fond of saying.

Grand crouched on a flat rock beside the small, silty opening. Hannah stood behind him.

The hole was approximately two-and-one-half feet across. Snagged on a rock on the south side of the opening was a black backpack. It was held there by one of the shoulder straps. Hanging from the backpack were long tattered ribbons that looked like they came from an orange poncho. The frayed pieces fluttered like seaweed as the silty water washed by.

"I'm guessing this opening wasn't here the last time you looked," Hannah said.

Grand leaned looked over the edge. "It sure wasn't."

"Obviously, our sheriff hasn't noticed that the creek bed is a little dry up ahead," Hannah said.

"It's not something he might have noticed," Grand pointed out. "The flow changes seasonally. I might not have noticed myself if I hadn't seen water pouring in when I was down there."

The deputies arrived then. The brawny Deputy Bright ordered Hannah and Grand to step back.

"Hey, we're the ones who found this," Hannah said. She remained where she was as Grand stepped back.

"We'd have gotten here in a few minutes," Scott said. "Please just do as the deputy asked."

Hannah reluctantly took a small step away as Deputy Bright got on his hands and knees in the water. The officer slipped his flashlight from its belt loop and carefully examined the backpack and the sinkhole without touching them. Deputy Scott crouched beside him.

A moment later Gearhart reached the sinkhole. He was followed by Victor Singer.

"Now how the hell did this get way over here?" Singer asked.

"Maybe one of the men slipped in the dark and went off the road," Scott suggested.

"If either of the engineers went off the road, they didn't slip down this rabbit hole," said Deputy Bright.

"How can you tell?" Singer asked.

"There are large rocks in there," Bright replied. "A guy falling through would have plugged the thing up."

"Can you see the bottom?" Gearhart asked, pointing east.

"No, sir," said Bright. "It slopes off to the west."

"Scott, check the creek bed in the other direction," Gearhart said. "See if one of the men might have wandered off."

"Yes, sir." Scott said.

The deputy set off. Hannah told the Wall to go with him but to keep an eye on his watch. They had less than forty-five minutes to file the story and any additional photographs.

Gearhart regarded Grand. Hannah didn't like the look in his eyes. Something was coming.

"What made you think to look all the way over here?" Gearhart asked.

"When I saw the lake below I assumed the creek was feeding it with overflow," Grand said. "It made geographic sense."

"So you didn't know that the backpack would be here."

"No."

"You just expected to find another sinkhole," Gearhart said.

"That's right," Grand replied. "Sheriff, what are you implying?"

"I was wondering that myself," Hannah complained. "What do you *think* we were—"

"Professor, I'm not implying anything," Gearhart said, cutting Hannah off, "I'm trying to find two missing men. You were up here when they disappeared. Now if you have any other special knowledge of this incident, I need to know what that is so I can locate them."

"Sheriff, come have a look at this," Deputy Bright said.

Gearhart looked at Grand a moment longer before stepping over. When the sheriff's back was turned Hannah gave Grand's hand a reassuring squeeze. His large fingers closed around hers for a moment, then he stuck his hand in his jacket pocket. Gearhart was doing his usual trying-to-provoke-people thing, get them upset so they open up. The problem was, Gearhart either didn't know or didn't care when someone was truly trying to cooperate. She couldn't imagine what was going through Grand's mind, but the sadness in his eyes was awful.

They watched as the sheriff knelt in the water beside Bright. The deputy used his flashlight to point on the underside of the backpack.

"See those?" Bright asked.

Gearhart nodded. "Lift it up," he said.

Bright carefully pinched one of the straps between two fingers and raised the bag.

Singer stepped closer, "What is it?"

"Gashes," Bright said.

"From what?"

"I don't know," Bright said. "They could be from hitting the rocks."

Gearhart studied them for a moment, then rose. "Except for my deputies, I want everyone out of the ravine."

"What?" Hannah said.

"This area is now a suspected crime scene."

"The entire ravine?"

"Yes," Gearhart informed her.

"Why?" Hannah asked. "What is it? What kind of gashes are they?"

"I'm not going to speculate," he replied.

"You're just going to dictate," she complained.

Gearhart turned from her to talk to Bright.

Since discussion was futile and the party was over, Hannah bolted toward the sinkhole. She was able to get a quick look at the gashes before the sheriff moved between her and the backpack. They were about five or six inches long, several inches apart, and clean.

"Ms. Hughes," Gearhart snapped, "I want you *back* on the road and in your car and I want you to recall your photographer at once."

"Sheriff, are they knife marks?" Hannah demanded. "Was there a fight?"

Suddenly, one of the road crew workers called from the edge of the sinkhole. *"Victor!"*

Singer looked up. "What is it?"

"Come here!" the man cried. "We found something!"

Singer, Gearhart, Grand, and Hannah went back up to the road. At Gearhart's orders Bright remained behind with the backpack. Hannah used her cell phone to call the Wall and get him back up to the sinkhole.

The crew had found Stan Greene's backpack. Unlike the other backpack, it was intact. Since this section of the road had fallen in after the rest, Dr. Thorpe suggested that the engineer might have removed it and set it aside before going into the sinkhole. There was still no trace of Stan Greene.

But granite was finally showing through the wet dirt; according to Dr. Thorpe, they had reached the bottom of the sinkhole. Tired but determined, the crew began clawing away at the sides.

Shortly after, the two volunteers of the Special Ops team arrived in the sheriff office's new Hummer, which barely fit on the roadway. The Junior SOV, young baby-faced Albert Moy, was a former Navy SEAL who worked as a tennis pro at the Santa Barbara Country Club. The Senior SOV, craggy, middle-aged Frank Lyon, was a retired movie stunt actor. Grand and Gearhart went off to confer with them and Hannah went back to her Blazer. She had to concentrate on rewriting the article, changing the emphasis from collapsing roads and missing engineers to a story that carefully insinuated an attack on at least one of the men. Despite the sheriff's silence, he had given her that much by declaring it a crime scene.

Hannah also wanted to start working on the follow-up. By tomorrow morning everyone was going to have the basics: what happened, biographies of the two men, interviews with family members, and any late news. *The Coastal Freeway* had to have those too but also something different.

She'd find it.

For the moment, however, Hannah listened to her tape, plugged in a few quotes from Deputy Bright and Professor Grand, and let herself savor something she rarely had: a breaking story. She also enjoyed something else, one of the things that had attracted her to this profession in the first place.

The sense of being in the middle of a human drama. Of knowing that with the world and the flesh in disorder, the devil could not be far away.

13

Grand and two Special Ops volunteers drove to the foot of Snyder Trail and walked to the slope. One of them carried a gym bag stuffed with gear; the other carted an aluminum case that contained a MarineScan UCM—the "You See 'Em," the Underwater Camera and Monitor. The Santa Barbara Sheriff's Office usually used this off-shore to examine everything from broken pipelines to shifting sand levels. Today it would be used to study the lake.

The other two men were in good physical condition and made it up to the cave without difficulty. It took less than an hour for Grand to rig their harnesses and get them down to the floor of the upper cave. By now the rains were lessening and there was enough light coming in through the swallow hole so they didn't have to use the night-vision goggles.

The three men walked toward the tunnel with Grand in the lead. The scientist's mood was slowly brightening. It had been dark when he left the ravine. He was angry about the way he'd let the sheriff manhandle him during the interrogation. It shouldn't have *been* an interrogation, it should have been an asking. A questioning. And Grand should have set the sheriff straight immediately. It was the same way Grand had responded to things all his life. He'd let someone push and push before finally giving a nudge back. And the nudge was never enough to gain back the self-respect he'd lost.

But he was back in his world where he felt safe. Where Gearhart and those like him faded to insignificance. Where the mission was to eliminate one's own ignorance, not learn to live with the ignorance of others.

The scientist looked up as they passed the steep cave walls. The two large paintings seemed subtly different from before. It appeared as though the lava and water were actually flowing. That impression could be due to shifting clouds changing the natural light or the fact that the men themselves were moving. Grand also wondered if the Chumash artist had created that illusion intentionally through the use of color, lighting, and slight variations in the rock surface. Maybe he was trying to suggest that the animal spirits were never at rest. It was an eerie and impressive creation.

The trip through the north-side tunnel was relatively quick and easy. Once they were inside the cave, the Special Ops team recovered the radio and placed it in a plastic bag. While they took detailed photographs of the ledge and the water flowing into the cave, Grand walked along the narrow stone outcropping. The ledge did not go all the way around the cave, so it was difficult to see where the water spilled after leaving here. Possibly it flowed into a series of caverns that emptied into the sea. That was how many of these so-called "mountain fountains" worked. They were carved by high-elevation runoff that began during the Ice Age, the water pouring through cracks and enlarging them over the centuries. But Grand had been right about the creek feeding the lake. Though very little light came from above, they occasionally heard the muffled, distant shouts of the men working above them on Painted Cave Road.

Surprisingly, Grand felt none of the apprehension he'd experienced when he was down here earlier. The air was as warm and close as before, the water was just as still, the gnats were equally as persistent. Perhaps the presence of the other men had somehow changed the dynamic. Or maybe something *had* been different then, something his senses had missed but his instinct hadn't.

After collecting their pictures, the men set up the UCM. The main unit consisted of a battery-powered, thirteen-inch color monitor with an antenna on top and a detachable joystick controller. The rest of the system was built on a white plastic raft the size and general shape of a mouse pad. On the underside of the raft was a plastic case with a halogen light, a small video camera, and a rudder. On the top, in the rear, was a small motor. After Moy placed the raft in the lake, Lyon steered it using the joystick.

Grand watched the monitor as the raft slowly crisscrossed the lake. The hum of the motor filled the cave with a soft, echoing drone while the camera's wide-angle lens broadcast sharp color pictures to the monitor. The lake was no more than five or six feet deep and the images showed a relatively smooth floor columned in places with stalagmites. Judging from the lack of erosion, the waters hadn't been here more than a few weeks. There was no sign of equipment, clothing, or anything else that may have washed down with the radio.

It took nearly an hour to cover the entire lake. When the men were finished, Moy packed up the UCM while Lyon radioed Gearhart. The Special Ops leader told the sheriff they'd found nothing except the engineer's radio and were planning on returning.

"Have you had any luck up there?" Lyon asked.

"Negative," Gearhart replied. "We're going to extend the search into the mountains."

"We'll be out of the cave within a half hour," Lyon said. "If you've got some place for Moy and me, we'll head directly there."

"Sounds good," Gearhart said. "Why don't you take the Arroyo Burro Trail. Work your way toward the Falls."

"Will do," Lyon said.

After the Special Ops volunteer signed off, Grand approached him.

"Do you think you can find your way out?" Grand asked.

"Sure. Why?"

"I'm going to stick around, look in some of the other tunnels," Grand said.

Lyon offered Grand his hand. "Stay safe, and thanks for your help."

"Anytime."

Frank Lyon turned and took a last look at the water spilling into the cave. "Professor, you've been around these mountains a lot. What do you think happened up there?"

"I don't know," Grand admitted. "The way the weather's been, the ground acting up—it's easy to get hurt or lost or swallowed up."

Lyon nodded. "Yeah. Lots of possibilities. We just haven't hit the right one yet."

Moy came over and wished Grand well. Then the men left, trailing light and clomping footfalls.

Grand fished his penlight from his jacket and clicked it on. He walked toward the far side of the cave. The sounds coming through the sinkhole dimmed and vanished as he approached the gentle waterfall. Because the lake was so shallow, it had probably been just a small pool before La Niña caused it to swell. The waterfall might not have existed before then, in which case the lower cavern might have been easily accessible to the Chumash.

Reaching the tunnel, Grand found a waist-high cupule on the right side of the entrance. He used the small, natural groove as a handhold and swung his left leg around. He placed his foot on the bottom of the opposite wall, just above the waterfall. Still holding on with his right hand, he shined the light along the narrow opening.

And looked down at the sky.

14

The cosmos was spread before Jim Grand. At least, that was what it seemed like.

Painted on both sides of the narrow tunnel were nearly linear arrays of white dots, crescents, circles, and semicircles. The images looked like stars, lunar phases, and what appeared to be several comets. The symmetrical objects ranged in size from several inches in diameter to over a foot across. Unlike most Chumash art, which was sharp-edged, all of the images were extremely fuzzy, as though they were twinkling. Like the two mountains painted in the upper cave, the walls down here were mirror images of one another, though only seven of the individual pictographs on each side were identical.

Grand looked down the center of the passageway. At the bottom, about twenty feet from where he was perched, the creek spilled into another underground lake. The lake below was shallower than the one up here, since Grand could see portions of stalagmites.

Grand would have to go further to see what was down there, but not today. He would have to go back home to get additional climbing gear as well as rubber boots, and he was also tired. He didn't want to make a mistake that might harm the paintings. Before leaving, he took a moment more to study the images. Though they looked like representations of the heavens, he didn't recognize any constellations among the smaller "stars." Perhaps the Chumash shaman was trying to explain celestial mechanics, imagining where the moons and stars went when they dropped below the eastern and western horizons.

That might be why there were no renderings on the roof of the tunnel. But if these images were heavenly bodies, why would the Chumash have painted them down here instead of in the upper cave?

It was possible the artist didn't want to offend the Great Eagle by putting his own stars and moons so close to the heavens. Or maybe it wasn't a shaman who had made these paintings. Perhaps it was a scientist who had to hide his ideas because they conflicted with beliefs about the animal gods. If so, this cave could hold unimaginable treasures.

Suddenly, something changed. It wasn't anything Grand could see or hear. He felt a chill, as though a cloud had moved in front of the sun. The sense of unrest returned.

Grand remained where he was, shining his light along the passageway. The waters glistened flatly as they spilled down the gentle incline. After a moment he thought he heard something moving in the water below.

"Roche? Greene? Is that you?"

The sound of the waters seemed to subside. Grand moved the light around. He didn't see anyone.

He agreed with what the deputy had said earlier. The men probably could not have slid down the sinkhole. Apart from the too-small size of the opening, the men would have dragged loose stones with them when they went down. There had been none of that along the sides. But freak events did happen. It was possible an animal had gone down the hole. Whichever it was, the cool along his back told Grand he wasn't alone.

"Roche! Greene!"

There was still no response and no further movement. If either man was here he might be injured. He thought of calling to the rescuers, but by the time they got down there the men could be dead.

Grand looked along the tunnel walls and floor for someplace to put his hands and feet. The first Chumash paintings were three feet away. He could go a little deeper without risking them. Grand tucked his penlight in his pants pocket, pointing up. He needed light but he also wanted his left hand free. He put his left foot in the water. The creek came up to his ankle and splashed over top of his boot, but the footing was good. He leaned back slightly to compensate for the slope and put his hands on the walls just inside the passageway. He simultaneously brought his right foot into the passageway and ducked under the low ceiling. He was now standing inside the tunnel.

He retrieved his penlight.

The first two designs on either side of him were crescents. They were sharp-edged, matching, and seemed to glow against the charcoal-gray rock. The Chumash were not known to have used phosphors in their art, but these designs seemed to be more luminous after having been exposed to the light. Or maybe it was another illusion.

There would be time enough to study the paintings. Grand looked down the tunnel. Nearly half the lower cavern was visible now but there was nothing new to see. More water, more stalagmites.

"Is anyone down there?" he shouted.

He began to wonder if his imagination had created a presence where there wasn't one. Caves could do that too, if not by their personality then through the release of gases like methane or nitrogen.

This time the rippling didn't stop. It grew louder as it moved closer to the bottom of the tunnel. That ruled out a geological bubble-blower such as an underwater spring or thermal vent.

Grand's arms and legs were growing tired. If whatever was down there didn't show itself soon, he was going to have to retreat—

Something bobbed up, startling him. As Grand watched, a large, black plastic cylinder surfaced like a submarine. It took a moment before he recognized it as a flashlight casing. Water spilled from the open back as the hollow container turned over in the lazy current. The casing flopped over and lay flat on the water as a series of big bubbles sputtered from the end. Then the flashlight began rotating in the flow like a rolling log. The face glass and bulb were both shattered. If one of the engineers had dropped the flashlight, it probably hit a stalagmite or two before sliding down here. Grand didn't see any threads on the back of the cylinder, which meant it must have had a spring-loaded battery cap. Those were easy to change one-handed in the field. A good knock could have caused it to pop open. If they scanned the shallow water below, they'd probably find the batteries on the bottom.

Grand thought about trying to retrieve the flashlight but the current carried it away again, toward the back of the cave. Even if he could make it to the lower cave without touching the paintings, he didn't know what the ground was like or how many other branches the cave had. He would tell the sheriff about it and then come back the next day, better-equipped, to examine the art. He didn't think Gearhart would insist on sending his Special Ops team back today. He needed his manpower outside, where it would be put to better use.

Grand took a long step back to the lip of the passageway. Before swinging onto the ledge, he had a final look at the pictographs. The images were unique and their meaning was a mystery. Perhaps they were stars, perhaps they were eggs, perhaps they were an attempt to create an alphabet. Maybe they weren't even meant to be taken literally.

But whatever the paintings were, they were haunting. A little part inside of Grand smiled.

After too long a time, it would be good to have a challenge keep him awake at night instead of sorrow.

A moment later the scientist turned and made his way back to the tunnel that led to the main cavern.

The empty flashlight knocked against the side of the cave and twisted gently away. It hit a stalagmite and changed direction, spinning into a flow that led from the cave to a steep tunnel. A moment later it washed down, plunging deeper into the mountain.

The cylinder was swept into a long, low cavern where the darkness was thick and unbroken. The smells were heavy, damp, and musty. The only sounds were those of the water as it rushed into a forked tunnel. That and a slow, deep, hollow breathing.

The wait was over. The breathing moved. So did the musty smell.

They moved into the forked tunnel and down one of the twisting branches. They moved swiftly, surely, through stalactites and stalagmites, around sharp corners, and across depressions where the water deepened. The breathing quickened as it moved and after a minute the rankness, too, was no longer the same. It sparkled with the hint of salt air. Even the darkness changed. It was no longer as full as it had been. Here and there the black shaded to dark gray.

At the entrance to another cave the movement slowed and the breathing turned around. The smell settled into a place above another tunnel.

There were other smells coming from below, the smell of salt and decay. And new sounds, the sound of water.

And the waiting began again.

15

The Coastal Freeway went on sale at noon.

Within two hours the office of the County Board of Supervisors—the six-person committee that represented the districts in Santa Barbara County—announced that a press conference would be held at 4:00 P.M. in the small auditorium of the county administration on Anapamu Street. In addition to Sheriff Gearhart, the mayor of Santa Barbara, the chairperson of the County Board of Supervisors, the chief of police, Caltrans spokesperson Carl Lessin, and Dr. Thorpe would be in attendance. Sergeant Marsha Levy, the sheriff's public information officer, said that Gearhart wanted to personally brief reporters about the status of the investigation in the Santa Ynez Mountains and then get back to work.

Use the press when you need them, Hannah thought.

Hannah and the Wall were there, along with reporters from the *L.A. Times,* the weekly *Santa Barbara View,* several local radio stations, and the network TV affiliates from Los Angeles. Hannah always sat in the front row of the small auditorium. It was tougher for Gearhart to ignore her from there. She set her tape recorder on an empty seat beside her—there was always an empty seat beside her—and took a stenographer's notebook from her shoulderbag. Hannah usually filled several pages with questions, though she always starred two or three of the most important. Usually, that was all she got to ask.

The press conference started nearly fifteen minutes after four as Gearhart was late getting in from the mountains. Hannah wondered if the delay was intentional. Gearhart was a skilled politician. He may have wanted to create the impression that only the responsibility of calming the public could tear him from the field. Chairperson Andrea Danza, a young Santa Barbara native, took the podium to introduce Sheriff Gearhart. Chairperson Danza claimed to have problems with Gearhart as well, though she only confessed those off-the-record, woman-to-woman. She, too, was a skilled politician.

In usual Gearhart fashion, it wasn't so much a conference as a recitation; the sheriff said he wouldn't take questions until the end when, of course, he would be in a hurry to return to the scene.

Gearhart began by saying that the sinkhole on the road itself had been cleared out. There was a map of the Santa Ynez Mountains behind Gearhart and he called on Dr. Thorpe to explain how there was a series of fissures that wound through the mountain, possibly connecting to the cavern where Jim Grand had found the radio. Though she and a deputy had made a cursory examination of the fissure Stan Greene had entered, they had found no trace of the engineer other than the backpack. The sheriff said that both backpacks had been removed from the site and were being studied by the crime lab for "the three Fs" —fibers, fingerprints, fluids—as well as any other "remnants." He indicated that while Greene's backpack appeared to be intact, there were gashes on Bill Roche's backpack that were also being analyzed. He didn't want to speculate about what had caused them, though he said that nothing was being ruled out.

Gearhart then revealed that "the team" had also found a flashlight, apparently belonging to Bill Roche. It was discovered in a cavern beneath the cave where the radio had been found. The sheriff speculated that it had been washed down with the radio and said that nothing else had been located.

Overall, Gearhart said, the search-and-rescue effort now consisted of twenty-four deputies covering the ravine, the roadway, and the surrounding mountains—a total of twenty square miles. He also indicated that helicopters would be watching the surrounding area for fresh sinkholes or persons such as hikers or campers who might have seen or encountered the engineers. When Dr. Thorpe returned to the site, she would lead a better-equipped unit into the Painted Cave fissures to make a more complete exploration.

Regarding possible explanations as to where the men had gone,

Gearhart still believed they'd be found in the area, possibly in the fissures. He acknowledged that a great deal of blood had been reported at the site and that it was lost in the second-phase collapse of the road. That was one reason he thought Roche may have ended up in the sinkhole. Looking directly at Hannah, he said that speculation regarding "criminal activity" was "irresponsible and premature." He said that he had declared the site a crime scene primarily as a precaution to prevent the accidental obliteration of clues.

Gearhart sat and Chairperson Danza returned to the podium.

"Thank you, Sheriff Gearhart." Danza looked out at the press corps and smiled. "We'll take a few questions before Sheriff Gearhart and Dr. Thorpe return to the field—"

Hannah raised her hand and rose. "Sheriff, I understand that you've checked the Honor Farm and other penal institutions for possible escapees, and have also looked into the backgrounds of the two engineers."

"That's correct."

"Can you tell us anything about those?"

"In all the places we've checked, the prisoners are accounted for," Gearhart said. "We've expanded our investigation into surrounding counties. Those results will be available through Sergeant Levy later in the day."

"And the engineers?" Hannah pressed.

Danza pointed to Carl Lessin.

The Caltrans information officer rose. Hannah had talked to him before on the land-sale fiasco. The smug young man was in his middle twenties and clearly delighted to be sitting there with the big boys.

"Psychological profiles are private and privileged," he said.

"I understand." Hannah persisted. "But if there's a potential risk to the people of this count—"

"There is no discernible risk," said Lessin, "and as Sheriff Gearhart indicated we do not intend to speculate."

A few reporters asked about the sinkholes—how they were created and whether the roads in other areas of the mountains were safe. Dr. Thorpe explained the process concisely and "Joe Caltrans" added that his department had dispatched emergency teams to other sections of mountains to "ascertain the stability of the tertiary road system."

Indicating that Sheriff Gearhart and Dr. Thorpe were needed back in the field, Chairperson Danza ended the press conference. She said that reporters would be contacted via phone or E-mail if there were new developments.

Gearhart left then, promptly and directly, by a side door. The TV reporters went over to Chairperson Danza to discuss going up to the Painted Cave sinkhole and taking videos. Hannah didn't understand what satisfaction any journalist could get being a gatherer instead of an investigator.

The Coastal Freeway was located in a two-story house down the block from the main post office on the corner of Anacapa and Canon Perdido streets. Hannah left the auditorium, got into her Blazer, and was sitting in her office less than five minutes later, reviewing her notes from the press conference. She was going to E-mail questions to everyone who had been present.

"Who knows," she muttered. "Someone might slip and answer one."

Hannah didn't think the sheriff knew more than he was telling. But she didn't believe the answer was as simple as two men being trapped in a sinkhole. And she didn't think the sheriff believed that either. There was blood on the road—a lot of it, according to the emergency team. If both men had gone under, where did the blood come from? If only Greene was buried and the blood belonged to Roche, where was he? Seriously wounded men did not travel far.

Hannah resented not being able to ask those questions. And she disliked the vanity or politics or whatever it was that prevented Gearhart from ever saying, "I don't know."

After submitting the questions, Hannah checked her E-mail. There were the usual jokes she didn't have time to read from people she barely knew, cover letters with attached press releases from local businesses, and updates from family members that went to siblings, cousins, aunts, uncles, and grandparents. She didn't have time for any of that now. Hannah's personal E-mail address was on the newspaper masthead and she'd been hoping for responses to her article on the missing engineers. Perhaps from someone who might have seen or heard something, maybe even a ransom demand.

There was nothing.

After talking briefly with Karen Orlando about other assignments, Hannah decided to visit the engineers's wives. They'd declined to talk to her on the phone, but they might feel differently in person. Before leaving, Hannah instructed Karen to phone her with any RT—radio traffic—that had to do with sinkholes old or new or a missing anything. She also grabbed what was left of Karen's tuna fish sandwich and took it with her.

The drizzle had stopped and the gray skies were a shade lighter than they'd been since morning. The rain left behind damp and darkened roads, an unseasonable chill, and a sense of calm that was somehow more ominous than reassuring.

16

On the way home Jim Grand decided to stop by the *Hutash* offices on Del Playa Drive to visit Joseph Tumamait. Maybe the paintings would intrigue him, maybe not. Maybe he would talk, maybe he wouldn't. It was going to be tough, but it was long, long overdue.

The robust, thorny eighty-two-year-old Tumamait was a leading anthropologist, an expert on Chumash culture and one of Grand's mentors. Born in nearby Camarillo, the scientist was a UCSB graduate who had worked with Margaret Mead at the American Museum of Natural History in New York before returning to the west in 1965. Mead's involvement with the mental and spiritual health of primitive peoples had fascinated Tumamait, who passed his love of primitive psychology on to one of his own students, James Grand.

From the first, the men were very close friends and colleagues. Tumamait often risked his reputation to back Grand's revolutionary ideas about the relationship between pre– and post–Ice Age peoples and the monsters they hunted. The ideas were revolutionary in part because they were not based on anthropological evidence but on Grand's own experiences in the field. Grand had become the modern world's foremost expert on prehistoric weapons. Collecting and studying ancient samples, then learning to make his own. Grand became convinced that the hunt was far more than just a matter of food-gathering. The use of weapons required daily refurbishing of blades, careful storage of feathered shafts in clean, dry places, and adjustments dictated by the weather—arrow wood, spearhead bindings, and even the herbal sleeping potions used in drinking water were affected by rain and snow, heat and cold.

Grand believed that the people best-suited to create these weapons—and perhaps to use them—were the shamans, the same people who rendered gods, animals, and tableaux of the hunt on cave walls. But if the shamans among the Chumash and other peoples believed that animals were holy, how could they hunt and consume them?

The answer, Grand felt—and Tumamait agreed—was that the entire process was aspirational. Preparing for the hunt, the shamans and their caste slowly became the animals—in spirit at first, tracking them as an animal would, and then in the flesh when they consumed them. The animal spirit and meat were then passed from the shamans to the tribe as a sustenance and religion.

The idea of warrior-shamans was a revolutionary one, and not wholly embraced by either the scientific community or most of the surviving Chumash. But Grand had the best kind of evidence. He had made weapons and he had dwelt in caves and hunted for food. The entire process made the hunter intimate with the stones and the trees from which he crafted his weapons; with his own thoughts and spirit when he set out; and finally with the elements, the land, and his prey. It was a process about creation, life, death, and spirit. If a young man were not a shaman when he first became a hunter, he probably became one in time. Apart from telling tales to the young or infirm or those who didn't hunt, the only way to express what he was feeling was through art.

Many scientists believed that prehistoric people were simple people, interested solely in survival. They regarded shamans as eccentrics who were feared because they knew some medicine and they knew a few tricks. Grand didn't agree, and Tumamait was his greatest advocate.

Then, seven years before—while Grand was working with the Smithsonian—Tumamait went up to one of the caves where a hiker had found pottery. While he was resting by his stone campfire, Tumamait was visited by the Great Eagle. The scholar later said the Chumash god gave him a mission: to protect the Chumash heritage by protecting the earth. The vision was so compelling that Tumamait came back to Santa Barbara, resigned his professorship, and put both his life savings and his passion into *Hutash.*

Grand understood how that had happened. He had felt the presence of spirits many times in the caves. They always came in the dark, when you were alone, when the senses were alert and the mind was open and undistracted. Sometimes they kissed the soul, sometimes they were an eerie prickle. But Grand had never been moved the way Tumamait had—perhaps, Grand suspected, because he approached experiences like these with the mind and not with the spirit. There were fewer roadblocks getting to the soul.

Tumamait's relationship with Grand changed after the elder's vision. He withdrew emotionally from those who were not Chumash. He tried to maintain his relationship with Grand until the young anthropologist began mapping the Santa Ynez Mountains and discovering new caves. Tumamait had come to regard the paintings as a resting place for the gods. To disturb them was to put the needs of men before the needs of the spirit world. He could not endorse that, nor could he share his insights with those who did.

However, Tumamait did not entirely close the book on the relationship. He also wrote, "Sometimes the gods test us. If they test you, then you will understand, as I have, that we are not masters but servants."

Because they had been so close, Grand always hoped there might be a way to reconnect at some time on some level short of a deific trial. Possibly through a Chumash find, one that would excite the anthropologist that was still somewhere inside Joseph Tumamait. One that would convince him of something Grand had always believed, that being Chumash—or any people, for that matter—was a matter of conviction and dedication, and not of blood.

Perhaps the tunnel art was it.

Hutash became an influential environment organization. Their chief rivals were powerful oil interests, construction industry, and transportation groups that used shell organizations to channel money into civic improvements, political campaigns, University of California scholarships, United States Geological Survey research, and other groups and causes. The implicit goal of these donations was to remind Southern Californians that—as a Caltrans executive had once put it—it was not always possible to grow the quality of life without the land to grow it on. Like his ancestors, Tumamait had been able to slow but not stop the encroachment of what he called the *Haphaps*—the destroyers. There were even those at *Hutash* who believed that Grand's grant was given for two reasons. First, so that Chumash cave sites could be identified in order for housing construction to be undertaken without damaging them. And second, to strike at Tumamait by engaging one of his former star pupils. Grand didn't know if any of that were true. All he *did* know was that the more sites he found, the more Chumash caves and former dwellings would be protected now and for all time.

Hutash's offices occupied the top floor of a modest, three-story building that overlooked Window to the Sea Park in Isla Vista. The tan walls were decorated with turn-of-the-century photographs of Chumash people and settlements. The only artifacts were wall hangings and wood carvings that had been made by modern-day Chumash.

The tall, bald-headed Tumamait received Grand immediately. The men hadn't seen one another since Rebecca's funeral.

Grand was openly happy to see his mentor. Tumamait's welcome was courteous, with a hint—just a hint—of satisfaction in the heavy-lidded eyes. The Chumash elder obviously knew something that Grand did not. The men embraced briefly.

"Hyvasti," Grand said, using a traditional Chumash greeting.

"Petaja," Tumamait said, a formal expression of gratitude. "I thought you might come."

"Oh?"

"There was an owl feather on my stoop this morning," he said.

"The messengers of the Great Eagle," Grand said. So that was it, the reason for Tumamait's smile.

"The feather was the color of your hair and eyes and the eyes were damp with dew."

"Are you pleased?" Grand asked.

"I'm always pleased when my beliefs are vindicated."

Grand grinned. He detected a whisper of the old Joseph Tumamait in his manner. Tumamait wouldn't give Grand the satisfaction of admitting he was happy to see him. But Grand sensed he was.

Tumamait took a step back and looked his former student over carefully. "You look tired."

"I am."

"I mean inside," Tumamait said, touching his own chest.

"That too," Grand replied, his smile softening. "It's been difficult."

"You are tired because you keep Rebecca trapped inside," Tumamait said. "Her spirit is free. You must let it go."

"I know," Grand said.

The Chumash believed that unless the spirits of "the beloved dead" were ceremoniously put to rest, they stayed with the living. Frustrated at being unable to touch and feel, the spirits became malevolent and destructive—sometimes physically, as *maniti*—poltergeists—and sometimes emotionally. Tumamait had offered to help him send Rebecca away through fasting and recitations of a ritualistic wedding ceremony, bonding the widower to the earth. That would allow Rebecca to become *nashu,* "the next thing," an animal closer to the gods. Grand had declined. He wasn't ready to let Rebecca go.

"But you know me," Grand went on. "I carry a piece of everyone I ever met. I carry a lot of *you* with me."

"My people call these 'scars,'" he teased.

"There are a few of those, but there are other things too," Grand smiled. "Mostly very good things."

"Not recently," Tumamait pointed out.

"No," Grand admitted. The smile softened. "Joseph, I came here because I need a favor. I need you to help me solve a puzzle."

"What kind of puzzle?"

The elderly man listened as Grand described the new discovery up in the mountains. Grand described the tunnel, the white circles and crescents, and the symmetry of the designs. When Grand was finished, Tumamait was silent, his expression unchanged. Grand had hoped that the nature of the discovery might spark some of the old curiosity. Apparently, it had not.

"I've never head of a Chumash shaman creating astronomical art," Grand continued. "If that's what I've found in the caves, it could be an extraordinary discovery."

"For whom?" Tumamait asked.

"For all of us," Grand said.

"You know what I believe," Tumamait told Grand. "Those works were not created for all of us. They were meant for the eyes of the gods and for other shamans."

"I also know that we aren't certain who they were meant for or who looked at them."

"And we will never know," Tumamait said. "Why not leave them, then, as the creators wished?"

"Because I want to learn everything I can about an amazing civilization. And I want to show others *how* great they were . . . how great you are."

"What others think won't change my people."

"But it might help improve the rest of us," Grand said. "We think that our communications and medicines and knowledge are greater than anything that has come before. That isn't necessarily so."

"James, years ago I told you that when the Great Eagle came to me I realized the paintings of my people are not meant to be talked about and analyzed," Tumamait said. "They are not stories to be read. They were painted by the enlightened. They are doorways into another realm meant to be opened only by the gods. I'm sorry, but I can't help you with this. If the earth has chosen to speak to you, you will know it in time."

"'In time' may be too late," Grand said. "Strange things are happening in the mountains. Disappearances, caves opening, the past emerging."

Tumamait said nothing.

Grand felt like he was back in school, being pushed by his professor to discover things on his own. In this case, though, he wasn't sure whether his mentor wanted him to continue searching or whether he really wanted Grand to stop.

"All right then," Grand said. "Let's try this. Have you had other visions since the first one?"

"Many," Tumamait said.

"Were they all of the Great Eagle?"

Tumamait nodded.

Grand stepped closer. "Be my teacher one more time. Tell me one thing he's taught you."

Tumamait thought for a moment. "I will tell you this. *Haphap* is dangerously near," the elder replied.

"The Mountain Demon," Grand said. "How do you know?"

"The Great Eagle comes to me when the world is in discord and he is no longer content to be spirit," Tumamait said. "He came to me recently. He was changed."

"In what way?"

"His feathers were those of an owl."

"Why?"

Tumamait didn't answer.

"Is he well?" Grand asked.

"He is a god," Tumamait said. "He comes because the earth is not well."

"In what way?"

"That is for us to determine," Tumamait replied.

"And fix."

"And fix," Tumamait agreed. "Good luck."

Grand smiled and offered his hand. "I'm not sure what I need good luck with, but thanks for your time." The smile turned bittersweet. "I miss the old days, sir. I miss talks like these, our explorations of mind and land."

"Perhaps we will have them again."

"I want to," Grand said. "It's been too long."

Tumamait clasped Grand's hand. "There are many roads to the same place. Hopefully, I'll see you at the end. Until then, James, be careful."

"I'll do my best," Grand said.

He left the office feeling—how had Rebecca put it once when she came back from church? *Lightened but not enlightened.*

Though he still didn't know much about the paintings he'd seen, he had reconnected with Joseph Tumamait. And that was something.

17

Grand pulled up to the curb just as Fluffy was coming in from his late afternoon walk. The scientist was looking forward to seeing the dog. He could use some unqualified support after the difficult encounter with Tumamait.

He didn't get it.

The Labrador retriever had a walker named Stanley Walker, which was one of the reasons Rebecca had hired him. The retired actor was conscientious and had good references, but Rebecca also enjoyed irony and silliness.

Fluffy usually greeted Grand by throwing his oversized front paws on his chest and barking until he drooled. Today he planted his paws on Grand's chest and just stood looking up at him, silently.

"What's wrong, boy?" Grand asked.

"He's been a tad weird today," said the short, white-haired, well-groomed Walker.

"In what way?"

"Our boy has been extremely quiet."

Grand put his hands under Fluffy's big ears and looked into his gentle eyes. "You got a problem you need to talk about? Was that collie next door teasing you again?"

"I don't think so," Walker said. "Marley was quiet today too. So were my other dogs."

Grand looked at Walker. "All of them?"

Walker nodded.

"Has that ever happened before?"

"Just once," Walker said. "Right before the Northridge earthquake. But this is different."

"In what way?"

"It's not like they're earthquake afraid," Walker told him. "They haven't been hiding under the bed or in the bathtub or any of that business. It's also not a sick quiet. I don't feed them the same brand of food, so it isn't poisoning. They're just—not excitable. That's the best way I can describe it."

Grand scratched hard behind Fluffy's ears. The dog took it without his usual panting enthusiasm.

"See what I mean?" Walker said.

Grand nodded. "It could be the weather."

"Too much gray?" Walker said.

"Maybe. Something else we can blame on La Niña. If we can whip up a little sun tomorrow maybe we'll all feel a little better."

"I know I would," Walker said as he gave Fluffy's ribs a strong pat. "I'm running out of dry shoes." He gave the big dog another pat and then headed for his station wagon. "Well, good night, Fluffy. Good night, Professor."

"Good night." Grand said.

Grand and the dog crossed the stone walk that cut through the center of the small, neatly kept yard. Grand had cut the seven stones himself after Rebecca's death. He'd carved them in the mountains and carted them down here; anyone who looked at them closely might notice that they were rough-hewn letters that spelled his wife's name.

Grand took a quick shower, dressed in sweatclothes, and snatched a cold chicken drumstick from the refrigerator. He usually bought a whole cooked chicken on Sunday and picked at it the rest of the week. It was only Wednesday; this bird wasn't going to make it. But it had been an active week and Grand usually didn't bother eating lunch.

He finished the chicken leg and sat down at his crowded desk. Fluffy lay on the mat beside the chair, as usual. As Walker had said, there didn't seem to be anything wrong with him other than the fact that he was quiet. Rebecca had always insisted that animals could get the blues, just like people. Maybe La Niña *was* that cause.

Grand booted the computer. Over the years he had built an extensive library of prehistoric and pictographic art, starting with books he had begun accumulating when he was six years old.

Back when he was Jimmie "Grand Canyon," he thought. The memory came with feelings that were both bitter and warm, loving and angry, polar emotions in careful balance. Two more things that were perched on the tips of the Great Eagle's all-encompassing wings.

Grand still had those original books on his shelves. Only now there were literally thousands of books featuring tens of thousands of illustrations ranging from the hieroglyphs of Middle Eastern peoples to the more recent designs of Native Americans. While many of the illustrations were in books, some were on videotape and some—most, in fact—were stuffed in file folders.

Undergraduate anthropology students at the university had been scanning the loose art onto diskette for Grand. He decided to check those first. The pieces had been indexed by subject and he began by inputting the keywords *moon, sun, planets, comets,* and *stars.* Grand was more familiar with the European and North and South American animal art than he was with celestial art and was curious to see what would turn up.

The search gave him star charts of prehistoric Polynesian seamen, carvings of constellations by the Naxca peoples of southern Peru, stars drawn in the Sacred Almanac of the Mayans, Babylonian lunar maps, and the Chaco Canyon, New Mexico, monuments of the Anasazi.

Grand accessed the Anasazi photographs, which were of artwork dating from A.D. 900 through 1130. There was a color petrograph of the 1,054 supernova which created the Crab Nebula. It consisted of carvings showing three concentric circles roughly a foot in diameter with flame firing off to the right. Above it were a large star, a crescent moon, and a handprint.

All of the renderings were interpretive rather than literal. So were the astronomical designs Grand found in other files. The Egyptians of the Eighteenth Dynasty visualized the omnipotent sun as a wide, glowing eye. The Hopi of the North American Southwest portrayed stars as flaming arrow tips. The Thules of prehistoric Alaska imagined shooting stars to be the dripping blood of wounded animals. Apparently, no early artists had rendered the heavens as literally as the Chumash painter. Grand checked some of his books and found the same symbolic art among other ancient peoples.

That made sense, he thought. Like the afterworld, the heavens were incomprehensible to ancient people. They would have personified or anthropomorphized the universe to make it understandable.

Grand sat back in his chair. It was getting dark and he switched on the fluorescent desk lamp. He thought for a moment. He went over what Tumamait had told him, but he didn't have any new insights on his single word.

"Exactly."

He put Tumamait from his mind for now and went back to the source. Maybe the old man *didn't* know the answer and was simply suggesting that the question itself was the problem.

The trick to solving mysteries like these was to try and free the mind from contemporary knowledge and references. Not to think of the earth or moon as huge spheres but as a fragile dirt shell and a bright eagle's eye in the sky, respectively. To imagine the gods living above and below and seeing everything and controlling the weather and the flow of water and the fertility of the land. To be aware of their spirit emissaries moving through the dark to give shamans visions and ordinary mortals dreams or nightmares.

To think like an ancient man.

When that was done, it was necessary to look at the designs for the first time—again.

He had found Chumash paintings of the Great Eagle soaring through blackness, but never any that represented the heavens. Perhaps showing the god was as far as the shamans went.

"Hold on," Grand thought aloud. "Maybe they're not stars at all, Fluffy."

Grand went back to his earlier thoughts and word-searched *eggs.* He found several designs from around the world. They ranged from perfect ovals to cracked ovals to hatched and broken shells. Some eggs were giving birth to animals, some to people, some to hybrid gods. Some were white, some were brown, some were red. He found nothing that looked like the Chumash designs. He checked *Native American alphabet.* The Chumash frequently traded with other tribes, perhaps they picked up some of their symbols.

He looked at samples of the Cherokee alphabet, of the Mohawk, the Blackfoot, the Cree, the Lakota, the Potawatomi, and others. There was nothing that looked like what he'd seen in the tunnel.

"Maybe you're still going about this the wrong way," he said to himself.

Typically, Chumash cave paintings were not interrelated. Designs within individual caves were often random, like the rooms in a museum. They were linked only by the artist or the era. Maybe these were different. Perhaps the mountain with the snake and the mountain with the dolphin were designed to lead to the paintings in the tunnel.

"The dolphin mountain is white," Grand said. "Maybe the pictures are supposed to be ice or snow."

But deep inside the mountain? That made no sense.

Maybe the designs were meant to be read the other way, from the bottom up. The circles and crescents could be leading *to* the mountains, flowing from inside the earth.

"What about seeds?" he thought out loud. "Maybe the Chumash thought that mountains were born from rock-eggs. Or maybe the designs are supposed to be clouds formed inside the earth—"

Grand liked that one. Maybe the shamans thought that clouds were smoke, that they were formed by fires that burned inside the earth. He decided to word-search *clouds,* see if there were other examples of subterranean origins. Even when ancient peoples had no contact they often came up with similar ideas, such as boats or rafts that took the dead to the underworld or newborn kings being sent to earth in baskets. The phenomenon was called "cultural parallelism" and it had helped Grand interpret cave paintings in the past.

As the computer searched for *clouds,* Grand looked down at Fluffy. The dog was asleep on his mat.

"What do you think, boy?" Grand asked. "Did the shamans believe that clouds were made from fire?"

Fluffy looked up and Grand reached down to scratch the dog under the chin. As he did, Grand saw something he hadn't noticed before.

"Shit," he said as he swung back to the computer, canceled the search, and started a new one.

18

The two luminescent eyes watched the long, deserted roadway from low on the gusty promontory. Moist and dark, like large oily pearls, the eyes shifted and widened almost imperceptibly at every movement a hundred feet below. They roamed among the dim lights and deep shadows, the tall waves of the sea beyond, the dark beach, the large sea animals that broke the surface in the distance, the night birds that soared and hovered above the rocks, the flat clouds, the misty raindrops, the signposts rattling in the wind.

Most of these things were familiar; a few were not. But new or old, it was a world of constant movement, a world where any motion could be enemy or prey. Which was why the eyes missed nothing. Nor did the ears, which were shaped like gold tulip petals. They stood high and faced the front or the sides, wherever they heard a disturbance. Nor did the light-brown nose, its finely cobbled surface flexing restlessly in the wind. And then—

It froze as the scent came suddenly, from the north. Unlike many of the smells, this one was familiar and welcome. Prey from the sea. A moment later, when it grew stronger, the head turned back. The black eyes were met by other black eyes and they all began to move, though not in the same direction.

Quickly and silently they slid through the brush and stones, causing mice to flee and rattlesnakes to freeze and commanding the foothills simply by moving through them. The color of the prey was different, the speed was greater than they had seen, but the size was familiar.

They knew just what to do.

Glen Grey was a happy man.

Ten years before, when he was an eighteen-year-old high school graduate—and just barely—the Pacific Palisades native was a beach bum. He sold himself to volleyballers who wanted a good game or a championship; he gave surfing tips for pay; and he held spots close to the water, then sold them to latecomers for a twenty. When there were no gigs to be had, he grilled burgers and hotdogs at Ma's and Paz on the corner of Via de la Paz. Grey slept on the beach or crashed with friends or found an open car door and dropped on the backseat. When there was nowhere else to go he went home. Actually, where he went was "house" since it wasn't really a home. Not with his unemployed actor dad who toked-up or coked-up and took out his frustrations on his only son, and his entertainment lawyer mom who was never home even when she wasn't on a case.

Things changed for Grey when his friend Bartok broke his leg on a new board. While Grey sat with him waiting for the ambulance, Bartok complained that he was dead shit: He drove a refrigerator truck from the Santa Barbara marina down the coast to Los Angeles with fresh fish for over two-dozen restaurants. How was he going to drive with a broken leg?

Grey offered to do it for him. He agreed to take only half the salary and tips, which was way above what he was making at Ma's. Bartok agreed.

Grey ended up loving the job. He would spend the entire afternoon on the beach, charging his batteries. Then he would drive south after midnight with the day's catch. He'd make the rounds, leaving it with early-rising chefs or in outdoor freezers, come back after dawn, and sleep in the truck or in an open boat at the marina until after noon.

The owner of the company, Caroline Bennett, also loved Grey. He was easygoing, reliable, and obeyed the speed limit and parking laws. When Bartok returned, the boss asked the young man to stay on. Grey agreed, and nine years later he was still here, taking rockfish, red snapper, yellowtail, whitefish, and sculpin on what he called "Their last trip along the coast."

Grey especially loved cool, rainy nights like these. Windows open, leather gloves snug on his hands, feeling cool. Doing the reverse commute at this hour, traffic was sparse. Especially here, on the fringe of Santa Barbara County. When the weather was bad, as it had been these past weeks, even the locals stayed off the coastal roads. It was mostly tourists who had no choice. They were here and they had to see Santa Barbara *now.*

The silence was sublime and the solitude was absolute. There was usually just Glen Grey, his ocean, and the growl of the diesel engine. Sometimes he talked to the "once and future-sushi" lying in barrels and lockers in the back—depending on whether they needed to be in ice or in saltwater—and sometimes he just listened to his groovily smoky Audra McDonald and Debbie Gravitte CDs. Sometimes, like now, he just enjoyed the quiet—

The bump startled him.

It was a hollow sound, like something had landed on the roof—maybe a falling branch or a rock or something from an airplane. The Santa Barbara airport wasn't far away. Grey slowed immediately and looked out the side mirror. If something had bounced onto the road he wanted to move it or call the highway patrol and set out a flare.

Nothing was out there. He looked toward the side. There were rows of grassy foothills leading up to a sandy slope and a two-hundred-foot-high promontory. Not much could have hit him from there. He wondered if a gull might have come down for some reason. Maybe it had been attracted by the smell of the fish. Those birds could be pretty aggressive. Grey once had a seagull land on a picnic table and snatch away the slice of sausage pizza he'd bought at the marina. The entire slice, for God's sake—

There was a second thump, much closer to the front of the truck. It was followed almost immediately by a third sound, more like a bang, directly on top of the cab.

"Friggin' *what?*"

Grey needed to stop. He looked out the passenger's-side window. If things were bouncing off the hills and onto the road he wanted to pull over on the ocean-side part of the highway.

As the young man turned, something banged on the windshield. He turned face-front just as the window blew in, showering Grey and cab with particles of glass. The drizzle and wind momentarily blinded him; he jammed on the brakes and shifted gears. Rubber screamed and burned and the cab twisted. Grey dragged the sides of his right glove across his eyes. As he did, the lids filled with motes of glass that had caught on his lashes.

"Fuck!" he screamed, wide-eyed. *"Shit,* god, *god!"*

Points of pain drove him mad and forced his eyes to open wide. He released the wheel and picked at his lids, trying to pull them down, as awful pinpicks danced on all sides of his eyeball.

The truck skidded on the wet highway. Grey screamed as the sharp edges stabbed the insides of his eyelids. Shrieking with pain, he squinted into the weather as he tried to regain control of the vehicle.

Suddenly, the darkness turned gold, then red. Pain flooded his body from neck to thighs.

A moment after that he went numb. And his eyes, which had been so anguished, shut for good.

19

Grand had spent several hours going through the computer files, books, magazines, and Web sites looking through Chumash art. Every time he found an image of an animal he enlarged and enhanced it.

Grand didn't find what he was looking for and at three-thirty in the morning he finally gave up and went to bed. He would start again when he was fresh. Or at least fresher. He was so far behind on sleep that it would take a week of doing nothing just to get back to normal.

Fluffy followed him to the bedroom. The Lab hopped onto the foot of the bed, circled his spot twice, then literally fell across the quilt. Grand envied the dog, who was asleep within seconds. The Chumash had had that right too. Animals were superior to humans in many ways. More efficient, certainly.

The scientist pulled off his sweatclothes and slipped under the covers. Grand sat there, his back against the headboard. He looked at the dog.

"We make a good team, Fluff," he said.

Fluffy's head rose an inch.

"You come up with good ideas and I do the legwork," Grand said. "I only wish I knew which one of us screwed up tonight."

Fluffy continued to look back at him, patiently and politely.

"I still like the idea," Grand said, "so it must've been me who screwed up. We'll try and figure this out tomorrow. Right now, sleep."

Fluffy agreed and lay his head down. Grand stretched out too, sliding his tired, swollen feet under the dog. He'd done a lot of climbing and it was good to give them a rest.

He lay there and thought about the idea. It *was* sound. What he'd seen tonight when he looked at Fluffy was something that a Chumash shaman would have seen and pondered and might have painted.

The fact that Grand hadn't found any precedent didn't discourage him. Perhaps if he could figure out whether the images in the passageway related to the paintings of the mountains—

Later, he told himself, looking over at the clock. *Do this later.*

Grand shut off the light, punched up the pillow, and settled his head in the middle. He closed his eyes. The rain was stopping. The night was still.

He wasn't going to have any trouble sleeping tonight. It had been a long day but a challenging and also rewarding one. If nothing else, he'd reconnected with Tumamait. It was a tentative step but one he'd needed for a long time. And he had a mystery to solve. Because of that, because his passion had somewhere else to go, his thoughts of Rebecca were dreamy rather than sad. He saw Rebecca sitting at the dining room table on her day off, catching up on newspapers, journals, and correspondence. He could still smell the sweetness of her neck, feel her under the pink terrycloth robe. He could smell the Kona coffee she loved, taste the melted butter of an English muffin on her lips. He smiled as he remembered a song she once improvised to get him away from his computer late one night. She had called it "Chumash," a love song about a man and his art, and she sang it to the tune of the old Association song "Cherish."

Rebecca was so alive in his mind and senses. How could he want to send her spirit away? If he did, then he'd lose these precious moments along with the bad memories.

Or would he? Wasn't there a place he could keep the happy times and still allow her spirit to rest, let himself get on with the business of living?

After a few minutes Grand was too tired to focus on the things Tumamait had said. Consciousness grew heavy and black. But before he surrendered it entirely, the images from the lower cave came back vividly, like the last, memorable bangs of a fireworks display.

Grand cracked his tired eyes. He didn't see how he could be wrong. He had seen the images from the cave in his living room.

The desk lamp gleaming in Fluffy's eyes. A pair of white crescents, side by side.

Grand shut his eyes again. He wondered where a Chumash shaman might have seen those same images. In what animal and under what circumstances? By sunlight? Moonlight? Firelight? And why would he have painted them in that passageway? Had that cave been inhabited by wolves or bears at some point in the past? Did the Chumash believe that one of their gods lived below? Did they think that this was the entrance to *C'oyinashup,* the lower world?

And if they did, were they right?

It was the last thought Grand had before surrendering to sleep.

20

Carl Fischer always took his morning jog just before sunup.

The middle-aged manager of the Montecito post office would suit up in his black tights, a singlet and waterproof windbreaker, running shoes, and a tiny "headlight," a flashlight that fit around his forehead like the reflective glass doctors wore when he was a kid. Then he'd do a brisk mile along the narrow, deserted strip of beach. *His* beach, since there was no other human out at this hour and precious few birds. When he got back to his small waterfront home, Fischer would shower, put on the post office blue-and-whites, make apple and cinnamon oatmeal and hazelnut coffee, and enjoy them on his deck facing the Pacific. Fischer loved sunsets over the ocean. He loved having dinner on the deck with his wife and teenage daughter. But the sunrise, lighting the sea as it climbed over the mountains, was even more thrilling. The texture of the water changed with every moment and was different with each new day.

He loved the run, too. Rain or sun, the air was always invigorating and it gave him the lung-cleaning he needed to work indoors from six to three. After thirty years he could literally *smell* the difference between oil- and water-based ink on third-class newsprint, knew when magazines arrived with perfume and cologne sewn into the bindings, and had been compelled by employee sensitivity training to be mute about mail carriers and clerks who needed showers or deodorant. He'd suffocate without this daily purging.

The air had a misty chill but at least it wasn't raining. There were a few breaks in the dark, blotchy clouds where crisp stars could be seen against the blacker sky. Occasionally a car zipped by on 101 and then, save for the breakers, it was quiet again.

Fischer knew the beach and he knew the air. And he knew when something was different. This morning, when he neared the cove that marked the half-mile point, he knew that things weren't right. There was a strong, foul smell in the wind. It grew stronger as he ran so he started breathing only through his mouth. He heard dozens of birds from somewhere in the cove just ahead. Since the occasional early-rising gull usually picked its meal from the sea, Fischer's initial thought was that a whale had beached here. The cove was lower than the highway and the tides reached their peak around nine P.M., so it was possible that motorists might not have seen whatever was here. Fischer continued toward the line of rocks that formed a small, natural breakwater on the near side of the cove.

The white beam of Fischer's headlight bounced as he ran. He saw the sea slam against the rocks on the inside and crest in low, white plumes. Gulls sitting on the breakwater hopped up with each new wave. Fischer counted at least twenty birds on the outskirts of the cove. There were more birds beyond; he could see them as he neared. He slowed. The rocks were coated with droppings, which meant the birds had been here a while.

When he was about fifteen feet from the breakwater, Fischer turned toward the sea. The rocks were too high to see over, especially piled high with gulls, so he would have to go around them. He removed his shoes and socks. The tide was out and he wouldn't have to go in very deep to get around the rocks, maybe waist-high. He walked toward the water, alternately looking toward the cove and watching out for sharp-edged seashells.

The rocks were lower the closer to the sea Fischer came. He could see now that the birds were piled on something. They were clustered together so thickly that they looked like a single wriggling mass. There had to be a whale under all that. He couldn't think of anything else that would attract so many birds. The birds were quiet and ignored the glow of the headlight.

Carl Fischer waded into the surf; the water was stinging cold and the sand felt like slush. He continued to look to the left as he made his way toward the cove. When he finally rounded the breakwater, he stopped. What was in the cove was not a whale.

There was a truck beneath the birds. It was lying on its side, the cab facing the sea; the top and one side of the vehicle were both caved in. The gulls were not only on top of the truck but inside as well, feeding on whatever was there. They were also spread out on the beach, picking at bones and bits of flesh from what looked like fish.

Fischer didn't want to get much closer and risk making the birds angry. But he felt he should have a look at the cab, see if someone was alive in there. The front of the truck was facing away from him, so he went back to the water's edge and walked to the south. Birds were clustered in the cab as well, which wasn't a good sign. Fischer stopped slightly past the truck. The top of the cab and part of the windshield were facing him. The exterior itself was free of birds but the interior was packed. Stepping back into the water, Fischer picked up a rock and threw it at the cab. The stone hit the driver's-side door with a loud clang and sent birds flying out the broken window. They settled lightly on the sand, the started walking back again. But in that brief moment, Fischer got to see what the birds had been poking through.

It wasn't a fish.

21

There was no rain or wind. The sun was well over the hills by the time the highway patrol had finished constructing the tent over the fish truck. The blue, four-sided valance—a so-called "banquet" tent—was thirty-by-thirty feet long and covered on all sides. Gunfire had been used to frighten and scatter the birds before the sides of the tent were laced up. Volunteers were piling sandbags on the ocean-side of the truck. It was 8:00 A.M., just past low tide, and the sea was still twenty yards out. The waves wouldn't reach here until after 2:00 P.M., but Chief Traffic Investigator Idestrom wanted to protect the site and any potential evidence for as long as possible. Three highway patrol investigators were outside the tent taking measurements and photographs, trying to figure out how fast the truck was going when it went off the road. Four more officers were examining the outside of the truck for signs of vehicular failure such as a blown tire, broken axle, or worn brake.

Sheriff Gearhart was standing inside the tent watching, which was all he could do for now. The accident had occurred in Montecito. Though the town was part of Santa Barbara County, Montecito had a contract with the highway patrol to investigate vehicular accidents. Until the highway patrol investigation was finished, Gearhart couldn't take charge of the site or the investigation. However, Idestrom had allowed four criminalistics technicians from Gearhart's office to work on the cab of the truck. The CTI was territorial, but he wasn't blind.

The cab of the truck was bright with blood. The blood was still damp where it was thickest and looked as though it had been poured on the driver's-side seat cushion and the back of the seat, splashed on the passenger's seat, on the floor and under the mats, and on the dashboard, and dribbled on the large and small slivers of glass that were strewn about the cabin. But there was no body. Not in the cab, not on the beach, not in the surf, and not on the road. Sheriff Gearhart knew the gulls hadn't done that, though he had no idea what did.

While he waited, he talked by radio with his field commander in the Santa Ynez Mountains. Though the search for the two missing engineers had continued through the night, expanding into the surrounding mountains and including twenty local volunteers, nothing had been found. Dr. Thorpe had spent until midnight in the fissure along with two deputies and a pair of bloodhounds who had been given the scent of both backpacks. They'd gone for over a quarter mile in both directions and found nothing. Thorpe was fascinated by the tunnels but the dogs were so unimpressed that one of them actually lay down and wanted to go to sleep toward the end of the trek.

Gearhart had finally gone home at 3:00 A.M., napped until 6:00, and was about to return to the site when he'd gotten the call from his communications officer about what Carl Fischer had found. Gearhart came right over, arriving just minutes after Idestrom. He was there when the driver's boss, Caroline Bennett, arrived to ID the truck. At least, that was the official reason she'd been called to the site. The name was painted on the side; the highway patrol knew who owned the truck. Having the owner come there gave the investigating officers a chance to talk to her while she was emotionally open and her lawyer wasn't present. According to Idestrom, the talk wasn't particularly useful. The CTI turned that part of the investigation over to the sheriff's office.

Andrea Danza arrived a few minutes past eight. She made her way through a small crowd of reporters, ducked under the crime-scene tape, and entered the tent. Hannah Hughes shouted after her that they should be allowed to take pictures inside; Danza said she'd ask the sheriff, which was the first thing she did.

"I think that's a bad idea," Gearhart told her.

"Why?" she asked.

Gearhart took her closer to the truck. The sheriff knew that Danza was a former emergency medical technician who had been to the sites of car accidents, gas tank explosions, and fires. The sight of blood was not new to her. But after seeing the site close-up she agreed with the sheriff. In addition to the shattered truck, there was a thick coat of bird droppings, blood, dead fish, and a few gulls that had been crushed or pecked to death. The big waterfront fire that nearly destroyed Stearns Wharf in 1998 had spawned a gruesome cottage industry of postcards, mugs, and placemats. She told Gearhart that this was not the image she wanted her administration to be remembered for.

They stood looking at the cab.

"My God, Malcolm," she said. "Have you ever seen anything like this?"

"Not in this country," Gearhart replied. "Even in 'Nam, I never saw this much blood without a body somewhere."

"There wasn't one?" Danza asked.

Gearhart shook his head.

"I assumed it was taken away—"

"Not by us," Gearhart said. "And the man who found this swears he saw nothing in the cab except gulls poking through the blood. If there was flesh here, they got it."

Danza looked unwell. "What can you—I mean, where do you—"

"Start to look?" Gearheart asked. "I'd probably have some of the birds shot and dissected. But then I'd have Joseph Tumamait and his shorehuggers up my butt and probably no real evidence to show for it."

"Then where did the body go?" Danza turned her face toward the sea. She breathed slowly, deeply. "Could the driver have still been alive after this? Could he have walked away, maybe fallen into the water and been washed out to sea?"

"I've got two boats out there looking," Gearhart said. "But I'm not optimistic. According to my forensics chief, most of the driver's blood is in that cab. I don't think he could have gone anywhere without it."

"What about a big explosion?" she asked. "The back of the truck looks like it was hit."

"The top of the truck was *im*ploded," Gearhart said, "and the back of the cab itself is intact. That isn't what got the driver."

"What if the truck hit the breakwater when it left the road?" Danza said. "The driver could have been thrown."

"There are no signs of scraping on top of the truck or on the rocks," Gearhart said. "That was the first thing we checked. And he wasn't thrown. The seatbelt is still buckled."

"Still buckled?"

"Yes. He was pulled out. Or torn out."

"Unbelievable."

"Yes," Gearhart said. "But what's most unbelievable is that we haven't even got a shoe or a piece of bone or any trace of the driver anywhere. Not even footprints, though the tide was probably a lot closer to the truck when this happened. The killer could have walked in the surf or even on the cab itself. The truck is also near enough to the road so that someone might have parked on the shoulder, hopped onto the truck, and stayed off the sand altogether."

"And then just drove away with the body," Danza said. "Or what about *flew* away in a helicopter?"

"That would have shown up on the airport radar," Gearhart said. "One of my deputies checked. There was nothing in the log."

"Did you get anything else from the man who found the wreck?"

"Highway patrol talked to him for over an hour. Unless he's a hell of an actor, he didn't make off with the body."

"What about the owner of the seafood company?" Danza asked.

"She said that everyone loved the driver," Gearhart said. "But according to Caltrans, Roche and Greene didn't have enemies either—"

"Hold on," Danza said. "Do you think these incidents are related?"

"It's possible," Gearhart said. "The emergency crew reported finding a lot of blood up at Painted Cave Road. Now we have this. Maybe some whacko's moving south, sniping at people from the foothills at relatively close range and then taking the bodies."

"Like a serial killer or cultist."

"Something like that," Gearhart said.

What he didn't tell Danza—he knew she had cooperated with Hannah Hughes in the past and didn't want this getting around—was that he wasn't ruling out Greene as the killer. The first patch of blood was found where Roche reportedly had been waiting for him, and there was no damage to Greene's backpack, only to Roche's. The men might have struggled and Roche could have had the backpack on while they fought. Since the search team started moving out from that site, Greene might be panicked or flipped-out and was doing the same. According to Chief Deputy Valentine, the senior engineer's psych profile indicated that he had been treated for severe depression and was taking medication to treat it. Gearhart didn't know what the hell could depress a guy with a secure, good-paying job and a couple of healthy kids. But he had never understood people who "broke" anyway.

"So how do we handle this?" Danza asked.

"With who?"

"The reporters waiting outside, for one."

"Assuming that Greene and Roche continue to be missing," Gearhart said, "we tell the press that both situations are still under investigation and we don't see any evidence that the disappearances are connected and that there is no evidence of criminal activity."

"That's probably best for now," Danza agreed. "Okay. That's what we *tell* them. Meanwhile, what do we do? We can't say there's no criminal activity and then put out a general advisory—"

"No, but we can take strong, reasonable precautions," Gearhart said. "I've ordered Chief Deputy Valentine to increase our vehicular patrols in the hills from Goleta to Montecito. He's also stationing lookouts along San Marcos Pass and at high spots overlooking other roads, which is another reason we need to keep this quiet. I don't want people spotting our guys up there with spyglasses and high-powered rifles and thinking they've found a killer. I'll be talking with Captain March at the highway patrol later this morning. We'll work out shifts to cover the highways and main roads throughout the county."

Danza nodded. "Do you want me to handle the—"

"Sheriff!"

The voice had come from the cab. Gearhart walked over, followed by Danza. The sheriff was surprised that he could smell the rubber of the gloves over the scent of the fish. Then again, maybe he'd just gotten used to the stench. He could also smell the tart scent of the IS vapors being used to search for fingerprints. The vapors were a combination of iodine and superglue, which could be sprayed onto any surface, including blood. They coalesced quickly on prints and revealed more details than traditional powder.

The sheriff stepped up to portly team leader Thomas Gomez, who was on his knees in the sand, right outside the broken windshield. The three other members of his group were working through the open passenger's side door and on the other side of the shattered windshield. There was a gentle hum coming from inside the cab. Gomez had hooked a small battery pack to the air system and was blowing the contents of the vents into plastic bags. The bags had pinholes that allowed the air out but kept particles in. Sometimes pieces of skin, strands of hair, or fluid samples ended up in the bags.

"What have you got?" Gearhart asked.

"A very weird case," Thomas admitted. "Sheriff, did the victim have a dog?"

"I don't know," Gearhart admitted. "Why?"

"Because we've got what looks like fur stuck in the blood and floating from the air vents," the balding man replied. "There's also what looks like spittle in the grooves of the floor mat. It's thicker than drool from any dog or bobcat I've ever seen, though I'll have to check it against samples from rabid animals. If it matches, that would lead us in a whole different direction. I'd also put in calls to all the local zoos and animal preserves."

Gearhart pulled his cell phone and notepad from his jacket. He was angry at himself for not having thought to ask about the dog. A lot of drivers traveled with dogs for companionship, protection, and to keep from having to put them in kennels. He checked his notes for Caroline Bennett's number and called. The woman had gone back to her office with a deputy to talk to the packers in the small warehouse, see if Glen Grey had seemed different from usual the night before. There was always the chance that he had to meet with someone on the road, maybe a drug dealer or someone who held a chit, possibly a gambling debt. If so, he might have been anxious or depressed.

Gearhart was only on the phone for a few seconds. "The driver did not have a dog."

"Well, that does complicate things," Gomez said. "There was almost certainly a long-haired animal here at some point."

"Maybe he picked up a stray," Danza said.

"I doubt that," Gomez said.

"Why?" Gearhart asked.

"Because I haven't found any nose-painting on the pieces of glass," Gomez replied.

"Excuse me?" Danza said.

"You're not a dog owner," Gomez said.

"No."

"If a car window is closed, dogs often put their paws on the dashboard and their wet noses on the windshield," Gomez said. "So I'm betting this was a predator, possibly drawn by blood after the accident and possibly it was a bobcat—though if a carnivore *was* here, I also don't understand how it managed to get the victim out without leaving footprints in the blood. A bobcat can't just *pull* someone through a broken window."

"I know," Gearhart said. He looked back across the smashed walls of the truck. "And an animal didn't cause those breaks."

"I also don't understand why there isn't a trace of the victim other than blood and a few strands of hair," Thomas went on. "A large boa constrictor could do that, but they don't have fur, they don't live here, and they leave slither marks, which pretty much rules that out. Like I said, it's a weird one. I'll know more after we get the fur and spittle samples over to the lab."

Gearhart nodded, then called Chief Deputy Daniel Mahoney, head of Support Services—as the sheriff's office floaters were known. The unit backed up all the other divisions. The sheriff told Mahoney to have one of his deputies check with the Santa Barbara Zoo and to call everyone in the database who might own or train big cats, wolves, Komodo dragons, or other predators, possibly for the movies. Gearhart wanted to make sure all the animals were accounted for. If no one picked up the phone or if Mahoney thought someone was not telling the truth—private owners occasionally lied to try to get their animals back before they were shot or confiscated—Gearhart told the chief deputy to send a car out. Mahoney said he'd have the answers before noon.

Gearhart put the phone away and went back to the cab. Danza excused herself to brief the press.

Though the sheriff had gone through the drill with Mahoney, he wasn't convinced that an animal had done this. Scavenged perhaps, but not killed or taken the driver. His gut told him this was a thrill-kill, as Danza had said.

In Vietnam and in Los Angeles, Gearhart had seen people do sadistic and bizarre things. Some of them were worse than this. Now, as then, he didn't spend time trying to understand why they did it. He tried to find evidence that pointed to *who* was responsible and where they might be now or the next day. And then, whether it was in a humid jungle or an overcrowded city, he did one thing more.

He made sure they didn't do it again.

22

Hannah Hughes wanted to tear someone's head off and throw it. Hard. Preferably Gearhart's, though the head of any bureaucrat would do. At the very least the reporter felt like tossing her small tape recorder into the banquet tent and running in after it.

Oops! Dropped it. Sorry.

What was the worst the sheriff could do. Arrest her? Gearhart wouldn't want to give her the publicity. But she *was* afraid that he'd bar her from other sites, so she behaved herself.

It was just before eight-thirty in the morning and a dozen reporters were packed into a small area ten feet from the tent on the north side of the beach. Sandbags and the breakwater kept them from getting closer on the other sides of the tent. Hannah and the Wall had been on the beach since six-thirty, ever since Karen Orlando came in and happened to pick up the highway patrol radio report of the accident. Hannah wished she had the money to hire someone just to monitor all the police and fire department communications during the night. Then they could get a jump on stories like these. By the time they got here, the tent had already been raised and Gearhart had put out the DO NOT PASS GO tape. The only information reporters had been given was that a fish truck belonging to Bennett's Surf had gone off the road and that the driver was dead. Hannah had tried to reach Caroline Bennett several times on her cell phone, but the line had been busy. Hannah left messages for her to call back.

In the meantime, Hannah paced the small patch of beach between the tape and the breakwater. She looked at the area around the sunlit rocks, at the steamy road—the tread marks were light, indicating only a modest application of the brakes—at the sea. There were a pair of the sheriff's patrol boats nearshore. That was unusual. They had to be part of the investigation, but why? Hannah was also disturbed by things she *wasn't* seeing and by the attitude of many of the reporters. Some of the print people had spent an expense-accounted night in Santa Barbara rather than go back to Los Angeles, Fresno, and Monterey. They were drinking coffee and eating croissants and apparently waiting for either the chance to photograph a colorful wreck or for something to break with the missing engineers. And that seemed to interest them only because it might involve blind thrusts. Freshly uncovered faults in Southern California were always newsworthy.

At eight-thirty, Andrea Danza finally came out to speak to the reporters. The woman had on her stern, official face, which meant she'd be giving tight-lipped, cautious answers to soften the bad news. Hannah had been down this road with her before. She wasn't in the mood for it.

Danza began the short "briefing," as she called it, by stating that highway patrol still didn't know what had caused the accident. The tires of the truck were intact but there was no information yet about the condition of the brakes, the steering, or other vehicle systems. Danza said that she was not authorized to release the name of the driver until his next of kin had been found and notified. She agreed to answer a few questions.

"Can you tell us anything we hadn't already figured out?" Hannah asked. Her frustration was showing. She didn't care.

Several of the reporters laughed.

"What would you like to know?" Danza asked.

"What do the police think *caused* the accident?" Hannah asked.

"That's still under investigation."

"Is there any speculation?" Hannah fired back. It was like Ping-Pong. She had to keep going until Danza missed.

"You know that we never speculate on situations of this nature," Danza replied.

"Was the driver drinking?"

"That has not yet been determined."

"Ms. Danza," said another reporter, "is there anything new on the missing engineers?"

"Sadly, no," she said. "That search has been expanded but nothing has turned up."

"Have there been ransom demands?" the report asked.

"No," said Danza.

"What are the patrol boats doing offshore?" Hannah asked.

"They're sweeping for contents of the cab that may have washed out with the tide," Danza replied.

"Was the driver alone?" another reporter asked. The way he asked implied something salacious.

"There is no one else in the truck at present and no evidence that anyone left it," Danza answered.

"It's been over two hours," Hannah said. "How long do you plan on leaving the body in the vehicle?"

That question caught Danza off-guard. Her pause, though momentary, surprised Hannah.

"Until the investigation is complete," Danza said.

"Shouldn't the coroner be involved with this investigation?" Hannah asked.

"By county law and policy, no," Danza replied. "It was the decision of Chief Traffic Investigator Idestrom of the highway patrol to treat this tragic incident as an accident. The CTI invited the sheriff's criminalistics team to work on the driver's remains, and their investigation had been in progress for over an hour. Unless Mr. Gomez and his group finds possible criminal cause and the crash site is turned over to Sheriff Gearhart, the coroner is not required to make an on-site evaluation. Now, if you'll excuse me—"

"*Has* the criminalistics team found anything to suggest foul play?" Hannah asked. "A stab or bullet wound on the body? Could the driver have picked up a hitchhiker who got off before the truck—"

"It would be premature to comment on any of that while the investigation is ongoing."

"It wouldn't be premature to *deny* the existence of any marks," Hannah suggested.

"I'm sorry," Danza said, "but I'm not going to comment on any details of this investigation." She excused herself and began walking toward her car, which was parked up on the shoulder with the other cars.

This was bullshit. Hannah knew Andrea Danza and she knew when Danza was stonewalling. There was no ambulance here. No hearse. Two patrol boats were searching the coast. Maybe they were looking for beer cans that might have floated from the cab—or maybe they were looking for something else.

Then it hit her.

"Madam Chairperson, *is* there a body in the truck?" Hannah asked.

The woman kept walking. Hannah was the only reporter who followed her as she opened the car door and got in.

"Ms. Danza, that's an easy question," Hannah pressed. "Can't you give me a yes or no? You said no when someone asked about ransom demands—"

The woman looked up at Hannah. "You don't know how to give a person room."

"For what, Andrea? Wiggling or lying?"

"Breathing," Danza said. "Right now, Ms. Hughes, I wouldn't answer if you asked whether the sun was shining."

"The body's missing, isn't it?" Hannah said. "That's why the coroner's not here."

Danza shut the door and started the car.

"Why are you keeping this from the people?" Hannah yelled as her phone beeped. "What's the problem here?"

Danza drove off. Snarling in frustration, Hannah fished the phone from the pocket of her windbreaker. "Hello?"

"Hannah, it's Caroline Bennett."

"CB, hi," Hannah turned toward the road, looked up at the mountains, tried to put Andrea from her mind at least for a moment. "Thanks for calling back."

"Sorry I couldn't talk before but I've been on the phone, "Caroline said. "Plus there's a deputy with me. He's interviewing one of the packers now, so I was able to catch a break. It's been a bad morning."

"I know and I'm sorry," Hannah said. "I was hoping you could tell me what's going on. They've got the crash site sealed off and they won't even tell us if there's a body."

"You're asking the wrong person," Caroline said. "I don't know what the hell's going on."

"What do you mean?" Hannah asked. "You were here before."

"Yeah, and I didn't see much more," Caroline told her. "I came to the crash site. I stood on the road, I identified the truck, and then I was taken to a highway patrol car to answer questions about the driver."

"Weren't you asked to ID the driver?"

"No."

"Did you see him?"

Caroline said she did not.

"Then I'm not understanding this at all," Hannah said. "Who is the driver?"

"Hannah, I can't. They'll know where it came from and Gearhart will give me and my drivers trouble—"

"I understand," Hannah said quickly. Screw Danza. She knew how to give a person room when they deserved it. "Can you tell me what kind of questions they asked you?"

"Routine stuff," Caroline told her. "The driver's background, who he hung out with, where he hung out, how long he was with us. The sheriff even wanted to know if he had a dog."

"A dog? Why?"

"Apparently, they found fur in the cab," Caroline said.

"Just fur? No paw prints in the blood?"

"Huh?" Caroline asked.

"I mean, a dog didn't come sniffing around after the accident?" Hannah asked.

"Oh, I don't know," Caroline said. "Listen, I'm getting motioned over by the deputy. I've got to deal with him and then talk to my insurance guy and also see if I can still get fish to my clients. If you need anything else, can we talk later in the day?"

"Sure," Hannah said. "Sorry to keep you and thanks again."

"You're welcome."

Caroline hung up. Hannah slipped her phone back in her pocket. The Wall shambled closer.

"Remember when we used to have to find a phone booth to do this?" the photographer asked.

"Yeah. But I'm not getting any more information than I used to."

"Technology. The great myth of our time."

"Not now, Wall," Hannah said. She was looking back at the tent. The other reporters were beginning to disperse. Then she looked back up at the mountains. "Something's not right here."

"What?"

"Something happened that they don't want us to know about."

"Maybe *they* don't know what happened," the Wall suggested. "Maybe that's what they don't want us to know."

"Possibly." Hannah glanced behind her, at the road and at the foothills. Helicopters from the search-and-rescue unit were visible in the distance. "But Sheriff Gearhart has to be thinking the same thing I am."

"Which is?"

"That this may be related to the disappearance of the engineers," Hannah said. "And if it is, there's something Gearhart may have missed."

Before the Wall could ask what that was, Hannah had her phone out again and was running to her Blazer.

23

It was seven o'clock in the morning when Jim Grand returned to the "volcano" cave. That's what he was calling it, since the volcano—the one with the serpent, not the dolphin—was the only image he could identify positively. He had a little more than six hours before his afternoon class and he wanted to use them productively.

The scientist had brought extra gear to explore the underground tunnels, including rubber boots and crampons for negotiating the sloping floors of the lower passageway. However, Grand knew when he got there that he probably wouldn't be needing any of it. The water runoff from the ledge was just a trickle now, not only because the rain had stopped but because the extensive drainage system built by the California Water Resources Department over the last twenty years was finally able to handle the overflow above ground. As a result, less of it was spilling into the caves.

After hammering a piton into the ledge, Grand tied a rope to the duffel bag and lowered the gear to the cave floor. Then he secured the other end of the rope to the piton and climbed down. Since he wasn't going to be studying the walls there was no reason to use the harness.

Grand spent nearly two hours exploring the fissure on the opposite side of the main cave. Before going back to the "white designs" tunnel and possibly descending deeper into the cave system, he wanted to see where the more accessible southern tunnels led. He also wanted to find out whether the Chumash had painted designs there. Driving up here he'd had a wild notion. If this complex of caves was as extensive as he thought, perhaps the Chumash had charted them and left the map on a wall. Though that would have been unprecedented for the Chumash, other ancient peoples had left similar designs on cave walls. It would be better to check before he went down rather than after.

There was nothing inside.

Unlike the tunnel on the north side, this section was extremely difficult to negotiate. Though it was dry in here—the slant of the ledge above sent the runoff to the north side—the tunnel was also small, narrow, and unventilated. According to Grand's compass he was headed southwest. It didn't surprise him when, after nearly two hours, he came across chalk markings on the wall. Unfortunately, the designs weren't made by the Chumash. They were a pound sign and an arrow pointing away from that spot, a geologist's notation that the tunnel had been explored to that location from the direction in which the arrow was pointed. No doubt Dr. Thorpe had come this far from the other direction, from Painted Cave sinkhole—probably a good quarter-mile—looking for the two missing engineers. The geography would be right for her to have reached this spot. He could picture the world above. Behind him, in the northern tunnel, was where the ravine sinkhole had dumped the creek water into the lake.

Grand made a similar chalk notation pointing in the other direction. Then he returned to the main cave. He wondered, as he always did when he made markings on a cave wall, whether some future archeologist would find the chalk marks and wonder who made them and why.

Shortly after 10:00 A.M., after taking a water and granola-bar break, Grand was ready to go back into the north-side tunnel that led to the underground lake. During the long night Grand had spent with the Chumash archives, he'd developed an adversarial relationship with the mysterious images. He was looking forward to spending more time with them, wrestling with them, trying to figure out whether they were eyes or something else.

The floor of the tunnel was dry and he reached the lake in less than twenty minutes. There was very little water running in from the creek and the lake had shrunk to nearly half the size it had been the day before. Crisp stalagmites split the softly rippling surface and the waterfall leading to the lower cavern was a smooth and gentle flow.

Grand made his way along the ledge to the tunnel where he set down his duffel bag. He put away his flashlight, donned his night-vision glasses, and stepped into the mouth of the tunnel. He'd brought along the video camera but decided not to take it with him until he'd reconnoitered. If the ground was solid and the footing secure, he'd come back for it.

Grand looked at the paintings, but only for a moment. Something else caught his attention.

The waters in the lower cavern had also subsided, leaving just a small, still pool in the center. There was detritus on the surrounding stone floor. Among the smooth pebbles, soggy pieces of tree bark, and leaves that had washed down from the creek, he saw a pair of batteries. They had probably fallen from the flashlight he found the previous day. Before he did anything else, Grand decided to retrieve them and see if there was anything else that might have washed down from the engineer's backpack.

Grand squatted and started down the tunnel. He didn't need his crampons to get down the passageway, though he moved slowly and was extremely careful not to place his hands on any of the images.

As he descended, Grand glanced at the paintings. Looking at them, he was less and less sure that the images were eyes. While they looked exactly like the shapes he'd seen in Fluffy's eyes, they were extremely fuzzy. Chumash work was typically sharp-edged.

Reaching the bottom of the passageway, Grand tested the ground with a foot and then stood. He had suspected that this cave was much smaller than the one above and that was confirmed. It was nearly one-third the size. The air was surprisingly musty and the cave was extremely cool and dry. He guessed that until the creek bed opened up there hadn't been any water down here for ages. The scientist stepped around a stalagmite, walked a few steps to the still, small pool, and took a quick look around. There were no paintings on the walls, so he removed his goggles and turned on the flashlight.

What he saw surprised him.

The walls were covered with a webwork of fine, jagged, superficial fractures. He'd never seen anything like them. His first impression was that they resembled the sutures of a human skull. The rock also had a strange, multicolored surface. Though the basic tone was steel-gray, almost like graphite, there were very pale reds, greens, whites, and blues swirled into the surface. The cave above had been entirely charcoal gray.

Grand began moving around and under the stalactites and stalagmites. The stalagmites rose about four feet from the floor and the stalactites descended five or six feet from a twelve-foot-high ceiling. Like the cave wall, they were stained with color and had wire-fine cracks up and down each one of them. Reaching up, he closed his gloved hand around the tip of one of the stalactites. The stone crumbled easily, like burned wood or charcoal.

"What the hell did this?" Grand murmured. He brushed off his glove on his pants and continued to look around. He couldn't figure out what had caused these cracks. He hadn't seen anything like them in the cave above and he had never seen two caves so close together that had experienced such obviously different geological stresses.

Then Grand noticed something on one of the stalagmites. He bent closer and shined the light on the stone. There were several long, straight hairs caught in one of the cracks. Grand removed his glove and carefully plucked the hairs out. He examined them carefully under the light. There were five of them, each one stiff and thick and approximately five inches long. The hairs weren't dark, though he couldn't tell precisely what color they were. Because they were bristly, one strong possibility was that they had been part of a Chumash paintbrush that had been left down here and torn apart by the swirling waters.

Grand placed the samples in a plastic bag, then looked closely at the other outcroppings. There were hairs caught in several other stalagmites as well. A dog or a coyote or a mountain lion could have been washed down here. They might have been caught in the sinkhole at the creek. But unless the water had been much higher down here, he couldn't imagine how the hair had gotten stuck three and four feet from the floor.

Grand had intended to spend time in and around this passageway measuring the icons, taking a few low-light video images, trying to see the designs fresh by looking at them from different perspectives: from the middle and bottom of the passageway, from the far end of both caves, and lying flat on his back in the center of the tunnel. He had planned to explore the extremely steep, narrow, twisting tunnel that led from the small cave to who-knew-what below. He had wanted to run the video camera around the lower chamber so he could study the site later, maybe share it with Dr. Thorpe.

But now he had another mystery and he had to get this one into the lab. For the one truism of science was never to let too many mysteries collect. Knowledge can't be built on leaps of faith.

The scientist took a moment to scrape mineral samples from the cavern walls. He used the edge of a small blade from his Swiss Army knife. Then he carefully brushed the rock fragments into a plastic bag. He would also bring those back to the university for analysis, see what had caused the discoloration and how long the non-native minerals had been present in the rock.

Grand exited the cave, then checked his watch before he began packing his gear. He would have just enough time to get the samples to the various university laboratories before teaching his class. He was looking forward to getting back in front of students. It was an enforced break, a time to clear his head. It was also a place to get a new perspective. Going back to basics always helped him to see things fresh.

With his finds safely stored, Grand left the cavern.

Behind him, the darkness was still, silent, and absolute.

24

Hannah loathed and detested the bullshit article she wrote about the truck crash.

The reporter didn't usually react that strongly to her work, not only because the topics weren't particularly controversial but because the stories tended to have a resolution by the time she wrote about them. An election. A race. A fire. But the mystery of the missing engineers and the dead driver was still ongoing.

What bothered her most was that she felt that she was misleading the public. It was probably like writing for *Pravda* under the Communists, but it was her own damn newspaper. Journalistic integrity kept her from saying what she really thought, that Sheriff Gearhart and Andrea Danza were hiding something and that the situation at Painted Cave and on the beach might be related.

Hannah was also frustrated that she hadn't been able to reach Jim Grand. She had left a voice-mail message at the office and at his home. When he didn't call back and her deadline neared, she rang the anthropology department at the university and asked if he had a cellphone number. She was told that he didn't have a mobile phone.

"The signals don't reach the caves he explores," said an assistant.

She had wanted to talk to him for that day's edition. The sheriff and his people were busy searching the hills. But Hannah wanted to know if any of the mountain caverns might reach from the Painted Cave sinkhole to the beach where the Bennett's Surf truck was found.

Having no cell phone wasn't going to help her do that. Hannah thought of asking Dr. Thorpe, but she didn't want Caltrans and Sheriff Gearhart to know what she was thinking. She had a feeling Gearhart's supply of crime-scene tape could cover most of the Santa Ynez Mountains. She also considered asking her friend Allen Daab, a traffic reporter for Los Angeles's number-one radio station, to take his chopper on a pass over the mountains and try to spot Jim Grand's SUV. But even if Daab agreed to do it, Hannah wouldn't have had time to drive up there and search the caves for the scientist.

All of which left her in a very pissy mood. Even the sun finally coming through the big cathedral window of her brick-walled office didn't cheer her. It warmed the room, lit up the wall-framed photographs of her family, gleamed off the plaques she'd won for college journalism and community service and editorial contributions she'd made to local business leagues. Even the plants on the shelves seemed happier. But not her.

She sat at her desk and glared at her computer monitor and reread the article she had written on the Caltrans engineers. It wasn't so much a story as an update: how many people were involved in the search and how it had expanded. The families had refused to talk to her and Caltrans had nothing to add to their upbeat bullshit statement that they were still hoping for a successful resolution to the situation. She reread the article she had written about the fish truck accident. It told where the crash had occurred and what kind of truck was involved, but not *who* was driving, *why* the accident might have happened, and *where the goddamned body was.* What kind of newspaper was she running if she couldn't get basic information like that? A shitty one, obviously.

The missing body thing annoyed her most of all. Not just the mystery but because Hannah couldn't even *say* the body was missing. Never mind a lawsuit from the driver's family for pain and suffering if she was wrong. She didn't like *being* wrong, especially not in print.

Shortly before filing the story she decided to give Grand's office one more try. To her surprise, he picked up.

"Professor!" she said.

"Yes?"

"This is Hannah Hughes."

"Ms. Hughes, hello," Grand said. "I was just listening to your third message—"

"Yes, I'm sorry about all those," she said, "but I really need to talk to you. Actually, I needed to talk to you about an hour ago, but now will do if you have a minute."

"All right," he said. "Unfortunately, I only *have* about one minute."

"I'll talk fast," she said. "Here's the thing, Professor. Did you hear about the truck crash this morning outside of Montecito?"

"No. I've been in a cave all morning. What happened?"

"A fish truck went off the road and I think the driver's missing. No one's being allowed near the truck, so I can't say for sure. But if it's true, and if it's connected to the disappearance of the engineers, it could be a big story. What I need to know is this. Is it possible that the caves, tunnels, and sinkholes connect the Painted Cave region with the foothills near the beach in Montecito?"

"Sure, it's possible," Grand said. "In one way or another all the underground systems are connected, from Baja California to Alaska, both over the land and under the sea."

"Great. I just want to make sure—we're not talking metaphysics, here?"

"I'm sorry?"

"You know, like in the East. That all things are connected throughout the universe."

"No, we're not," Grand said. "Though I don't repudiate those beliefs."

"Of course not. Do you know of any direct routes from the place where we were to the beach?"

"Not offhand," Grand replied. "I'd have to look up some of the geologic charts—"

"Could you?" Hannah said.

"You mean now?"

"Please."

"Ms. Hughes, I've got work to finish up and then a class to teach."

"Hannah. And I'll call you Jim. Look, I know this is an imposition, but it's very important.

"It also may prove irrelevant," Grand said.

"Why?"

"Because of the rainfall," Grand told her.

"I don't understand."

"Some of the old, charted tunnels may have collapsed and some new ones may have opened up," Grand told her, "like the one I was exploring this morning, which lead to a series of tunnels and the subterranean cavern where I found the engineer's flashlight—"

"*You* found that?"

"Yes."

"Gearhart, you lying SOB," she said. "He said he found it."

"He can have it," Grand said. "The point is, the only way to be sure of any connections would be to find a cave, sinkhole, or fissure near the beach and work your way backward, to the northeast."

"Couldn't you go the other way?"

"Not if you don't want Gearhart to know."

"Oh, right," she said. "Good point."

Shit, Hannah thought. A hive of "be's," a journalist's nightmare. The maybes, could be's, might be's. Though Hannah was taking notes, she knew she wasn't going to get much of this in today's already-late paper. She wouldn't be able to prove most of it in time.

Okay, she told herself, she was semi-resigned to that. But if there were anything to her theory she was going to get it into tomorrow's edition. And to do that, she was going to need help.

"Professor," Hannah said, "would you possibly, please, consider working for us?"

"What?"

"As a paid, independent consultant," she said. "Accompany me to the foothills and look around. Help me see if there's an opening that could connect to the Painted Cave sinkhole, and if so whether it looks like someone or something has been using it."

"And if the answer is yes?"

"Then we'll call in Sheriff Gearhart," she said. "Not to show him up, I swear," she added quickly. "I just want to be in there getting dirty. He can't blow me off if I have some kind of evidence."

Grand thought for a second. "Ms. Hughes, ordinarily I'd be happy to. But I've got some important research to do right now."

"Professor—Jim, I understand but I'm begging you. This is breaking news and you're the only one who can help me get it right."

"I'm not the only one—"

"You're the only one I trust," she said. "And I don't want to go nosing around up there alone or with the Wall."

More silence.

Hannah had to fight to resist playing the don't-you-hate-Gearhart-too? card. She was afraid that bringing Grand's late wife into this, even obliquely, might shut him down rather than fire him up. Grand's hesitation was killing her, but Hannah pressed her lips together. She didn't know if even a gentle *please* at this point might push him the wrong way.

What the hell, she decided. "Please?" she said softly. "I need this."

Grand was silent for a second longer. "You're obviously not going to make today's edition," he said.

"Correct."

"Then I'll tell you what," Grand said. "I've got to run some tests. I should be done with those in two or three hours. Can we meet somewhere around four o'clock?"

"Four would be terrific," Hannah said. "How about I swing by the school and pick you up."

"All right," Grand said. "I'll be at my office in the Humanities and Social Sciences Building. If you miss me there I'll be in the physical sciences lab. That's off Mesa Road, parking lot eleven—"

"I'll find it," Hannah said. "Got an interesting project working?"

"I found something in one of the caves," Grand told her. "I want to run the basic DNA tests, try to figure out what they're from and how they got there."

"Anything newsworthy?"

"Not for the *Freeway,*" Grand said. "Just some hairs, probably from an animal—"

Hannah felt as though she'd raced over a speed bump. "You found what, where?"

"Excuse me?"

"You found animal hair in one of the caves?"

"I think that's what they are, yes."

She was still feeling the jolt. It could be nothing. She didn't want to get too excited. She also didn't want to scare Grand off. She forced herself to calm down. "Professor, you said your classes are over at four?"

"Right."

"That'll give me enough time to finish up. I'll see you then."

"I don't understand—"

"I'll explain when I see you," Hannah promised.

The young woman hung up. It took her a few moments for what she'd heard to settle in.

It could be a coincidence: fur in the truck on the beach and fur in a cave in the mountains. One could have come from a dog, another from a bobcat or bear. But if it weren't a coincidence, it could be the biggest local story ever. Her mind raced from rabid animals to a mad killer in a fur coat. It was possible. That was the wonderful thing about journalism. Though nothing could be reported until it was proved, nothing could be discounted until it was disproved.

Hannah added some of the information Grand had given her. She wrote that the sinkhole the two engineers had been investigating could lead anywhere, even to the shoreline, and that—to hell with caution and to hell with Gearhart—a lead was being investigated that could link the men's disappearance to the crash of the fish truck.

Hannah read the new material. She frowned. She didn't say or imply that the driver was missing. And what she wrote was true: *She* was investigating the link. Reluctantly, Hannah added a line to that effect. She didn't want to imply that the sheriff's office was following the lead. She reread the addition and was satisfied that she hadn't written anything inaccurate or misleading. If it turned out there was a connection between the two incidents, the *Freeway* would be the first news source to have reported it.

Hypercharged, Hannah spell-checked the stories, E-mailed the crash feature and the search-and-rescue update to the printer, then went to work on the rest of the newspaper, meeting with Karen, talking to her writers and art director, and reviewing manuscripts.

But her mind wasn't on the work. It was on caves and fur.

There was a trick one of her investigative methodology professors had taught her, to play word association when you had no other clues or leads. First impressions were a good guide.

Butcher knife wound and dead husband? *The guy was a philanderer.*

Single woman strangled from behind? *She got in a last word for which her boyfriend had no other comeback.*

Caves and fur? she thought.

Fred and Wilma Flintstone, she answered.

Hannah frowned. She hadn't done well in the course, either. She wasn't good at making blind jumps. She needed to examine things closely, follow them from point to point to point. That was one reason this was so frustrating. Gearhart was holding information that prevented her from doing that.

But Hannah was dogged in that pursuit and, unlike Gearhart, she had only one goal. Not self-aggrandizement, not a bigger audience, not wealth or fame. She had the only goal you could reach by going straight ahead.

The truth.

25

The University of California, Santa Barbara, in Isla Vista was founded in 1891 as a trade school. Brought into the University of California system in 1944, the school moved to its present site in 1954. Set on the cliffs overlooking the Pacific Ocean and wrapped around its own moody lagoon, the sprawling, spectacular 815-acre campus is the home of Nobel and Pulitzer Prize–winning professors in engineering and mathematics, humanities and fine arts, and physical and social sciences. The centerpiece of the campus is the 175-foot-tall Storke Tower, which sounds its sixty-one-bell carillon twice every hour.

Grand pulled on his windbreaker and headed over to the physical sciences lab. He was intrigued by Hannah's insistence on coming over and wondered why mentioning the fur samples had gotten such a strong reaction. He had a feeling he'd be finding out. Hannah Hughes did not seem like the kind of woman who held back whatever was on her mind.

Grand walked into the large, bright lab. He didn't come here often but he had fond, very strong memories of the place. He and Tumamait had some of their most impassioned debates here, starting with the day the twenty-four-year-old Grand tested the penetrating power of his first re-created bow and arrow. *Could* a yew shaft launched from twenty feet away with a granite tip have broken through the skull of a woolly mammoth, and is the skull of a cow really an acceptable substitute? The answers were unequivocally yes to the first and maybe to the second. Years later computer simulations supported Grand's view. But win or lose the debates, Grand had always appreciated Tumamait's questions, which were relentless, unforgiving, and brilliant.

He missed that.

Grand unzipped his jacket but he left it on. Away from the sun at this hour and situated so close to the ocean, the lab vacillated between a stiff late-morning chill and suffocating afternoon heat. With all our science we were still effectively living in solar-heated caves.

Grand wanted to get the hair sample into the DNA soup before class so he'd have the results when he finished up. With luck, DNA fingerprinting would tell him most of what he needed to know. The other morphology tests he wanted to run—carbon-14 dating and gas chromatography to determine the age of the hairs and the ratios of certain key elements of both the hairs and the mineral samples—had to be done elsewhere on campus and would take several hours longer.

Fortunately, the graduate student in charge of the DNA lab during the weekday morning shift was Tami Colgan, a former student of Grand's. A wait of days or even weeks for test results was not uncommon as students, professors, and local attorneys—"the paying customers," as Tami called them—came to the lab for workups. She took his hair sample right away, putting some of it in the soup and having an assistant bring several samples to the Engineering II building around the corner. One of the engineering students had built her own radiocarbon dating unit, so the age of the hair could be determined relatively quickly. Tami also sent the mineral scrapings over to the geology lab for gas chromatography analysis. With Dr. Thorpe off campus, a number of students had declared an unofficial holiday. As a result, the lab was free.

The DNA test facility was located in a windowless, closet-size room off the white-walled main lab. The first part of the analysis consisted of placing a small hair sample into a liquid enzyme that dissolved the DNA from other matter. Once the separation was complete, Colgan would place the DNA on a thin nylon membrane and bombard it with X rays. Since different parts of DNA react differently when exposed to radiation, they form distinctive autoradiographs on the nylon. This pattern resembles a distinctive bar code, the so-called DNA fingerprint. The fingerprint can then be scanned into the computer and compared to other patterns on file. Using the high-speed, state-of-the-art equipment, the process of creating a fingerprint would take slightly over three hours. Because radiation was involved, the walls were lead-lined and Tami would only be in there to get things under way.

The young woman promised to get the other tests he requested started, then thanked him for bringing the hairs over. She said she was glad to have had the opportunity to help with real research for a change.

Grand thanked her, then went to teach his once-a-week class on the cave art of the Americas.

26

Five minutes.

That was all blond, lithe, twenty-year-old Patrick Vlaskovitz decided to give The Stratum Lady, their old but still sexy guide through the unwanted subtleties of the earth's crust.

When Professor Thorpe didn't show up for class again, and the usual graduate student substi-dude was missing and presumed jerking off, sophomore and aspiring naval officer Vlaskovitz—warming a seat here because it was required—glanced over at superskinny, dark-haired Tim Douglass and stocky Pancho d'Escoto, who were sitting in the last row. Vlaskovitz gave his college roomies the high-raised eyebrow "fuck it?" look, to which they responded with the pursed-lip, single-nod "fuck it!" response. And together the three of them walked out of Dr. Thorpe's Geological Sciences 1103A, Structural Geology class. They left the building and strolled into the brilliant orange sunset and out to Douglass's van.

Twenty minutes later they were changed into their black sailing spandex and pulling their Hobie Cat from the garage of the off-campus student residence where they lived.

Forty-five minutes after that they were in the choppy, wind-slapped waters off Goleta Beach.

Ninety minutes after that they were over two miles from shore between Montecito and Summerland with a broken rudder and seriously unhappy dispositions.

27

Hannah Hughes reached Jim Grand's office in the Humanities and Social Sciences Building just over a minute after he did. The reporter was wearing tight black jeans, a loose white blouse, a stylish black blazer, and a very unhappy expression. She had hair-clipped her bangs from her face. The rest of her hair hung straight as a result of the sea spray baking on her sweaty head on the beach during the morning.

"So tell me," she said.

"What?"

"Do I look more like my photo now?"

Grand smiled. "Yes, you do."

"Well I feel like it," Hannah said. "It's been a day and a half without much to show for it."

"Then relax," Grand said. "I'll be right back."

Grand left to appropriate a chair for her from the office of Associate Professor Wildhorn, who was teaching.

Hannah slid her red bag from her shoulder, put it on the floor, and dropped a pair of paper bags from Chris's Crinkles beside it. She stood there, enjoying the moment of peace. The window was open and the room was filled with cool sea air. Fading sunlight turned the bare white walls amber. There was a small television and VCR on top of a filing cabinet beside the desk, and a map of the region on the wall behind her.

Darker patches of wall above the desk marked spots where pictures had once hung.

Grand came back with a swivel chair. He put it down and shut the door. Hannah sat down.

"I brought us late lunch or early dinner, depending on how you look at it."

"It'll probably be both," Grand said. He cleared a space on the gunmetal desk between a pile of overstuffed folders and videotapes on the right side. He placed the thick bags of take-out there. The desk was also stacked high with ungraded papers, rubberbanded diskettes, unread journals, uncatalogued photographs, and boxes filled with stone arrowheads and spearheads.

"How was your class?" Hannah asked.

"Fine. So tell me about your day and a half. What's the latest from the front?"

"From the sheriff's office? Not much," Hannah said. "Gearhart's a master at presenting this image that everything's under control without telling you how, why, and whether it really is. It's infuriating."

"What did he say?"

"According to the afternoon press conference the search is continuing, widening, and there's no cause for worry. But enough about the dog-and-pony show." Hannah shook her head. "Jim, I don't know what to make of everything that's been happening. Maybe there isn't anything *to* make of it, but I had to talk to you."

"Okay," he said patiently.

"I told you about the truck accident in Montecito and the possibly missing driver and the fact that none of us was allowed close to the site."

"Right."

"What I didn't tell you was that Gearhart called the owner of the fishing company, who happens to be a friend of mine. He asked if the driver was traveling with a dog." She paused. "Jesus, you know what?"

"No."

"Now it sounds crazy."

"What does?"

"This whole unformed idea of about a million parts," Hannah said.

"Tell me."

Hannah took a short breath. "I'd been thinking that the disappearance of the two engineers was related to what happened to the truck driver, which is why I wanted to ask you about a possible tunnel route from Painted Cave Road to the foothills overlooking the beach. When the sheriff found hairs in the truck cab and my friend told me the driver didn't have a dog, and then *you* said you'd found hairs in one of the caves, I thought that an animal might be killing people."

"Has that been ruled out?" Grand said.

"I don't know. No one's talking."

Grand thought for a moment. "It could have been a scavenger in the truck. I've seen raccoon footprints on deserted beaches. But there is something else that might suggest the involvement of an animal."

"What?"

"Remember the backpack we found in the creek? The lacerations?"

"That's right," Hannah said.

"I'm sure the crime lab will give them a complete examination," Grand said. "They'll check for animal hairs, any saliva the fabric may have soaked up—"

"And we'll never find out the results," Hannah said bitterly.

"Everything comes out in time," he said.

"Maybe, but I don't have your kind of eons to wait," Hannah replied. "When will you know what kind of animal your cave hair belongs to? I'd love to hit Gearhart with that before tomorrow's edition."

"That data should be ready now," he said as he booted his computer, "along with the results of the radiocarbon and gas chromatography tests."

"Radiocarbon I know about," she said. "Gas chromatography is. . . ?"

"A process in which a substance is broken down to molecular pieces which are hitched to a carrier gas and then sent through a liquid or solid absorbent," Grand said. "The components are then sifted so they can be identified and measured."

"Oh. *That* gas chromatography," Hannah said.

Grand smiled. "It's like blowing smoke through a tissue and seeing the gunk that's left behind."

"Ah," Hannah smiled. "That I get."

"Every living thing metabolizes chemicals in very distinctive proportions," Grand said. "In case the first two tests aren't enough to tell us where the hair came from, the breakdowns give us a precise map to compare to other chemical maps."

"Got it. I want you to know I really appreciate this," she said as the computer's hard drive whirred. "Not just the information but being able to talk to someone. Someone who understands."

"I'm glad I can help," he said.

"I just don't want to drag you into the politics of it," she added quickly as she punched in a number. "Gearhart is my problem, the stonewalling son of a bitch. And now he's got Andrea Danza on his side—"

Hannah stopped as her phone beeped. She excused herself and pulled the phone from her bag. She spoke quietly while Grand returned to the computer. The conversation was a conference call with her advertising rep, who apparently wanted Hannah to run a series of feature articles about new trends in beach footwear in exchange for a six-month advertising guarantee from a manufacturer of a new kind of beach footwear. Grand was impressed by Hannah's insistent refusal to do "advertorials." He was also impressed by her ability to shift from an outpouring of rage to making quick, calm, confident decisions. Grand had never been able to make fast changes like that. Rebecca, who was always upbeat, used to have to nurse him from his pensive moods, something that usually took the better part of the morning or evening.

Maybe it's a gender thing, Grand thought. Males were territorial carnivores who found it difficult to leave anything without a struggle, even a state of mind. Females were more adaptable.

Hannah hung up and opened the Chris's Crinkles bags. The smells brought back memories for Grand and he tried not to think about them. He concentrated on the list of data options. All the results on the hair sample tests were completed; the results of the mineral scraping would be done by early evening.

Grand booted the DNA results first.

As he looked at them, he shook his head.

"What's wrong?" Hannah asked.

Grand said without triumph, "I was right."

"About what," she said eagerly.

He pointed to the bags of food. "This is going to be dinner."

28

The DNA results presented Grand with an impossibility.

They showed the presence of metabolic activity in the hair samples, most actively in the gene that regulates the chemical breakdown of glucose. That ruled out the hairs having been part of a Chumash paintbrush. But the test did not produce a match in the database of mammals indigenous to Southern California. It was possible and not unprecedented that an animal from outside the area had escaped from a zoo, circus, or private collection. Either no one had noticed it or was afraid to acknowledge it for fear of lawsuits or insurance claims.

It also meant that he would have to run a lengthy series of tests comparing the DNA of the hair to the DNA of all the mammals that were in the database.

Before Grand did that, though, he decided to have a look at the other test results. What he found there might help to narrow the search. As he loaded the data from the radiocarbon dating, Hannah asked Grand to explain how the dating process worked.

"Carbon 14 is a more massive form of carbon, one that's radioactive and loses electrons as it decays," he told her. "Since carbon 14 is created by interaction between solar radiation and earth's atmosphere, it becomes integrated in carbon dioxide and is found in all living things. When something dies and the carbon in the system is no longer replenished, the carbon 14 already present begins to decay. Because the rate of decay is constant, we're able to accurately determine when living tissue last absorbed carbon 14."

"Understood," Hannah said. "Then how do you determine the age of nonliving things like rocks and pottery and the Shroud of Turin?"

"All rocks, minerals, and other nonliving matter contain different kinds of radioactive material such as uranium, thorium, potassium-40," Grand said. "Those decay into different states which are also measurable."

"I see," Hannah said. She plucked several fries from the bag and ate them. "So we could test these fries using radiocarbon dating because they were once alive."

"That's right." Grand smiled at Hannah. "At least, you're assuming they were. You have to read the fine print at a place like Chris's Crinkles."

"What do you mean?" Hannah said.

"The last time I went to the movies with Rebecca they had something they called 'buttery topping' for the popcorn and a 'frozen dairy product' where they used to have custard—"

"Are you saying that these may be fake spuds?"

"It wouldn't surprise me."

Hannah shrugged and ate several more fries. "You could be right. But Chris Sheehy is a local businessperson and an advertiser, so I've got to patronize her place. Anyway, who knows? Maybe next week one of your scientific colleagues will find out that eating dead things with carbon 14 is bad for us. Potassium-40 may be all the rage."

Grand smiled as the results of the radiocarbon dating began to appear on the monitor. While he read the data his smile evaporated. "It can't be," he said.

"What?"

Grand finished the file, then scrolled back and began reading the figures again slowly.

"*What* can't be?" Hannah pressed.

"The radiocarbon dating results," Grand said. "They say these hair samples are nearly eleven thousand years old."

"You're joking," Hannah said. "But according to the DNA findings the hairs came from a living creature," Hannah said.

"They did," Grand replied.

"Is there any way something could have contaminated your samples, like microbes or germs?" Hannah asked. "Maybe they were mistaken for signs of life in the hair."

"That can't happen at the DNA level," Grand said. "The tests Tami ran take apart the hair itself. There's no way of mistaking that for a microbe."

"Well something's obviously wrong," Hannah said. "And if the DNA tests are foolproof—"

"Then there must be a mistake in the age," Grand said. "I'm going to check the DNA analysis. The tests also give us a chemical breakdown. There may be something in the hair, a chemical, mineral, or radioactive element that could have skewed the radiocarbon result."

The fan in the computer hummed quietly as Grand asked the computer to identify elements and chemicals that were present in the hair. There was nothing unusual. Hydrogen, oxygen, carbon, magnesium, nitrogen, phosphorous, sulfur, and various salts.

Grand brought up the proportions of organic materials and other compounds. When those were on-screen he compared them with elements and compounds found in the hair of local bobcats, gray wolves, foxes, elks, field mice, and rabbits. He wasn't trying to determine that the hairs had come from one of those animals, only that the ratios were relatively similar.

They were, with two exceptions.

"The average water content of the other fur samples is 68.7 percent," the scientist said as he read the ratios. "The hair samples I brought in have an elevated saturation level of 87.6 percent."

"That sounds pretty high," Hannah said.

"Yes, but explainable. The hairs were probably submerged at some point down in that cavern. What I don't understand is this other figure."

"Which is?"

"Carbon dioxide," Grand said. "The random fur samples have levels that are an average of 300 percent *higher* than the hairs I found in the stalagmite. That shouldn't be. The air my creature breathed shouldn't have contained such low percentages unless—"

He stopped.

"Unless what?" Hannah asked.

"No. There's got to be a mistake," the scientist said as he went online to the UCSB Web site and accessed the Biological Sciences database.

"What are you doing?" Hannah asked.

"I'm asking the computer to give me the levels of atmospheric carbon dioxide eleven thousand years ago and today," he said as he typed. "If the older figures correspond to the CO_2 levels found in the hair samples, it will corroborate the date the radiocarbon test gave us."

"In which case we have an eleven-thousand-year-old specimen with reliable DNA findings that tell us the specimen is alive," Hannah said.

"It's impossible, but that's pretty much what we'll have."

"I don't think I'll be running that information in tomorrow's paper," Hannah said. "I wonder if Gearhart's crime lab gave him the same results on the hair samples."

"That's a good question," Grand said. "If they did, that could be one reason he's being so tight-lipped. He doesn't want to look foolish either."

"After we've checked this out, maybe I should tell him what we've found," Hannah said. "See if that opens him up a little, maybe fills in a few missing pieces for him."

The scientist nodded and sat back.

As the computer worked on finding the data he tried to think of explanations that might reconcile the findings. The only thing he could come up with was that one or the other of the tests had somehow been compromised. If that were true, then the concentration of atmospheric carbon dioxide eleven thousand years ago could not be in the same proportion as the ratios the DNA test found in the hair samples. Otherwise, the tests would prove one another to be correct.

"How do we know what earth's atmospheric levels were eleven thousand years ago?" Hannah asked.

"From studying ancient ice," Grand said. "Scientists have taken thousands of deep core samples from ice in both the north and south polar regions. They've analyzed air trapped in bubbles in the ice and found a steady increase in carbon dioxide levels from prehistory to now."

"Increased why?"

"Mostly due to volcanic activity," Grand said. "Volcanoes pour massive amounts of carbon dioxide into the atmosphere. They also caused a greenhouse effect that was probably what ended the Ice Age and caused the spread of deserts and the destruction of countless ancient forests."

"So human burning of fossil fuels wasn't the initial cause of global warming?" Hannah said.

"No. In fact," Grand said, "some scientists believe that humankind may actually be helping the planet. By keeping it warm enough, we may have prevented the Ice Age from returning."

"Do you believe that?"

Before he could answer, the figures appeared on the screen. Grand and Hannah both looked at the monitor.

"This is incredible," Grand said. "Eleven thousand years ago there were eight parts per million of carbon dioxide in the atmosphere compared to twenty-five parts per million now."

"That's an increase of 300 percent," Hannah said with open astonishment. "Just like the hair samples."

Grand felt the same galvanizing frustration he did when he tried to understand the Chumash paintings from the passageway. The material was there, the answers were there, true and immutable. He simply didn't know how to interpret what he was seeing.

Maybe he wasn't seeing because he was looking too closely. Perhaps he needed to put the data in a larger picture.

"If the DNA test results can't be wrong and the age of the hairs has been confirmed, what's next?" Hannah asked.

Grand ignored the raspy voice of Professor Wildhorn as he walked around the department asking if anyone had seen his chair. He leaned forward and began typing again.

"What's next," Grand said, "is we take a step back. In math, a point doesn't tell you much. But two points define a line. We need to draw a line from our sample to another one just like it."

"Word association," Hannah said.

"Pardon?"

"Never mind," Hannah said. "What do we have to do?"

Grand went back to the UCSB Web site and opened a comparative research program on the Biological Sciences Web site. He dropped the results of the DNA test into it.

"I'm having the computer search every biological file it has access to until it finds a match for the DNA," Grand said. "This could take five minutes or five hours, depending on how lucky we get. If you have other things you need to do I can phone you."

"No," Hannah said. "Getting this story is all I need to do. So unless you mind—"

"Not at all," he said.

The computer hummed, the breakers broke, and Grand suddenly felt warm behind the ears. The space between him and Hannah was small and the silence made it seem even closer. Intimate.

He reached for his hamburger and unwrapped it. As he did he noticed Hannah absently work a finger through the top of her blouse. She was rubbing what looked like a piece of jewelry.

"What have you got there?" Grand asked. He had to say something.

"Excuse me?" Hannah said.

He pointed at her neck.

"Oh." She smiled and pulled out a tarnished pair of dog tags. "My good-luck token."

"Were you in the military?"

"No. They belonged to my dad, in Korea. See how they're dented?"

She leaned closer to show him.

"I see," he said.

There was a moment, just an instant, when everything else in the room and in Grand's brain disappeared. He blanked on everything but the smell of the woman and the soft light on her throat. He felt warm and probably looked red all along the jaw. He hoped she didn't notice.

Hannah sat back. "The dog tags deflected a piece of shrapnel the day my father got there," she went on. "So every day after that, when he woke up, the first thing he did was hold them in his fist and pray for life and good luck. After the war he put them away until my junior year of college."

"What happened then?" he asked, the heat fading quickly from his neck and face.

"My dad read some of my stuff in the college paper," Hannah said. "He was convinced that one day someone I wrote about would try to kill me."

"So he gave them to you as a good-luck token."

"I thought it was a little over the top," Hannah said, "but I appreciated the thought. I mean, I didn't see my life being *quite* like a war zone—though I did start touching them for good luck."

"And now it's a habit."

"I do it without even thinking. I guess it's weird."

"Not at all," Grand said. "Totems and amulets are as old as civilization. They can signify a unity with something—with your father, for example—or they can symbolize the protection of a deity."

"So I'm actually very cutting-edge New Age," she said. "Do you have anything like that? A rabbit's foot or a lucky squeezed penny with a picture of something on it?"

"No, but my father used to have this little ritual he did. He drove a bus in Los Angeles and every time he got in, he'd step up with his left foot first. When I asked him why he did that, he said the left was his heart side and it always made him think of life, his family, and how precious both of them were."

Hannah looked at him. "Now *that's* sweet."

"My father's a great guy," Grand said. "He used to love talking to the regulars on his route. He's totally outgoing. My mother liked staying home, taking care of the house, and listening to opera. But as different as they were, somehow they just fit together."

"And they love you."

He nodded.

"What was the best thing they ever did for you?" she asked.

He looked at her. "That's an odd question. It's a good one, but strange."

"So what's the answer?"

He smiled. "The best thing they ever did was to take me to the Grand Canyon when I was six years old," he said. "When I was a kid I loved to collect comic books. I loved the art and I couldn't get enough of the most dramatic characters: Thor, the Spectre, the Flash, Sub-Mariner, Iron Man. Other kids were into kickball and dodgeball, but I was overweight and I didn't enjoy them."

"You were overweight?" she said.

"Yeah."

"My God," she said. "You could be a poster child for fitness."

"That also came from what my folks did for me," he said. "The kids at school started calling me Grand Canyon because I was so fat. So I just shut myself off from everyone. Comic books became my universe and my mother and father decided that probably wasn't a good thing. So during the summer between first grade and second, my parents decided to show me that the Grand Canyon wasn't just big, it was majestic and wonderful. They packed me and my younger sister Victoria in a car and we drove out there. I'd grown up knowing the mountains and the ocean but I have never imagined actually seeing anything like the awesome alien worlds and colorful subterranean realms I'd read about in comic books."

"That must have blown you away."

"Completely," he said. "Not only that, but the people who lived there loved the same things I did. They made animal fetishes—dolls of frogs, turtles, bears, and other creatures that were supposed to have magical powers. They made little corn maidens—witches that lived since the beginning of time. And some of the inhabitants even carved and painted their own forms of comic books on cave walls and mountainsides, pictures of great hunters and extraordinary animals. I came home from there with a new sense of my name." He smiled. "I also came back with an armload of books, postcards, Brownie Starflash photographs, and a purpose. The mythology of ancient peoples—the stories of *real* superheroes—became my new passion. I got my pilot's license years later, but I never flew as high as I did on that trip."

Hannah was smiling. "Thanks for telling me that."

Grand smiled back. "Thanks for asking. I didn't mean to get carried away."

"You didn't. And I liked it. Do you still see your folks much?"

"On Christmas and their anniversary, mostly," Grand said. "They moved to Cornwall, England, which is where my sister lives and my mother's family came from. They have a little farmhouse there. They don't raise anything but they love it there. What about you? Do you see your parents?"

Hannah's smile twisted. "I'm expected to make the pilgrimage back to Rhode Island every few months. My mom keeps setting me up with this yacht-guy and that stock broker–guy because she's the only one at the club who doesn't have grandchildren and I don't have any siblings. My dad wants to make sure I'm still alive and that the newspaper isn't being printed in red ink."

"Is he one of your investors?" Grand asked.

"No, he's my *only* investor," Hannah said. "Nineteenth-century railroad money is underwriting my—"

Hannah stopped speaking as the computer pinged. Grand swung to the keyboard.

"What happened?" Hannah asked.

"I'll be damned, it found a match," Grand said.

"After just eight minutes?" She jangled the dog tags. "Thanks, Dad. What is it?"

Grand stopped the search and clicked on the highlighted file.

"It's in paleoanthropology, my department," he said. "That's why it came up so quickly."

"Doesn't your department only deal with ancient things?" Hannah asked. "Extinct races and animals?"

"Yes," Grand said.

The file opened and the database DNA map was displayed side by side with the original DNA fingerprint that Grand had given the computer. The database map was from a sample that Grand had discovered himself in Mexico, the only fossil minutely detailed enough to yield a complete DNA fingerprint.

He stared at the two sets for a second, the stacks of horizontal dashes that signified genetic sequences. The loci—the individual patterns—were identical in both samples. Everything was right.

Yet everything was wrong.

The sea seemed louder, the air somehow different as he tried to process what the search had turned up. Even the suggestion of it being true did, for an instant, make Grand feel as though two points in time had somehow folded back on themselves, like a ribbon being twisted round. The campus, thousands of years, all of human knowledge seemed to vanish for that instant.

The moment itself passed quickly, though the aftershocks stuck in his mind like the remnants of a nightmare.

Or a vision?

"So what is it?" Hannah pressed. "What does it say?"

What does it say? Grand thought. No one would play a trick like this and risk expulsion. And though he'd have tests run again, they were rarely wrong.

"Jim?" Hannah pressed.

"According to this, the hair I found belongs to a living animal that's been extinct for at least eleven thousand years."

"What animal?"

"*Smilodon fatalis,*" Grand said. He looked at her. "A saber-toothed cat."

29

The sun had gone down, the moon was rising, and the wind and currents were finally cooperating to bring the Hobie Cat almost within "walkin' distance" to shore. At least, that's how Patrick Vlaskovitz described where they were—six fathoms from the bottom at roughly a quarter of a mile out, which the young student knew he could swim if he had to. Whether Tim Douglass and Pancho d'Escoto could swim it, he didn't know.

Vlaskovitz also didn't care. After a shitload of hours just drifting out here, with the Cat's tail busted and d'Escoto not having remembered to bring the freaking phone, which was his responsibility, they were lucky to be within sight of shore at all. Only Vlaskovitz's skill with the sail had kept them from heading out to Japan or frigging Tonga on currents that were slightly stronger than the wind. At least Douglass had stuffed some Twix bars under the seat pad, so they had something to chew on while they waited for the tides and currents to become more favorable and help them toward shore.

In a way, as d'Escoto had lamely pointed out, it was a good thing they hadn't sailed shoreward sooner. When it was still daylight the southbound coastwise traffic lane—which was farthest out—and the northbound coastwise traffic land were clogged with big motorboats going way too fast to watch out for stranded Hobie Cats. Hell, they'd almost gotten clocked by a weather buoy, and that sucker was standing still. Douglass didn't share his enthusiasm. The navy's Pacific Missile Range was located just north of San Miguel Island and they could easily have drifted into that. None of them had bothered to check in with the twice-daily radio warnings because they didn't expect to be stranded the hell *out* here.

But stranded they were, so the three young men just sat on the teal trampoline slung between the peapod-shaped blue pontoons, getting colder and colder and waiting—as Douglass put it—"for air and water to return us to the earth."

Douglass was the poet of the group. At least, he was the only one who didn't look out the window during English lit.

And they would be returned to the shore relatively soon, unless they got caught and stranded in kelp, which was all along this coastline stretch of the Santa Barbara Channel, according to the small, laminated chart they had. That would be the final indignity. Three hunky sailors, suntanned and cool, with a busted rudder, chocolate Twix smears on their mouths, and a Hobie Cat with a proud red, orange, and yellow sail snarled in large bundles of seaweed.

The skies darkened, the planets and stars began to show, and the Hobie Cat continued to bob in the right direction. The waters were insistently choppy and Vlaskovitz knew that by the time they got back to shore it would be the land that seemed unsteady. Hopefully—since they'd also left the cell phone in the car—they'd be close enough to a pay phone to call for someone to come and get them and bring them back to their own wheels.

Vlaskovitz consulted the chart by moonlight. The Hobie Cat was now about four hundred feet from shore. They were headed to an area of the beach that was only one fathom deep. As soon as they cleared the mooring buoy, he'd get off the damn Cat and pull it to—

The Hobie Cat shuddered violently and then stopped dead. The trampoline bulged in the center. The three men, who had been more or less lounging, were quickly alert.

"What the fuck?" d'Escoto blurted. He grabbed the forward crossbar, which rested between the pontoons, to keep from being tossed over.

"Submerged rock—" Douglass shouted.

"Shift to port," Vlaskovitz told the others. He wanted to try to alleviate the pressure on the center to keep the fabric from tearing. He held onto the halyard but let it go slack as he moved.

As the men slid to the left side of the vessel, the bulge suddenly sagged and vanished. The sailors stopped moving as the Hobie Cat once again bobbed restlessly on the restless sea.

"Ohhhhkay," d'Escoto said.

The other two sailors continued to watch the trampoline in silence. The slap of the dark water on the pontoons seemed unusually loud and active. It *was* stronger, Vlaskovitz decided as beads of water popped higher than before as the wavelets struck the pontoons.

Vlaskovitz tightened his hold on the halyard. They weren't far from shore and he wanted to get moving again. He didn't know what they'd hit, but he didn't want to run into it again.

As he began maneuvering the sail to catch the wind, the world flipped over. The Hobie Cat went up on its forward end, dropping the three men in the water, then stood on-end for a moment. The sailors popped back up just in time to see the catamaran pulled straight down. The vessel went under so hard and so fast that the mast bent back and snapped. The sail and heavy guylines whipped around before they submerged and then the catamaran was gone.

The cool waters calmed almost at once. Vlaskovitz dog-paddled in place as he waited for the Cat or some part of it to bob back up. It had to. They were only in ten or eleven feet of water and the vessel was nearly that long. But nothing came back up. Not even the chart.

"We got a fucking shark!" Douglass cried, spitting a mouthful of seawater across his chattering teeth.

They might. Vlaskovitz couldn't think of anything else that would have pulled the Cat down like that.

"Shit!" d'Escoto yelled.

The young man started swimming madly toward shore. Vlaskovitz and Douglass started after him.

"Slow it down, Pancho!" Vlaskovitz screamed. "If it's a shark, the motion may—"

D'Escoto stopped abruptly, straightened, and went down.

Vlaskovitz and Douglass stopped side by side. Moonlight swam across the still-swirling waters where the student had been.

"Shit sticks," Douglass said. "This is bad."

Vlaskovitz looked at his companion. They were vulnerable to attack and their body temperatures were dropping. They had to get out of there.

"Listen," Vlaskovitz said. "It's only about four hundred feet to shore. If we go in about a hundred feet more we can ride the breakers home."

"What about Pancho?"

"Swim," Vlaskovitz said.

"You mean we just leave him—?"

"We leave him or we join him," Vlaskovitz said. "Now let's go—but slowly. Don't kick if you can help it."

Vlaskovitz started out doing a slow, steady breast stroke. Douglass went with him.

"It's going to get us," Douglass said as he gulped down breaths.

"No way," Vlaskovitz said. He kept his eyes on the white-gold sand of the deserted beach. It wasn't that far away; all they needed to do was get there.

Their bodies rose and dipped with the swells, the water chilling them through their black, water-resistant suits. Despite his efforts to concentrate on the shore, Vlaskovitz was thinking about d'Escoto. He wondered if his friend died instantly or if he was alive long enough to realize what was happening to him. Maybe not. He hadn't screamed; he just seemed to freeze. Or maybe he was underwater by the time he figured it out, when it was too late to scream.

Jesus.

The current suddenly picked up beneath him. When Vlaskovitz felt the initial upward bump he thought it was something moving toward him from below. But then the wave began to roll him forward, fast, and he and Douglass were swept closer to shore. When the swell dissipated about one hundred feet from shore, the young man felt a slight undertow as the current pulled back. He resumed swimming slowly. Though the waters were probably only six or seven feet deep here, he didn't want to try and touch bottom yet. They'd get to shore faster if they continued to ride the waves.

He glanced at Douglass. His friend was keeping his head entirely above water, which was an awkward way to swim, with his eyes fixed on the shore. His strokes were stiff and the muscles of his shoulders were tight; he looked like he wanted to erupt. But he was keeping it in check.

Another wave caught them, hoisting them up and ahead. Vlaskovitz rode it on his belly. The moonlit beach was reassuringly close, just twenty or so feet away. He wasn't even sure the water was deep enough here for a shark large enough to have done what this one did to the boat.

They were going to make it.

Vlaskovitz let his legs drop. They touched sand before they were fully extended. He stood. The water was up to his waist.

"Yes!"

He shuffled forward, the water sloshing against his backside, the cold grains of sand sliding from under his toes with the backwash. Douglass was beside him and then in front of him and then running way in front of him. The lanky man reached the deserted beach and simply dropped, facedown. He was lifted by an incoming breaker that plopped him down a few feet ahead. He crawled forward and turned his face to the heavens.

"I made it!" he cried. "You gray killing bastard, I *made* it!"

Vlaskovitz staggered to shore seconds later. He was breathing hard but remained standing. Shivering with relief, he stopped beyond the breakers and turned to look back at the sea.

"What do you see?" Douglass yelled over.

"Nothing."

"Nothing?"

"Nada." Vlaskovitz scowled across the moon-sprinkled sea. He watched the wave crests for flotsam from the Hobie as he looked north along the shore. "It's weird, man. I don't see *anything.*"

Douglass sat, flopped his wrists across his knees, and shook his head. "Pancho. Man, he can't be gone."

Vlaskovitz didn't want to believe it either and kept searching.

"Where the hell are we?" Douglass asked, looking around.

"Loon Point," Vlaskovitz said.

"Right, right," Douglass said. "I see that now." He got to his feet. "Hey, I'm going to find a phone and call for help."

"Solid. There should be one—"

Vlaskovitz stopped suddenly. He squinted to the right as something moved offshore. It was about thirty feet out and to the north.

"Hold on," Vlaskovitz said.

"What's up?" Douglass said.

"I see something!" he said. "Check it out!"

"Where, man?"

Vlaskovitz pointed and Douglass looked.

The twisted body of the Hobie Cat was coming ashore—in pieces. Both pontoons spearing through the water, the trampoline being dragged behind one. The mast and sail rolled in separately, the sail apparently perforated in spots.

But that wasn't all. There was something in the water, just beyond the wreckage. Something alive.

"Hey, I see it too!" Douglass said. "It's moving." He started running toward it. "*Pancho!* Yo, Panch!"

Vlaskovitz ran toward it as well. It was moving, a shape outlined by moonglow. As it came nearer the young man thought it might be Pancho crawling, since the shape was longer than it was tall. Then he realized that it wasn't Pancho d'Escoto at all. It had fur, enormous paws, and a short, slender tail.

"What the hell—?" he muttered.

From where he was standing it looked like a large dog with its head hung low. But it didn't walk like a dog. Its movements were slow and low and steady, oblivious to the waves and shifting sands.

Tim had reached the surf, nearly in front of the thing. He stopped. The thing turned its head toward him, which was also toward Vlaskovitz. Ten feet of water separated the animal and Douglass.

The pieces of the shattered Hobie Cat came to rest on the beach. After its spiraling, disjointed arrival, the scene seemed suddenly serene. But only for a moment.

What happened next came so quickly that it didn't register on Vlaskovitz until it was over. The dog—or whatever it was—continued to look toward them and also continued walking slowly. It was a soft-angled creature with a bright white outline and a perfectly balanced gait.

Then, suddenly, something flew at Douglass from the crest of the next falling wave. It was almost as though the plume itself had taken form and broke off, like a cell dividing. The shape shot forward so fast that it was on him before he had even turned to look at it. Douglass was driven back hard. He landed on the sand about four feet from where he'd been standing, his arms flying up as the thing's massive front paws struck his shoulders. As the young man's arms fell back down, the creature's head went up. Its jaw opened ninety degrees, silhouetting a pair of long, hooked fangs against the brilliant moon. Then the animal's head dropped hard and swift between its forelegs.

There was a pop, and while Douglass shuddered on the beach, the beast raised its head and rushed back toward the sea.

Douglass's body went with the beast's head, stuck to it. The young man hung limp and uncomplaining.

The attack on Douglass took only a second or two. By the time Vlaskovitz looked back at the other creature, the one that had been walking ashore slowly, there was nothing he could do but that.

Look at it.

The animal had turned while Vlaskovitz had watched Douglass die. It was now racing at him so fast that he only had a moment to observe it in the bright moonlight. He could see now that the thing wasn't a dog. It was a cat—a monstrously large one. Just how large Vlaskovitz couldn't be sure, since it was moving and there wasn't enough light to tell for certain. But two things definitely stood out. One was its large, deepset eyes. They were dark and reflective on the surface with a gleaming white-amber core. The other was its teeth. Up close, in the brief snapshot view he got of them, Vlaskovitz saw that the sleek, ivory fangs were larger than butcher knives and as glistening-sharp.

A wave broke, or was it a roar? There was warm sea wind on his cheeks, or was it angry breath? He couldn't be sure, it was happening too fast—

An instant later Vlaskovitz flew back.

He felt the sand on his palms.

He saw the stars.

He saw three moons in the sky. And then two of the moons moved.

The great head went up and came down. Vlaskovitz experienced two hard, sharp punches just below each shoulder. He felt the air leave him, though not through his wide and silent mouth. His hot breath puffed up at him from where he'd been struck in the chest.

He felt something wet under both arms. He closed his eyes and felt himself being jerked up.

And then he felt nothing.

30

Hannah and Grand looked at the side-by-side DNA maps on the computer monitor.

"This has got to be a joke," Hannah said. "Maybe not your guys pulling it, but someone—"

"No," Grand said. "The computer did the analyses. It's working fine."

"But it can't be right," she said. "How long have saber-toothed tigers been extinct?"

"Eight thousand years," Grand said. "This particular species has been extinct for nearly eleven thousand years."

"There can't be an animal that old eating people in Santa Barbara."

"I agree."

"But there has to be an answer to the missing people and strange fur," Hannah said.

Grand had to agree with that. *And yet,* he thought.

The sun had set and it was getting cold. Grand stood, closed the window, and looked out at the sea.

What if the answer was *Haphap*? Joseph Tumamait didn't just *believe* the demon was near. He said that he *knew* it, absolutely. The Chumash elder had become more spiritual over the past few years but he hadn't lost his mind or his empirical judgment.

"Maybe this isn't a joke but an accident," Hannah said. "Someone in the lab could have run a test on a saber-tooth fur sample and sent you the results by mistake."

"They couldn't have," Grand said. He sat back down.

"Why not?"

"Because we don't have any fur samples from saber-tooths."

"You don't, but someone may."

"I mean scientists don't have any samples," Grand told Hannah. "We've found swatches of fur from woolly rhinoceroses, woolly mammoths, peccaries, short-faced bears, snowshoe hares, dire wolves, and giant sloths. We've got fur, skin, and even organ samples from all kinds of prehistoric mammals from around the world, samples that were frozen in ice or submerged in tar. But we've never found any specimens of fur from a saber-toothed cat. We haven't even found a cave painting that shows a saber-toothed cat."

"Why do you think that is?"

"Probably because no one who ever saw one lived to paint its picture," Grand said. "From everything we can gather—including computer simulations based on skeletal remains—saber-tooths were the greatest hunters that ever lived. Fast, stealthy, powerful. As for why there are no fur samples, we suspect that most of the cats died in open fields where they probably hunted, and that their remains were scavenged by animals or early humans for food, clothing, and weapons. Their fangs would have made excellent knives."

"Good point," Hannah said. "No pun intended. So if our knowledge is so thin, where did the original DNA sample for your *fatalis* tiger come from?"

"We got that from bone and tooth fossils," Grand said. "The fossilization record has left a very clear imprint of saber-tooth DNA."

"I see. Then maybe someone used that DNA to genetically engineer fake hair," Hannah suggested.

"Why?"

"I don't know," Hannah admitted.

"It would take tens of millions of dollars and a very sophisticated lab to fake something this convincing," Grand told her.

"Besides, if someone did that they'd probably want to make the discovery themselves, get the acclaim and funding that comes with it."

"True," she admitted.

They were silent for a moment. Grand couldn't stop thinking about *Haphap,* about Tumamait's utter conviction, about the caves, about the presence he felt when he was down there. Chumash lore did not describe *Haphap*. Perhaps the demon was meant to personify everyone's greatest fear. Or maybe he was never seen clearly in visions.

Or perhaps the stories came from real life?

The legends about *Haphap* could have risen from tales of a fearsome predator that lived inside the mountain caverns and struck swiftly and terribly. And if that were true—

"I wonder," Grand said.

"About what?"

"The caves," he said. "I wonder if there might not be another reason we never found any saber-tooth fur."

"Such as?"

"Maybe they lived and died underground," Grand said. "Bobcats live in dens. Foxes make their homes in underground burrows. Bats roost in caves. Early humans dwelt there as well."

"Sounds reasonable."

"Even more so when you consider that the cats may have gone underground when things froze up during the Ice Age," Grand said. "Generations of them living in caves. And when saber-tooths migrated south, where it was warmer, they stayed in the caves."

"No one ever thought of this before?"

"Not that I'm aware of," Grand said. "Paleontologists believe strongly in 'habitual parallelism,' an assumption that the lifestyles of past and present species are somewhat similar. Ancient turtles lived the same way as modern turtles, ancient birds lived like modern birds, and so on. We've always assumed that saber-tooths were like modern-day lions and tigers. But what if they weren't? What if we haven't seen any paintings of them because, like bats, like many other predators, they hunted at night when prehistoric people were in their huts or caves."

"That makes sense," Hannah said. "But how does that help us? Are you suggesting that a species could have survived unseen for thousands of years?"

"No," Grand said. "I'm just thinking out loud, looking for new ideas, directions."

Grand turned to the keyboard and checked for the results of the gas chromatography tests on the rock scrapings he'd taken. The computer at the lab told him the tests were still working. He sat in silence, staring at the DNA maps, doing what a man does if he hasn't had an epiphany in the form of a vision. Wrestling with science and spirit.

"The Flintstones," Hannah said softly.

"Excuse me?"

"First instincts," she said. "I always thought they were a little crazy but now I'm not so sure. Let me ask you something. Forget about it being 'impossible' for the moment. Is there any way you can imagine that one of these saber-toothed tigers might have survived?"

"Any way I can *imagine* it?"

"Yes," Hannah said. "Like they do in Scotland with the Loch Ness Monster. Do you believe in the Loch Ness Monster?"

"I'm not convinced that it exists."

"But you don't rule out the possibility."

"No."

"Or the Abominable Snowman."

"Where's this going?" Grand asked.

"What if we start from that same place with the saber-tooths?" Hannah asked. "With a possibility, however remote. When I toured Loch Ness, the guide on the boat said things like, 'Ages ago the Loch was closed off from the North Sea and a family of prehistoric animals could have been trapped here . . . and so on and so forth.' Assume we have a saber-toothed tiger. It certainly seems to fit the profile of our killer. How did it get here?"

Grand shook his head. "First of all, any species with just one living example couldn't survive. There would have to be parents and offspring."

Hannah shrugged. "If we can allow one saber-toothed tiger then we can allow two. Just like in Loch Ness."

"I suppose so," Grand said. "But even if there were a pair of specimens and they lived in caves and only came out at night, there would be some evidence of habitation. Feces. Carcasses of prey."

"Maybe they live deep in the caves or defecate in underground streams," Hannah said. "Maybe they bury the bones like dogs or maybe they eat the bones as well as the meat."

"That's a lot of maybes, Hannah."

"I know," she admitted. "I don't like them either. But let's keep going. How much would these creatures eat?"

"A modern lion, in captivity, needs about twenty-five pounds of raw meat each day," Grand said. "In the wild, where it needs energy to hunt, a lion consumes thirty to forty pounds of meat a day. And that's a four- or five-hundred pound animal, six or seven feet long. *Smilodon fatalis* weighed from fifty to one hundred pounds more than that on average."

As they were talking, the gas chromatography analysis of the cave scrapings arrived.

Grand immediately opened the file to have a look while Hannah tapped her leg anxiously. She was as intense a person as Grand had ever met. Even in the middle of this—or because they were in the middle of it?—he found it invigorating.

"Talk to me," Hannah said. "What have we got?"

"Another piece to the puzzle that doesn't seem to fit," Grand said. "The rock scrapings from the cave where I found the hair were laced with tephra residue—volcanic ash. There are also significant traces of silicate glass, sulfur, chlorine, aluminum, and sodium and other minerals that, according to the report, are not indigenous to this region."

"Translation, please."

"The mountain passageways could be vents for local volcanic activity or for volcanoes that erupted hundreds of miles away," Grand said. "That would account for some of those elements."

"They got blasted here."

"Right. What I can't understand is the presence of minerals I've only seen in artifacts from the far north."

"Which means?"

Grand sat back and folded his arms. "Stone and wood that have been buried in glaciers become permeated with the waters that comprise the ice," he said. "They have a distinctive chemical signature. We didn't have glaciers this far south, but what we've got here are the same chemical signatures."

"Maybe the chemicals were blasted down here too, carried by a volcanic explosion," Hannah said.

"That's possible," Grand agreed. "But it would be —"

He stopped as he thought of the two paintings on the cave wall. A volcano of fire and a mountain of ice. But not a mountain.

A glacier.

Hannah's cell phone rang and she reached into her bag to answer it. As she talked, Grand just sat there looking at the screen.

All of this was an academic exercise being performed by tired, stymied minds. As much as Grand had always loved comic books and fairy tales, he never confused them with reality. Even though one of his favorite stories in Egyptian mythology was about the phoenix reborn from ashes, myths were fiction. For all of their power and portent, even the Chumash tales of animal spirits were fantasies. Besides, the leap required—from feeling some kind of spiritual presence in a cave to having an animal spirit take form and kill—was a large one. Even when Joseph Tumamait knew it, absolutely. And Hannah's reasoning, while fascinating, had more holes than Painted Cave Road.

Hannah folded the cell phone and put it back in her bag. "That was my managing editor. She just intercepted a radio broadcast from the communications officer at the California Highway Patrol dispatch center in Ventura. The call was to all cars in the area of Summerland. We appear to have more missing persons."

"Where?"

"At the beach not far from Toro Canyon," Hannah said. "A motorist saw a wrecked catamaran and stopped. There were no bodies, no remains. Just bloody sand and something else."

"What?"

"Footprints from some kind of animal," Hannah said as she shouldered her bag and rose. "Big ones."

31

With any luck we can get there before Gearhart does," Hannah said. "The Wall is going to meet us there."

Grand was driving as they sped along 217 headed toward 101. Hannah was on an open phone line with Karen, who promised to provide her with any updates. Unlike the sheriff's office, the highway patrol didn't have a policy of maintaining public radio silence while en route to crime or accident sites. Since a patrol car had only just arrived, no news had come in.

As they reached the highway and headed southwest, Hannah kept a lookout for Gearhart's black-and-white. He might have been up in the mountains, delaying his arrival. Grand's mind was on the paintings he'd seen in the upper caves.

A volcano and a glacier, he thought, *with Chumash gods inside of them.* A snake symbolizing the inner earth, a dolphin representing the sea—water. According to the geological record, it was uncommon but not unknown for volcanoes to erupt beneath glaciers. It had happened to Mount Rainier in Washington forty thousand years ago, and in several regions well south of that.

Suppose a volcano erupted beneath a glacier in the American Northwest. Suppose the force was so extraordinary that the blast broke into fault lines and followed them south, deep into Southern California. Extreme heat and intense cold together, burning new vents in the mountains, sealing other vents. An eruption so cataclysmic that it inspired a Chumash shaman who may have witnessed it to record the event in two oversized images in a cave.

But then where did the lower cave come in, the white icons?

They reached the site twenty minutes after leaving the university. Two highway-patrol cars were parked between 101 and the train tracks that ran along the coast. The Wall's car was already there; Gearhart's was not.

Grand pulled up behind the Wall's Jeep. He grabbed a flashlight from the glove compartment. Then he and Hannah hurried to where other lights were moving along the beach at Loon Point.

It was 7:30 P.M. and less than an hour from high tide. The pieces of the catamaran had been lined up on the beach and the four highway patrol officers were walking along the shoreline, the lights playing over the surf.

The Wall was busy snapping pictures of something in the sand, near the water line. When he saw Hannah and Grand he motioned them over.

"They actually *asked* me to do this," the photographer said with a smile. "They wanted me to get a record of these before the tide erased them completely."

Grand shined the light on the sand. He squatted beside the vestiges of two footprints. They were facing the railroad tracks and were approximately three feet apart. Though they were significantly eroded by the incoming tide, they appeared to be the prints of a feline about three times the size of a bobcat.

"What do you make of them?" Hannah asked Grand.

"It's difficult to say," Grand answered. "The prints might have been smaller when they were made. The water may have filled them in and enlarged them. Even so, they're too far apart to have been made by a bobcat or even a wolf. I'd say we're looking at an animal much bigger than that."

Hannah didn't say anything. She didn't have to.

"What's interesting," Grand went on, "is the way the prints are facing. Away from the ocean."

Hannah looked out toward the road. "And there aren't any prints between here and the tracks. Wall, where's the blood?"

"Gone," he said. "One of the officers soaked some into a handkerchief for the lab and I got a few pictures before the tide took it out. It was just a foot or so behind the prints."

"*Behind* them," Hannah said. "That doesn't seem to make sense."

"Actually it makes a stronger case for the idea that whatever made these prints is the killer," Grand said.

"Why?"

"I'll tell you in a second," Grand said. "Let's have a look at the catamaran."

They walked over. One of the officers intercepted them, but Grand explained that he wanted to check for signs of predation on the wreckage—claw marks, bite marks, bloodstains. The officer said he could look as long as he promised not to touch. Grand agreed. He and Hannah hurried over.

"How many people does it take to work one of these things?" Grand asked as they jogged across the beach.

"A Hobie Cat? After it's in the water, one good sailor could handle it," she said.

They reached the wreckage and Grand shined his light across it. The sail was shredded and there were gashes in the trampoline and on the pontoons that resembled the sharp, clean marks they'd seen on the road engineer's backpack at the creek sinkhole.

"Are they teeth marks?" Hannah asked.

"I don't think so," Grand told her. "There are three and four in spots. They look more like claw marks. But check out the pontoons—the attacker was *under* the catamaran."

Hannah bent and examined the gashes. "Then I guess that rules out our strange little theory."

"This wouldn't necessarily rule it out," Grand said. "While big cats don't particularly like the water, they're excellent swimmers when they want to be."

"Selective habitual parallelism," Hannah said.

"It does occur," Grand said. "So let's try this on. The predator, whatever it is, is either walking along the shore or is in the sea. For all we know the tunnels have an outlet right off shore. Many cave systems do. The animal sees the boat and goes under. It attacks from beneath—using its claws because its mouth is closed. It chases the sailor ashore then kills him and turns back the way it came, its prey in its mouth. The victim bleeds on the sand as the killer retreats."

Just then they heard a distinctive, two-siren wail in the distance, one sound high and the other low.

"The herald angels of Malcolm Gearhart," Hannah said. "I say we tell him the killers are land sharks and see how he reacts."

"Pardon?"

"Land sharks," Hannah said. "Didn't you ever see them on *Saturday Night Live*?"

"The Travolta movie?"

Hannah looked at him and smiled. "It's okay," she said. "Never mind."

For a moment Grand felt the way he used to when Rebecca would make fun of what she called his "*not-getting-it-ness*"—like a big dumb rock. His wife used to follow it up with a peck on the forehead or a hug and an explanation, which more often than not he still didn't get.

Hannah started back toward where the Wall was and Grand followed. But he really missed Rebecca right then.

32

Dressed in new overalls, her sad freckled face framed in long, curly red hair, six-year-old Eugenie Budette sat eating microwaved macaroni and cheese and drinking iced tea at the small Formica table in their camper. Eugenie's stuffed, scruffy white rabbit, Blankie, was sitting on the bench beside her. There was a window to her right but the amber drapes had been drawn—by her. Eugenie didn't want to see where they were because she didn't want to be where they were. And though the drapes didn't make it all go away, at least they were familiar, more like home than this place whose name she didn't know because she hadn't really been paying attention when her father had said what it was.

All she knew was that they had parked here in these stupid hills just a few minutes ago after driving for nearly five hours. Her father had wanted to get an earlier start but the movers took longer to get the truck loaded. Because it was late, Eugenie's parents decided to stop at some stupid campgrounds instead of going to a stupid motel. Her father said he needed to stretch his legs and her mother needed to get fresh air, so they'd gone outside. Eugenie hadn't wanted to go with them so she made herself and Blankie food, pulled the drapes, and sat here quietly sharing bites of dinner and hard swallows of sadness.

"Frizzuh brassa mugga lugga?"

"Shoomy noomy, hahahahaha!"

That's what her parents sounded like, talking on the other side of the wall. They were happy. That made Eugenie feel even sadder, lonelier. They didn't understand how dumb this was.

There were more voices now. There had been five or six RVs up here when they arrived. These people were probably from another camper. Eugenie knew from other trips, more fun trips, that campers liked to get to know each other, even though they did it by always saying the same things, asking the same questions.

"Hi, we're the Happy Dappy family from Arizona. Where are you folks from?"

"Hey, we're Joe and Sue Dumbhead from Minnesota. Where are you folks from?"

"We're from San Di-e-go," Eugenie said defiantly, possessively stressing each syllable. That's where she was born and that's where she was still from.

A moment later the young girl sighed.

"No we're not, Blankie," she said unhappily. There were tears behind her eyes. "We're not from there anymore."

Eugenie took a forkful of macaroni. She chewed it slowly, without pleasure. Whenever they went camping she usually didn't mind the talk. She and Blankie talked too. But this wasn't a trip the young girl wanted to make. The Budettes were leaving their home in San Diego and driving up to Seattle, where her father had taken a new job. Eugenie didn't know why her father needed a new job. She thought he liked working for the navy.

Eugenie put her plastic fork down. "I'm not really hungry, Blankie. Are you?"

"No, I've totally lost my appetite," the rabbit answered from the side of Eugenie's mouth.

Eugenie put her left fist under her left cheek. She looked across the table at the bathroom, the shower, and the little sleeping area of the camper. She didn't want to sleep here. She wanted to sleep in her own bed, in her own house, where she'd always slept. She didn't want to move. She didn't want to make new friends, she wanted to keep the old ones—not on E-mail but in real life. She wanted to be able to watch TV with her best friend Ana and videotape the plays that they put on and—

Something thumped hard against the side of the camper, just under the window. It rocked the RV back and forth and then it was quiet outside. There was no more *shoomy noomy* or laughing.

Eugenie listened carefully after the RV stopped moving.

"Mom?"

The young girl's mouth twisted. She picked up Blankie and slid off the bench.

"Mom?"

She walked toward the door at the front of the RV. There was no one talking at all now and she was scared. She'd seen a TV show about the world's most ordinary serial killers where people had gone to the store and parked next to killers, who seemed like friendly people until they followed them home and killed them. Serial killers probably went to campgrounds too.

She reached the door and hesitated. She turned to Blankie, who was huddled in her left arm.

"What do you think?" she asked the rabbit.

Eugenie didn't bother answering. She thought that everything was all right, that maybe another RV had arrived and backed into theirs and her father was going to inspect the damage. But why hadn't her mother come in to see if she and Blankie were all right?

Eugenie reached for the knob. As she did the door suddenly swooshed open. Her mother was standing there, the top half of her body leaning across the door of the RV, her bottom half still outside. There was blood all over her forehead and cheeks, in her long red hair, and down her green sweater.

"Mom?"

"Get back!" her mother screamed at her.

Eugenie just stood there, scared and confused, as her mother put her right foot on the first of the two steps. The woman grabbed the sides of the doorway and tried to pull herself inside. But something stopped her. Cold. The woman's mouth pulled tight on both sides and her eyes shone white beneath the blood.

Eugenie started to cry.

"Stay inside!" her mother screamed. *"Close the—"*

Her mother vanished as she was speaking. She just disappeared to the side, like a balloon someone had popped. Here—then gone.

The door was still open. Eugenie heard gurgles and growls and things moving, but no voices. No talking.

Eugenie was squeezing Blankie so tightly that a finger went through his scraggly neck. But she wasn't even aware of it. She was only aware of the sounds and the cool air coming through the door—

The door. Her mother had said to close it.

Eugenie sniffed back her tears as she took a tentative step toward the door, then another, and then another before she could finally reach it. She stretched out her small hand and when she did she saw outside, not because she couldn't help it but because she had to see what was there.

Eugenie nearly fell as her legs went wiggly. She had been to the San Diego Zoo many times but she'd never seen anything like the thing that was holding her mother facedown and sideways in its mouth. The woman was so limp and the animal was so large that it seemed almost like her mother was Blankie.

Eugenie screamed. And screamed. And then she turned and ran, not because her mother had told her to but because her legs got their strength back and were telling her to.

She heard a roar behind her, one that filled the RV and shook her ears, but she didn't look back. She just screamed and ran and didn't even stop when Blankie's head dropped and rolled under the Formica table. . . .

33

Sheriff Malcolm Gearhart crossed the dark, deserted beach like Douglas MacArthur returning to the Philippines. At least, that's how it seemed to Grand. The sheriff was still all stride and command, despite what had to have been a long and frustrating day.

Gearhart walked directly to the ranking highway-patrol officer, Sergeant Bonnie Crellin. Hannah was also hurrying across the sands, pulling her tape recorder from her handbag as she did.

Grand walked after her, his longer steps making up for her hurried pace. He hadn't been on the beach since Rebecca's death and, now that he had a moment to think about it, he absolutely didn't want to. Feeling the sand under the rippled soles of his boots, hearing the ocean so close—it was almost as though he could reach out blindly and she'd find his hand. He held and savored the moment until it became unsettling. Until that which had been so deeply fulfilling was followed by an almost unbearable sense of loss.

Grand needed to let Rebecca go, not just for his sake but for the sake of the here and now. He needed to focus on whatever was killing people. He continued the process Rebecca had started before—

He corrected himself. *It was Hannah,* he thought. Hannah had started the process, not Rebecca.

Grand continued the process of assuming that saber-tooths were alive and worked backward. The size of rib cages suggested the giant cats had remarkable lung capacity, which could be used for extended running but also for holding their breath underwater. Carrying off two hundred pounds of dead weight was also possible for them. Scarring from muscle attachments on fossils indicated that the animals had very strong neck and jaw muscles. That was presumed to be for accommodating their powerful biting and gutting ability—killing prey with a single, penetrating attack of the two fangs, then ripping up chunks of flesh for consumption. But what if the neck muscles were also used for hauling the dead prey off to dens? Gutting it later?

Then there'd be no sign of a victim, except for blood.

This part of Southern California was the heart of where *Smilodon fatalis* had lived, from the shore to the mountains and all the way down past Los Angeles. In addition to the killing style, the geology would certainly explain everything that had happened, from the disappearance of engineers Greene and Roche to the attack on the catamaran. Not only had the rains opened new tunnels, but many of the existing caverns opened into underwater grottos, formed over the millennia by the rise and fall of the sea.

Yet while so many things made sense, the notion itself was highly improbable, if not impossible. How could saber-toothed cats have remained hidden for so many years?

By living underground and eating wild animals.

But without a sighting?

His own words came back to him: *Probably because no one who ever saw one lived to paint its picture.*

Gearhart was talking to Sergeant Crellin. As Grand and Hannah neared, the reporter turned.

"I want to tell Gearhart what we've found out," she said as they walked. "Are you okay with that?"

"Sure."

"He may want answers more than he wants me to just disappear," Hannah said. "Maybe we can pool what we know."

Gearhart was turning away from Sergeant Crellin just as Hannah and Grand neared. The sergeant was instructing her men to break out the yellow tape and to admit only Gearhart's lab team. The sheriff glanced at Hannah and Grand, then started toward the wreckage of the catamaran.

Hannah caught up to him. "Sheriff, we need to talk."

"Ms. Hughes, this is now officially a crime scene."

"I know."

"You'll have to leave."

"I know the drill."

"But I would like copies of the pictures your photographer took," Gearhart went on. "He can drop them off at my office. You'll be reimbursed for his time and material."

"You can have copies on me. All I want to do is talk."

"There's nothing new about that."

"Sheriff, this is important," Grand said. "Give her a few minutes."

"I once asked you for something to help this town," Gearhart said. "You—the two of you—told me to piss off. You don't have the right to ask for a damn thing."

"We know things you don't," Grand said. "Things you need to know."

"Do I?"

"If you want to find who did this, yes," Grand said. "Your lab team wouldn't have run the same tests that I did."

"Such as?"

"Radiocarbon dating."

Gearhart looked from Grand to Hannah. He continued walking. "Talk," he said to her.

"As the professor said, we've been doing a little research on our own," Hannah told him. "Professor Grand was down in one of the caves this morning—the one where he found the engineer's flashlight—and he discovered something down there. Fur from a large predator."

"And?"

"It was from a big cat," Hannah replied. "Possibly the same one that attacked the fish truck."

Gearhart reached the shattered Hobie Cat. He squatted and looked at the gashes with his flashlight. "We're looking into that possibility."

"Not this possibility," Hannah said.

Gearhart looked up. "I'm listening."

"Without doing the carbon-14 test you wouldn't have thought to go to the same database we did to find a DNA match," Hannah said. "Sheriff, this is going to sound weird, but the fur comes from an animal that is supposed to have died out about eleven thousand years ago. I say 'supposed to' because the samples Professor Grand found came from a living creature. The spacing of the gashes on the catamaran and the size of the footprints in the sand seem to corroborate the identity of the animal."

"Which is?"

Hannah just blurted it out. "A saber-toothed tiger."

Gearhart didn't flinch or roll his eyes. He looked from Hannah to Grand. "Do you believe that?"

"Until a theory can be discounted I always keep an open mind," Grand told him.

"That isn't exactly an endorsement," Gearhart said.

"No. It's a possibility."

"But I notice that you're not dismissing it either," Hannah said. "Why, Sheriff?"

"Ms. Hughes, today I've listened to explanations ranging from UFO abductions to actors wearing movie monster makeup to people who change into tigers to attacks by angry Chumash spirits," Gearhart said.

"What makes you so sure there are no spirits?" Grand asked.

"I've received offers of help from psychics, exorcists, and even a lion tamer," Gearhart went on. "Now you're saying that prehistoric cats are using the beach as a litter box. Off the record, I don't believe any of it. But until I find who or what is responsible for the disappearance of these people, I'm going to listen to any respected professional."

"This isn't about ghosts and space aliens and you know it," she said. "*Why* didn't you dismiss the idea of these tigers?"

Gearhart excused himself and started toward the car. Hannah followed and Grand went after her.

"Why won't you *talk* to us?" Hannah demanded.

"Ms. Hughes, this is why I hate these little discussions. Because everything turns into a goddamn interview, a negotiation for information."

"But we can help!" she said.

"How?" Gearhart asked.

"Like we just did," she said. "Gathering information, talking to people—"

"Your kind of help can also cause panic," Gearhart said. "Or it can inform a perpetrator about what we're doing so he can plan his next crime."

"Animals can't read!" she said.

Before the sheriff could say anything else there was a call on the patrol car radio. Gearhart jogged over.

"Look," Hannah said to Grand. "The call is out of range of his personal radio." They hurried after him. "It's either from the mountains or another town. Something's up. I can feel it."

Gearhart reached the car, opened the door, and removed the handset from the console under the dashboard. "Gearhart here. Go," he said as he slipped into the vehicle and shut the door.

Hannah and Grand arrived a moment later. The car window was up and the voices were muffled inside. A moment later he started the engine and revved it. The voices were lost entirely.

The Wall had finished taking his pictures and ambled over. "Did he offer to put us in for a responsible-citizenship medal, being here before the critical evidence was obliterated?"

Hannah said nothing.

"Then the answer is no," the Wall said. "If nothing else you've got to admire Gearhart's consistency."

A moment later Gearhart turned on his flashing lights and drove off.

Hannah watched for a second and then ran toward Grand's SUV. "Come on," she said. "Something's up."

Grand and Hannah got into the SUV and the Wall jumped into his Jeep.

"Let the Wall go first," Hannah said. "He's done this before. If we lose Gearhart he'll call me."

Grand obliged. After the Jeep rattled over the train tracks and sped after the patrol car, Grand set out. Meanwhile, Hannah had her phone out, ready to take the call.

As they followed the Wall back onto the 101 and then up into the foothills, Grand realized that he had gotten this all wrong.

It was Hannah who was Douglas MacArthur.

34

As he raced to the Upper Santa Ynez River Canyon, Sheriff Gearhart thought about the call he'd just received. Screams and gunshots had been heard by a ranger near the Juncal campsite. It had happened less than a half hour before—probably a camper who had had too much to drink at dinner and went a little bonkers. Things like that had happened before. Though he wanted to be sure, Gearhart didn't see how this situation could be related to the others.

The highway patrol had checked out the Hobie Cat serial number and found that it was owned by a Patrick Vlaskovitz, a student at UCSB. He and two friends were seen going out in the late afternoon, so they were probably killed when they came ashore early in the evening and the beach was deserted. Poor guys at the wrong place, wrong time. But if other attacks were a model, the killer needed more time between kills than an hour or two. And the killer tended to tackle isolated persons, not groups. A campsite just didn't fit.

His flashing lights lit the surrounding slopes as he headed into the hills. The siren was muted by the closed windows and the whir of the air conditioner driving icy air through the vent. He needed the cold air to stay alert. He wasn't a young Marine anymore. Being on the go for two days straight with only a few hours sleep was rough. And it wasn't just the work itself that was exhausting. It was dealing with people like Hannah Hughes.

She had no idea, Gearhart thought angrily. *She had no mortal foggy notion what it was like.*

Hannah Hughes ran a self-indulgent newspaper. If it failed, she still had her multimillion-dollar trust fund to live off. Even Professor Grand probably didn't get it. He taught college kids and solved mysteries that were thousands of years old. If he failed to figure them out, no one got hurt. Neither of them knew the burden of protecting lives and property, order and security, sanity and peace. And Hannah just didn't know how to cut him any slack.

Gearhart didn't particularly like either of them, but that wasn't the issue. As a Marine, he'd learned to look past personality and talent. What would help them realize a goal, complete a mission, and get out alive? Hannah and Grand were both smart, resourceful, and relentless and if Gearhart thought they could help he'd be happy to listen. But Hannah wanted to sell newspapers and Grand probably wanted to write papers. Whatever else Gearhart wanted, he wanted above all to perform the job he was elected to perform.

Yet as sprawling as Hannah's net tended to be—or because of that—she had managed to be right about one thing, though. Gearhart knew more than he was telling about this case. While he wasn't willing to buy the idea of a saber-toothed tiger, he wasn't dismissing the notion that some nutcase was murdering people in the fashion of a saber-toothed tiger. And that the killer was planting evidence to fool wanna-believers like Hannah and Grand. One of Thomas Gomez's lab boys had made that suggestion after examining the backpack they found in the creek sinkhole. The chemist had just taken his son to see the saber-tooth fossil displays at the George C. Page Museum in Los Angeles. The boy had posed for a photograph with his head in the tiger's mouth; the depth and spacing of the gashes reminded the chemist of that mouth, so he had E-mailed the museum for exact measurements.

They fit.

The fur specimens the lab boys found in the fish truck supported the notion that someone was trying to emulate a saber-tooth, though Grand was correct about that. They hadn't radiocarbon-dated the sample or tested to see whether it came from a living creature. According to the experts at Page, there weren't any existing examples of saber-toothed tiger hair. The fact that Gomez and his team hadn't found a match meant that the sample in the truck probably came from some obscure animal like a platypus or wombat. As soon as the technicians got a spare minute they'd nail that down for sure.

Gearhart kept people like Hannah Hughes at a safe distance because he knew from his experiences in LA that all he had to tell her was that there might be a lunatic pretending to be a saber-toothed tiger. He could see the headlines now: COPY-CAT KILLER! Gearhart could live with that, but only after they'd found the perpetrator and any accomplices. He didn't need his investigators pressured by front-page yipping and editorial scare-mongering. That was how mistakes and wrongful arrests happened. There were thirty experienced police and search personnel in the field. They were just about finished searching the mountains and would be moving into the caves soon. They'd get whoever was doing this.

Get him and make him extinct.

35

Grand was accustomed to driving the hills and was having no trouble keeping up with the Wall. Not that there were many places the photographer or Gearhart could lose them, especially with his flashing lights bouncing off the slopes. In about a quarter of a mile, the Divide Peak RV Route would end and intercept a very short spur of East Camino Cielo. From there, they could only head west in the direction of the Painted Cave or east toward Pendola Road. Pendola Road ran toward the northwest and was the location of four campsites: Juncal, Mid–Santa Ynez, P-Bar Flats, and Mono.

"What makes you think Gearhart will let us stay?" Grand asked Hannah as they neared the end of the Divide Peak Route.

"He won't," Hannah said. "But he can't chase us away without a reason and, with luck, it'll take him at least a minute or two to get one."

The Wall reached East Camino Cielo and turned east.

"They're headed toward campgrounds," Grand said.

Hannah shook her head. "This is amazing."

"What is?"

"All of this," she said. "Discovery, a story unfolding, piecing things together, danger."

"Going nose-to-nose with Gearhart on his turf?"

"Busted," Hannah said with a guilty grin. "Yeah, that too."

"I guess it's different being part of the news instead of just covering it," Grand said.

"Totally."

"But I can't get it out of my head that people are dying out here. It puts a different imperative on the process."

"That's what I mean," Hannah said. "What we do can make a difference. It's the main reason I got into this business."

They started up Pendola Road and immediately turned off at the Juncal campsite. The site was located in the Santa Ynez river drainage. As Grand pulled up he saw seven campers parked well apart on the thickly treed grounds. There were four motor homes, two pop-up campers, and a large fifth-wheel trailer. The lights were on in some of the RVs, off in others. High, grassy hills rose beyond the site, blocking most of the moonlight.

Gearhart and the Wall were moving toward the campers. An officer from the Pendola Ranger Station was already there; Grand recognized the green Chevy truck. A flashlight was moving toward Gearhart. Grand pulled up near the fifth-wheel trailer, a thirty-six-foot Gulf Stream Conquest. He and Hannah got out. Hannah hurried after Gearhart.

"Sheriff," said the short, middle-aged, clean-cut ranger in a brown uniform.

"What've we got?" Gearhart asked.

"Blood," replied the ranger nonchalantly. He jerked a thumb over his shoulder. "Looks like party night in 'Nam over there."

The men started walking into the heart of the camp. "How many victims?" Gearhart asked.

"So far I haven't found a one," the ranger said, "But I haven't gone into all the campers yet."

"You said there were guns."

"Two," the ranger replied. "They were different locations. Each one got off a round, but that was—"

"Help!"

The cry was small, thin, and high.

Everyone stopped talking, stopped moving, and listened.

"Daddy?"

The voice was coming from inside the Gulf Stream Conquest. Grand had stayed by his SUV and was the one nearest the trailer. The door was only ten feet away. He ran toward it.

"Grand, wait!" Gearhart shouted.

Grand did not intend to wait. Whoever was inside might be hurt. Seconds could matter.

The door was located in the front of the trailer. There was a large pool of blood to the left of it, large, ugly scratches on the wall beside it. Grand opened the door with the sleeve of his jacket so he wouldn't smudge any fingerprints. He stepped back and listened.

"Grand, dammit!" Gearhart shouted.

Grand didn't hear anything from inside the trailer. He went up the stairs and looked in.

The lights were on and the camper was relatively neat. There was part of a stuffed animal on the floor and uneaten dinner on the dinette. The drapes of the bay window were drawn. He moved down the center of the RV toward a side aisle. There was another room in back.

"Hello!" Grand said as he moved into the master bedroom. He stopped and looked under the queen-size bed. "Is anyone in there?"

"I'm here," said the small voice.

It came from a bath suite in the back. Grand hurried over. The door was shut. He didn't know if it was locked, but he didn't want to open it. Not if the girl was hiding from something. He knocked.

"Are you in there?" he asked.

"Yes."

"Are you okay?"

"Uh-uh."

"May I come in?"

"Where's my dad and mom?"

"We're looking for them," Grand said softly. "But we found you. My name is Jim. Could we talk just a little?"

"It was here," said the voice.

"What was?"

"The lion."

Grand felt his bowels tighten.

Gearhart arrived.

"Where was the lion?" Grand asked.

"It was outside and then it was on the roof."

"Well, it's gone now. Listen," Grand said carefully, "I've told you my name. It's Jim. Remember?"

"Yes."

"What's your name?"

"Eugenie."

"Eugenie? That's a *very* pretty name."

"And my rabbit's name is Blankie. But he lost his head when I was running."

"He did? Well guess what, Eugenie."

"What?"

"Blankie's head is out here. And if you open the door, there's this very nice man, Sheriff Gearhart, who will be happy to put Blankie's head back on his body."

The girl was silent again.

"Eugenie, are you all right?"

"Yes," she said after a moment. "I was just looking."

Grand felt a chill. "At what?"

She didn't answer.

"I've had enough of this," Gearhart said. He moved close to Grand. "Open the door. Whoever did this is getting farther away and she's our only witness."

"Sheriff, this girl is scared," Grand said. "She says she saw a lion. There's something else in there. You startle her and she may not want to talk at all." Grand took a breath and knocked softly on the door. "Eugenie?"

"Yes?"

"The sheriff would really like to fix Blankie. And maybe there's something you'd like. A snack?"

"I'd like my mom."

"Okay. How about you come out, tell the sheriff a little about what happened. Then maybe we can see where your mom went."

The girl was silent again. A moment later they heard clumping; it sounded as if she was walking in the shower or tub. Then there was a click and the door handle turned. A small, red-haired girl stood in the open door, a headless bunny tucked under her arm.

Grand smiled and crouched in front of her.

"Hi, Eugenie," he said. "I'm Jim Grand."

"Hi."

"And this is Sheriff Gearhart," he said, pointing up.

"Hi," the girl said.

Gearhart half-smiled.

"Now," Grand said, "if you go with the sheriff, he'll take you to Blankie's head. And maybe the three of you can sit down and talk."

Eugenie looked from the sheriff's face to his gun. "Okay," she said. "You go first, Mr. Sheriff."

Gearhart turned and left the bedroom. Eugenie was close behind him. She turned and looked at Grand before leaving the bedroom. She tried to smile but it stopped short of her eyes. They were guarded.

Grand smiled back. When she was gone, the smile faded and he looked into the bathroom. It was a small, brightly lighted room with oak-panel cabinets and a garden tub. There were pieces of cotton in the tub; stuffing from Blankie, he guessed. She must have been huddled there. He couldn't imagine what she was looking at until he looked up.

There was an oblong skydome over the tub. Ordinarily the stars would be visible, but not tonight.

Tonight, the sky was red.

36

Professor, you didn't know who or what was in that camper," Gearhart snapped. "You could have caused that girl's death and your own by going inside." The sheriff glanced at Hannah Hughes. "*This* is why I take control of a site when I get there."

"He helped you," Hannah said.

"He slowed me down," Gearhart said.

Grand and Gearhart were standing beside Grand's SUV, at the foot of a high slope. Hannah and the Wall were standing behind Grand. A helicopter hovered over the light, illuminating the grounds. In front of them, newly arrived deputies sealed off the campgrounds and examined the blood-covered tops of several of the vans. As in the truck crash, blood was all that remained of the victims. To the north, in the picnic area, an emergency medical team and trauma counselor examined Eugenie at a park table.

"I want the three of you out of here, now," Gearhart said.

"She said she saw a lion," Grand said quietly.

Gearhart looked at him. "Man, you know how to push but not to listen. She *thinks* she saw a lion."

"Sheriff," Grand replied evenly, "something scared that little girl enough to cause her to hide in the smallest place in the smallest room of that camper and to stay there."

"She also thinks her stuffed rabbit is alive," Gearhart said. "She has an imagination."

"Having an imagination doesn't mean the girl was using it," Hannah pointed out.

"She was eating dinner when this happened," Gearhart said sharply. "The drapes are neatly drawn. She wasn't looking outside."

"But she could hear. Maybe she heard something near the door and went to check it out. The door closes by itself. She could have opened it, seen something, and run."

"It was dark," Gearhart said. "And there are no footprints."

"The cat could have been on the tops of the campers," Grand said.

"If there *was* a cat."

"There was definitely something there," Grand said. "That's where the blood is. The scratch on the wall of the fifth wheeler is pretty high—it could have happened when a big cat reached down."

"Could have," Gearhart said. "That scratch could also be an old one. And there are at least eight people missing. Why would a lion take them all? No, Professor Grand. Only the girl knows what she really saw, if anything, and my people will find out what that was. Even then, until the evidence—*evidence*—tells us otherwise, there is no lion."

"Barring a lion then," Hannah said, "what do you make of this?"

"It's under investigation," he replied and walked away.

Grand, Hannah, and the Wall stood there silently under the clear, cool sky. A brisk wind was blowing from the southwest and riding up the hill. Grand looked to the north, along the steep slope. He still had a feeling that something was out here, beyond the reach of the lights. Something—the only word that came to mind was *unhealthy.*

"Do you guys really think there's a lion running around up here?" the Wall asked.

"It's possible," Hannah said.

"You know, I'm wondering," Grand said.

"About what?" Hannah asked.

"The killer apparently fed at the beach. There was no reason to attack the campsite."

"There's an 'unless' in your voice."

Grand nodded. "Unless the gunshots came first. Maybe the cat was walking past here after leaving the beach. It could have been carrying a body. Maybe someone saw it and opened fire."

"I like that," Hannah said. "It could have been headed to another cave."

Grand nodded. "Let's move the cars and do a little climbing."

"Where?" Hannah asked.

Grand pointed to where the edge of the spotlight from the helicopter barely illuminated a section of the slope.

"See the boulders up there?" Grand said. "About a hundred feet up, just past the light?"

"Yeah—"

"Look right above them," Grand said.

"I see what looks like a shallow ditch there," Hannah said.

"It's not a ditch," Grand said. "It's a slide path. When large rocks become dislodged from higher elevations they slip down the mountainside leaving gouges or ruts."

"And?" Hannah asked.

Grand said, "That's how I've found most of the new caves up here."

Hannah looked at him. "Let's go," she said as she climbed into the SUV.

37

Grand and the Wall drove their vehicles out of the campsite and back onto Pendola Road. They pulled off on the nearest shoulder where Grand took out the flashlight and started up the slope. The Wall followed with his own flashlight and cameras.

Hannah was scared but excited. She felt the way she did just living in Southern California, where the earth could shift and cause the seas to swell over Santa Barbara or the mountains to rain down. Only more so. If they were right and Gearhart were wrong, there wasn't going to be a doorway where they could hide or high ground they could run to.

Though Hannah had to be cautious and conservative in print, she refused to embrace Gearhart's parochial view of what was happening here. Not just because it was Gearhart's view but because Hannah had learned—in these hills, in fact—that nature could surprise you.

When she'd first moved to Southern California, the young woman had come up to this very place. Because she was such a beach baby she *had* to see the sea at dawn from someplace high. So she'd climbed up one of these hills, and as the sun rose behind her she looked out at the ocean. It was whitecapped and green and filled the world to its ends. The hills smelled of the sea and she felt safe. It was a spectacular experience. But what was most unforgettable about that morning was that when she started back down the mountain she happened upon a field where monarch butterflies were hatching. There were thousands of them with their brown wings, dark veins, and matte-black borders with white spots. Some soared with the joy of new flight, some rested.

But the wings of each one were moving, catching the light, changing from moment to moment. The sense of safety was replaced by a sense of fragility, her individual life less important than the awesome cycle she was witnessing. She felt less permanent than a butterfly's wings.

Right now she felt even less permanent than that. Not just from the possible danger but from the exertion of the past few days. The young woman's ankles began to hurt almost at once from pushing her heels into the soft earth. But she wasn't going to let that slow her down.

Grand had told them not to speak. The wind was moving up the mountain. An animal would smell them but a human wouldn't. A human would have to hear them.

"Unless, of course, we've got to phone him for help," the Wall said.

Grand had said he was going to lead the group around the side of the mountain as they climbed. He said he wanted to bring them back on the camp side just above the helicopter searchlight. He didn't want Gearhart seeing them and calling them back.

They made their way up the steep mountainside, Hannah in the middle. She could tell the Wall was unusually anxious. They weren't going up to track the killer, and none of them expected that he or it would still be there. They were only going up to look for more footprints or fur samples. But Hannah didn't blame the Wall for his anxiety. She was usually so determined to get her story that she bulldogged ahead without always factoring in all the what ifs. That was how she'd almost burned to death at the wharf fire, trying to talk to fire fighters on the line. And he'd had to pull her from a sea cliff that was collapsing in Goleta during the storms of 1997. She'd wanted to know what it was like to be banged around by winds and rain. In addition to taking pictures, it was the Wall's job to reign Hannah in.

The mountainside was alternately rocky and muddy, with thick grasses in some places and none in others, steep inclines in spots and gentle slopes in others. The first and last time Hannah had been up here it wasn't the rainy season, which made a big difference. It also wasn't nighttime then, where every *click, hooo,* and *crunch* wasn't a potential danger. When the wind was refreshing and not a gentle betrayer.

As they climbed, Hannah watched Grand in the glow of the Wall's flashlight. The scientist moved with such poise and balance that it was suddenly difficult to picture him sitting still in a chair back in that small room at the university. Yet he had seemed at home there too. Also when he was wisecracking about Gearhart running for governor.

Outer and inner strength, humor, and intelligence, Hannah thought. And from the way Grand smiled each time he mentioned her name, still very much in love with his late wife.

Hannah had never met anyone quite like him. She felt safe around him, something she'd never felt around Sheriff Gearhart.

They continued up and around the slope, sometimes ascending so steeply that they were literally on their hands and knees going up. As they climbed, Grand occasionally pocketed large, flat stones. She was curious about them but didn't want to talk and break her concentration on the climb.

Eventually they saw the edge of the spotlight. There was enough light spilling over so they could see, and Grand had them shut off their flashlights so that they wouldn't be noticed from the ground or, possibly, from whatever was above. Then he led them around the arc, toward the slide path. It was interesting feeling her way: Her other senses truly did compensate for not being able to see as well, her sense of touch in particular. She was much more aware of the stability, texture, and even the temperature of each rock or ledge or tree trunk she used to climb.

The air was cooler and the wind nippier as they ascended. Hannah could see the moon-speckled ocean in the distance, the white clouds, the stars, the misty lights of Santa Barbara.

They passed the boulders and followed the slide path straight up.

Suddenly, Grand stopped and pointed ahead. "Look."

About forty or fifty feet up the mountain leveled off. It was as though a massive piece had been sliced from the top. A forest of oaks had grown there, the outermost trees slanting sharply outward, bent and shoved but not dislodged by decades of rain. The slide path started at the edge of those woods, bounded on both sides by boulders that hadn't come free. They were too low to see whether or not there was an opening.

Grand started climbing again. So did Hannah. With a deep sigh, so did the Wall.

They reached the summit ten minutes later. Breathing heavily, her hands cold, swollen, and throbbing. Hannah stood beside Grand as he looked down a sinkhole. He turned on his flashlight, using his body to shield it from the campsite. The sinkhole wasn't as large as the one by Painted Cave, only about four feet across. Like the hole in the creek bed, this one sloped away sharply inside. The interior was studded with root tips and rocks, many half-buried in the wall. The soil was dark, rich, and damp.

Grand turned and shined his flashlight into the thick woods. So did the Wall. The twin beams met on a dirt path that led to this point, which was probably a scenic stop for hikers. The narrow, deeply rutted path slanted toward the ledge; rainwater had obviously followed it down, backed up behind the boulders, and created the sinkhole. They couldn't see very far into the woods as ground fog and clouds merged to form a misty cloak.

But they discovered that this hole had something they had not found at the other holes. Something they saw when Grand's light moved slowly across the woods, along the heavy cover of leaves and high grasses.

Another set of eyes, watching it.

38

The two eyes were about one hundred feet away, maybe four feet off the ground. Large and milky-white, they possessed an eerie luminescence in the gleam of his flashlight. Almost immediately upon spotting the eyes in the deep thicket, Grand shut off his light. If the owner hunted at night and lived in caves, the glare would only antagonize him.

"Wall?" Grand said.

"Yes, sir?"

"Shine your light on the ground."

The Wall did.

"Is it one of them?" Hannah asked.

"I don't know," Grand replied. "It could be an elk or an owl on a low branch—anything." Grand handed his light to Hannah to free up his hands. "Both of you back away from the sinkhole, slowly."

The Wall did as he was told.

Hannah hesitated. "I'm staying with you," she said.

"No," Grand insisted. "Right now we're a pack. If it's a cat we don't want to scare it into attacking."

Hannah started moving away.

"Keep your arms relaxed," Grand whispered. "Don't look at whatever's out there and don't crouch. It might think you're going to lunge. And don't take any pictures. Just a click could set this thing off."

Hannah and the Wall backed around the rocks along the outer side, near the edge of the slope. The boulders there were waist-high and would afford some protection if the animal attacked, maybe buy them a little time to start down the mountainside.

Grand didn't move. He wasn't surprised to find a large animal up here. He had felt its presence throughout the climb. Experienced predators, including humans, had an energy that the ancient Dorset Eskimos of northern Labrador had called *maat*—literally an unspoken voice that communicated strength. The earth elements had it and communicated it simply by "being" in a great number—rocks as mountains, water as the sea, and air as wind. In most wild species, the great number of *maat* is enhanced by a display of plumage, by inflating the cheeks, by shouting and chest-thumping, or by exposing teeth or a large set of horns or antlers or a large, shaggy mane.

Here, this close, the creature had *maat* that was off the chart. It was stronger than anything Grand had ever felt in the wild. It reminded him of how he felt on that childhood Grand Canyon trip, when his family went to Hoover Dam and he stood at the foot. Without seeing it, hearing it, or smelling it, Grand was still very much aware of the awesome might of the lake gathered on the other side. And Grand wasn't the only one who felt it. Whatever animals were in the thicket and surrounding area, they were not active like their brothers and sisters on the mountainside. They were deeply hidden.

When Hannah and the Wall reached the point where they'd come to the summit, the Wall backed over the side. Hannah stopped.

"What are you going to do?" she asked Grand.

"Try and learn something about what's out there," Grand replied.

"How?"

"By waiting here and seeing what it does."

"Why don't we let the sheriff do this?" the Wall asked.

"Because he'll come up here with a small army to try and take the animal down," Grand said. "A lot of people may die."

"Instead of just us," the Wall said.

"We're not going to die," Grand said. He began gathering small branches that had washed down from the treeline.

"This is crazy," the Wall said. "We're standing next to the animal's home. What do you *think* it's going to do?"

"That depends," Grand said. He was speaking in a very soft, melodic voice which he hoped would help put the creature at ease. At the same time he removed his Swiss Army knife from his pocket. He pulled the blade out slowly, silently. Then he knelt and cut slits near the thick end of the branches he'd gathered.

"What are you doing?" Hannah asked.

"Making a starburst," Grand said. When he was finished cutting the slits he took the flat stones from his pocket. He fit one end into the slit and pushed the other end with his thumbs. The fit was snug, as it was supposed to be. "Twenty-five hundred years ago the Dorset Eskimos of northern Labrador used these to catch sea birds. When they were swung around in a crowd of seagulls, each hunter could kill several birds at once." After he finished inserting four stones into four branches, he bunched them two in each hand and rose slowly. "The ends were weighted to fall with just a snap of the wrist. They would get two hits with each snap."

"If the animal does come after me, I want you both to get down the mountainside and into the spotlight," Grand said. "Make as much noise as you can to get Gearhart's attention."

"You don't have to worry about that," the Wall said as he hunkered down beneath his boss, just below the ledge. "If that thing charges they'll hear me down in Santa Barbara."

Grand continued to look out at the creature's eyes. As he did, he held the ends in his hand. With the rocks in his pocket as projectiles, he had the kind of slingshot used in the Maori *haka* war dance. The native weapon was designed to be used at close range. After stunning the enemy or prey with a blow, the warrior was able to release one end of the slingshot and use it as a whip. The Maori also used it for capturing wild animals to use in religious rites, since the strap could also serve as a muzzle.

Holding the starbursts lightly in his hands, he stepped away from the sinkhole. The animal's dark, liquid eyes moved with him. The scientist sensed that the animal wasn't so much watching him as studying him.

Grand studied the animal back. Apart from the eyes being reminiscent of the paintings, they reminded him of something else. At the moment, he couldn't place what that was.

The creature stayed still, silent, and focused. The breathing or rustling of very large animals like bear and deer could usually be heard. Not this thing. There was vigilance but no hint of unease. It appeared undistracted by the distant buzz of the Bell-412 helicopter and the faraway shouts of the sheriff's team. And it certainly did not seem to fear.

The animal could be a lion as Eugenie had said. Ignoring for the moment how a lion might have gotten loose here, big cats had the capacity to command entire regions with their presence, their stature. But what if the DNA and radiocarbon dating were correct? Could this *possibly* be a creature that hadn't walked the earth for millennia? And if so, how had it returned? A genetic experiment? There were enough government laboratories in the region to pull off cloning, but DNA restoration on this scale?

And then, in a cascade of what ifs, Grand thought, What if the animal had never left? The Chumash believed in eternal animal spirits. What if this were one of them? Or what if there were a reality behind the lore; a way, a place, a *something* that had enabled a prehistoric creature to survive to this day? The fact would contradict knowledge but it wouldn't necessarily contradict science. If the animal were here there had to be a reason.

In the primeval setting on the windswept mountaintop, civilization and the new millennium seemed very far away. The groan of soggy, fallen branches underfoot seemed louder than the helicopter hovering over the campsite. The sea air smelled of eternity. And for a flashing moment the feeling that Grand had in his office, of time folding back on itself, was very real again.

Grand stopped several yards from the sinkhole and the eyes stopped with him. It was then that he realized what they reminded him of:

Security cameras.

They were just *there* in the dark corners of life, taking things in, processing images and data, doing nothing as long as nothing was done. Is that what this creature had done for tens of thousands of years?

From where he stood the trees were pale, tapered columns, like the entrance to an ancient temple. In his imagination the angled, upper branches formed sloping cornices while the twigs and leaves described a chaotic frieze. The ground mist was the smoke of sacrificial braziers, with wisps from censers hanging in the higher branches.

Having gone about ten feet from the sinkhole, Grand began moving forward just to see what the animal would do. The wind picked up as Grand walked toward the oaks. Its lively howl and the shuddering leaves smothered the noise of the helicopter entirely. The sounds and motion made Grand feel isolated even from his two companions. Yet never once, in all his years of exploring mountains and caves, had the scientist felt so much a part of a place. He was connected to the ground, the air, the heavens. Grand wondered if this was what Joseph Tumamait's vision had been like. Not a mystical coagulation of smoke and light but something very real and surprisingly personal.

The eyes continued to watch him. The moonlight filtering through the leaves picked out hints of a massive shape in the blackness. There were the lines of huge shoulders and hindquarters. But the animal was still mostly in shadow, impossible to define.

Grand stopped again, approximately fifty feet from the woods. The wind was whistling here, split by the trees. But beneath that sound he heard a rumble, like a low, steady drumroll. It took him a moment to identify it as the creature's deep breathing.

Then Grand stopped. He listened and turned very slowly toward the left.

And made a disturbing discovery.

39

Hannah had watched anxiously as Grand approached the thicket, his pale yellow jacket a dim ghost in the darkness. He was the only place of calm in a world that seemed to be made of nitroglycerin. Hannah didn't know what moment, what action, what impulse might cause an explosion.

A part of Hannah—a very large part—wanted to go to Grand. Not to help him, because she didn't see how she could, but to experience what he was experiencing. She once interviewed an astronaut after the space shuttle *Challenger* exploded, and it shocked her when he said he envied them in a way: that they had died with their boots on.

Now she understood.

It seemed worth the danger, even the risk of dying, to be out there getting this story and phoning it in to Karen as it happened. The only reason she didn't was because it might hurt Grand. The scientist obviously had a feel for these things; if anyone could find out what was in the thicket and live to tell about it, Grand was that person.

So Hannah watched. Scared for Grand, frustrated at being on the sidelines, and also proud about having found the thing before Gearhart but now questioning the wisdom of not summoning him. She wished Grand would let them know what was out there, whether it was a stag or an owl or possibly their killer. But he was just standing there.

She crawled up slightly and stuck her head a little higher. Maybe Grand would see her and make some kind of sign.

He didn't. She inched up a little more. Stones fell from underfoot and clattered down the mountainside.

"Hannah—" the Wall quietly warned her.

"I know," Hannah whispered back.

She did. She was supposed to keep still and quiet. But the eyes weren't on her, they were on Grand. She turned back and looked down at her photographer. The Wall was lying against the mountain, cheek to rock, as though he were hugging the side of a trench.

"Wall, give me the camera with the telephoto lens," she said, softly but insistently.

"Why?"

"Please?"

"The professor said no pictures—"

"I know," she said. "I only want to try and get a better look."

"No," he said. "Just sit still."

"I can't! I promise I won't take any pictures," Hannah said. "I have to see."

The Wall hesitated. Then, with a sigh, he rose up slightly on his left hand. As he did stones fell away from under his feet.

"Shit!" he snarled.

The Wall froze as more stones fell. They clattered into rocks below and caused a small cascade. But the cliff-side didn't give out beneath him. Slowly, he lowered himself down.

"That's it," he said.

"What's it?"

He hunkered back down without removing the camera. "We're going to do what the man said. Wait."

"Wall—"

"You'll know what's out there soon enough," he said.

Hannah didn't bother arguing. She continued to look out at the milky, cloud hazed forest.

This was maddening. Hannah was *extremely* disappointed at herself for not having gone with Grand. A reporter shouldn't be hiding behind a bunch of rocks. She should be in the middle of the investigation. Two could move as quietly as one, and the animal was as much her find—her responsibility, her *risk*—as it was Jim Grand's.

Just then, Grand moved. Instead of the back of his head she saw his face. But he was too far away for her to make out his expression or hear if he was saying anything.

She shrugged with her palms up and widened her eyes even though she knew he couldn't see them. If he wanted her to come over, he would have gestured in some way. So what did this mean? Was he getting ready to walk back or run back or go farther into the woods?

What? she screamed inside, her fingers curling slightly as she shook her upturned hands.

As the young woman watched, something moved. Not in the woods, but to her immediate left. Hannah turned and looked in that direction. A moment later she slowly raised her right hand, reached into her shirt for her dog tags, and held them tightly.

She swore silently.

She *should* have phoned in the damn story.

40

Only once in his life had Malcolm Gearhart gotten to a point of frustration and rage that was so absolute that he lost it. That was when Company A, 3d Reconnaissance Battalion, 3d Marine Division, was in action against the Vietcong near Danang. Gearhart, his best buddy Emanuel "the Man" Slatkin—"of the Brooklyn, NY, Slatkins," as he was proud of saying, always pronouncing his home state *En-Why*—and three other men were part of Lieutenant Leonard Ax's advance party that had deeply penetrated heavily controlled enemy territory. The Vietcong suddenly opened fire from six different concealed positions, cutting off the five men from the main party. When Lieutenant Ax was cut down at the start, Slatkin took over the deployment of the remaining troops, organizing a base of fire while managing to kill four Vietcong and silence an automatic weapons position on his own. While Gearhart concentrated on the killing, that short little pecker Slatkin kept everyone's spirits up, kept them fighting, and helped keep them alive until the main body could cut through, drive the Vietcong back—the bastards usually didn't like to hang around for a fair fight—and get them the hell out.

That was when Slatkin stepped into a Hanoi Two-Fuck. They called it that because first you got screwed in a figurative sense; and second you literally got fucked when a thin, sharp eighteen-or-so-inch stake, usually bamboo but sometimes steel, attached to a horizontal arm, came slashing at you from camouflage hiding and penetrated your belly. Penetrated with such incredible force that it came out your back and dragged you with it, pinning you to whatever was behind you. Often, it was another soldier.

There's a moment, just before the Hanoi Two-Fuck impales you, when you know it's coming. It's a moment filled with the worst sound in the world: a click that means you stepped on the hidden trigger, like a tiny landmine, that launches the arm. Even keeping your foot on the trigger won't save you. Once it's sprung, it's sprung. Dropping won't save you either because the stake comes too fast and will still get you in the chest or head.

Gearhart was to the right of Slatkin, about three feet away, when they heard the click. They looked at each other. They knew what the sound was, though for a second they weren't sure which of them was going to get two-fucked. The ground was thick with vines and rocks and it was impossible to know whether you'd stepped on the trigger or not.

They just stared into one another's eyes for what seemed like forever until the Two-Fuck came shrieking from behind some goddamn plant and, covered with leaves, smashed through Slatkin. Two-Fucks were often set up in pairs, since the instinct of a soldier was to go to his buddy and the Cong could get two for the bloody price of one. So all Gearhart could do, all anyone could do, was watch as Slatkin was dragged back, his toes lifted off the ground, his heels digging through the ground, and was whammed into a tree.

They had to leave Emanuel Slatkin of the Brooklyn, En-Why, Slatkins hanging from the tree there while they searched the ground for the other Two-Fuck and disarmed it. Fortunately, Slatkin only lived for about a half minute after being skewered. But during those thirty seconds, Gearhart screamed inside with a helpless pain that he'd never experienced before or since. Only after he was sure the man was dead did he let it out. And there were times he thought he was still screaming, still wanting to punish the fucking Cong. Or any one or thing that killed with that kind of cold sadism.

Like now.

Standing by the fifth wheeler, looking again for anything that might tell him who or what was behind this, Sheriff Gearhart was getting close to popping—very close. He hadn't been able to finish the job in Vietnam or in Los Angeles, but he was damn well going to finish the job here. The job he was *supposed* to be able to do better than anyone else.

People were dying in increasing numbers, a prowler was still out there, and he wasn't getting anywhere. His lab team was still at the beach, so he'd had to request a forensics unit from nearby Ventura County in order to get this site sampled before it rained or the wind blew away clues or camera crews arrived and saw them doing nothing here except scratching their asses while they looked again for footprints or tracks that just weren't here.

And then there was the problem of failing to apprehend this thing before it spilled into another county. Not only would Gearhart lose control of the manhunt to the state police or—worse—the National Guard, he'd lose face. Even when he came home from Vietnam, there was nothing Malcolm Gearhart had been ashamed of personally.

As the sheriff was about to get on the radio—again—and ask for another update from Thomas Gomez and his lab team at the beach, stones suddenly struck the top of the RV and the ground around it. He looked up at the mountainside to the north. Ground appeared to be giving way somewhere near the top, dropping rocks and dirt.

It could be nothing. It could also be the killer.

Gearhart switched the radio from Gomez's frequency to the frequency of the helicopter.

"Officer Russo!" he said to the woman flying the chopper.

"Sir?"

"Take yourself up about two hundred feet," Gearhart said. "Ride the spotlight along this side of the northern peak to the top. I want to see if there's anything there."

"Yes, sir," Russo said.

A moment later the spotlight was crawling from the center of the campsite toward the northern rim.

41

Jim Grand had once read a zoology paper about the interaction between apes and humans. More than once, the lifestyle and activities of the great apes gave him ideas about how Neanderthals and other human ancestors might have organized social hierarchies.

According to the paper, it was not uncommon for a male ape to stand watch while the female ate. However, there had been several recorded instances where a male ape would appear to stand watch while the female circled and attacked intruders. Grand had never heard of any other species doing this, since it required a level of deception and intelligence that most animals did not possess. But that didn't mean it never happened.

Even before Grand was sure exactly what was standing in front of him he became aware of something moving to the side and then behind him. It was moving quickly. He heard the low drumroll of its breath as it stalked away, deeper into the woods. Then he saw a large shadow move from the far side of the thicket toward the cliff.

Toward Hannah and the Wall.

There are two animals, Grand realized.

He had speculated about that possibility before, when he and Hannah were tossing ideas out at the university. Grand should have kept that in mind here, in the field.

The scientist was angry at himself for having underestimated these creatures. The animal in front of him had been the decoy while the other one flanked them. Fortunately, the animal to the side was hugging the ground and moving toward Hannah at a slow, stealthy crawl.

Perhaps it didn't intend to attack. It might just be positioning itself to protect its home or enter the sinkhole. The animal in the thicket could be covering for it.

Still, Grand didn't intend to take chances. He started back toward the ledge. He wanted to get back to Hannah and the Wall, be there in case the big cat did go after them. Make sure they got a good start down the mountainside and cover as they descended.

By this time Hannah had seen what Grand was looking at. She froze. That was a good thing; this wasn't the time to make any sudden, panicked movements.

Grand moved confidently but not hurriedly. As the seconds passed he became more and more in tune with the land, the *maat* of the two animals, and his own center. He looked to the east. The second animal was still moving without haste or menace. At this rate, Grand would reach the ledge first. Now that he'd had a clearer look at the animal, he could see that it was definitely a large cat, though he couldn't tell what kind.

Grand listened carefully. He didn't hear anything behind him. The encounter would probably end without a confrontation. Though they didn't get everything they came up here for, at least they now had some idea what they were dealing with: animals that apparently weren't hostile unless hungry or provoked. The first thing he and Hannah should probably do upon getting back to town was bring in the State Department of Fish and Game, Wildlife and Large Animals Division. Try to figure out a way to track, encircle, and tranquilize the cats—

Grand's brow darkened as the slap of the helicopter rotor suddenly became louder. He looked out and saw the chopper rising higher above the campsite, thc sky brightening in front on him.

No—

A moment later the darkness turned bright white and the mountaintop flooded with light. From behind and from the right, Grand heard a roar that ripped through the din created by the helicopter, the wind, and Hannah screaming his name.

42

The light and the bellowing collided somewhere over Grand's head. "Hannah, get down!" he yelled.

Hannah turned back toward her photographer. "Wall, get a picture!"

"What?"

"There's time to get a shot—"

"No!" Grand screamed. "Get down!"

"Jim, we can do this—"

"Dammit, call Gearhart to get the chopper out of here then get the hell *down!*"

The Wall had had enough. He wrapped his big arms around Hannah and pulled her back. Hannah shouted at him. He didn't care.

Good for him, Grand thought. He admired Hannah tremendously, but she could be completely reckless.

Grand kept running but took a moment to look behind him at the animal in the thicket. It was moving now. It emerged at a slow-motion gallop—big, strong steps powered by muscles that were so taut, propelling a body so long, that it took several moments for the animal to build up speed.

Incredibly, the creature was exactly what they had thought it might be: a saber-toothed cat.

As the giant came forward, the fine white fog rolled around its low-slung head and shoulders. It was almost as though the animal had taken form from the cloud itself.

Grand couldn't tell much about the saber-tooth from this distance. The animal had long, golden fur—not shaggy, but longer than the coat of a lion. It seemed stiff, like bristles. Because the creature's head was down, averted from the spotlight, Grand could only see its eyes. They were dark, wide-set, and very narrow now.

The scientist also didn't have much time to study it. Looking back, he ran across the white-lit terrain toward the ledge. The chopper was just hovering, level with the cliff. Grand waved for it to go back, but the helicopter remained. The cat on the east was just outside the light but also running toward the ledge. It would be in the spotlight within moments. Hopefully it was headed toward the sinkhole and not toward Hannah and the Wall.

Grand watched the cat as it ran. The animal was easily over six feet in length and its tail added nearly another foot to that, held straight behind with a teardrop-shaped tuft of hair at the end. The cat had to be moving at least forty miles an hour and gaining. It moved like a cheetah, its torso extending with each long stride. But it was much larger and more muscular than a cheetah. And just seeing it turned something on in Grand. It aroused something primal, a competitiveness he didn't feel in real life. Certainly not in academia. His legs moved harder, faster, and his senses seemed more acute somehow. Challenge, stretching and expanding the human template.

Or was it the animal spirit of the earth itself entering him, he wondered, the way the Chumash said it was supposed to?

Behind him, Grand heard the stones crunch faster as the other cat picked up speed. The scientist started turning the starbursts at his side and then raised one of them above him, a dervishlike display of *maat*. He whistled loudly. Grand wanted the cat to know that he was running not because he was afraid but because he was protecting his own.

This was what the Maori must have felt during haka, he thought. Moving in a way that appeared mad and uncontrolled to outsiders but was sane and necessary in the context of preparing for war or intimidating an enemy.

It was liberating, not just physically but emotionally. Frenzy took the place of fear, burning away everything but the warrior within. He resisted the urge to cry out, only because Hannah or the Wall might think he was hurt and come running. But the energy to do so was there.

And yet the paleoanthropologist was still present in him too. The cat was just coming into the light on the right and Grand watched as it emerged from the darkness.

Against all logic and defying any known precedent, the animal was a saber-toothed cat. It was not a vision but a living *Smilodon*—genus *fatalis,* from the awesome size of it. And it was magnificent.

The animal was indeed nearly seven feet long from point to point, with longish, dark gold fur save for a stiff, slightly raised brownish tuft that ran along its back from the neck to the base of its tail. The animal's seven- or eight-inch-long fangs grew from a thick pocket of bone beneath those patches. Their backward curve was slight and graceful, ending in incisor-sharp points. The creature's mouth was shut; on each side flaps of skin bulged over the tops of the fangs. The animal's large ears were pointed sideways and slightly flared, almost like those of a bat. There were small white tufts of hair on the tops of the ears, like those of a bobcat. The neck was much thicker than that of a modern-day cat, packed with muscles that supported the heavy upper jaw. The animal's foreleg shoulders were massive and the hind legs were even greater still. The paws were the size of baseball mitts with claws like sharks' teeth. The body between them appeared to have scars—healed scars. The creature had to weigh a half-ton.

Grand took in these details quickly since the saber-tooth was only illuminated for a moment. The chopper finally withdrew, throwing the mountain back into darkness.

The scientist reached the sinkhole moments before the cats did. He raced around it, stopped swinging the starbursts, and vaulted the nearest boulder. Then he turned quickly to look back. He was prepared to face the two saber-tooths if he had to.

But both cats were gone.

43

The Wall was stretched over Hannah, huddling her against the mountainside. When Grand landed on the ledge above them, Hannah waited and listened. When she heard nothing she squirmed from the photographer's big arms.

"You're fired, Wall," she growled.

"Good."

Grand was still crouching behind the rock and looking out at the misty mountaintop. Hannah looked behind her, down at the bright campsite, then squatted beside Grand.

"Talk to me, Jim," Hannah said in a flat, low voice. "Were they what we thought?"

"Yes," Grand said as he rose slowly. He dropped the starbursts. He was still staring across the dark tor.

"Saber-toothed cats."

"That's right."

Hannah rose. "My god. This is amazing. But why didn't they attack? Was it the light?"

"It might have been that or it might have been my retreat. A lot of animals won't fight if they don't have to."

"Maybe it was your star-things," The Wall suggested.

"That's possible too. But there's another possibility." Grand put the rock in his jacket pocket and took the flashlight from Hannah. "The sound of the helicopter. Roaring is a ritualistic display."

"Then why didn't they attack when they first saw us?" Hannah asked.

"They weren't hungry and they didn't feel threatened," Grand said. "I think they were just up here to watch the sinkhole."

"Why?"

"I'll let you know when I'm sure. Where's your cell phone?"

"Back at the car."

Grand turned around. "Wall, do you have a cell phone?"

"Yes."

"Can I borrow it?"

"Sure," he said as he reached into his equipment case. "I won't be needing it in the North Pole, where I'm moving tonight because there aren't any monsters there."

"That we know of," Grand said.

The Wall seemed to freeze.

"Jim, what's going on?" Hannah asked. "Who are you going to call? And—shit. How can these tigers be alive?"

"Deep freeze."

"Huh?"

"One of the cats had large, healed scars," Grand said. "They were long uppercuts. The cat was in a fight with an animal that sliced from bottom to top, head bowed. Possibly tusks. Possibly mammoths."

"Prehistoric elephants?" she said. "What have we got, an entire Ice Age population?"

"I don't think so," Grand said, "which is my point. Mammoths wouldn't be hiding in caves. We'd definitely have seen them before now. Back at the university we had radiocarbon reactions from tissue that was metabolically alive. That can't be. In order to be alive, the creature would have to be processing carbon dioxide. If it were processing carbon dioxide, we wouldn't have gotten a reading."

"Okay—"

"With one exception," Grand said. "Cryogenesis."

The photographer handed Grand the cell phone.

"Wall, is Hannah's number programmed in?"

"It's number one."

"Hold on," Hannah said. "Are you telling me the cats were frozen?"

"Remember the elevated water levels in the fur samples?"

"Right," Hannah said.

"That could have come from the ice," Grand said.

"But how?" Hannah asked. "There were no glaciers this far south, were there?"

"No," Grand said. "But there may have been subterranean ice."

Hannah shook her head. "This is impossible."

"A lot of things seem impossible until they happen," Grand said. He slipped the phone into his jacket pocket, turned on the flashlight, then swung back over the rocks.

"Where are you going?" Hannah asked.

"To get some answers." The scientist walked over to the sinkhole and cautiously peered over the edge. When he was sure the cats weren't there, he shined the light down. "The cave will probably block the phone signal but I'll find a place to call you."

"Like hell." She turned. "Wall?"

"Yo!"

"My phone's in the car, in my bag. Get it and keep it with you."

Grand looked at her.

"I'm coming with you," she said.

Grand shook his head once. He sat on the edge of the sinkhole.

Hannah crouched beside him. "The chopper has already landed at the campsite and El Gearhart is probably on his way up. He's going to close off this site and I'm *not* giving up another lead. With or without you, I'm going in."

Grand didn't think she was bluffing and there wasn't time to argue. "All right," he said. "Wall?"

"Still here."

"Your flashlight?"

The photographer climbed the boulders and ran the light over.

Grand looked at Hannah. "Step where I step and watch out for stalactites. If you knock yourself out I'm leaving you where you fall."

"Fair enough."

"No talking," he added as he shut off the phone and handed it to Hannah. He glanced over at Wall. "We'll call if we find anything."

"Just give me time to get down the mountain," the Wall said.

"And back," Hannah added. "We need pictures of the site."

The Wall groaned.

Meanwhile, Grand was moving the light around the sinkhole. The sloping passageway went down about seven feet and was lined with sharp-edged stones, most of which appeared to be part of larger, buried rocks. Grand handed Hannah the flashlight and told her to shine it down. He pushed his heel down against one of the stones and it held. He eased down, his back to the side of the sinkhole, and put his full weight onto it. Then he climbed down to the others. When he reached the bottom he had Hannah toss him the light. He considered running on without her, but knew she'd try to follow. Instead, he helped her down.

The passageway was just over five feet high and about four feet wide; the air was musty and close. The tunnel led west toward the Pacific and east; he could hear the faint sound of breakers and assumed the cats had used this passageway to go from the beach to the mountain.

Grand motioned Hannah toward the east. He didn't think the cats would be going back to the sea; since this started, they hadn't seemed to backtrack. Where they were headed, whether by instinct or design, was one of the things he hoped to discover by tracking them.

That, plus the meaning of the Chumash paintings—the mountains in the upper cave and the circles and crescents in the lower cave. By virtue of what he had seen tonight, Grand believed that the paintings were more than a shaman's expressions of faith.

He believed they could be a warning.

44

Grand made his way through the increasingly narrow tunnel as he had made his way up the mountainside: fast and sure-footed. Holding her flashlight in her right hand, at her side, and keeping her left arm up to block and shift around stalactites, Hannah struggled to keep up with him.

She had come down here hoping to pick up more information, more understanding, and more news. She hadn't expected to actually catch up to the cats, though that really seemed to be Grand's intent. Hopefully, he had something in mind for what they would do then. Despite what Grand had said, Hannah didn't think the cats would welcome them with open paws.

As Hannah walked, she watched Grand. The quiet-university-professor aspect of the man seemed even more deeply buried than it had been on the mountainside. Climbing to the tor, he had been focused. But here it was almost as though he'd become the thing he was tracking. The movement of his shoulders reminded her of a stunt pilot who had once performed off the pier. Grand's "wings" kept ducking this way and that to avoid rock projections, to turn his light into narrow fissures, to move him around stalactites. Like the pilot, he did all of this at a fast walk. His legs also moved with fluidity and confidence. It was almost as if he could anticipate the terrain, like a driver who had been along a road so often that the ride was almost a coast, even at night. Obviously, all caves and tunnels weren't the same. But maybe the senses one used were. If so, Grand was certainly using them.

The tunnel sloped down, which didn't surprise Hannah. After several minutes it turned sharply to the north and dropped away faster, nearly at a forty-five-degree angle. Grand turned so that his right side led and leaned back slightly as he continued down. Hannah did the same. Grand would frequently turn quickly to make sure that she was all right. Despite his attitude before they descended, his attention—and expression—showed concern for her.

As they walked, Grand also swung his flashlight over the floor and walls of the tunnel looking for signs of passage. Twice so far he'd stopped to examine scratch marks on the ground. He would turn and nod to Hannah that they appeared to be going in the right direction.

The deeper she and Grand went, the more the tunnel turned and twisted, sometimes in a tight S-shaped pattern. There were thin, deep ruts here and there. They looked like cracks but Hannah realized that they were probably caused by water dripping from stalactites and dribbling downhill over the millennia. Hannah tried to picture lava being forced up slowly to create these passageways, burning through the softest strata of stone, the path of least resistance. It probably piled up in these lower caverns until the pressure became so intense that the magma just blasted through the upper sections of rock. Hannah imagined heat so intense that higher areas of the tunnels, areas that weren't submerged as long, were liquefied, then solidified into the oddly shaped bubbles she saw around her. It was strange. The bubbles looked so new, ready to pop, while the stalactites—which were formed much later—appeared vastly older.

As Hannah thought about these awesome natural forces, she realized that she had been at this newspapering game for too many hours of her life, far too intensely. She was actually writing the antediluvian volcano story in her head, as if she were publisher of the *Ice Age Gazette*.

Hannah had no idea how far they'd gone. A half mile? Maybe more?

It certainly felt like more. The tunnel became tighter—Grand was ducking now, and she had to as well in spots—and Hannah began to feel closed in. The air was cool and wet and it was scary, the idea that it was probably longer to go back than to go forward. Her legs had been weak after the climb and they were getting wobbly now. Blisters were forming on her heel and big toes. But she pushed herself on, then on some more, because she had asked for this. And she was actually glad she had exhaustion and claustrophobia in the front of her mind. It was something to think about other than what they were searching for. If she thought about the cats for too long she might freak or freeze, the way she did when she first saw them back on the mountaintop. They were frightening, yet so overpowering in their form and hypnotic in their movement that she couldn't look away.

There were no turn-offs from the tunnel, no side-tunnels. Hannah didn't know if that were unusual or not, but she was glad about that. At least there was no question which way the cats had come.

After what had to be another quarter mile or so—some of which they had to walk bent over, since the roof of the tunnel was less than five feet high—Grand stopped suddenly. Hannah stopped too. She listened. She heard nothing except Grand breathing deeply through his nose.

She breathed through her nose too.

And tasted fresh air.

Grand started up again. When he could finally stand up straight he ran, weaving and moving through the stalactites and outcroppings and getting well ahead of Hannah. She wasn't worried about losing him. The air was getting sweeter. The tunnel was coming to an end.

The ground leveled off and then rose slightly. The final leg was about fifty feet up a steep slope, which she took on her hands and knees. Though the rock scraped her knees and the heels of her palms, it was the quickest way up.

She reached the top and climbed out. She stood beside Grand.

There were near the base of a mountain and looking across a wide gully. Hannah couldn't place where they were or even what direction they were facing. There were more hills beyond the gully and peaks on either side of them.

Hannah looked straight ahead, where Grand was looking.

"This isn't good, is it?" she asked.

"No," he replied gravely. "It is not."

45

The Bell chopper touched down lightly on the mountaintop, in the center of the clearing. Gearhart climbed out, not lightly but with a clear sense of purpose. That purpose was to find the animals the pilot said he saw. Find them and kill them before the night was over.

The rotor-blown grasses whipped around Gearhart's feet as he approached the edge of the mountaintop. The Wall was taking pictures around the sinkhole. He stopped as Gearhart approached. The sheriff didn't see Hannah or Grand. He didn't like that. He didn't like it at all.

Snapping on his flashlight, Gearhart removed the point-to-point radio from his belt. After debriefing the pilot back at the campsite, Gearhart had spoken to Chief Deputy Valentine and given him his instructions. As soon as the chopper lifted off Gearhart called him again.

"What's the status on Dr. Thorpe?" Gearhart asked.

"I spoke with her and she's pulling her charts together," Chief Deputy Valentine informed Gearhart. "I've sent a deputy to the house. She should be here by the time the second chopper arrives."

"Good. What about the rest of the team?"

"Felice is calling everyone in now. Frank Lyon has begun organizing squads and putting together gear."

"Has he got extra night-vision equipment?"

"The police department and Sheriff Shooter are sending over their hardware," Valentine said. "Shooter is ready to offer his people if we need them."

Gearhart didn't want help from the Ventura County Sheriff's Office. It was bad enough the situation had spread as far as it had in his own county. "Will the teams be ready to move out when Dr. Thorpe gets there?"

"They'll be ready," Valentine said.

"I'm counting on it," Gearhart said. "I want these killers, Mike. I want them out of commission, tonight."

The sheriff switched off the radio and slid it back into the belt loop. He stopped a few feet from the Wall and glared at the photographer. "Where did they go?"

The Wall pointed down the hole.

"Does your boss have her phone?"

The Wall shrugged.

"Call her."

"I can't."

Gearhart advanced on the photographer. "Mister, you *call* her. I want those two back here."

"Sheriff, I physically cannot do that."

"Why?"

"Grand turned the phone off," the Wall said. "A ring at the wrong time—the cats might hear."

Gearhart swore again. "That's the *reason* I keep you people out of places like this."

The Wall said nothing.

Gearhart calmed slightly. "Tell me about the cats. Did you get a good look at them?"

"Not really."

"Is that a *no?*"

"I didn't get a good look at the cats, no, sir," the Wall said. "I saw a big *thing* for about a half a second when I jumped up and pulled Hannah behind the rocks. After that all I saw was Hannah's butt."

Gearhart shook his head. *That was a big help.* The guy was supposed to be a goddamn journalist. The sheriff shined his light down the sinkhole. He didn't believe what the pilot said he saw—lions with fangs. And if that *was* what he saw, then this was someone's idea of a sick gag. He didn't believe there was a pair of saber-toothed tigers in the hills.

"Walter, I'm closing off the entire area," Gearhart said. "I asked you to drop the film off at my office. Would you do that now?"

"If I leave the mountain, Sheriff, it may block the phone call when Hannah gets out."

"Then give me the phone," Gearhart said.

The photographer stood there. "You want my film and my cell phone. Anything else?"

"Yes, I want your fucking cooperation! I'm not running a summer camp."

The Wall hesitated, then handed him the phone. "I'll need Hannah's okay on the film," he said.

The sheriff slid the cell phone into the back pocket of his pants.

"You know, Hannah *is* trying to do good," the Wall said.

"Save it—"

"And she's got guts," the photographer added. "It wouldn't hurt you to cooperate a little."

"Cooperation is trust and trust is earned," Gearhart said. "Now please get yourself back down the mountain."

The helicopter had resumed hovering over the campsite. The north side of the peak was once again spotlit and the Wall walked toward it. He climbed the boulders and started down the mountainside.

As soon as the Wall was gone, Gearhart turned and ran the powerful flashlight over the flat field and the woods beyond. He had told Chief Deputy Valentine to organize the deputies and volunteers into teams of three and four, all of them armed. It was clear now that the killers were moving southeast through the mountain caves. Whether they were people or animals or some twisted combination of both, they had to sleep sometime and emerge somewhere else in the range. The plan was for Dr. Thorpe to define an outside perimeter with the beach and this sinkhole as southern and eastern boundaries. Once the map was drawn his teams would take up positions at the base of foothills and close in. If the squads found cave openings, they would make their way inside. With helicopters spotting from above, there was no way the killers could get away.

Again.

The sheriff walked toward the foggy woods. He was impatient for the operation to begin. If he didn't hear from Hannah and Grand before his teams were in place, Gearhart would warn his personnel that two people might be inside the caves and to watch out for them. But he wouldn't hold up the operation. It wasn't personal; his job was to protect citizens whether he liked them or not. He wouldn't delay this for anyone.

Chief Deputy Valentine called to say that Dr. Thorpe had arrived and the second chopper was ferrying her up. She was accompanied by Shooter and Deputy Skitch Kline of Search-and-Rescue, Mountain Tracking Division. Gearhart turned toward the ocean. He could see the Bell's bright flying light from where he stood. Valentine said that the rest of the teams, over fifty men in all, had arrived and would await Gearhart's instructions before heading into the mountain range.

Gearhart thanked him and signed off.

As he did, the cell phone in his back pocket beeped.

46

Grand and Hannah took a moment to stare across the gully. On the opposite side was the mouth of a large-diameter pipe made of concrete and approximately six feet in diameter. The bottom of the pipe was about two feet off the ground; the thick steel mesh that was designed to keep children out had been torn back and was hanging from the lower left corner. Water and detritus was flowing from the opening like spillage from a log flume. The runoff was pouring into a narrow, jagged channel that had been eaten from the pipe to the large gully.

This was bad news, Hannah knew.

Two years before, the municipal water districts of Santa Barbara, Ventura, and other counties down to Los Angeles had pooled their resources to create more efficient, interconnected drainage in the coastal ranges, a system that not only prevented flooding and channeled overflow from dams, but helped to fill the reservoirs of those communities. Given the lack of staining inside the pipe, Hannah assumed this pipe was part of that project. If that were true, then the cats had a new route through the mountains. One that had dozens of egresses, many of which would take them right to where the food was: the towns along the drainage route.

"Are we going in?" she asked.

"We have to," Grand said as he hurried down the steep, stony wall of the larger gully. "There are dozens of openings like this. If the cats leave we probably won't find them until they kill again." The gully was only four feet deep and Grand quickly crawled up the other side.

Hannah punched the speed-dialing code, then climbed down the side of the gully. She was connected after two beeps.

"Hello," said the voice on the other end.

Hannah reached to top of the gully. "Hello, Wall?" she said.

"No. It's Gearhart."

Hannah scowled. "What happened to the Wall?"

"He's gone. Where are you?"

"I'm not sure," Hannah said. She felt ambushed and violated. "We came to the end of the mountain tunnel and found a pipeline. We think the saber-tooths went in there. We're moving towards it."

"You're sure they're prehistoric cats?"

"We're as sure as we can be without getting up close and personal," Hannah said.

"Are you looking at the pipeline?" Gearhart asked.

"Yes."

"What's the gauge of the pipe?"

"I don't know, exactly," Hannah said. "The opening's about five or six feet across."

"That's one of the new pipes. They're using them in the Gibraltar Dam system expansion," Gearhart said. "Both of you stay where you are. We'll triangulate the call and pick you up."

Hannah looked over at Grand. He had reached the pipe and was examining the base. After a moment he climbed inside.

"Sorry, Sheriff, but we won't be here," she said.

"Listen to me," Gearhart said. "My SWAT teams are moving into that area. You pop out somewhere and they may not be able to distinguish between you and their prey."

"We're the ones on two legs," Hannah said. "I'll leave the phone here. You can follow the signal while we follow the cats."

"You may not get to follow *anything,*" Gearhart yelled. "Those pipes have been flushing regularly since the rains started—"

"We'll be okay," Hannah said.

The young woman set the phone on a flat rock beside the drain and climbed into the opening. She wondered if Gearhart had been concerned about their well-being or about the possibility that they might interfere with a kill shot.

The pipe was large enough for Hannah to stand. She splashed over to Grand, who was on his hands and knees about a yard in. He was using the back of his left hand to divert some of the flow as he studied marks on the floor of the pipe.

"What is it?" she asked.

"More claw marks," he said.

"Two sets?"

Grand nodded. "Both cats came in here, though there aren't any marks on the lip."

"Which means?"

"The cats didn't climb into the pipe. They jumped from somewhere outside and landed a yard inside." Grand stood, though he had to bow his head slightly. "The leap was precise and powerful."

"Just like when they disappeared into the sinkhole."

"Exactly." Grand sloshed ahead.

Hannah followed, her sneakers soaked with icy water. Even so, her feet weren't as cold as the backs of her shoulders. The chill of fear trickled down to the small of her back and settled there.

There had been awe in Grand's voice but it was tempered by concern. Hannah wasn't sure whether the scientist was worried about the power of the animals or whether it was something else, whatever it was he'd alluded to back on the mountaintop. But as she walked deeper into the pipe, the sounds of their footfalls splashing off the circular walls, she decided this much: She would give Gearhart the benefit of the doubt. He *was* worried about them.

Somehow, just thinking that made Hannah feel like she and Grand were a little less alone.

47

Sheriff Gearhart ran over to the chopper as soon as it landed. Special Ops senior officer Frank Lyon was the first one out of the helicopter. He was followed by Deputy Kline and Dr. Thorpe.

Gearhart was edgy. He wanted this action ready to go *now*. Chief Deputy Valentine had just radioed to say that he'd located the cell phone by tapping into the signal from three different points—the sheriff's office, the police station, and a car with the highway patrol. The spot where the three lines overlapped was where the cell phone was located, a place three miles southwest of Divide Peak, nearly one thousand feet up in the foothills. Gearhart instructed Valentine to radio the exact position to the chopper pilot.

Reaching the helicopter, Gearhart pulled the Special Ops senior officer aside. The sheriff had to shout to be heard over the roar of the rotor. "Did Valentine brief you?"

"He told me the pilot saw big cats."

"They may be all or just part of whatever's hitting us," Gearhart said. "Apparently, they've been located in the Gibraltar Dam drainage system."

"*In* it?"

Gearhart nodded. "Jim Grand and Hannah Hughes are there. They've been following the cats. Their last known position was southwest of Divide Peak. You've got night-vision gear?"

"Yes, sir."

"Okay. I want you to go back up. We'll get you the exact locations of the drain openings as soon as we have them. In the meantime, crisscross the area. See if you can find these things."

"If I do?"

"If it's an animal, take it out," Gearhart said.

"If it's not?"

"Don't let the sonofabitch get away," Gearhart said.

"He's yours," Lyon assured him.

The Special Ops leader hustled back to the chopper. A minute later he was airborne.

Gearhart went over to the line of boulders beside the sinkhole. Dr. Thorpe had booted her laptop and they began studying her maps, including those of the municipal water districts. Deputy Kline had water district supervisor Dean Rede on the phone and was using Thorpe's maps to find out exactly where each of the pipes opened up.

Though things were ready to pop, Gearhart felt like he was on a leash. In Vietnam he'd been able to turn everything he had on enemies, from M40 sniper rifles to napalm, from surgical strikes to blanket assaults. Here, as in Los Angeles, it was tough to get the job done. There were too many rules and too many special interest groups.

But he promised himself that this job *would* get done.

48

Though Grand was mentally and physically spent, there was something vitally alive inside of him. Whether it was a survival instinct, naked curiosity, or both, it kept his senses and limbs running at top speed.

Curiosity was certainly a large part of it. Grand had to fight being distracted by the creatures—by the wonder of them, by the questions he had about them, by whatever had apparently roused a pair of saber-tooth cats from eons of hibernation. He had to remember that he was the hunter and they were the prey. If Grand allowed his *maat* to weaken, if he let the roles become reversed, then he and Hannah would die.

And there was something else that concerned him even more than the cats. Something about the painting in the lower cave. A suggestion that danger was greater than what they'd see. Far greater.

Grand was able to move quickly in here. The pipe was on a slight up-slope, and he was able to straddle the water as it flowed down the center. There was debris in the water—branches, water bottles, the occasional drowned field mouse and rattlesnake. That meant the grate had also been torn out from somewhere up ahead. He hoped it was an old break, that the cats weren't so far ahead they were already in the mountains or in other tunnels already.

The water flow was becoming heavier the farther they went. Grand didn't know how often the system was flushed, but he suspected it would get pretty rough in here before long. He picked up the pace.

At least Grand didn't have to look back and check on Hannah. He could hear her splashing through the middle of the pipe. Whatever the young woman's motives for being here, whether it was altruism, journalism, or a combination of the two, Hannah Hughes had a great deal of courage and stamina. Despite the danger, she was here, and that inspired a maelstrom of emotions.

Protectiveness. Respect.

Affection.

Grand hadn't felt that toward a woman since Rebecca died. When the feelings first started, turning his head to look at her, for no reason other than to look at her, he felt that he was being disloyal to his wife, experiencing warmth toward another woman. Back on the mountain he had tried to justify it, telling himself that Hannah's presence helped to keep his instincts sharp. That if anything happened to her he would blame himself. And that was true, as far as it went. Now, he couldn't lie to himself. Hannah wasn't just a jump start for his survival skills.

He cared for her, more and faster than he'd expected. He didn't know what Rebecca would have thought; all he knew was that if the roles were reversed, and Rebecca were alive and alone, he would feel happy for her. He would know that he had a special, irrevocable place in her life.

After a few minutes they reached a juncture. On the left, a downward-sloping pipe met the main conduit.

"Wait here," Grand said. "I want to check the pipe."

"Why can't I come?"

"I'm on point. That's my job."

"Seriously," she said.

"Seriously," he replied. "If I run into a cat and it attacks, I need someone to take the information back to Gearhart."

Hannah didn't argue.

The pipe was about eight feet away. Hannah shined her light ahead.

Grand crouched slightly, ready to spring ahead or back. He removed his belt as he neared the pipe. There wouldn't have been room to use the starbursts here but his belt might prove useful. He let the strap hang from his right hand while he held the flashlight in his left. He listened carefully for breathing or splashing, though it was difficult to hear anything other than the echo of the rushing water.

The pipe was a yard away. Grand approached cautiously and very, very slowly. He was aware that the cats could be getting away while he checked, though he didn't think they'd feel any urgency. They probably couldn't hear him because of the water, nor smell him because there was no wind. The cautious approach was for his own benefit—to give him time, even an extra second or two, to defend himself. If one of the cats did attack, he wanted to be able to detain it long enough for Hannah to get a good head start. He was also using the time to think of ways he could manage the tight space to his advantage. To brace himself against the side of the conduit, or use the water and slope to slide back toward the entrance. If he did encounter one of the cats, and it was hostile, Grand had decided he would have to noose it somehow, either around the mouth or throat, and hope to hold it. Get onto its back, where it wouldn't be able to reach him with teeth or claw. With any luck, their struggles would block the conduit and prevent the other cat from passing.

Until that second cat bites me in the ass and lifts me off like a rubber ball, he thought. But even that would be all right, as long as it bought Hannah time to get away.

Despite the danger, Grand was overwhelmed by a breathtaking sense of discovery. Not only about the cats but about the origins of modern humans. For the first time in his life Grand truly appreciated the awesome courage of his forebears. And he also understood the forces that necessitated the invention of weapons and their constant, painstaking refinement. It was like watching anthropological history unfold inside and out.

He reached the juncture. The flow from the left conduit and from ahead joined here, creating two separate currents that made it difficult to stand. Grand took a quick look up. The flow was heavy. Though he didn't see any claw marks at the bottom, a good-size leap might have taken them several yards up. He shined the light up the pipe, did not see a cat. If a cat had gone up there, the only way to be sure was to climb up himself. And there wasn't time for that. He didn't see any detritus washing down, which meant that the grate was still in place. He was gambling that the cats had gone ahead.

Grand motioned Hannah forward. The young woman sloshed toward him. He started ahead.

Suddenly, Hannah screamed.

Grand swung around and stared into the wide flashlight beam.

Hannah was hopping and stomping at something in the water. She stopped when she saw what she was fighting. It was a dead rabbit. Hannah stepped aside and let it flow past.

"Sorry," she said when she reached him. "It scared me."

That was interesting, Grand thought. If the cats were here they hadn't eaten on the carrion. Either they only ate when they were hungry or they only ate what they killed. Just like most modern big cats.

The two resumed their trek.

The pipe turned gently toward the left after several minutes. Shortly after that it forked. One branch continued straight ahead and the other went up, to the right. That one was dry.

Of course, Grand thought. He turned to Hannah and leaned very close to her ear.

"Wait here," he said.

She made a face but nodded.

Grand started toward the conduit, which was slightly smaller than the pipe they were in. As he neared he could see that there was no soiling on the bottom. As he suspected, it was a service conduit built to give maintenance workers access to the pipes. There were several such conduits in other parts of the mountains, all of them ending in large blockhouses.

The scientist grew angry with himself. He should have thought of those large, mushroom-shaped structures before. They were thick, windowless, and warm at night. They'd make perfect dens.

Grand reached the base of the pipe, which was about four feet up the side of the conduit. He saw claw marks all along the concrete. He pulled himself in and squat-walked up, using his belt hand to steady himself on the side of the pipe. There was something up there. He could feel it. As he continued to ascend he could smell it, dank and musky. He snapped off the light. There was enough illumination from Hannah's flashlight to climb.

He neared the open top of the conduit. It was stuffy in the pipe and Grand was perspiring heavily. There didn't seem to be a break between his heartbeats. If he were attacked in here, his only defense would be a rapid retreat, a backslide into the main conduit.

Grand reached the end of the pipe. The blockhouse was dark. He put the front of his flashlight against his hip and turned it back on. There was a very slight, yellow glow from the plastic lens setting.

There was also something else.

Death.

49

Hannah was becoming anxious.

She was standing just beyond the downward-sloping conduit. The dry conduit was ahead, to her right, but she couldn't see Grand and she couldn't hear him because of the water. She'd seen how quiet the cats could be, and she was worried for him. There was something special about the man. It wasn't just his imposing physical presence, which was—*humid* was the word that came to mind. Or maybe that's how he made her feel; she wasn't sure. It was also his humility, his sense of wonder, and the well-being she experienced when she was around him. It was as though nothing could harm her.

She felt that more acutely in his absence. Now that he was gone, menace seemed to be everywhere. Hannah felt the way she used to feel in the unfinished basement of their seventy-year-old mansion in Newport. The bare bulbs, dampness, and brick walls were great to play in when she had a couple of friends over. But when her friends left and she had to turn off the lights and run up the steep wooden stairs, the basement became a den of monsters. They never caught her, but she knew they were there, hidden beneath the growl of the oil burner or the washing machine or the water tank.

They were there. And they were here too.

Hannah kept turning around, flashing the light behind her and checking the other conduit. The water was splashing down vigorously over there, washing the opposite direction and carrying along bark, leaves, and branches that must have been torn from trees by the storm. The flood from ahead was also getting stronger. Hannah had no idea how high Grand had gone but she hoped that he could see or hear the water.

A moment later she saw him backing from the mouth of the dry conduit. She smiled as Grand hopped into the main pipe. With his shoulders hunched and his head bent, he walked toward her. He kept his light turned slightly away to keep from blinding her.

"We've got to get back," Grand said when he reached her side.

"What's wrong?" Hannah asked.

There was something different about his voice. It was tense, urgent.

Grand didn't answer. Holding the flashlight and belt in his left hand, the scientist grasped the young woman's hand firmly in his right and jogged ahead. Pulled along by Grand and pushed by the water, which was now well above her ankles, Hannah had never felt so leg-weary. Her thighs were actually trembling from all the climbing and running she'd done today. The water in her shoes didn't help. She found herself leaning forward, putting more of her weight on Grand's hand. He took it easily.

They continued for twenty or thirty yards when Grand stopped abruptly near the first juncture. Hannah stood close behind him, still holding his hand. She was breathing hard and looking at where he had fixed his light. He was shining it on the mouth of the pipe, which was now on their right, about ten feet away. Water crashed down, slapping high against the sides of the pipe and sending the flotsam from behind them faster and faster down the main conduit. But that wasn't what had caught Grand's eye.

"Turn off your light," Grand said.

Hannah did.

The scientist released her hand. He switched the belt to his right hand and kept his own light on the mouth of the pipe. There was something moving there. Hannah could tell by the way the rushing water came together. Something had parted it just beyond their line of sight. Debris that would have come down the center were spilling out on the sides.

A moment later the black nose, then the muzzle, and then the fangs of one of the cats came into view. The eyes came next, golden and looking ahead. The animal's head hung low in the pipe. The saber-tooth turned toward the intruders as it continued its slow, careful descent. A moment later its huge front shoulders appeared, the cable-taut muscles visible as they moved beneath the fur. The claws, longer than an adult's fingers, flexed and relaxed each time one of the animal's paws was drawn from the water.

Grand had turned slightly so that he was facing the pipe. "Hannah, stay behind me," he said as he began sidling toward the pipe.

"What are we doing?" The words barely made it from her dry throat.

"Leaving."

"Shouldn't we go the other—"

"We can't," he said.

Hannah assumed the other cat was there. She stopped talking and concentrated on staying alive.

The cat poised on the edge of the down-sloping conduit for a moment, just watching them. Then, with easy grace, it took a long two-legged step into the main pipe and immediately turned toward them. It nearly filled the conduit from side to side.

Grand stopped. Less than six feet separated them.

Hannah peered out from behind Grand. She was accustomed to house cats, bobcats, and even tigers at the zoo. But this creature was enormous, even in its details: the whiskers that hung from its snout, the large golden eyes, the sparkling ivory fangs that were the size and thickness of a telephone receiver. Its head was slung low, making its powerful shoulders seem even higher and more massive. Its tufted ears faced forward and there were great knots of muscles on the sides of its thick neck. Its forelegs weren't tapered like those of big dogs. They were stocky and ended in huge paws.

The cat stood there moving its head in a slow circle. It probably couldn't see them and was apparently sniffing.

After a moment it snorted.

"Jim, I really think we should go back—" Hannah said, just as she heard a heavy splash behind her.

She didn't have to turn to know what it was. The other cat, coming toward them.

She nearly tripped over a branch and clutched at Grand's shoulders. She was shaking all over now, and not just from exhaustion.

She watched as the cat in front of them lowered its great head even further. It crouched.

Then it ran at them.

50

Grand did two things in the instant before the cat in front of them charged.

First, he flung his flashlight at the second cat. The animal growled as the flashlight struck it. Grand hoped it would also distract and confuse the cat in front, for just a moment. As the submerged flashlight filled the pipe with a dim, rippling glow, Grand dropped his belt by his feet and grabbed the branch that Hannah had stumbled over. The thick limb had become wedged diagonally against the sides of the conduit. Wrenching it free, Grand wrapped his belt around the bottom to protect his hands, then immediately flattened his back against the pipe and lifted the branch slightly.

The charging cat stopped right in front of Grand. The animal landed on the branch and the forward part cracked beneath its forepaws. As the animal opened its jaw and lunged toward him, Grand shoved what was left of the limb forward, into the cat's right front shoulder. The scientist leaned all his weight into the push, growling and focusing his *maat*. The cat hadn't had time to dig its claws in and, helped by the water's buoyancy, Grand was able to shove the animal back against the far side of the conduit. The beast snapped and struggled but Grand had it pinned.

For the moment.

"Go!" Grand screamed hoarsely at Hannah.

The young woman scrambled behind Grand on her hands and knees. The churning water nearly reached her chest as the flood increased. She made it past the scientist, stumbled forward until she could get her feet under her, then ran into the darkness.

The big cat began to duck and wriggle to get away from the branch.

"No!" Grand cried and pushed harder, his feet braced behind him, against the side of the pipe. The animal's cries filled the conduit. So did its twisting struggles, which prevented the second cat from squeezing around it.

Grand saw the second cat finally give up trying to get past. It crouched and prepared to leap over the other cat.

This was it, he told himself. He was going to have to release the first cat and run.

Suddenly, a second, deeper roar filled the pipe, sounds that didn't come from the cats or from Grand. When the massive flood hit seconds later, it filled the pipe more than halfway, slamming the cats one into the other and driving them forward while washing around them.

Grand immediately released the branch, bent to scoop up his belt, and was knocked back hard before he could find it. The waters washed him forward, back first, which may have prevented him from drowning. He was able to breathe by stretching out and floating on his back, his mouth facing up. Buffeted from side to side, he extended his arms to keep from being rammed against the walls of the conduit.

It was dark. Grand did not see or hear the cats. There was only the din of the flood. Thoughts came at him quickly and disconnectedly. He hoped that Hannah was all right; he knew they were both going to take a bad hit when they emerged from the pipe; and he was sorry he'd had to hurt the cat, as magnificent a creature as he'd ever seen. A creature whose right to life and to the earth itself transcended his own.

And there was another thought. A thought spurred by what he'd seen in the blockhouse. Confirmation of what he'd suspected and the certainty that there would be more death before this matter was concluded.

Grand's thoughts were cut short when he felt himself drop. The roar of the water changed from loud and thunderous to loud and strident. The dark of the pipe was replaced by sky, though he was still on his back. He was swept to his left, felt the grate against his shoulder, and reflexively grabbed it to break his fall. But Grand couldn't hold on and he hit the rocky ground hard. From cave falls he knew not to take the entire hit on his back and he immediately slapped-out, striking the ground with his arms extended and his hands palm-down. That helped brace him and spread the force of the impact. His shoulders and lower back still struck hard but at least he didn't break anything.

He also didn't come to a stop. Water continued to wash over him, pushed him toward the larger gully. He leaned on his right side and tried to swing over on his hands and knees but the water knocked him forward. He tumbled down the stony wall, water and branches pouring over him as he struggled to move away from the flow, toward the rear of the gully. He got out of the cascade, scratched at the wall with his left hand, and managed to pull himself to his feet.

"Hannah!" he cried.

There was no answer. He looked around in the dark.

"Hannah!"

"Here," she moaned.

He looked ahead and saw Hannah curled on her side several feet ahead of him in the gully.

Struggling forward as the water and debris spilled onto him, Grand reached Hannah's side. Water from the pipe flowed under and around her. Though her eyes were shut, she was breathing and coughing. Grand felt her neck. It didn't appear to be broken. It was probably all right to move her.

He slid his arms carefully under her legs and shoulders.

"Where are we?" she asked, her eyes still shut. It was as though she was waking from a dream.

"Outside the pipe," Grand told her. "Now hush. I'm going to get you out of here."

"Okay."

There was something sweet and trusting about the *"okay."*

Grand picked her up gently and, shielding her from the water with his body, carried her to the back of the gully.

Half-walking, half-stumbling, but making sure that Hannah didn't hit the ground, Grand climbed from the channel. He set her down on the soft grasses at the far end. Still barely conscious, Hannah moved her leg, her head, her arms. Except for a few cuts and bruises, she didn't appear to be seriously hurt.

"Where are the tigers?"

"I think they're staying inside. We're not a threat anymore," he said.

"Good . . . good."

Grand turned to look back at the pipe. The water continued to pour out but he saw no sign of the cats. He wasn't surprised. Once those claws and forelimbs dug into something, he didn't imagine there was very much that could dislodge them.

Grand sat on the grass to Hannah's left. He took her hand in his and held it as he caught his breath and thought about what he'd seen in the blockhouse. About the Chumash painting. About how it all made sense now.

Suddenly, the terrain began to brighten. Grand looked behind him as a light appeared in the sky. A moment later he heard the sounds of a rotor.

Less than a minute after that a chopper was settling down on the hilltop above the conduit.

51

When Frank Lyon's chopper arrived, he had spotted Grand and Hannah and immediately called Gearhart for medical assistance. While they waited, Grand had told the Special Ops supervisor everything he'd seen. Lyon listened without comment, then left them to find the blockhouse.

A half hour later, Sheriff Gearhart came in the second chopper along with a three-person emergency medical team. Protocol, established by Gearhart, required that an emergency medical unit be on active call when any search-and-rescue operation was underway in the county. The sheriff hadn't changed the EM status since his people started looking for engineers Greene and Roche. The four teams rotated every eight hours, during which time they had to be within the county and near transportation.

Gearhart talked to Lyon on the radio while two of the technicians treated Hannah Hughes by the gully. They had both been draped in warm, red wool blankets; a portable heater and work lights had been set up nearby. Hannah was lying on her back on a field air mattress. There was no need to stabilize her with plastic splints or straps, since a quick check revealed that nothing had been broken. The only reason Hannah wasn't on the phone to her office was because the cell phone had been washed away in the flood and Grand hadn't bothered to look for it. She needed to take a break. They both did. It had been a long, strenuous couple of days and things were only going to get worse.

Grand was standing next to Hannah's air mattress. He was thinking about the encounter, about what he'd seen in the pipe. He was searching for habits, patterns, explanations, anything that would help him make sense of this. He'd already been checked by one of the emergency medical technicians. Except for bruises and lacerations on his hands, shoulders, and forehead, the scientist was in pretty good shape. The medic, an elderly white-haired woman named Mrs. May, was dressing the last of Grand's wounds and telling him that he should check himself into the hospital for the night, just for observation.

Grand appreciated her concern. These medics, all of them volunteers, did what they did because they cared about people.

The medics finished a few minutes later. Gearhart met them at the foot of the hill and spoke with them briefly. At his request they left the lights and heater and headed back toward the hillside to wait. Then Gearhart had a talk with the chopper pilot by radio.

This was the first time that Hannah and Grand were alone since he'd pulled her from the gully. Hannah propped herself painfully on an elbow. She winced but refused to lower herself back down.

"You shouldn't be doing that," Grand said. "Lie back down—"

"I'll be all right," she said, wincing. "Never retreat or you'll stay there. That's my motto."

Grand shook his head. He sat beside her and moved close with his legs stretched out. He pulled her toward him gently so she could lean against him.

"Is that better?" he asked.

"Much," she said. "Thanks."

He held her a little tighter.

"Now—will you tell me something?" she asked.

"Sure," he said.

"What did you see before the flood?" Hannah asked. "What was in that conduit?"

"There's a blockhouse," Grand told her.

"One of those concrete storage bunkers with big mushroom-cap tops and heavy metal doors?"

"Yes," he said. "The one we came across was an access point for workers to service the conduit system. There was mostly repair equipment in there—welders, bags of concrete and troughs for mixing it."

"That's all?" Hannah said.

Grand held her. He didn't answer her.

"Jim?"

"What I saw were scraps of bone, hair, and clothes," he told her. "I don't even know how many victims there were. A half-dozen, maybe more.

Hannah squeezed his hand.

"I'm not sure who everyone was, but there was part of a backpack like the one we found in the creek."

Just then Gearhart walked over. He looked down at the young woman.

"How are you?"

"Fine," Hannah said.

Gearhart looked at Grand. "You?"

"Apart from feeling like a cat toy, I'm okay," Grand said.

Gearhart seemed to be studying Grand, like his eyes were little x-ray machines.

"Where are we, by the way?" Grand asked.

"Nearly halfway between Gibraltar Reservoir and Jameson Lake," Gearhart said.

"That far east?" Grand said.

"That far east," the sheriff replied. "You did some serious traveling."

"Have you been able to check out the blockhouse?" Grand asked.

Gearhart nodded. "Lyon got the keypad access code from Dean Rede. He went in."

"Is it definitely the missing men?" Hannah asked.

"I can't say anything more until we've run tests and notified next of kin," Gearhart said.

"But it's definitely human remains," Hannah said.

Gearhart didn't answer. He continued to study Grand. "I'm more interested about what you saw in the conduits."

"We saw two saber-tooths," Grand said.

"You're sure."

"I'm positive."

"They weren't just big cats."

"No. And these animals are smart. One of them stayed behind and let us through. Then he came after us."

"And obviously went back into hiding," Gearhart said. "Lyon's chopper is circling the mountaintop. So far he hasn't seen a thing. Not even a bobcat."

"The bobcats are probably scared," Grand said. "They must have run. That's common when a powerful new carnivore moves into an ecosystem. The smaller predators start to sense what's out there."

"You have any idea where they're going?" Gearhart asked.

"Not exactly," Grand said. "But so far they've struck at the sinkhole on Painted Cave Road, the two beaches, the campsite, and the blockhouse. Except for the attack on the catamaran, which veered to the southwest, the cats have been moving southeast."

"But you don't know why."

"Not yet," Grand admitted. "But animals do things for a reason. If I were you I'd have Officer Lyon concentrate his search on caves, sinkholes, or drains in that direction."

"I'll do that," Gearhart said. "Is there anything else?"

"There is," Grand said.

Gearhart waited.

"You musn't hurt these animals. Call the Fish and Game people," Grand said. "Get them involved."

"They've been notified."

"No," Grand said. "You have to *tell* them what we have here. Tell them we've got to take these animals alive."

Gearhart pulled the radio from his belt. "Professor, my only interest is keeping *people* alive."

"I understand that," Grand said, "but with a little planning we can accomplish both."

Gearhart said nothing. "The pilot will evac you both. Can you make it up the mountainside?"

"Yes," Grand said. "But first I want your word that you'll work with me on this."

"If there's time."

"There is," Grand insisted. "If the saber-tooths are anything like modern cats, they'll find a new den and then they'll probably be finished moving for the night."

"Probably isn't good enough," Gearhart said.

"Even if they keep moving we'll have until tomorrow at sunset before they hunt again. And as long as we don't do anything to antagonize them, they may not kill anyone.

"Why?" Gearhart asked.

"Because there were only about six or seven victims in the blockhouse," Grand said. "It's possible the cats took the bodies from the campsite elsewhere."

"To eat later."

Grand said nothing.

"And you want me to save them," Gearhart said. "Whatever these animals are, this stops tonight."

Gearhart turned to go; Grand got up and stepped in front of him.

"Sheriff, please. Don't rush into this. It's not just for the sake of the animals but for the safety of your people. These cats have been moving with precision and intelligence. I told Lyon and I'm telling you. They use decoys and feints and they can jump farther than any creature alive today. Wherever they stop for the night it will be in a place they can protect."

"Maybe they can protect it from clubs and stone arrowheads, but I plan to go in with real firepower," Gearhart said. The sheriff stepped around him. "But thanks for the warning."

Gearhart turned and walked toward the hill, simultaneously radioing Lyon instructions about patrolling the southeastern section of the mountains.

Hannah watched him go. "I've said it before and I'm sure I'll be saying it again. He's a licensed bully."

Grand said nothing. He was thinking.

The medics were still waiting by the hillside. Gearhart sent the two male medics back to collect their lights and heater. Then the sheriff helped Mrs. May up the slope to the chopper.

Hannah tried to stand as the medics approached but her left leg buckled. Grand caught her and put her arm around his shoulder.

"Thanks," she said.

"Are you sure you can make it?" one of the medics asked.

"I'm sure. It's just exhaustion. I'll be okay after a little rest." She looked at Grand. "You should get some too. It'll be at least a few hours before he can find the animals and put a SWAT team into the field."

Grand nodded. Though his tired mind was already tearing desperately through options, Hannah was right. He needed rest.

He also needed to make a call. He needed to make that before he did anything else.

52

Gearhart's radio beeped as the sheriff watched the chopper take off. He switched it on.

"Gearhart—"

"Sheriff, I think I've got one of them." Special Officer Lyon told him.

"Where?"

"Where the Santa Ynez River and Agua Caliente Canyon meet," Lyon said. There's a drain with a sinkhole about a hundred feet away. It looks like what Grand said—big sonofabitch."

"Do you have a clear shot?"

"Not really—there's a lot of tree cover."

"Where's the second one?"

"I don't see it yet," Lyon said.

"I want to get them both, now," Gearhart said. "Is there some way you can keep either of them from going into the sinkhole?"

"I can try firing on either side," Lyon said, "keep it out in the open. Or I can go down—"

"No," Gearhart barked. "Keep your distance. Take them out if you can—I'm going to get a highway patrol chopper to take me over. I'll meet you there with a team."

There was no answer.

"Lyon, do you read me?"

"Yes, sir," Lyon said.

"I'll get back to you," the sheriff said and signed off.

Gearhart immediately radioed his nighttime communications officer and asked him to patch through a call to Assistant Commissioner Lauer at home. Lauer was head of the highway patrol's field operations, which oversaw the Office of Air Operations. When Gearhart needed an additional fixed-wing plane or helicopter fast, that was the man he went to. The California Highway Patrol had larger, longer-range choppers than the sheriff's own hill-and-beach sweepers. That was what he wanted now.

Gearhart explained that they had their "animal killer" in sight and needed to airlift personnel to the site. He asked Lauer to have the chopper pick up his sharpshooters at the sheriff's office, then collect him and head on to Lyon's position. Since there was a CHP pilot on duty at all times, Lauer told Gearhart that he'd have the helicopter at the office parking lot in under ten minutes and at the sheriff's position five minutes after that.

Gearhart thanked him.

The sheriff briefed Lyon, who said that he thought he saw the second cat in the conduit. There was a clearing between the pipe opening and the sinkhole. With a little luck, he felt he could pick at least one of them off as it passed through, then hold the other one.

"There may not be anything left for you to do when you get here except to mop up," Lyon told him.

"I'll settle for that as long as you're careful," Gearhart told him. "This isn't a freakin' movie set—there are no safety rigs."

Lyon promised he would be very careful.

Gearhart clicked off then made one more call. It was to Thomas Gomez. The forensics scientist was en route from the beach to the campsite. The sheriff ordered the lab team to divert from there to the blockhouse. He wanted them to positively ID the remains at the site. Gomez complained that he and his team were exhausted but said they'd be right up.

Gearhart put the radio back in its loop. He made a fist and shook it tightly at his side. This *wasn't* going to get away from him. He had good people in the field and on the way. And though he was furious that these killings had transpired in his community, on his watch, he was nearly at the end of this ordeal. He would display the dead carcasses of the animals and the people who counted on him would understand that while they probably couldn't have prevented this, it could have been far, far worse.

All Gearhart had to do now, he hoped, was the thing he hated most.

To wait.

53

His leathery features creased with frustration, Frank Lyon looked out at the canopy two hundred feet below.

When he was still working as a movie stunt actor, absolutely nothing daunted him. He raced chariots, drove motorcycles off cliffs, and once parachuted from a plane onto a hot-air balloon. If he hadn't busted his leg while he was skiing, the fifty-one-year-old would still be stunting instead of training new talent—and working as a Special Ops officer to get his jollies.

In the old days, it would have been nothing for him to sling his M21 sniper rifle and night scope over his shoulder, rappel to the treetops, find a position in the high branches, and take the kitties out. But he hadn't done any rope climbing or Tarzan-type bits for a while so that would be dicey.

Still, he didn't want to let these fuckers get away; Gearhart was counting on him. When a guy like that counted on you, you wanted to deliver.

He turned to the pilot, twenty-something Deputy Russo who did time in the Air Force as a medical evacuation flier.

"How close to the treetops can you get us?" Lyon shouted.

"I can sit you down right on top of them," the young woman replied.

Lyon thought for a moment. Then he attached the night-vision scope to the rifle. "I want you to kill the searchlight and go down slow," he said. "If it looks like our pals are getting scared again, I'll let you know and you shoot back up. If I get the first one down I'll let you know. I'll need the light back on fast so I can spot the second."

The pilot said she understood.

Lyon had seen the first cat moving slowly toward the sinkhole. The second cat had finally emerged from the drain. Lyon opened the door. It was about two hundred yards to the sinkhole. After he shot this one he would have an okay shot at the sinkhole—certainly good enough to put a wall of bullets ahead of the surviving cat and make it think twice about going in. As long as he could keep it in the open, he had a good chance of nailing it.

The pilot shut off the light. Lyon found the cat in his scope and the chopper began to descend. The cat looked up, then moved under some branches. The slow build of the rotor didn't appear to alarm it.

"Move south a little!" Lyon told the pilot.

The chopper slid to the side so Lyon could keep the cat in view. He didn't want to take a shot unless it was a clear one; wounding the animal, especially not mortally, might only make things worse.

Parts of it came and went though the leaves as the chopper descended. They were about one hundred feet up, then eighty, then sixty. The clearing was ahead. That was where he'd get the cat. Right there. Then he'd swing to his right and be ready to fire at the sinkhole. He wanted a kill shot, though, on the first cat. If he had to fire a second round, that would give the other cat more time to escape.

The trees were about thirty feet below. Lyon's palms were sweaty but he felt just like he used to before a big gag—pumped, ready, *there*.

They were down to twenty feet. The leaves were whipping madly, which actually gave Lyon a clearer view of the ground and his target. He could see the cat's hindquarters through the branches.

"Go west a few feet," Lyon said. Hopefully, that would stir the leaves where he needed a clearer view. Lyon's left foot was on the step at the bottom of the door and his right in the corner of the door itself. It was a secure perch even though it didn't give him a wide target area; the helicopter's landing skid was too far below the cabin for him to lean on. That was why they had to keep the cat in a fairly narrow range.

The chopper shifted slightly and continued to descend. They were roughly ten feet above the trees and thirty-five feet above the target. The leaves parted and blew off ahead of the cat and it moved toward them. Lyon took a moment to drink the creature in.

Grand hadn't been kidding. The thing was a giant, like nothing Lyon had ever seen except maybe in some of the monster movies he'd done. He'd have its head in his sight in just a few seconds—

Something flashed past his sight and the helicopter shuddered violently. The Special Ops officer looked up from his rifle just in time to see the impossible. Lit by the green glow of the control panel, he saw one of the cats land on the skid, stretch itself up, and fill the open doorway.

The damn thing had jumped from the treetops.

Lyon's last thoughts were of something Grand had said before he went to the blockhouse. *Decoys and feints,* he had warned. *They use military-style tactics.*

The cat lunged at Lyon. The gun fell overboard. Blood sprayed from an upswipe of the cat's claw, ripped from somewhere on the left side of Lyon's chest. It spotted the windshield, controls, and Deputy Russo. While the pilot tried desperately to focus on the controls, the special Ops Officer was screaming beside her, flailing at the monstrous weight on top of him.

The creature's powerful motion, weight, and the repeated lashings of claw and fang made it impossible to steady the helicopter. The skids crunched on the upper branches and then the cabin thumped with an ugly, loud bump on the treetops. The helicopter settled unsteadily on its perch.

Russo sought to abandon the craft. She released the controls and turned toward the door. Before she could reach it, the cat surged over the mangled Special Ops officer and put its two long teeth into Russo's left shoulder. The pilot shrieked as the cat bit down and away.

The helicopter tilted toward port, Lyon's side. The slanted rotor was still turning at top speed as it cut into the trees, filling the air with wood, leaves, and the clacking of the rotor as it struck the branches.

The narrow blades bent and folded, one of them slamming through the windshield and filling the cabin with glass. A moment later the rotor hub stopped turning when it hit one of the heavy lower branches. The helicopter settled noisily into the trees, on its side. The trail rotor continued slicing downward, kicking up dirt and sparks as it struck the ground. The rear rotor cap cracked, causing the unit to fly off. It cartwheeled across the ground, stopping only when it embedded itself in a tree trunk.

Except for falling particles of leaf and the occasional groan of a branch, the night was nearly still. Nearly, but not quite.

While one cat waited and watched, the other leaped from the cabin of the fallen helicopter. It landed heavily on the ground then shook itself off from head to tail. The fur of its face and shoulders was splashed with blood. Some of the blood was from the occupants of the cabin while some of it belonged to the cat itself. One of the rotor blades and several pieces of glass had cut it on the right shoulder when the blade struck the windshield.

But it would survive.

It was not time to feed and, leaving the bodies behind, the cats walked toward the sinkhole, slipped inside, and thought nothing more of this strange new creature that had tried to take the night from them.

54

There's something I need to understand," Hannah said.

Grand was behind the wheel of his SUV. The helicopter had placed Hannah and Grand back near the campsite. Wet and exhausted, they'd climbed into Grand's car and headed down from the mountains toward Hannah's apartment. The heat was on full and the windows were open, keeping them warm and awake for the half-hour ride.

"Cryogenesis," she went on. "*How* has that kept these animals alive until today?"

"I honestly don't know," Grand said.

"But that has to be how it happened. They couldn't have been living underground."

"I don't see how," Grand said.

Hannah was amazed that after all she'd been through she had the energy to get revved up about this.

"But there are a lot of problems with cryogenesis," Grand went on. "As you said, glaciation didn't reach this far south," Grand said. "Even if it had, simple freezing wouldn't have done the job."

"Why not? Remember those three Incan children who were found a couple of years ago, twenty-two thousand feet up an Argentine volcano?"

"Mount Llullaillaco."

"That's the one," she said. "Those kids were sacrificed five hundred years ago and freeze-dried by the climate. When they were discovered there was still blood in their heart and lungs."

"They were also dead," Grand said.

"The children were dead before they were frozen," Hannah said. "What if they'd been alive when that happened?"

"Then all of their biological systems would have stopped immediately," Grand acknowledged.

"And preserved?"

"Theoretically."

"Which is what happens in cryogenics."

"True," Grand said, "but there's a big difference between preservation and successful reconstitution."

"I know," Hannah replied. "But first things first. Biological entities have a very high chance of surviving cryogenics and being revived if their systems contain glycerol-related oils and fats. Those compounds can be added to a specimen or they can be inherent, part of a diet. Typically, a diet that includes fish."

Grand glanced at her. "Another article?"

Hannah nodded. "About a local company that freezes donor embryos," she said. "As we know, the saber-toothed tigers like fish. But they could have gotten the substances from any number of animals. Back to my point about the Incan kids. At some time in the past, after they were frozen, one of those kids was hit by lightning. Despite having been dead *and* freeze-dried, there were signs of biological activity where the lightning had struck."

"I read about that, but it was extremely limited activity," Grand pointed out. "There was some cellular growth but not the full-scale metabolism we're seeing here."

"Yes, but maybe conditions were different in some way," Hannah said. "Some *significant* way that we're missing. Let's go through them."

Grand was tired but Hannah wanted to push him. Not just because she was curious and not just because she'd have an article to file in the morning. They were obviously missing something that would explain the reemergence of the cats and she wanted to know what that something was.

"We've had an incredible amount of rain and lightning over the past few weeks which could be a factor in some way," Hannah said. "What else? Give me words. Ideas. Anything."

"All right," Grand said. "I found the fur in what was apparently a volcanic vent."

"Volcanoes," Hannah said. "Intense heat. Could that have played a part in this?"

"Possibly."

"Things in Pompeii were preserved by ash and pumice."

"Again, not alive," Grand said. "But you mentioned something a minute ago that wasn't entirely accurate yet may have something to do with this."

"What?"

"You said the kids in Argentina were freeze-dried. They weren't," Grand said. "They were frozen."

"What's the difference?

"Freezing is intense cold," Grand said. "Freeze-drying is intense cold followed immediately by a exposure to a complete vacuum. That one-two hit preserves the object in its frozen state, but without ice. Then the object, whether it's coffee or fruit, can be restored by adding water."

"Which makes it easier to store or ship than something that's frozen," Hannah said. "Okay. What does that have to do with our situation?"

"You asked how the saber-tooths were preserved," Grand went on. "They wouldn't have been exposed to a vacuum but they might have been exposed to intense heat, which can have the same desiccating effect. When anything is burned, the water content vaporizes first, then the vessel itself disintegrates. But I wonder what would have happened if the biological matter were preserved in the nanosecond before the heat destroyed the shell."

"You mean the water is evaporated but the heat dies before the animal does?" Hannah asked.

"Yes."

"Is that possible?"

"In theory."

"That doesn't help us."

"It might," Grand said. "One of the reasons scientists have always assumed there was no volcanism in Southern California is because we don't have calderas here—volcanic craters. But I saw volcanic *vents* down there. So there definitely was lava flow."

"So you're saying—what?"

"Vents without calderas. That means the eruptions occurred somewhere else. Somewhere there might also be glaciation. Intense heat, intense cold. The one-two punch."

They fell silent. Hannah felt like her body had been mugged; she was suddenly very aware of the warmth from the heater, the heaviness of her arms, and the weight of her eyelids.

"Are you thinking?" Hannah asked.

Grand said he was.

"Good. Because my brain just shut down."

"Hannah, are you on line back at the apartment?"

"Yes. Why?"

"There's something I want to check," he said urgently. "Something that may explain the cats and a painting I saw."

55

Grand and Hannah entered the spacious, high-ceilinged living room of her condominium. While Hannah booted her computer on the dining room table, Grand went to the second phone line, which was located in the bedroom. He stood beside the night table and punched in Joseph Tumamait's home number. The Chumash elder answered the phone after the first ring.

"Hello, James," Tumamait said.

"How did you know?" Grand asked.

"There is unrest in the spirit world," Tumamait said. "The Great Eagle came to me in dreams. But he was different tonight."

"Different how?"

"The owl was riding his back."

"Meaning?"

"He is not alone."

More riddles. Grand didn't have time for them.

"Joseph, there's unrest in the *real* world. This is going to sound incredible but there are saber-toothed cats in the mountains. They're responsible for killings over the past few days."

"The *haphaps* are returning," Tumamait said calmly.

"I don't believe that these cats are the destroyers," Grand said. "I've been with them. There's no cruelty in the creatures. If there were, they'd have been kings of the earth."

"Instead of us," Tumamait said.

Hannah appeared in the doorway; Grand held up a finger.

"Sheriff Gearhart is going after the cats with the intent to kill,"

Grand said. “He’s doing this now, tonight. I want to save them but I need your help.”

“What do you want me to do?”

“This is an environmental issue. Call people at Fish and Game, people on the state level. Try and get them to intervene.”

“They don’t always listen to me.”

“Joseph, we have to try. Please.”

“Of course,” Tumamait said. “And what are you going to do?”

“Try and learn more about the animals,” Grand said. “Figure out where they’re going and try to get there ahead of Gearhart.”

“All right,” Tumamait said. “Good luck.”

Grand thanked him and hung up. He walked over to Hannah.

“Joseph Tumamait?” she asked.

Grand nodded.

“Interesting man,” she said. “I should have realized you’d know him.”

“He was my mentor in college. We went on a lot of digs together.”

“Is he going to help?”

“He said he would,” Grand said.

“Good,” she said. “I’ll interview him in the morning. We’ll talk about exterminating a race. It will have more meaning coming from him.”

That was true, the scientist thought. It scared him a little, the way Hannah knew how to spin things. He worked with facts—just facts.

He looked at Hannah. She had gotten out of her wet clothes, pulled on a white bathrobe, and looked very cozy. She also looked smaller somehow. In need of protection?

“I hope you don’t mind the informality,” she said, pulling the robe a little tighter. “I was cold and you were in here.”

“I don’t mind at all,” he said.

“I’ve got another robe in the bathroom, if you want it,” Hannah added. “I keep it here in case I have a guest—like my dad.”

“Is it his?”

“No,” she said. “It was actually stolen from a hotel by some jerk I was with and then added to my bill.”

“Your bill?”

“I paid for all the trips we took,” she said. Her mood darkened.

"Actually, I was engaged to the asshole but he was a gold-digger so I dumped him. I keep the robe here to remind me that he was an opportunist and to not make the same mistake again."

"Well, I will take the robe if it's all right," Grand said. "I don't want to mess up your chairs."

"I also put some water on," Hannah told him. "Do you want instant coffee or tea?"

"Coffee," he said. "Black."

Hannah showed him to the bathroom. Grand left his clothes on and slipped the bathrobe over them. He felt wet and stupid. He took the robe off, took his clothes off, then put the robe back on. That felt better but still not right.

To hell with it.

This wasn't the time to be modest. He took the robe off, took a shower, and then put just the robe back on. It might not be appropriate but it was definitely more comfortable.

Grand went back to the living room feeling self-conscious. He was used to being in caves, in dusty fields, and in cluttered surroundings. Not in a woman's home where everything looked clean and coordinated and the chair even *felt* expensive. He was glad Hannah was still in the kitchen. That gave him a chance to sit in her seat and start typing on the laptop.

He entered the keywords *American Ice Age Volcanoes* and waited. When the list of topics appeared he began scrolling down.

Hannah returned as he was reading the list. She set a mug of coffee beside the computer and leaned close.

"What are we looking for?" she asked.

Grand picked up the mug and took a sip. "Remember the other day at Painted Cave, when I told you about some Chumash art I'd discovered?"

"Yes."

"The paintings showed a volcano and a snow-covered mountain," he said. "There was a serpent in the volcano, which is consistent with Chumash eruption images, but I couldn't figure out why there was a dolphin in the white mountain. The answer may be that it wasn't a mountain."

"What was it?"

Grand found what he was looking for. He clicked on the heading. As the Web site was accessed, he said, "It was a glacier. A volcano and a glacier, side by side."

The site opened. It was an article from *Geologue Monthly.* The piece was titled, "When Ice and Lava Clashed."

"This could be it," Grand said.

Hannah got behind him. Holding her own mug, she leaned closer to his shoulder, almost to his cheek, and read along with him. Grand knew that for the rest of his life, wherever he was, whoever he was with, when he smelled Lipton he would think of Hannah Hughes and this moment.

The article described an eruption that occurred eleven thousand years ago, when Mount Rainier erupted beneath two miles of glacier in what is now west-central Washington state.

"Here it is," Hannah said excitedly. She reached over Grand and moved the mouse. The screen scrolled further. She read, "The explosive forces built beneath the unyielding ice until the surrounding terrain gave way. Chunks of ice were forced through the earth like subterranean comets, propelled by superheated gas and magna. Some of these sections of glacier may have been blasted as far as five or six hundred miles." She stood. "That's it, Jim. It has to be!"

Grand nodded and continued to read. The article said that in newly burned volcanic vents where the ice came to rest, the walls were often fractured by the intense heat and cold—which would explain the flaking he found in the subterranean cavern.

It would also explain something else. The painting in the passageway.

"What do you think?" Hannah asked.

"Two of them could have been trapped, frozen where they were, or carried along."

"It's possible," he admitted.

"Encased in ice or freeze-dried?"

"Probably the latter," Grand said. "It can get very warm in those caves. A block of ice wouldn't have lasted for thousands of years."

"And lightning couldn't have reached them if they were frozen solid," she said. "Maybe it struck them and did a Frankenstein number, brought them back to life."

"I wonder if it was lightning or something else."

"Such as?"

"The rainwater that spilled in there could have contained electrolytic elements from any number of sources," Grand said. "Hydroelectric, acid rain, chemical—any of that could have been absorbed in their skin, jump-started their metabolic processes."

"I *like* that," Hannah said. "So the tigers wake up and they continue doing whatever they were doing back then."

"It's possible," Grand said, though he was only half-listening. He was thinking about the cavern, the walls, the passageway. There weren't two Chumash paintings, there were three. And they all meant something.

"This is *incredible,*" Hannah said. She leaned over Grand and bookmarked the Web site. "Okay. I've got to calm down. What we should do is rest for a few hours. Then I'll get up and write this in a way that doesn't sound impossible. Maybe get a few quotes from you, from biologists at the university, some cryogenics people. I'll also have to put someone on the environmental angle, take Gearhart to task for his blood-and-guts approach." She looked at Grand. "How's that sound to you?"

He didn't answer.

"Hey, are you okay?" Hannah asked.

Grand shook his head slowly. "I'm not sure."

"What is it? Gearhart?"

"It's more than Gearhart."

Hannah's enthusiasm quieted. She squatted beside him. "Jim, talk to me."

"There was a third painting down there. At first I thought it was a celestial design. Then I thought they were eyes."

"And what do you think now?"

"That I was right the second time."

"Eyes?"

Grand nodded. "They're staring out from the cave where a Chumash artist found them thousands of years ago. Eyes that were painted white because the artist was trying to say that they were frozen. Eyes that belonged to petrified saber-tooths inside the caves."

Hannah's expression crashed. "Oh Jesus, Jim. How many eyes were there in the painting?"

He looked at her. "Dozens."

56

Sitting in the passenger compartment of the highway-patrol helicopter, Gearhart was concerned when he couldn't raise Lyon on his radio. Poking his head into the cockpit, the sheriff asked the pilot to call Deputy Russo in the Bell.

There was no response.

Gearhart sat back in the vinyl seat. He looked out the window as they made a thuddingly noisy pass over the dark terrain. He felt, for a flashing instant, that he was back in Vietnam, being airlifted from a combat zone and waiting to find out if the rest of the platoon made it out in the second chopper. He hated that feeling then and he hated it now.

The flight took less than five minutes, though Gearhart knew before they reached the site that something had happened. There was no light in the sky and no call to indicate that the chopper had followed the cat to another location. His initial concern was that the chopper might have collided with one of the peaks in the dark; though Deputy Russo was an experienced night flier in the mountains, she did not usually travel this far southeast. Then he began to hope that they'd experienced mechanical trouble and had set down somewhere.

But Gearhart's hope was blasted when the highway-patrol pilot reported seeing wreckage among the trees up ahead. Gearhart jumped from his seat. He squeezed into the cockpit between the pilot and copilot and looked out as the chopper approached the site. They had cleared a five-hundred-foot hill and dropped to two hundred feet.

The scene was horrific. Brightly lit by the jiggling white searchlight,

Gearhart saw that many of the trees had been stripped of leaves. As they neared he could see the helicopter nestled among them. Worse than the horribly twisted rotor was the sight of the chopper itself. Lying on its side, it reminded Gearhart of a beached whale—helpless despite its formidable size and power.

But the helicopter wasn't badly damaged, and Gearhart still hoped that Lyon and Russo might be alive. The pilot dropped lower. Only then, as the remaining leaves parted, could they see inside the cockpit.

"Oh, shit," murmured the pilot. "Sheriff—"

"Go lower!" he yelled.

The pilot obliged.

The sight was shocking, even to Gearhart. Lyon's body was lying across that of Russo. They were savagely mangled and bloody beyond imagining. Though the windshield was shattered, the dismemberment hadn't happened in the crash. Gearhart had seen rotor wounds and crash injuries. These two looked as though they'd been pushed through a paper shredder.

"Put me through to the California Army National Guard," Gearhart said. "The Fortieth Division Support Command in LA, General Brewer."

The pilot obliged.

While he waited, Gearhart looked down at the wreckage. He didn't know what had brought the chopper down; that would be for the investigating engineers to figure out. But he knew what had mangled the passengers. Except for the presence of the bodies, the blood distribution was the same as in the fish truck they'd found on the beach. The cats had probably gone in after the chopper went down and finished the two off.

Gearhart looked out at the sinkhole. He wondered if the animals were there watching, waiting for them to make a move.

They wouldn't have to wait long, Gearhart vowed.

Not long at all.

57

Except for the thick roar of the waves behind Grand, the living room was silent.

Hannah took a slow sip of tea, then walked toward a white leather sofa in the center of the room. She sat down in the middle and huddled around the mug. She looked past Grand at the sea.

"You know, we could be wrong about this," she said. "There may be another interpretation of that painting."

"I don't think so," Grand said.

"Why not?"

He picked up his coffee and walked toward her. "Since this started I've been bothered by the amount of carnage we've seen, especially at the campsite. Two cats could have been responsible for killing all of those people and carrying them away, but this—"

"Makes a lot more sense."

Grand stopped beside the sofa and nodded. "The cats we saw are probably point cats watching the pride's flank."

"Like an army."

"Yes. There are probably one or two more serving as scouts. They're going to be tough to bring down alive *or* dead," Grand went on. "The question is, where are they going? What were they doing eleven thousand years ago when they were incapacitated? Seasonal homes, hunting grounds—we have no idea what their migratory habits were back then, assuming they had any."

"I just had a thought," Hannah said. "One you may not like."

"What?"

"We better let Gearhart know about the other cats," she said. "Even if we convince him to use tranquilizers, he'll still need enough darts and guns to deal with a dozen or more animals."

"Good point," Grand said. "I'll make the call."

"You know, this is incredible, Jim. Just incredible."

"I know."

"Thanks for sharing it with me."

He smiled and took a swallow of coffee as he walked toward the bedroom phone. That was a sweet, heartfelt thing to say. It made him feel good. A flower in the midst of carnage and chaos.

Grand left a message with Deputy Young in the sheriff's office communications center. The scientist explained that he had no evidence of a larger pride, only suspicions, but that care should be taken before pursuing the saber-tooths into any caves, tunnels, or drains. Grand added that the heart of the pride might have been using the blockhouse for a den, which would explain the remains Senior Officer Lyon had found. Grand told them it would be okay to phone if they had any questions. That was the only way he could keep on top of what they were doing.

Grand hung up and returned to the living room. Hannah had curled up on her side on the sofa.

"What did they say?" she asked sleepily. Exhaustion had caught up to her. He knew the feeling.

Grand walked over to the desk. "The sheriff is up in the mountains and they'll forward the information. I told them to call if they needed anything." He took a sip of coffee.

"You better keep the phone with you," she said. "I'm bad at middle-of-the-night calls. I sound like I have socks in my mouth."

Grand still had the coffee in his mouth. He held it there, then swallowed slowly. "I told them to call me at home."

"That was dumb," the young woman mumbled. "Call back and tell them you're here. You can have the bed. I'm comfortable where I am." Hannah snuggled in a little deeper. Her voice continued to fade. "I should take a shower. All that running, the rainwater . . . but I don't want to get up."

"Don't," Grand said.

"Okay. Good night, Jim."

"Good night, Hannah."

"Thanks again for everything."

"You're welcome," he said.

Hannah passed out.

Grand continued to look at her. He felt awkward standing there, but he didn't turn away.

It was strange. Grand had held both of Hannah's hands, carried her, felt her neck and limbs for broken bones. She had rested against his chest back at the foot of the mountain where they fought the cats. Yet this was more intimate than any contact they'd had.

He liked it.

Grand didn't bother to call the sheriff's office again. He called his home phone and programmed it to forward calls to this number. Then he phoned Walker and left a message asking him to give Fluffy a very early once-around-the-block in the morning. Walker was up at dawn, and Fluffy would be pretty unhappy by then. Finally, Grand lay down on the bed. He shut off the light.

The oversized pillow was rich with Hannah's scent, mostly perfume or hairspray or whatever it was women put on. Rebecca had never bothered with any of that. She smelled of sea breeze and Rebecca.

But this was nice. Grand realized, suddenly, that he was smiling. For the first time in months he felt a sense of contentment.

Sleep came easily, which he happily embraced even as thoughts of ice and fangs played on the fringes of his mind.

58

Hannah was already showered, dressed, and working at her laptop when Grand walked into the living room. He winced as he glanced through the wide-open glass sliders at the white beach. The sands were blinding. He turned away and looked around the room for a clock. He saw one on the VCR. It was seven-forty. Hannah wasn't the only one exhaustion had caught up to. He hadn't slept this late in years.

"Good morning," Hannah said.

"Good morning," he said groggily.

Grand walked toward Hannah. The young woman was dressed in a sky blue blouse and faded jeans. The long sleeves of the blouse were rolled back. There were scratches and bruises on her forearms, cheek, and neck. Despite the wounds, she looked fresh. It was her attitude, he decided.

"There's coffee in the kitchen. I brewed it this time."

"Smells good," Grand said. He went in and poured himself some. "Do you want anything?"

"No, thanks. Listen—there's been news."

Grand woke up fast.

"My managing editor called a few minutes ago. It may not have anything to do with the tigers, but the helicopter with Officer Lyon went down."

"The Special Ops officer?"

Hannah nodded.

"Is he all right?"

Hannah shook her head. "Both he and the pilot were killed."

"In the crash?" Grand asked.

"I don't know," Hannah said. "The coroner is doing an autopsy, but of course no one is telling the press anything yet."

"So there were bodies this time," Grant said.

"Yes," Hannah said. "Besides, how would the tiger have gotten inside the cockpit of a helicopter that was airborne?"

"We've always suspected that saber-tooths may have been climbers," Grand said. "*Are* climbers," he corrected himself. That would take some getting used to. "They have the claws and strength for it. They could have jumped off a treetop, off a cliffside. Or maybe the helicopter landed and tried to take off again."

"But why would they attack?"

"To protect their territory. I told Gearhart to have Lyon follow a route southeast, remember? He may have found what he was looking for and tried to take them out. Is there any other information?"

"Not about that," Hannah said. "The only other news is that Gearhart has requested assistance from the Army National Guard to seal off the area. He's going to get it."

Grand turned back toward the sliders. Since the night before, when Gearhart had threatened to kill the creatures, Grand had been wondering how they would fare against automatic weapons. These very saber-tooths had probably faced prehistoric hunters with spears or arrows. They might understand the concept of projectiles. If so, they might also have come up with a strategy for dealing with humans and their weapons.

He needed to collect his thoughts, make a plan. He slipped his hands into the pockets of the robe and breathed deeply. The sea air smelled good. He looked along the beach toward the south. There was a wharf with a pair of workers hanging over the side painting the pilings. There was a faint smell in the air, one he couldn't quite place that was coming from the wharf. His mind was sidetracked as he thought back to when he lived on the beach with Rebecca. There was something different and he realized at once what it was. There were joggers but no dogs. Usually the beach was full of them at this time of day. He wondered if the animals sensed the presence of the saber-tooths and were refusing to come out. Maybe that was the reason that Fluffy had been so quiet the day before.

"Finished," Hannah said as she typed the last period with a flourish. "Last night's adventure as we lived it."

"Did you mention the saber-tooths?"

"I fudged," she admitted. "I said they were big cats that looked like saber-tooths. I usually don't run anything without two sources, and I try not to be one of them. Let me ask you something."

"Sure."

"If the tigers are traveling southeast, their trip to the beach was pretty far off course for them."

"Very."

"Why do you think they went there?"

"I'm not sure," Grand admitted.

"What do you think about this idea then," she asked, "that the cats might have been looking for something familiar. These tigers wake up, things are totally different from what they were. The ocean could have been the only smell they recognized. Maybe they went to check it out."

"It's possible," Grand agreed.

"That could also be why they attacked the fish truck," Hannah said. "It was a familiar smell."

"The saber-tooths could also have mistaken it for a giant herbivore," Grand said. He slid the door open a little further and watched the workers. "The truck growled, it smelled of fish, and it moved quickly. Modern cats like to attack running prey."

"Why?"

"If prey is running they're already scared of something, possibly a fire, army ants, that sort of thing," Grand said. "Which means they probably aren't going to pay close attention to something that's stalking them. Prehistoric herbivores were probably the same."

"I see," Hannah said. "What else do we know about these animals in particular?"

"Not a lot," Grand admitted. "As I said, we suspect that sabertooths were territorial. We tend to find their fossil remains clustered in areas that were once plains or fertile valleys."

"Why did they become extinct? Changes in the environment because of the Ice Age?"

"Only partly," Grand said. "They may have been forced out of many areas when prehistoric humans crossed from Asia to North America over the Bering land bridge."

"That's when the Bering Strait was frozen so you could literally walk from Asia to here."

"Correct."

"So migrating humans hunted them out of existence?"

"Not directly," Grand said. "We believe they preyed on many of the same herbivores for food. Eventually, humans outnumbered them and overran Southern California."

"Starving them to death."

"Effectively," Grand said.

"Why didn't they hunt us?"

"We suspect they did," Grand said, "which is why we accelerated the invention of weapons to protect ourselves."

"The first arms race," Hannah said. She shook her head. "I still don't see how people fought those things with primitive weapons."

"You and I did it in the pipe."

"We had a flood and a branch to help us," Hannah said.

"If it hadn't been those things it would have been something else," Grand said.

"Such as?"

"A hubcap, a bottle, our own shoes tied together and used as a bolo or garrote. There's always something."

"Really? Suppose all you had was a bunch of leaves," she said. "What would you do then?"

Grand thought for a moment. "Stand up."

"What?"

"Just stand up," Grand said.

Hannah did.

The scientist took a piece of paper from the stack in her printer tray. He crumpled it.

"Pretend you're one of the cats," he said.

Hannah made her fingers into little claws and growled.

Grand threw the crumpled piece of paper to the right, toward the sliding glass door. Hannah looked at it. When she did, Grand reached to the other side and pulled a letter opener from a stack of mail. He flipped the blade in his hand and held it to her throat.

She recoiled, then frowned. "That's cheating."

"Why?"

"Because there wouldn't have been a letter opener on a mountaintop."

"It could have been a chunk of rock."

"To do what with, bop me on the nose?"

"That, or stab you," Grand said. "Cut your throat. Many of the shales up there can be split with a good whack on another rock. The edge you'd have would be scalpel-sharp."

Hannah sat back down. "I still say it wasn't fair. You didn't use the piece of paper as a weapon. You used it as a distraction."

"The best weapons *are* nonlethal, psychological ones," Grand insisted. He replaced the letter opener on the pile. "According to leather pouches I've found in ancient graves, prehistoric hunters carried what we call 'startlements,' which may have been used to distract predators. Crushed leaves or feathers to catch their eye, ground bone to make them sneeze. Anything to gain time so they could run or grab a weapon or cry for help. Maybe next time I won't need the letter opener, just the crumpled paper to remind you that I can *get* a letter opener. Many evolutionary scientists believe that something simple like that—a crumpled piece of white paper—can change the course of genetics. If you preyed on butterflies, they might notice your reaction to the paper. Through genetic mutation they might slowly turn white to intimidate you."

"Are you saying that living things can actually *will* mutation?"

"We don't understand the mechanism, but it happens," Grand said. "The perception of threat, the ability to respond, and the desire to survive—they're all directed from in here," he tapped his temple.

"I guess if you can make yourself sick or get ulcers, anything's possible," Hannah said. "So with any luck I'll grow myself a sixth finger on each hand to help myself type faster."

"And then your brain will start to think faster and then you'll need a seventh finger," Grand said. "That's how it happens."

"I'll take that faster brain now," Hannah said. "What about those Chumash paintings you were talking about. Not the ones of the volcanoes but the eyes. What do you think the Chumash were telling us?"

"I don't know," Grand said. "The paintings in the upper cave told how the cats became trapped. By volcano and glacier. I suspect the eyes in the passageway below were a Chumash 'keep out' sign. Another shaman would have understood them. The caves are full of warnings like that."

"Fascinating," she said. "The things we don't know that are all around us. It's awe-inspiring."

"It's also scary," Grand said.

"In what way?"

"I was just thinking that I'd better get in touch with Environmental Protection Agency and pest-control people."

"Why?"

"Because there were gnats in the lower cave," he said. "They were bigger and buzzier than any I'd ever encountered. I wonder if they might have been frozen with the tigers."

"Shit," Hannah said. "Prehistoric bugs."

"If they are, they can cause a serious imbalance in the insect ecology of the region."

"And what about any bacteria or viruses the tigers may be carrying?" Hannah asked.

"There's that too," Grand agreed.

There was a lot to consider, which was all the more reason to take the animals alive, to study them without obliterating whatever they might be host to. Grand had to make that his immediate priority.

Hannah read what she'd written, then E-mailed the story to the copy editor. "This is all completely amazing," she said. "What are you going to do?"

"I was just thinking that," Grand said. "Gearhart probably won't do anything else until the National Guard arrives."

"That'd be my guess," Hannah said. "Otherwise, why call them out?"

"I want to make some calls, see if Joseph Tumamait had any luck, and also find someone to cover my classes. Then I want to get to Gearhart, try and talk to him, explain why we need to capture the cats alive."

"You haven't got a prayer," Hannah said. "Besides, if those animals did kill Officer Lyon then this is now a personal matter."

"But won't the operation be out of Gearhart's jurisdiction if it crosses the county line?"

"Technically, yes," Hannah said. "That's probably why he called in the Army National Guard. He has friends there. They'll cut him slack if this spills into other counties."

"It can still be his trophy," Grand said.

"You've got it. And trust me, if he can stop the cats he'll make the most of it. We'll see Gearhart standing beside dead saber-tooths on all the evening shows. The national ones."

Grand finished his coffee. "I've got to go."

"You know, if I were you I'd appeal to people's pocketbooks," Hannah said. "Tell the county leaders how much they can make from a Live Prehistoric Animals attraction at the zoo."

"I'll have to think about it," Grand said.

The thought of caging these beasts also sat like a stone in Grand's gut. He knew he'd do it if it were the only way to keep them alive, but he suspected that captivity, even in a wildlife preserve, would kill them over time. There was something about these animals that seemed to require the open environment, the hunt, a connection with the earth itself. It was as if they became part of the land they ranged, drew strength from it.

Just like the gods in Chumash mythology, he thought, *which was why they fought over it.*

Grand put the coffee cup back in the kitchen. As he turned to go he suddenly realized that he had to say good-bye to Hannah. But just good-bye wouldn't quite cut it.

"I'll be done with everything around noon," Hannah said. "Can we link up then?"

"Sure," Grand said.

Hannah wrote something on a piece of paper and handed it to Grand.

"What's this?" he asked.

"My other cell phone number," she told him. "Let me know if anything interesting happens."

"Sure. How many cell phones do you have?" he asked.

"Three," she admitted. "Well, two now. I'm a reporter. Can't afford a dead battery or busy signal." She looked at him. "Do me one other favor?"

"Of course."

"Stay out of trouble."

"With?"

She grinned. "If you want to knock Gearhart's block off, that's fine. I mean with the tigers."

"I'll try to avoid them both," he said. "And by the way—there's something I should have told you before."

"What?"

"These animals—they're saber-toothed cats. People call them tigers because they look like tigers. But they aren't related to tigers. Or lions. They were their own species."

"Damn." She wrote a quick E-mail to the copy editor asking her to make the change.

"Sorry. I should have told you before."

"It's okay. You're a guy. The truth takes a while."

Hannah sent the E-mail, then looked at him. He looked at her.

"Well," he said after a long pause. "I better get going."

Hannah smiled—a little sadly, he thought. "Thanks again for everything," she said.

He smiled back, then turned and left. And kicked himself for that.

Rebecca is gone, he told himself. *You can't let yourself die with her.*

Grand continued kicking himself on both sides of his conscience all the way out to his car and as he drove home and as he walked along the path to his front door and took Fluffy, who was much more animated than he had been—and certainly more cheerful than Grand was at the moment, damn his own cowardly skin—out for a short walk.

59

Gearhart got Grand's message about there being a pride of cats in the mountains. The sheriff wasn't entirely surprised. He didn't think the deaths at the campsite had been caused by two animals. He still didn't believe that the cats were what Grand claimed them to be: resurrected prehistoric animals. He might as well say they were ghosts.

No. Whatever these animals were they had a reasonable, credible explanation. If they weren't tigers gussied up and set loose by some homicidal nutcase, maybe—*maybe*—they were mutations. And that was a reach. In any case, Gearhart would know for certain before long.

After placing his call to the 40th, the sheriff worked out a deployment plan at his desk. Then he went to the small cafeteria in the back of the building and took a nap on the couch. He was awakened at 8:00 A.M. by Deputy Valentine, who said that the sheriff had a call from Brigadier General J. D. Dori, commander of the 40th Division. The fifty-eight-year-old Dori and Gearhart went back over thirty years, to when Dori was a Marine drill instructor. Dori left the Marines in 1969 and joined the California Army National Guard two years later. He had been Gearhart's DI and they reconnected years later, when Gearhart moved to Los Angeles.

Dori's 40th Infantry Division, mechanized, is headquartered at the Southern California Disaster Support Area at the Los Alamitos Armed Forces Reserve Center. Nicknamed the Sunburst Division—after its distinctive sun-patch—it has an authorized strength of just over fourteen thousand. Because of its involvement with the Los Angeles Riots of 1992, as well as flooding and earthquakes that struck with regularity, two of the division's busiest components have been the 40th Division Support Command, or DISCOM, based in Los Angeles; and the Engineer Brigade, which is based in Santa Barbara.

Dori's subordinate had called the brigadier general at home and informed him of Gearhart's request for support troops. Dori was calling back to say that forty division soldiers had been assigned to Gearhart under Lieutenant Anthony Mindar. An additional five troops would be sent in CH-47D Chinook helicopter to provide air reconnaissance only. Though the young lieutenant would be there to assist Gearhart in whatever way was required, the officer would be commanding his own personnel in any engagement.

Gearhart said he understood. What that meant, of course, was that other sheriffs would be prevented from taking command of the operation if it spilled into neighboring counties.

The troops would be trucked in. Because Gearhart didn't want to create panic in downtown Santa Barbara he asked that the armed troops drive directly to the junction of Ballinger Canyon and the Cuyama River. That was right before the border of Ventura County to the east and San Luis Obisbo County and Kern County to the north. Gearhart would personally inform the sheriffs of those counties about the operation and invite them to provide personnel.

Dori told Sheriff Gearhart that the troops would be bringing night-vision gear, as requested, and would leave Los Angeles later in the morning. The sheriff thanked him.

After making the calls to his colleagues, Gearhart buzzed Chief Deputy Valentine and asked if there were any updates. When he'd returned from the field, Gearhart had left spotters on the ground and in the air around the site of the chopper crash. The ground personnel, heavily armed groups of four, were in constant radio contact with one another and with the highway-patrol chopper. The helicopter stayed in touch with them even when it returned to base to refuel. The spotters were all situated on high ground, which would have been impossible to access without the animals being seen.

Valentine said there had been no sightings.

At least Grand was right about that. The killers were night creatures. That would give Gearhart time to find possible places of egress and time set up a wall of armed National Guard personnel. He would leave his own teams behind the lines, covering the sinkholes and caves the animals had already been through, just in case they tried to double back.

Gearhart looked at his watch. It was nearly nine o'clock. He went to get a cup of coffee. Before turning to his map, there were two other tasks he had to do. One was to brief Santa Barbara officials about what was going on. The second was to brief Sergeant Marsha Levy, his public information officer, about everything that had happened so that she could hold a press conference. Gearhart would not be present for this one. There was too much to do and nothing to gain by answering questions about how the animals had managed to avoid capture. Levy was far better at apologizing and fudging.

Gearhart had no intention of standing before the press until he had something to show them.

The carcass of one of the killers.

60

The California Army National Guard troops arrived at the mountain site ready for a siege.

They came armed with flares, flashlights, M16 rifles, handguns, and motion detectors. Though the soldiers wore camouflage fatigues, some were also dressed in clothing designed to protect them from animal bites. These included protective vests made of high-density polyethylene with floating rib plates on the side and spandex pants with heavy foam pads for the thighs, hips, and tailbone. The team also brought shin guards, hard hats, and elk-hide gloves that reached nearly to the elbow. Only the dozen soldiers of the "armored" unit—or the "padded" unit, some of Gearhart's deputies joked—those men who were going to place the motion detectors inside caves, sinkholes, and pipes, put on that gear. The rest of the soldiers wore their standard drab green uniforms. Six of those soldiers would be stationed in the air in case they needed to enter one of the caves in pursuit of the prey.

Gearhart quickly became impatient with their preparations and with Lieutenant Mindar's quiet command style. It wasn't that the soldiers really needed to be ready faster. Gearhart didn't imagine anything would happen until sunset. It was just that these men didn't move like Marines. They didn't act like they were the best at anything, or wanted to be. They were just two-year men doing a job with diligent professionalism, nothing more. The young, blond, clean-cut Mindar watched from his tent command post without saying much; he had his well-oiled machine and either didn't see the need to increase its efficiency or else knew that it was working at its peak. The

Chinook sat on a hilltop waiting for the motion detectors to be put in place so it could oversee the monitoring efforts from the command center in the main cabin. Gearhart had flown in 47B's in Vietnam. If there was any one image of what Gearhart hated up here it was that: the Chinook, a powerful two-rotor bird, sitting idle in the hills. The only reason the sheriff didn't climb on Mindar's back was because they still had a cushion, time-wise. If and when it became necessary to get more from the men, Gearhart would push.

Hard.

At least Lieutenant Mindar agreed with Gearhart that capturing the animals would be extremely difficult and possibly counterproductive. Men could die in the effort. The lieutenant had experienced sedating animals from dogs to deer to mountain lions during fires and floods. He said that not even seasoned gamekeepers knew how much tranquilizer it took to knock out a large predator without overdosing and killing it. They also didn't know which animals were allergic to tranquilizer ingredients such as nicotine and even how an animal would react after being sedated. Some became calm and then suddenly went manic. Some appeared to pass out only to waken and attack everyone around them. Some took a long time to even feel the effects of the dart.

The wait was punctuated by occasional, frustrated calls from Chief Deputy Valentine. Since no one in town had Gearhart's cell phone number, and the mountain roads had been sealed off on all sides, no one could reach him. Reporters, university professors, environmental groups—not just in the county but on the state level—and even Joseph Tumamait had left word for the sheriff to get in touch. Gearhart did not return any of those calls, nor did he ask Mike Valentine what they were about. Plausible deniability plus a true and unshakable belief that he was working for the public good was a potent rebuttal against any form of opposition. Particularly against special interests.

By early afternoon the motion detectors were all in place and everyone was ready to move out. Some of the men were airlifted by the Chinook and others got underway on foot, all of them following the course that Gearhart had laid out. He had consulted with Dr. Honey Solomon at the Santa Barbara Zoo and had learned that on average a lion rests between twelve and fifteen hours each day, most of that after feeding. The zoologist agreed that it was more likely for migrating animals of any kind to move after resting rather than before. Given the distance between the previous kills—approximately five miles—Gearhart calculated the outside radius of where the predators would appear tonight. This time his people would be there, ready to stop them.

Gearhart slipped on a weapons vest that included a serrated hunting knife, a Beretta, and extra ammunition, and accompanied the teams who moved out on foot. When they were in place, he would link up with the chopper and follow the motion detectors from there. The sweet, fragrant scent of monkeyflower and manzanita complemented the golden, late afternoon glow. In places, those sweet, refreshing scents were overpowered by the pungent odor of the sage and buckwheat that spread across large swaths of hillside.

Gearhart was more aware of the mountain smells than he had ever been before. It was like being back in the war, where enemies could be anywhere and were clever about concealing themselves. The ground was too rocky here to hold footprints, and Gearhart told the National Guard troops to examine the sharp-pointed scrub oak and needlelike chamise looking for traces of fur or blood, just in case the animals had emerged to change passageways. Though Gearhart was not willing to accept that the killers were prehistoric monsters, most of the time they *had* been moving southeast, as Grand had said. So Gearhart concentrated on caverns in that direction. Dr. Thorpe came along to help determine which tunnels and caves were too narrow to accommodate large predators, helping them to focus on the most likely routes.

Just before 3:00 P.M., everyone was in place across a twelve-mile stretch of mountain. The placements stretched into two of the other counties, Ventura and San Luis Obispo, and deputies from both sheriffs' offices were present to assist, advise, and monitor.

Gearhart and the Chinook were airborne shortly after three. The Boeing chopper had a range of slightly over thirteen hundred miles, which would give the units coverage for a good portion of the early evening. The plan was to refuel, if necessary, at nine. Gearhart had a feeling these creatures would show themselves long before then.

The sheriff was right.

Shortly after 4:00 P.M., the pilot of the chopper informed Gearhart that there was movement in a passageway, at an old cave nearly five thousand feet up in Monte Arido.

Gearhart went into the cockpit and looked at the thirteen-inch monitor between the pilot and copilot. It showed a green sonographic image of the throat of the cave. The monitor showed three distinct pulsing white blips moving northeast.

"Could they be hikers?" Gearhart asked.

"No, sir," reported the copilot. "Not unless they're riding dirt bikes. These blips are moving at twenty-plus miles an hour."

In dark caves, Gearhart thought.

Troops and deputies who had been stationed at sites in the region immediately surrounding the cave were notified and picked up by the Chinook.

As the chopper rushed over, the radio operator at the site confirmed the signals. There were definitely "animals" somewhere in the mouth of the cave.

The copilot asked the unit radio operator, "What kind?"

The operator was silent for a moment. And then he replied, "Big ones."

61

Sergeant Andy May peered through his binoculars at the cave. The headset was part of his helmet, a thick unit that put four pounds against the young man's forehead and on the outsides of his eye sockets. In the evening, the regular binoculars would be replaced with night-vision goggles. Four months before, when he had completed basic training and started AIT—Advanced Individual Training for specialized equipment and night-action—May had hated the heavy feel of them. Now, the National Guard full-timer only felt whole when he had them on. When he was equipped and in the field, he felt as though the terrain was his. Just like he used to feel when he went duck hunting with his dad and they'd wade waist-deep in Crescent Lake in his native Crescent City, Florida.

The four other men who were with him also seemed comfortable with their goggles. Three of them were guardsmen and one of them was a sheriff's deputy; all of them were cool and "ready to rumble," as the deputy had put it.

The cave opening was actually a ten-foot-tall, rightward-leaning gash in the face of the mountaintop. It was about five feet wide at the bottom and three feet wide at the top. There were boulders on either side and a ditch in front worn to underlying rock by the recent rains. In front of the cave was about an acre of flat ridge, barren except for dirt and low, tangled scrub. Beyond the cave the mountaintop continued up another thousand feet; around it, on either side, was a light blue sky free of clouds. The air was cool up here, a combination of the ocean wind, the height, and the chill of rainwater that had evaporated during the early afternoon and was beginning to condense.

Private, first class, Arnie Ruhf was the small group's communications officer. Two minutes before he'd been notified by the Chinook copilot about the movement in their cave. He'd immediately informed the other two people at the cave: May, Private, first class, Markle, and Deputy Bright of Sheriff Gearhart's team. The men were told that reinforcements were being rushed to the site.

They took up predetermined positions behind boulders, picked up their rifles, and aimed at the cave. May was on the left end of the line with Ruhf beside him. The sergeant felt a little anxiety coming from Ruhf and Markle, but he himself felt confident. He was an excellent shot and even at twenty-five miles an hour there was enough distance between the men and the cave—about one hundred yards—to give them time to aim and fire.

"We verify the identity of the target and the nature of its intentions before firing," May reminded the others. They were clustered in a fifteen-foot arc directly in front of the cave. "No one fires without authorization from myself or a direct attack—"

"Sergeant!" said Private Ruhf. "I see something."

"Where?"

"Right side of the cave, about three feet up."

May looked over. He saw it too: a pair of large, golden-white eyes hovering near the wall.

"Confirmed," said the sergeant. "Report to the sheriff, then wait until it tries to escape or to attack. Otherwise, hold your fire. Let's try to wait for the armored guys to get here."

Ruhf did as he was ordered. He settled uneasily into his firing stance behind the boulder, one leg bent, the other knee on the ground.

"What the hell is in there?" Private Markle murmured. "I've never seen eyes like that."

"Quiet," May said. He raised his rifle and looked down the site. "Remember. If they come at us everyone keeps to his line of fire. If you cross-shoot we may end up double-firing at the same target."

The men fell silent, a fire wall of guns and determination.

After a very long moment the two eyes were joined by two more, then two more. The eyes didn't move from the shadows. May wasn't able to see more than the floating orbs and an occasional downward-pointing tusk, a sliver of brightness against opaque black. The animals were remarkably quiet, though the blood rushing through May's ears drowned out any sound the creatures might be making. He thought he heard squeaks coming from the cave, but they sounded like bats. Maybe they didn't like the intruders either.

After nearly two minutes of waiting the men heard the distant beat of the Chinook's twin rotors. Part of May wanted to move in now, shoot the animals and take the score home on his résumé. That would mean a lot in the security world, where he wanted to go after this. But there was the well-being of his men to consider, so he waited for the chopper. He'd have to settle for the assist.

Because of the noise of the approaching Chinook, and because of the attention the men were paying to the eyes in the jagged cave opening, none of them heard the two cats come up behind them. The only indication May had that the unit was under attack was when Ruhf suddenly cried out, lurched backward, and disappeared down the slope.

Sergeant May spun to his right. He was just in time to see a pair of tusks—much larger and nearer than the ones in the cave—flash down at him, a green haze of motion.

There were strong punches on either side of his neck. They drove May down so that he was sitting. He whimpered and his arms shook uncontrollably; he dropped his gun without realizing it. There was hot breath in the young man's face and where he'd felt the punches there was now sharp, deep pain. May wanted to scream, but he couldn't breathe as his breastbone was torn outward.

He was dead before a sheet of blood splashed up from his shattered chest, covering his face and goggles.

As soon as the man went down the cats that had attacked them were joined by the others from the cave. The giants came quickly, sinking their fangs into the bodies, lifting them from the mountaintop, and turning back toward the cave.

They paid no attention to the bright star that came early in the southern sky.

62

"The blips are moving again!" the copilot exclaimed as the Chinook neared the mountain.

"Which way?" Gearhart asked.

"Out of the cave—only now there are five of them!"

The sheriff was once again standing in the cockpit doorway. The Chinook had collected fifteen soldiers and six deputies from four separate sites and was rushing to the cave on Monte Arido. The sheriff was peering out the front window at the distant peak.

If the cats were out of the cave, why weren't the soldiers and Deputy Bright firing? Realizing that he might not hear the gunshots because of the rotors, Gearhart grabbed a pair of binoculars from the equipment rack to the right of the cockpit. He looked out the window. Though the chopper was shaking and the magnified view was unsteady, he didn't see any flashes. But he did think he saw movement behind the rocks.

"Get your man on the radio," Gearhart said.

"Sir, the sergeant asked for radio silence—"

"Now," Gearhart insisted.

The copilot obliged. Gearhart continued to look out the window. He wasn't surprised when the copilot informed him that there was no response from the field unit.

"Get us over there *fast*," Gearhart said.

"Yes, sir," the pilot said.

Gearhart went back into the main cabin, a cargo hold that had been fitted with canvas sling-seats hung from the ceiling. There was also a winch beside the door and a sling for lowering equipment. He grabbed a rifle from the weapons rack toward the rear of the cabin. Then he went back to the outside door, which was located behind the cockpit. He slipped a harness around his waist, fastened himself to one of the hooks beside the door, and opened it. He wasn't going to lose these bastards again.

The Chinook dove and picked up speed. It was moving at about 120 knots. The wind was rough, the chopper was slanting down at a twenty-degree angle, and Gearhart had trouble standing. It would be tough to aim and fire from here. He wished he had fucking Sidewinders; he'd light the rockets and blow the entire mountaintop to hell.

Then Gearhart saw his enemy for the first time. He saw long, slinky golden figures moving through the sharp afternoon light. They appeared to be carrying things.

Prey?

No, Gearhart realized. Not just prey.

Bodies. Bodies dressed in drab green. The entire Monte Arido unit.

Gearhart slung the binoculars around his neck.

"Wilson!" he yelled over his shoulder.

The portly, balding first sergeant in charge of the armored unit hurried over. "Sir?"

"Sergeant, pass out weapons and send three men over here *now.*"

"Yes, sir."

The door was wide, though three men was all Gearhart felt the doorway could accommodate without them falling over or shooting each other. As the chopper neared the cliff, three guns lined up behind Gearhart. The sheriff turned so he could be heard over the rush of the wind.

"It looks like the entire unit has been taken out," Gearhart told them. "When I give the order, fire at any animals you see on the cliff. Shoot to kill; use multiples to clean up any vital signs."

Gearhart turned back to the door. The animals were halfway between the cave and the boulders where the soldiers had been. Because they were slowed by the weight of the bodies, the sheriff was able to see them more clearly now. They were definitely tigers of some sort.

The chopper was about one hundred and fifty feet from the mountaintop. Gearhart leaned into the cabin.

"Hold us here, steady as you can!" he shouted at the pilot.

The Chinook slowed and leveled off. Gearhart raised his rifle.

"Fire at will!" he shouted to the men behind him.

The air exploded with short, hot pops from the M16s. The cats were peppered with fire and began twitching, hopping, and snapping at the air as sprigs of red exploded from their shoulders, backs, and hindquarters. The gunfire was constant, some of the animals taking four and five hits as the gunmen shifted targets and their fire overlapped.

The two cats nearest the cave went down almost immediately, their backs and hind legs chewed apart, their skin hanging like bloody rags. Shots to the neck and skull finished them both off. Two other cats, wounded in the rear haunches, dropped their prey and tried to drag themselves forward, only to be pinned to the ground by additional fire. The last cat went down when it paused and used its fangs to scratch at a bloody hole in its right shoulder. It was hit by a succession of bullets that caused it to stagger sideways, though it managed to stay on its feet until it tumbled over the side of the mountain.

When the last cat went down, the other men lowered their rifles and high-fived each other. But Gearhart continued to watch the site as the Chinook hovered. After a long moment the last cat climbed back onto the ridge. It was moving with obvious difficulty.

"You should've been less loyal, you sonofabitch!" Gearhart yelled.

He watched and waited until it was back on top. Then he put a bullet between the cat's large, luminous eyes. Its great head flew back and then the cat dropped forward, its front legs splayed.

The site was still.

"Let's go down and see to our people," Gearhart said.

Gearhart looked at the ridge as they descended. The dusty tan surface was mottled with blood. Some of it in pools and some in threadlike streams. The pools were spreading and the streams were crawling forward, mixing the blood of man with the blood of cat. Except for the blood, the dark brown scrub, torn clothing, and fur stirred by the rotors, nothing on the ridge was moving. They would land, gas the cave, and make sure there was nothing moving inside either. Though Gearhart was saddened by the cost in human lives, he was satisfied that the objective had been achieved. He didn't know whether these tigers were throwbacks, mutations, or animals made from spliced genes. He didn't really care. That was for Grand and his kind to figure out. All that mattered to Gearhart was that the animals wouldn't be leaving that ridge under their own power.

There would be complaints about the fact that these animals were killed rather than captured. But there would be far more complaints if the animals had been able to lose themselves in the hills for days or maybe weeks more.

There would be mourning for the men who died here, though much less than if the cats had been allowed to prey on dozens of other people in Santa Barbara and adjoining counties.

There would be criticism, but there would also be praise. The most important thing was how Gearhart felt.

He had done what he'd set out to do.

He had ended a lethal threat.

63

Grand spent the morning making the calls to local environmentalists and animal rights groups. He also got an entomologist at the university to agree to go out to the creek to check for gnats that might have escaped from the cave. But the area was still closed off and she had to turn back. Hopefully, the insects hadn't escaped from the cave and would still be there when this was all over.

After that—with Hannah's blessing—Grand had spoken to several other newspapers and TV interviewers about what he thought was out there. He wondered if Hannah had not bothered to put up a fuss because she knew how they'd treat him. Like an alumnus of *The Weekly World News.*

Not that any of Grand's colleagues rallied behind what he had to say. When he spoke with them their reactions ranged from polite doubt—they were clearly humoring a man who had been under a lot of stress—to cautious interest to outright dismissal.

Only Joseph Tumamait put credence in what Grand had to say. Just like the old days.

Grand finished his calls and interviews late in the afternoon. He was about to try and plot possible routes for the cats when Hannah phoned.

"I just heard that the sheriff and the National Guard have literally closed off about two hundred acres in the mountains," she said. "There were reports of gunfire up there."

"Any information?"

"None."

"I've got to get up there," Grand said.

"The mountains are shut up tight—"

"No, Gearhart just thinks they are," Grand replied. "I can get wherever I need to. Do you have any idea where his command post is?"

"A traffic copter friend of mine said he thought he spotted it somewhere up near the intersection of Ballinger Canyon and Route 33."

"Thanks," Grand said.

"Whoa, wait! When are you going?"

"Now," he said.

"Can you swing by?"

Grand didn't want to expose her to further danger. But the idea of doing this without her seemed strange. "Sure," he said.

Hannah and the Wall both joined Grand in his SUV. They kept the windows down and the air conditioning off so they could hear the comings and goings of trucks, choppers, or other vehicles, possibly get a read on the direction they were headed. They heard nothing until they were about two miles up Route 33 when rifle fire began echoing through the mountains. Though sportsmen often took target practice in the open fields this was different: It wasn't sporadic but a continuous roar, like a fireworks finale.

Grand stopped the SUV suddenly, got out, and listened. A moment later he jumped back in the SUV.

"Could you tell where it was coming from?" Hannah asked.

"The northwest," Grand said.

"But I thought—"

"I know," he said, "that they were headed to the southeast. But Jameson Lake is to the west—it's possible they went that way for some reason."

Grand turned west on Barbara Canyon Road, followed the Cuyama River for several miles, then swung north. He stayed off the main and secondary roads, pushing the SUV through the rocky terrain of the Santa Ynez foothills. Grand and his passengers were silent the entire time. The scientist did not want to believe that the sheriff had found the cats already. Perhaps his officers found them in a cave and had been firing to pin them there—

When he heard the sound of a chopper, Grand followed it until the vehicle could go no farther. He stopped between two and three thousand feet up Monte Arido.

"Come on," he said, getting out of the car.

"Where to?" Hannah said.

Grand pointed up the mountain. "A chopper is hovering somewhere up there. They may have spotted the cats and are staying with them."

"Waiting for the cavalry to arrive," Hannah said.

"Maybe," Grand said.

Grand looked for the most accessible slope, the one with the easiest incline, and started up. He half walked, half ran so he could reach a point that was clear of the lower peaks and ridges so he could see the top of the mountain. The section they were climbing would give them both a view and access to the top.

Grand climbed for nearly forty-five minutes before reaching the top of the slope. The first hint of twilight was touching the sky. Perspiring and breathless, he had a clear view of the rest of the mountain. He looked ahead. What he saw was not promising.

A long-bodied helicopter was hovering approximately one hundred feet above a wide, level ridge. What looked like a large canvas sling had been lowered from the side of the chopper, just behind the cockpit. Grand could only see the ends of the sling; the rest of it was lying flat on the ground. There were at least a dozen people moving around the ridge.

Hannah and the Wall had fallen behind but Grand didn't wait for them. He scurried up, frantically clawing over rocks and grass toward the top. After climbing another thirty or forty feet he stopped again and looked up.

The sling had begun to rise. Now he could see what was in it. It was one of the cats, its golden hide blossomed with red.

Grand fell to his knees. And for the first time since Rebecca died, he reached into his soul for a scream and tears.

64

By the time Hannah and the Wall reached Grand, the scientist was just getting back onto his feet. Hannah didn't have to ask what had caused him to cry out. She saw for herself. The sight was vulgar and revolting. In addition to the one bloody cat in the sling, she saw others lying around the ridge. It was disturbing enough to be around death but it was more disturbing to be present for an extinction. Hannah wasn't a religious woman but the air felt chill and its whistle seemed mournful. She could swear she felt God frowning. Or Nature. Something.

The Wall snapped several pictures. The small, quick click of the shutter made the deaths seem more real, more tragic. It made Hannah think of the Chumash artists who had put so much effort into rendering animal likenesses on the cave walls. They made the paints, maybe spent hours getting in touch with the animal spirits, then sketched what they felt. They put living images on the cold stone. The Wall's images were of death.

They climbed the mountain, though their movements were now a blur. The smell of sinkholes being paved on nearby Route 166 wafted over. All Hannah could think about was the loss of these last surviving members of a magnificent race. She could only begin to imagine what was going through Grand's heart and mind.

When the trio finally reached the site it was worse than Hannah had imagined. Army National guardsmen were milling about different sections of the ridge. There were four dead cats still on the ridge and four red-flag markers near them. That meant human bodies had been removed from those spots. She wondered, coldly, whether those deaths had been what drew Gearhart to the ridge or whether they were a result of the sheriff having attacked the cats.

Grand reached the ridge first and ran toward the nearest of the cats. One of the National guardsmen moved to intercept him; Grand knocked him aside. Two other soldiers rushed forward to grab him. Grand reached the nearest of the cats before the men got to him. The soldiers tried to pick him up by his arms but Grand shook them off and stood.

"Leave him!" Gearhart shouted.

The soldiers stepped back as the sheriff approached. Grand crouched beside the cat. Hannah and the Wall arrived as Gearhart did. The photographer immediately started snapping pictures in case they were chased away. But Gearhart didn't seem to mind. To the contrary. He was obviously pleased with himself and seemed almost to be inviting coverage of his grotesque triumph.

Gearhart stood on the other side of the dead cat. He spoke loudly to be heard over the chopper.

"This is a restricted area," the sheriff yelled, then looked at Hannah. "But I'll tell you what. If you want some good shots, some really choice pictures that are sure to sell papers, go to the base camp where we've evac'ed the bodies of the guardsmen and my deputy. You'll spot them easy enough. They're the ones that look like sharkfood."

Hannah watched as Grand touched the cat—its ear, then its muzzle, then its bloody shoulder. She'd once seen her father's groom touch a sick horse the same way, with tenderness and great sadness. Hannah wished there were something she could do for Grand.

"You didn't have to do this," Grand said.

"No?"

"You see what these animals are now—"

"Yeah. Killers."

"And what are you?" Hannah asked.

"Why don't you ask the people in town?" Gearhart said. "Ask the families of Roche and Greene, if they'll talk to you. Ask the Rangers who work in the mountains. See if they agree with you."

Grand's hand moved along the lithe, muscular body. "It still didn't have to end this way. It wasn't necessary to kill them *or* lose any men."

Gearhart squatted and looked into Grand's eyes. "Is that your professional police opinion?"

Grand looked at the blood on his hand. "It's a fact."

"Is it? Sorry, but you were only batting .333 in your own field. There were more than two cats, you got that right. But you had the direction they were moving wrong and they came out in daylight." Gearhart reached across his body and slipped the hunting knife from his belt. "Deputy Bright was part of the unit up here. He had a wife and a young son who adored him." Gearhart wrapped his fingers around the cat's foot-long tail. Then he slid the knife underneath it and sawed across the base of the tail.

"Oh Christ, don't—!" Hannah said.

The tail came free. Gearhart held it, replaced the knife, and stood.

Grand just stared at him.

"I know Mrs. Bright very well," Gearhart said, "and I don't give a good goddamn whether the animal rights people picket my office round the clock, throw red paint at my house, or build a shrine up here and burn me in effigy. I don't care whether I get voted out of office and run out of town. Knowing that I did my duty here is the only thing that matters."

"Is it?" Grand asked.

"It is."

Grand's eyes swept across the ridge and then he looked back at Gearhart. The scientist stood and walked over to the cat that was being loaded onto the sling. He examined it and then he looked at the other cats. Finally, he walked back to Gearhart.

"You know what really matters, Sheriff?" Grand asked. "Patience. It gets you everything. Respect, cooperation, and most important—knowledge."

"What are you talking about?" Gearhart asked.

"Killing these cats may have created a bigger problem. They're just part of a larger group."

"You mean, the Chumash painting of the eyes?" Hannah asked.

"Not just that," Grand said. "The other group is almost certainly moving southeast, as I said. These cats were here for another reason."

"How do you know that?" Gearhart asked.

"A little zoological police work."

"Grand, don't fuck with me—"

"I'm not," Grand said. "I'm telling you that the worst is still to come. These dead cats are all female."

"So?"

Grand said, "The cats Hannah and I faced in the pipe were males."

65

Grand's remark took Gearhart by surprise.

The sheriff slid the severed tail through a belt loop. He looked around at all the cats. While he did, Grand turned toward the north, toward Route 166. He picked up sand from the ridge, sifted some of it through his fingers, and watched as they fell to earth.

As the Wall took pictures, Hannah walked over to Grand.

"What are you doing?" she asked.

"Checking something else," Grand said. "Something that might explain why some of the cats were here."

He released more of the granules. Like the first batch they drifted to the southeast, as he expected. Grand sniffed the air. He found something else that he expected. Something he should have thought of before.

"Well?" Hannah said.

Before Grand could answer, Gearhart walked over. The sheriff was once again a focused professional with a mission.

"Professor, I need to know how many more cats we're talking about," Gearhart said.

"Seven or so, assuming a full pride has survived," Grand replied.

"Would the remaining animals split up, go off in groups of two or three?" Gearhart asked.

"They might," Grand said. "They're looking for something."

"What?"

"I think I know but I won't tell you unless I have your assurance that the cats will be tranquilized and not executed."

"Executed?" Gearhart screamed.

"That's right."

"You twisted *shit!* You think your goddamn cats are more important than human beings?"

"Not more important or less," Grand replied. "I told you before we can save them all."

"Mister, you tell me where those cats are headed or you won't be able to save your *own* ass!"

"I already told you they're moving to the southeast," Grand replied. "And Sheriff? Don't threaten me."

"No? What'll you do?"

Grand didn't answer.

Gearhart raised both hands and gave Grand a big push to the chest. Hannah hopped back to avoid being bumped aside.

"Hey!" she cried.

"Don't do this," Grand said to Gearhart.

"Why not? You think you can take me, pro*fess*or?" Gearhart shoved him again.

Grand suddenly threw what was left of the dirt to the right. Gearhart glanced at it. When he did, Grand's right hand shot down. The scientist drew the hunting knife from the sheriff's belt. It was still wet with the saber-tooth's blood. Grand pointed it down and pressed it against the top of the man's groin. At the same time, Grand used his left hand to grab Gearhart's belt and yank him closer.

"I know I can take you," Grand said.

Gearhart tried to shove away from Grand but the scientist twisted the belt, pulled tighter, and pushed the knife down. The blade tip penetrated the fabric just above the zipper.

"Push me again," Grand said through his teeth. "Please."

Hannah hurried toward them. "Stop this!" She eased her hands, then her arms, between the men.

The men continued to glare at each other.

"Jim, *please*," Hannah said. "We don't have time for this."

Grand released Gearhart. Gearhart stepped back.

"When this is over, we settle up," Gearhart said, thickly.

Grand flipped the knife over and handed it to Gearhart hilt-first. "You know where to find me."

"And I will," Gearhart promised. "Now I don't have time to argue. What buys your cooperation?"

"I want to talk to the National Guard field officer at your base camp," Grand told him. "We can work out details of tranquilizing the cats while we move to intercept them."

"What the hell is wrong with you?" Gearhart yelled. "Sedation may not *work!*"

"I'm an optimist," Grand said. "Let's try it anyway."

Gearhart hesitated, but only for a moment. He pulled the radio from his belt and told the chopper pilot to lower the harness. Then he turned away and radioed Lieutenant Mindar.

As Gearhart talked, Hannah stepped in front of Grand.

"A pair of cowboys, that's what you two are. And I stress the 'boys.' "

"He'll cool down," Grand said. He looked at her. "Listen, Hannah. While we work this out with the National Guard I need you to do some things for me."

"Name them."

"Would you call Joseph? If things don't work out between the National Guard officer and myself, I'll need him to crawl up the command ladder until he finds someone who will listen about saving the cats."

"Okay," she said. "Maybe there are Chumash in the guard ranks. He can go to them."

"Good idea," Grand said. "Then I'd like you to call Dr. Thorpe. Tell her I need to know if there are any geological vents that open up between Hollywood and Beverly Hills. We also have to find out if there are any new sinkholes, maybe in the Hollywood Hills. And is there anyone you can call to find out where the drain pipes and viaducts open up in that same Hollywood–to–Beverly Hills corridor?"

"I'll have my City Hall stringer call the Department of Water and Power in Los Angeles," she said. "But why there?"

"Remember what you said earlier, that the cats might be looking for a remnant of their world?"

"Yes."

"You were right."

"I was?"

Grand nodded. "That's what I was checking over here," he said. "I smelled something before outside your apartment, but I didn't make the connection till now. The cats went to the beach because the wharfs are sealed with pitch. They came up here because of the repair work being done on the roads. Asphalt."

"Pitch and asphalt," Hannah said. "I'm confused."

"Tar," Grand said.

"My God, Jim. Why didn't we think of that before?"

"Because it's not a living place to me. It's a graveyard. But to them it was a buffet."

"I don't follow."

"Eleven thousand years ago Los Angeles was dotted with tar marshes," Grand said. "Rain doesn't mix with tar, so the pits were often covered with water or dust or fallen leaves. Large animals would wade across the pits thinking it was solid ground, or stop for a drink and get trapped. Saber-tooths used to prowl the edges of the marshes, leap onto the backs of the larger animals like ground sloths, long-horned bison, and mammoths, and tear away large chunks of meat before the prey went under."

"How do we know that?"

"Because the cats didn't always get away," Grand said. "Sometimes the animals rolled over and trapped them."

"And those remains are the ones that have been dug from the pits," Hannah said.

"In many cases, yes," Grand said. "Now suppose our saber-tooths were forced to leave the tar pits for some reason. Maybe they were driven out by a series of natural disasters tied to the eruption that eventually trapped them—forest fires or earthquakes or underwater eruptions that sent a tsunami inland. What if they sought refuge on the high ground of the Santa Ynez Mountains until they thought it was safe to return. Maybe it was smoky so they went underground. What if they were trapped in the cave before they could go home?"

"You're a genius," Hannah said. "So they emerged a few days ago, thinking that no time had passed—"

"And continued toward the tar pits," Grand said.

"But why would they have separated into two groups?"

"I'm not sure," Grand said. "Male and female lions often hunt separately, in relatively close proximity. Maybe the females headed to the smell of tar, thinking that vulnerable prey or the saber-tooth males would be there. Maybe they became disoriented and were separated from the males."

"God, what a story," Hannah exclaimed. "Male saber-toothed tigers headed for Beverly Hills."

"Hannah, this is still speculative—"

"I know," she said.

"The worst thing we can do is cause people to panic, start shooting everything that moves."

"I know that too," Hannah said. "And I won't run any of this. But you'll keep me in the loop?"

"Of course."

She handed him a cell phone. "I'm going back to the office. I'll call you on this. See why I carry three phones?"

He put the phone in his jacket pocket. "Because you're obsessive," Grand said. "But I'm glad, Hannah. Thanks for your help. Thanks for everything, Hannah."

She smiled. "Just stay safe, okay? If those cats figure out that they lost their mates, they aren't going to be very happy."

"I know," Grand said.

"And *I* wouldn't be very happy if I lose you."

Hannah stood on her toes, kissed Grand on the cheek, then quickly walked away.

Grand turned toward Gearhart. The carnage was awful. But there was the future to think about. And for the first time in a long time he had a reason to care whether or not he ended his day as the mummified Brooding Mountain Man . . . .

66

There was a time, early in the twentieth century, when the long and winding Sunset Boulevard offered spectacular views of the sun as it disappeared into the Pacific. That was before the avenue became so built-up that it was impossible to see the horizon over the homes, trees, and buildings in Beverly Hills and in the Pacific Palisades.

To see breathtaking sunsets, one of the best vantage points in the Los Angeles region is high in the Hollywood Hills. Located north of Los Angeles, the Hollywood Hills are a terminus of the sprawling Coast Ranges, a system comprised of the Sierra Madre Mountains, the San Rafael Mountains, the Santa Ynez Mountains, and many others.

One of the highest and most scenic spots in the Hollywood Hills is the high area where Coldwater Canyon Drive and twisting Mulholland Drive intersect. Not only are the sunsets awe-inspiring as they turn the hills and valleys from forest green to flame red, then from brown to black, they're followed by lights winking on across the wide, flat floor of the San Fernando Valley. Rippling heat gives a distinctive shimmer to the tiny white lights as they spread out for miles, more plentiful and brighter than the stars in the skies above.

Six-foot-four-inch Jason Broughton stole a moment from his guests. He pretended to be on his cell phone but what he really wanted was to look across his backyard and savor the view of the valley. He used to be daunted by those lights. When the unemployed actor worked as a valet for a Japanese restaurant on Ventura Boulevard in Sherman Oaks, he would drive into the hills at night and see the lights as places he didn't want to be: the boulevard where he worked, which was a commercial drag that had nothing to do with movies; an apartment he shared on Kester with two other aspiring actors; the valet job at night and clerking at a video store during the day.

Now the thirty-seven-year-old saw the lights as something magnificent. They were the map of a place he owned. After years of clawing his way up from bit parts, Jason Broughton was the star of the smash hour-long adventure series *The Legendary Adventures of Mighty Samson*. He was the new owner of this sprawling house that once belonged to one of the founders of Hollywood.

He had arrived. Those lights were *his* now. So much was his.

Jason turned. He looked at his sprawling, all-white Mediterranean-style home and his three-quarter-acre yard. The grounds were surrounded by ten-foot-high hedges, stonework, and poplar trees. Iron torches with flickering electric lights were mounted on the trees, house, and cabana and gave the small estate a Greco-Roman look. He had had those put in, replacing the garish spotlights that had been buried about the property.

A small pool in the center of the yard was lit by candles floating on miniature wooden barges. Jason looked at the tents arrayed around the pool. The sheer fabric blew lightly in the soft early-evening breeze. The tents were supported by columns and surrounded by statues that had been used on his show. The meats and vegetables roasted on open fires in stone pits. The waitstaff, dressed in Philistine attire, offered beverages in real silver goblets. He knew that guests were chatting with each other but looking at *him* and smiling. Actors and actresses. Agents and managers. The press.

They were his now, too.

Life was good.

Jason closed up his phone. He tucked it back into his white dinner jacket. It was time to return to his guests.

Suddenly, something leaped over the hedge, landed on the actor's back, and pounded him face-first into the lush green grass. Jason's spine and both of his lungs were crushed. In the moment of life that remained he saw a monstrous golden thing jump to the ground in front of him, jag suddenly to the left, and launch itself at Lizz Hirsch-Horn, his Delilah.

At the same time, the hedges and walls of the estate were being breached on all sides by other giants, some of them nine and ten feet long and standing five feet high at the shoulder. They flew down into the perimeter like dark angels, drawn by the smell of meat and the shimmering water of the pool. They tore into the fresh game that was standing around the yard, bounding one way and then the other, thick claws and fangs savagely pulling down prey by an arm or leg. Some cats would twist their prey by the head to break its spine, while others simply left it crippled where it fell so it couldn't get away. Then they would turn on another victim. Half the forty-odd guests were down in a matter of seconds.

The initial charge was followed by the choked screams and panicked flight of a disoriented mob. Guests who had been networking seconds before were now trying vainly to survive. The flame pits filled with stumbling waitstaff and panicked producers, the tents were splashed with the blood of actors and agents, and the pool filled quickly with reporters and managers who sought safety in the water. But the cats followed them in. Some of the saber-tooths jumped while others slid into the pool like crocodiles. The water turned cherry-red as the cats bit into their victims and shook them violently from side to side. The guests flailed and gurgled, groping hands and looks of wide-eyed terror occasionally bursting through the surface. Before long the cats climbed back onto the tile, dripping water and blood from their dead prey. The bodies were dropped on the edge of the pool while the cats pursued the few who had managed to get as far as the driveway.

Soon everything was silence. As the flickering fires threw distorted shadows on the hedges, the cats speared the party-goers with their fangs and began carrying them through the hedges to the valley whence they'd come.

He watched from a hilltop that overlooked the preying ground. On either side were two golden warriors whose yellow-white eyes, like his, were focused on the attack. A brown creeper clung to the back of one of them, using its long, curved bill to dig insects from the fur of one of the subordinate animals. Their fur rippled in the wind, the three of them sniffing the air as it gusted by. They ignored the strange smells, of which there were many. Only the familiar ones mattered, and one in particular.

Like the smells, the landscape itself had changed. The hills were different. They were smoother, with many caves above ground and creatures dwelling inside them. There was more water than before, clear and bright and collected in small ponds like the one below. There were tiny fires everywhere, including lights that moved through the sky—

Suddenly, he detected something on the wind.

His great silver head turned slowly in the direction from which they'd come. It wasn't a smell he'd sensed but a presence. He'd sensed it before only it was nearer now, more powerful.

More dangerous.

He didn't wait for those below to finish. They would follow soon enough. Moving quickly and resolutely, but not with haste or fear—never with fear—he strode down the hill followed by the two at his side.

Soon they would be home. He could smell that too. And when they reached it, they would make a stand against the thing that hunted them.

Death.

67

The Chumash believed that Death was dangerous company, a tangible thing that stayed behind after it claimed a victim. They believed that it inhabited minerals and also infiltrated living things, piggybacking itself on the soul or in the mind. Sometimes it killed the host outright, sometimes it drove them mad before killing them.

In the end, of course, Death always won.

Grand didn't believe that. But as he rode in the noisy chopper with the dead saber-tooth, he felt more than just the loss of the cats. The scientist was sitting in a sling-seat near the door and the animal was lying on the canvas, trussed and uncovered. Yet there was still a sense of menace about it. It was almost as if the saber-tooth could rise again.

If a cat has nine lives, how many would a saber-toothed cat have?

The scientist looked around the cabin. Gearhart was riding in the cockpit. He had the copilot's headset pressed to one ear. There was only one guardsman in the back and he was looking out the window.

Suddenly, Gearhart turned and shouted into the rattling-loud cabin. "Professor!"

Grand slid from the sling and went to the cockpit.

"We've got a new destination," Gearhart said.

"Where?"

"The Hollywood Hills," the sheriff said. "There's been another attack.

"When?"

"Within the last half hour or so." He offered Grand the headset. "Lieutenant Mindar wants to talk to you."

Grand switched places with Gearhart. The severed tail of the sabertooth swung and bounced on the sheriff's left hip as he moved. It almost seemed alive. Grand looked into the cockpit as he slipped on the headset and adjusted the microphone. This was the first time he'd used one of these while standing up. Usually he was sitting in the pilot's seat of his small plane.

"This is Jim Grand."

"Professor, this is Lieutenant Sam Mindar. Did Sheriff Gearhart tell you about the attack?"

"Yes. Do we know how many cats?"

"No. The police are talking to someone who apparently arrived moments after it happened. The person saw large animals and the police found gold fur on the hedges. They're organizing a search of the hills right now."

It took a moment for all of that to register. The Hollywood Hills were to the southeast of their position. Depending on where the saber-tooths struck, they were within ten miles or so of the La Brea Tar Pits. They must have kept moving through the night. Perhaps the females had broken off to rest.

"The LA Chief of Police wants to divert your Chinook to help with the air search," Mindar went on. "Sheriff Gearhart also said you know where the cats are heading. I need that intel now. They're moving into a densely populated region and they have to be stopped."

"I agree," Grand said. "But they have to be stopped with tranquilizers, not bullets."

"Professor, I've discussed this with Sheriff Gearhart. Sedatives are notoriously unpredictable—"

"I understand," Grand said. "Keep your guns as backup. I'm not asking for guarantees, just a chance."

"To do what?"

"Capture them."

Lieutenant Mindar was silent for a moment. "Professor Grand, I can't give you my word about how this is going to be handled. Now that the situation has entered greater Los Angeles I won't be in charge of the operation. I'll talk to the police chief about sedating the creatures but it would help if you gave me some good-faith information to work with."

"All right," Grand said. "Tell him I may be able to figure out the exact route the saber-tooths are taking through the mountains. When I do, I should be able to get ahead of them and lure them to wherever they want."

"How will you do that? If they've already eaten, food won't—"

"I won't be using food," Grand said.

"What, then?"

"I'll be using tar."

"The La Brea Tar Pits," Mindar said. "Of course. That's where the animals are headed."

"Yes, but there are many ways they can get there and you can't cover them all. Look, I've fought these cats close-up. I think I can get near enough to bait them and get out again."

"You'd risk that to save them?"

"Absolutely."

"Fair enough," Mindar said. "I'll do what I can. Please put Sheriff Gearhart back on."

Grand handed the headset to Gearhart and they switched places again. The lieutenant had sounded like a reasonable enough man. Perhaps this wouldn't be as bad as he'd thought. But as he stood beside the sling-seat and looked back at the dead cat, curiosity, concern, and fear moved his mind in countless directions. He picked one.

Maybe he'd asked the wrong question before.

If a cat is slain, how many lives does its spirit demand in exchange?

Grand didn't believe that, yet he couldn't help but wonder if he was doing the right thing. Of course it was right to try to save the cats. At least on an emotional and scientific level, and certainly on an ecological one. But what about on a spiritual level? Even if the cats could survive in captivity, was it fair to take away their predatory imperative? The world *was* different from the one they'd known. They couldn't roam free.

Not that it mattered. It wasn't his decision to make. Providence had kept these cats alive. And not for science but for that fact, he would do everything possible to keep them alive.

Grand remained standing where he was as the scuffed floor vibrated and tilted beneath him. He had to call Hannah with this new information, get her to narrow her search. As he reached for the phone, his mind moved somewhere else. The scientist had devoted his life to studying the hunting techniques of ancient peoples. He wondered if they'd ever attempted what he was about to try.

Most likely, he decided. Pleistocene hunters were pretty resourceful. Grand wondered then, with a flash of concern, if it had actually been tried on these very cats—and if so, whether the saber-tooths had fallen for it.

Probably. So far they seemed to.

But primitive humans almost certainly never had to deal with the other questions that nagged at Grand. They had relied on one another to make weapons, shoes, and water pouches that wouldn't break. They had needed each other to guard their backs during a hunt, to watch campsites while they slept, and to protect the mates and children of men who were out searching for prey.

As his mind took yet another path the question that bothered Grand was whether he could do the same.

68

Save for Hannah, the Wall—who was finishing up in the photo lab—and the night editor, Charlie Wong, the newspaper office was empty.

Hannah had written up the Monte Arido attack and collected the information Grand had requested. She called the cell phone. She hoped Grand had some ideas: What she had to tell him did not leave her optimistic.

Grand answered. The connection was weak and Hannah had to cover one ear to hear.

"Hello, Jim?"

"Hannah—I was just about to call. There's been another encounter, up on Coldwater Canyon in the Hollywood Hills."

"What happened?"

"The cats attacked an outdoor party," he said. "I don't know much more than that."

"Coldwater," she said. "That's right on your southeast beeline."

"I know. Have you got anything?"

"At least fourteen possible exits all around the Miracle Mile," she said. She looked at the geological charts. "But the route from Coldwater shouldn't be as difficult to trace. I can't read these things too well—but it looks like five or six trenches and faults lead in that direction."

"I'll look around the site and see what I can find in the way of sinkholes or tunnels," Grand said. "Thanks, Hannah. Would you be able to gather up the maps and meet me at the Page Museum?"

"The one right at the tar pits?"

"Yes."

"I can be there in about ninety minutes," Hannah said.

"Great. See you there."

Hannah hung up. She immediately called her Los Angeles stringer to send him up to Coldwater; he said he'd just gotten a call from one of his sources at the fire department and was on his way. Hannah then rushed to the small photo lab where the Wall was surrounded by hi-tech processing gear and computer monitors for the digital work. He was examining his color prints.

"All this bloodshed. These are heartbreaking," he said.

Hannah glanced at them. "Completely."

The Wall looked at her. "Is that the best you can do?"

"What do you mean?"

"'Completely.' This is tragic."

"I know Wall," she said. "But it's like my dad said about war. Fight now, mourn later. Give the best shots to Charlie and then get your stuff."

"What's happening?"

"We're going to meet Jim at the George Page Museum in Los Angeles," Hannah said.

The photographer shook his head. "Can't you leave me here?"

"Leave you? Hell, no, Wall. You're my photographer, remember?"

"For *The Coastal Freeway,*" he said, "Covering greater Santa Barbara County."

"Which is where this story started, which makes it ours. Now let's go."

He didn't move.

"Come on Walter. I don't have time for this."

"Time," he said. "You know what happens to reporters who don't take the time to sleep, eat, and reflect on life a little?"

"They get scoops," she replied impatiently.

"No," the Wall said. "They lose perspective. They get desensitized."

"Wall, what the hell are you talking about? What brought this on? The photos?"

"Partly. I've been standing here looking at these photos and thinking that we may be part of the problem. Gearhart wants to save human lives, Grand wants to save prehistoric monsters. Gearhart doesn't want people to know what's going on, you want people to know everything." The photographer shook his head. "We're fighting each other over creatures that are fighting each other. Somewhere, sometime, someone has to say, 'No more fighting.'"

"Wall, we're fighting to keep people informed, to try and improve the quality of human life."

"Not to prove something? Maybe to a father or to ourselves?"

"Hey, I want respect," Hannah said. "But that's not the reason I'm doing this and you know it."

"No, to do good."

"That's right!"

"But you're never the one who gets seriously knocked around," the Wall said. "Remember our last year at Brown when we did the series about mobsters and jocks making book on college sports?"

"Of course I remember. We were nominated for the Anna Prize."

"*You* were nominated for the prize. When we showed up at one of the bars where they did their betting, *I* was the one who got hit with a blackjack. A year ago when we did that Lone Rangering about Caltrans and the right-of-way land they bought cheap up here then sold at a big-bucks auction, who got roughed up trying to get into the public meetings? The guy without the lucky dog tags hanging from his neck."

"You survived," she said, "and I was able to be there when upper management voted themselves big pay increases using that money. A week after our article appeared they got voted out. We won."

"That's just my point," the Wall said. "We never really win. We just keep fighting, and they just keep fighting—whoever 'they' are on that particular day—and we all just keep getting more and more worn down." He gestured toward the desktop. "I look at pictures like these and you know what I see? Not death and blood. I see a great page one. We'll sell a lot of copies, outsell the *L.A. Times.* Another battle won, until the next day and the next day and the day after that."

"Wall," Hannah said patiently, "you're tired. You're stressed. But I need you to do this for me. When it's over we can talk about life, your future, a new studio, anything you want."

He looked at her. "You always say that. And it's never over."

"Sure it is," she said. "My great-grandmother once said to me,

'Hannah—squeeze every dime out of your life because it's over way too soon.' I don't say you're completely wrong, Wall. Maybe we do need to step back from what we're doing and how we're doing it. But Jim needs the information I have and I want to see this one through."

The Wall looked at her. "You like Jim."

"Yeah." She flushed.

"I do too, even though he's a little *Twilight Zone*-y."

"He's a good man, Wall."

The Wall sighed. "I guess." He turned to the coat rack where his cameras were hanging. "I'll do this one more time, Hannah. Once. And then we have a heart-to-heart."

"You've got a deal," she said.

The Wall removed his cameras, slung them over his shoulder, and followed Hannah through the dark, quiet office into the dark, quiet night.

He savored it while he could.

69

The Chinook landed at Fire Station 108 on the top of Coldwater Canyon, then immediately took off to help with the search. Meanwhile, Grand and Gearhart were driven by a Los Angeles Police Department patrol car down the road toward Sunset Boulevard and the site of the massacre. The driver maneuvered through a crowd of TV and print reporters who were clustered at the edge of the driveway behind police guards and yellow crime-scene tape. It did not escape Grand, the irony of being taken inside the one time he really wanted to be outside, searching for evidence of where the cats had gone.

Like the Juncal campsite, the hedged-in estate was spotted with large patches of blood-drenched grass. All the spots were marked by stakes with red flags. The bodies had obviously drained of blood where they fell; holes from nine-inch teeth would have caused that to happen very quickly. That was obviously the reason there was never a trail of blood to follow. Though it was a savage panorama, the absence of bodies made it possible to concentrate on the predators and not the prey. Grand wondered if the cats always brought kills back to their caves. He couldn't imagine that they were challenged by other predators. Perhaps they brought the food back to share with older cats or cats that had unsuccessful hunts in the colder times. If so, it suggested a level of socialization far greater than modern cats possessed. He had to study these creatures at greater length.

There were also the remains of roasts in the open fire pits, though the food was untouched. That didn't surprise him. Most animals in the wild did not eat cooked meat.

Lieutenant Mindar had arrived minutes before. He did not look happy as he greeted the two men. He took a moment to introduce them to young, blond LAPD commander Heeger, who was in charge of the police side of the investigation. Heeger was standing by the rear gate and was on the radio, talking to his field commanders. As Mindar walked Grand and Gearhart toward the pool, he informed them that Chief of Police Gus Maller was conferring about the next course of action with Mayor Greenburg and with Deputy Chief Janet Dumaman of Beverly Hills Operations and Deputy Chief Kurt Maser of Wilshire Operations, which included the area around La Brea.

"I was afraid of that," Sheriff Gearhart said. "They've got the timid leading the incompetent."

"What does that mean?" Grand asked.

"It means that for now, Professor, the sheriff and myself are on the sidelines," Mindar told him. "The Los Angeles city charter stipulates that the mayor has to declare a level-one state of emergency before the governor can order the National Guard to run security and logistics and also authorize law officers from other counties to become involved in an operation."

"What will change their minds?"

"I don't know," Mindar said. "The chief of police is tight with the mayor. He's apparently convinced him that we should make a stand here in the hills, stop whatever is out there before it reaches downtown."

"It didn't work in Santa Barbara but let's try it again here," Gearhart said. "Show Gearhart how it's done. The bastards. That's the police chief's fuck-you to me."

"Not entirely," Mindar said. "The chief is also concerned that if we move in prematurely with our trucks and hardware, it could cause panic worse than the actual attack. Cars jamming the freeways, end-of-the-world parties, looting—"

"Are they at least evacuating people from the area around the tar pits?" Grand asked.

"Just from the Page Museum itself," Mindar said.

"That's not good enough—"

"They feel that if there is an attack in the area, night staff, cleaners, and security personnel in surrounding buildings are probably safer being inside than out," Mindar said.

"They're wrong. Don't they realize these cats are used to moving through tunnels?"

"Actually, it's worse than that," Mindar said. "They also won't shut down Wilshire Boulevard without a damn good reason."

"Isn't *this* reason enough?" Grand asked, sweeping an arm toward the blood-stained yard.

"Frankly, Professor, part of the problem—a big part—is that the head scientists at the Page Museum and USC don't believe there *are* saber-tooth tigers roaming the hills," Mindar added. "They aren't signing on to your idea that their destination is the tar pits."

"This is unbelievable," Grand said. "You've got five specimens up on Monte Arido!"

"Five specimens that only you and Hannah Hughes think are saber-tooths," Gearhart pointed out. "I still think they could be mutations, maybe lab hybrids or bad clones running around out there."

"They're not. I saw where they came from, where they were frozen."

"In any case, a paleontologist from UCLA is en route to examine the specimens," Mindar said.

"That's an hour or more, wasted. What about transmitting video?"

"We can't," Mindar said. "Our uplink signal could be picked off. In fact, as soon as news choppers started snooping around we had to tarp the tigers over. The governor and his advisors don't want those images getting on the news. Until there's a positive ID the police want to remain open to the possibility that they're escaped tigers."

"Escaped from where?" Grand said.

"There are a number of licensed, private owners throughout counties all the way up to Frisco," Gearhart said. "Big cats are the chic thing to own. Kitties of the rich and famous."

Grand couldn't believe what he was hearing.

"If it's any consolation, Professor," Mindar said, "Police Chief Maller has taken the precaution of moving several barrels of tar to the site, in case they okay your plan."

"I hope there's time for all this caution," Grand said.

"For once, we agree on something," Gearhart pointed out. "Welcome to why I run my town the way I do."

Grand ignored him. "Lieutenant, do you have any idea how many people were carried off?"

"According to the guest list at the front gate there were eighteen people here when the cats struck," Mindar said. "The guest who found the massacre didn't see how many animals there were, and he only caught a glimpse of a few of them as they moved through the hills carrying a body each."

It would have taken most if not all of the rest of the pride to kill and then make off with twenty people. Obviously, the cats were staying together for the rest of their journey. Some of the cats would have had to make two trips, so wherever they came from couldn't be far away.

Grand looked out at the hills. He saw a few flashlights bobbing beyond the top of the hedges. "I've got to get out there and try to find out which way the cats might have gone."

"We've already got a small army out there looking for blood, footprints, pipes, large earthen openings of any kind," Mindar said.

"I know. I'd like to go anyway."

Mindar looked at Gearhart. The sheriff nodded.

"All right," Mindar said. "But we've got to do this through channels. Let me get an okay from Commander Heeger."

The lieutenant jogged over to Heeger and the men chatted briefly. When Mindar came back he called over an aide.

"Commander Heeger had no problem with you going out as long as you stay out of the way of his people," Mindar told Grand.

"No problem," Grand said. They were in the wrong place anyway.

Mindar asked his aide for a radio and a flashlight. The young man ran off to the Jeep to get them.

"The commander will let the field commander know you're coming out," Mindar said. "He doesn't want anyone mistaking you for a cat."

"Thanks." Grand looked at Sheriff Gearhart. "Would you care to come along?"

"I'll leave the zoological police work to you," Gearhart said. The sheriff looked at Mindar. "I want to go to the tar pits, see what kind of preparations they're taking. I've still got friends on the force. I want to see if I can ratchet things up a bit."

Mindar's eyes shifted to the tail hanging from Gearhart's belt. "There'll be press down at the tar pits too. You should probably put that away."

Gearhart raised it slightly. "It stays. It's like we used to do with Cong scalps in 'Nam."

"This isn't Vietnam."

"It will be before the night's through," Gearhart said confidently. "Saigon, Day Omega. People shitting and running when they see what's coming at them."

"It's your ass," Mindar warned. "The press will eat it up."

"I've seen teeth today," Gearhart said. "These people are amateurs."

The lieutenant shook his head slowly, then called over a guardsman to give Gearhart a lift to the tar pits. Grand suddenly understood something about Gearhart. He didn't care about his town. He cared about his *side*. Those who were on it got his support and protection. Those who weren't were his enemies. There was no middle ground.

As Gearhart left Mindar's aide returned with the flashlight and radio. He gave them to Grand.

Mindar looked at the scientist. "Let me know what you find out there."

"I will." Grand said. "Thanks for your help."

"Sure. I wish it were more. I truly do."

Grand thanked him. As the scientist walked toward the gate at the back of the estate, he felt as though he were having an out-of-body experience. He was watching things happen with an inevitability and momentum he couldn't stop. Bureaucracy, politics, territorialism, fear, misinformation, stupidity—everything bad was coming together to make the worst possible decisions. But he couldn't allow himself to focus on that. He had to try and find out where the cats were and then get to the tar pits. He had a very bad feeling that if the cats did show up, tranquilizing them would be the last thing on the minds of the LAPD. Especially if Gearhart had anything to say about it. He had to convince them otherwise, even if it meant taking point in any attack and trying to save at least one or two of the cats.

Heeger let Grand out and alerted his own units that the scientist would be moving through the hills. Flashlights poked through the trees and brush while a police helicopter and the Chinook circled the hills, its spotlight blanching the color from the trees and rocks. Despite Mindar's claim that they were being as careful as possible, the officers were crunching loud enough for Grand to hear and they were all walking upwind. If the cats were out there, these people didn't stand a chance. And while the officers were all over the map, they had missed two things. First, they should be concentrating on the southwest. The wind was blowing in that direction from the estate. Though wild animals shied from cooked meat, the smell coming from the fire pits might have attracted the cats. The second thing they should be focusing on was high ground. Animals preferred to run on level or downward-sloping ground to conserve energy and build up speed.

Rather than give the others an education, Grand looked around the surrounding hills.

There was a stilt-house under construction on a lot overlooking the estate, about two hundred yards up. It was in the right place and there was a high pile of dirt near the foundation. Grand made his way to the site and approached the mound. There appeared to be remnants of claw marks in the loosely packed earth. He walked around to the other side.

Sewer pipes lay beside the foundation. The ground had been dug to connect them to the main pipelines. The hole was about five feet high and went under Coldwater Canyon. He could hear the distant sound of water, possibly sewage in the main pipe or water draining from the hills.

Grand ducked down and looked in. The opening was five feet across. He didn't feel the presence of the saber-tooths the way he had before. He listened and heard nothing. He turned the flashlight from the opening, let it play over the house and through the surrounding hills. He didn't see any eyes, a flanking cat watching him. That wasn't a good sign. If he didn't find one inside, then maybe the pride had already moved on.

Holding the flashlight in one hand, Grand crawled in.

The tunnel was snug and when Grand hit basalt, the walls became extremely tight and jagged. He was in an earthquake fissure where the rock had simply split. The saber-tooths obviously had the capacity of a modern-day cat to twist and slink through tight places. The adaptability of the animals was astonishing. They had to have been hunted out of existence. No wonder humans were an irresistible target. Food plus one less enemy to deal with.

After a few minutes Grand found a diamond bracelet on the ground, then large pieces of bone and clothing. Then he saw human hands and feet. His fears were confirmed: The cats had eaten and moved on. That was uncharacteristic of large migrating predators and it seemed to be uncharacteristic of what he'd seen these cats do. He wondered if the saber-tooths could possibly have smelled the tar from here or whether they were moving along a path they had moved eons ago—perhaps only days before, to them.

Or was it something else?

Grand tried to raise Lieutenant Mindar but the signal wasn't getting out of the cave. He edged around the body parts and continued on. After a few minutes he found the sewer conduit. It was a thick white pipe set in the soil overhead and held there with bands bolted into the surrounding rock, flat steel sheets that gave the pipe play whenever the earth shook. The pipes were intact and the water sounds weren't coming from there. They were coming from somewhere ahead. An underground stream, probably, flush with rain water from La Niña.

One that could lead to drain pipes, caverns, or God knows where else, he thought. His plan might not work. Not if they'd already dispersed into two or even three separate groups. Unfortunately, he had no way of knowing.

It was a long way from Monte Arido to the Hollywood Hills, but maybe the cats hadn't bothered to rest tonight. The creatures were at home in water. They might have heard the stream and decided to move on. It would certainly make the journey quicker and easier.

But why go now? What was so urgent? Were they afraid of losing a particular tar pit to another pride? Were there actually two prides continuing a struggle, a race, that had begun millennia ago? Or had something else pushed them on? Fear? Did they sense an earthquake coming or maybe a larger predator of some kind? Had something happened within the pride? The pride probably had a leader. Was he young or old, fit or dying? Maybe he was hurt in the long-ago holocaust. The saber-tooth Grand fought had been scarred. Perhaps the leader was being threatened by another male and felt compelled to bring his pride home.

Grand backed out. He felt more anxious than he did when he knew the cats were near. For whatever reason, the saber-tooths were making the final part of their journey tonight. There wasn't time to research, check, double-check, and confer. There might not even be time to coat a tunnel with tar. The saber-tooths could be there in a matter of minutes. The area had to be completely evacuated and police had to be set up around the pits *now.*

The scientist got on the radio as he returned to the mansion.

"Lieutenant," he said.

"Here, Professor."

"I found body parts in one of the tunnels I checked, but no cats."

"What does that mean?"

"They moved on," Grand said. "They probably saw or heard all the activity and wanted to get to familiar territory as soon as possible. You've *got* to inform whoever's in charge there may not be time to set a trap for the saber-tooths. Tell them to cordon off the entire area around the tar pits and fall back as far as they can."

"Why?"

"Because those cats may get there in just a few minutes, coming at them in ways they can't begin to imagine!"

70

Millennia ago, as plants and animals died, their remnants became buried beneath wind-blown sand and water-borne rock. Over time, pressure caused the incompletely decomposed material to mix with sediments to form petroleum. Over the eons, this thick liquid—its composition varying from location to location—was covered over by streams and seas, by volcanism and earthquakes, by storms and other upheavals. The pools of petroleum ended up hundreds, sometimes thousands, of feet beneath the surface of the earth.

The planet's crust continued to shift over the eons, causing cracks and folds in the overlying rock. Occasionally, superheated gases from inside the earth would force the petroleum to the surface through these slender cracks. Often, the gases would mix with this petroleum creating a brownish-black mixture called asphalt, commonly referred to as tar.

The same forces that made Southern California and the adjoining seabed rich with oil made many of the low-lying areas rich with tar. A gradual warming of the climate caused many of the beds to harden and dry up. However, several remained active, the largest of which was the sprawling Rancho La Brea—Spanish for "the Tar Ranch." Late in the nineteenth century and on into the twentieth, many of the pits on the ranch were pumped dry of tar, which was sold for use in paving, sealing, and other commercial enterprises. But in one twenty-three-acre section the earth still forced tar to the surface, a process that continues to this day. Like their ancient forebears, animals still occasionally tumble into the pit, squirrels and dogs, insects and birds. Sucked into the tar, along with plastic water bottles and litter, the animals will lose their soft body parts to bacteria and time, though their bones and teeth—enveloped in tar—will one day return as the earth cycles through the percolation process.

Some of the smaller active tar pits are surrounded by concrete fences and occasionally blow large bubbles over the walls. Others are redirected through concrete and metal viaducts into the larger pits. Roads and construction have risen on top of many of these. The larger, open tar pools sit where they always have, impervious to the encroachment of civilization, ready to swallow human enterprise as they have hundreds of thousands of animals over the centuries.

The main thoroughfare of the area, Wilshire Boulevard, runs directly beside the largest of the many open pits, the Lake Pit. The Lake Pit is situated in the heart of the rich Miracle Mile, renowned for its upscale shopping, dining, and fashionable office towers. Behind the pit is the recently renovated George C. Page Museum of La Brea Discoveries, home to fossil displays, reconstructions of Pleistocene animals, paleontological research, and a spectacular atrium. The museum is named for the businessman-philanthropist who endowed the facility. Ongoing excavations take place in a series of smaller active pits that sit to the west, at the intersection of Ogden and Sixth Streets. To the west of the tar pits is the renowned Los Angeles County Museum of Art.

As an access to the vital San Diego Freeway, Wilshire Boulevard was a busy thoroughfare around the clock, and when Hannah and the Wall arrived, the reporter was surprised to find nothing different as she approached the museum. It wasn't until she arrived and saw reporters that anything looked different. The museum is set back from Wilshire, behind the Lake Pit and several acres of rolling green grounds. The wide, low, one-story white-brick museum is accessible by a flight of stairs guarded by saber-toothed statues. To the west the white sculptures stand alert on their pedestal looking to the east. They appear to be watching the other statue, a pair of saber-tooths locked in feral combat.

According to Hannah's LA stringer, reporters had gotten wind of an increased police presence at the museum and had collected on the spotlit walk between the two sculptures. Hannah told him to stay with the Coldwater situation, that she was headed for the tar pits. She and the Wall parked in the lot behind the museum, on Sixth Street. Telling the Wall to leave the art portfolio in which she'd stuck the charts and diagrams in the car, she hurried ahead to join the others. She looked for Grand at the front of the museum but she didn't see him. There were a few police officers present, but they were in street uniforms, not riot gear or body armor. She didn't sense any urgency. A few reporters were sitting at the picnic tables in front of the museum, drinking coffee.

Hannah called Grand. He picked up at once.

"Jim, where are you? I tried you before but couldn't get you!"

"That must have been when I was in the sewer tunnel up at Coldwater," Grand said. "I'm on my way down the hill with Lieutenant Mindar and some of his National Guard personnel. We're just crossing Santa Monica Boulevard. Where are you?"

"At the museum. What did you find up there?"

"The saber-tooths are on the move," Grand said. "They'll probably reach the tar pits in a matter of minutes."

Hannah looked around. "Does anyone know that? I mean, no one's acting like we have an emergency here."

"The lieutenant is talking to the police chief now. You've got to get out of there."

Just then Hannah saw a flatbed truck stop on Curson. The shield on the door marked it as belonging to the LAPD Anti-Terrorist Division. She saw Sheriff Gearhart standing on the back with a group of seven police officers. They were standing amidst a half-dozen waist-high black barrels. Unlike the other reporters, Hannah knew what was probably in there.

"Gearhart just got here," she said. "Probably with some of his old buddies. Looks like they're bringing barrels somewhere."

"That's probably tar," Grand said. "Hannah, don't worry about him. Just get out—"

"I'll be okay, Jim. I'll call back as soon as I know something."

Hannah clicked off and ran over with the Wall.

Gearhart's back was to Hannah. He was studying a map spread on one of the drums. There were equipment chests along the back of the cab. Gearhart didn't turn until one of the police officers looked past him. The sheriff frowned as he looked down on the young woman.

"Go back with the rest of the press," Gearhart said.

"Jim just told me the cats are on the way."

"We know. We got a report from Lieutenant Mindar. Now get out—" Gearhart suddenly looked across the street. "Shit."

Other reporters had noticed the truck and were starting to wander over.

Gearhart rapped hard on the back of the cab. "Let's get moving!" he shouted. "We'll take this to W-17."

Hannah grasped the wooden slats on the side of the truck. She pulled herself up as the truck rolled out.

"Whoa, stop!" Gearhart yelled to the driver.

Hannah pulled herself higher onto the truck. Two officers grabbed her arms and tried to lift her off and move her backwards. Hannah held on tighter, slipping one of her feet between the slats and hooking it around. The Wall ran over to catch her in case she fell.

"Get off!" Gearhart yelled at her.

"W-17!" Hannah shouted at Gearhart. "They're antiterrorism coordinates, right?"

"I said get off—"

She jerked a thumb behind her. "I'm sure one of those reporters will be able to find out where that is. Take me with you or I'll tell them."

Gearhart looked past Hannah. The reporters were now hustling across the museum lawn. "Pull her up and let's go!" the sheriff said.

The officers who were holding Hannah's arms pulled her onto the truck. The Wall remained behind, shouting for Hannah to be careful as the police team roared off.

Gearhart bent back over the map as the truck crossed Wilshire and headed south. He was pointing to a small square on the grid. "W-17 intersects the underground stream that starts up in the Hills. It looks like the only secure spot we can tap into."

His companion, a captain, pointed to the map. "We've got these other tributaries—"

"I know," Grand said. "If we don't stop all the cats at W-17, they'll probably continue along the main stream and come out here," he pointed to a square seven blocks away, "at a construction site at the corner of Western and Olympic."

"They can do a lot of damage doubling back from there to the tar pits," the captain pointed out.

"Exactly. So we lure the cats into the garage and pin them down. It should be a skeet shoot."

Captain McIver nodded. "I'm with you."

"Good," Gearhart said. He turned and glared at Hannah. "You want this story?"

"You know I do." She pulled her microcassette recorder from a back pocket.

"No moneybags to hide behind, no safe and comfortable press conferences where you can push people around."

"That's not me and you damn well know it," Hannah said.

"I don't know it."

"I'd rather be in the field covering a story," she told him.

"Fine." Gearhart came closer to her.

"I didn't come to Los Angeles for glory or to win allies. I came here to finish what I started. To protect people. I don't want any bleeding-heart bullshit from you. I didn't come here to carry out Jim Grand's agenda. There's no time to get tranquilizer darts. The cats are to me what I am to them: prey. Got that?"

"In quotes," she replied.

Gearhart backed away and Hannah looked into his eyes. They were more intense than she'd ever seen them. As they swung into the entrance to the Wilshire Courtyard office complex, she didn't doubt what he'd said. He was back to save Los Angeles, to do it in a way his old bosses could not. There was nothing wrong with that, but to call it civil service wasn't exactly right. It was also payback.

Still, for now, she'd let him have this his way.

The truck turned down the long, gently sloping ramp into the yellow-lit darkness. The driver stopped to give the night watchman the emergency order that would allow them to do what had to be done. The guard was instructed to let no one else down without first checking with Captain McIver, and not to bother checking if they were reporters.

Only as they continued down, toward level P3, and one of the officers opened the first of the four equipment chests did Hannah begin to realize that she was in this not with Jim Grand, a man who understood his quarry, but with Malcolm Gearhart, a man who understood firepower.

She wondered if that would be enough.

71

While the Anti-Terrorist team had been driving from the museum, the communications officer in the passenger's seat had used the dashboard computer to access the blueprints for the six-story redbrick office complex. It indicated that the foundation had been poured twenty yards north of a "stable thrust." That was the stationary side of a rift created when the ground to the south had pulled away at some time in the past. Though earthquakes had rent the ground since then, and the foundation had to be patched several times, the integrity of the building itself had been unaffected. However, building records indicated that several large cracks had split from the main fissure. Gearhart told Hannah he hoped they'd be large enough for the men—and the cats—to enter.

True to his word, the sheriff was tolerating, even cooperating with Hannah. She couldn't help but wonder if his changed attitude had to do with wanting his story told at home or the fact that Gearhart perceived her as being tight with Jim Grand. It could be a control thing. Or maybe, she thought, it was something else: vulnerability. Like a knight going into battle, maybe it made him feel better having a lady's colors on his lance.

That plus the tiger's tail, she thought with a flash of disgust. It was funny how both Gearhart and Grand were warriors, yet they were so, so different.

The truck rattled over a large drain grate. Reaching a spot in the corner of the lowest section of the garage, Gearhart and three other officers began unloading MP5s—heavy duty automatics. Meanwhile, the gray-haired Captain McIver handed his com-officer a portable ultrasound unit. The beam-forming unit, which was used in detecting solid masses like bombs and rifles in luggage, vehicles, or buildings, looked like a large oxygen tank with a metal-detector-style arm attached to the top and a coaxial cable running from the bottom. The cable ran to a small color-TV monitor mounted in one of the equipment chests. The com-officer held the arm in front of him, positioning its flat "hand" a few inches above the concrete and slowly running it back and forth over the ground. Thick lines began to slash across the monitor, filling it in from top to bottom as it built a picture of the subsurface geology.

After several minutes, he found what looked like a fissure. It started close to the foundation of the building and almost certainly to the main fissure. He concentrated on mapping the small section so they'd know just where to go through the floor.

Once the weapons were unloaded, one of the police officers removed a jackhammer from the locker while two officers plus Gearhart began breaking out the tactical gear they'd need: high-intensity flashlights; "Scott packs," small, self-contained breathing apparatuses with two one-hour bottles of air; a hundred-foot, half-inch nylon life-line which would be strung between the men; heavy electrical gloves in case any underground cables were broken during the ingress; and protective blue "Fritz" hats which were modeled after German army helmets from the 1940s. In the meantime the driver of the truck filled three buckets of tar from a spigot in the side of one of the barrels. Hannah asked the driver what the plan was. He said it was down and dirty: to go as far as possible into the fissure, pour the tar, and wait here for the animals to emerge.

The ultrasound picture was ready in five minutes. It showed a three-foot-wide crack under the floor near the southern wall of the garage. According to the blueprints the concrete was four inches thick. The officer with the jackhammer began punching through. One of the men explained to Hannah that they needed to make an opening large enough for the biggest man and his equipment to fit through easily. That was not so much for ingress as for a quick retreat if it became necessary.

The sound was so crashing-loud it almost seemed solid. Hannah covered her ears, then stepped well away as a cloud of white dust filled the large garage. It turned the police officers, the side of the truck, and the few cars in the vicinity into ghostly, ashen images.

The living looked dead and the dead had come alive. Hannah was starting to feel a little like Gearhart did back at the beach. She couldn't decide whether to write this story as news or myth.

The officer with the jackhammer slowly circled the spot he was working on, pounding away at the lip. Chunks broke off and fell into the fissure below. Eventually, a jagged hole opened up that was nearly four feet across. When the officer was finished, Gearhart made sure the mouthpiece of his Scott pack was securely in place, then he moved forward. The sheriff lay on his chest at the edge of the hole, shined a flashlight down, and moved it around. The beam created what looked like a white starburst above the hole, its glow illuminating countless particles of dust. A few moments later Gearhart nodded to the two men who were waiting. The sheriff slid into the opening as the officers came over carrying the tar buckets and their automatic weapons.

Small pieces of concrete fell in as Gearhart dropped down. His weapon and belt scratched against the ragged opening. After all the jackhammering, every sound seemed like the treble was turned way up.

Hannah walked closer to the hole as the buckets were handed down to Gearhart. Her shoes squeaked and her eyes were misty from the dust. She drew her lapel over her mouth to serve as a filter.

The second police officer went down, and then the third. The remaining three men removed their own MP5s from the equipment locker. They also wore service revolvers. They moved behind the truck and waited.

Hannah joined them. Only then did it hit her: The men had gone down to draw the tigers here, to this place.

She had faith in Gearhart; he'd killed a small group of the animals before. But she'd also seen what the tigers could do. And as she stood there waiting, listening to the men make their way through the fissure, she couldn't help but wonder if she'd be around to write her story in any form.

72

Gearhart was leading the way with the flashlight in his left hand and the MP5 in his right. The other two officers were carrying a bucket of tar each and their weapons. The smell of the tar was strong here. He'd be very surprised if the tigers didn't pick it up.

The fissure was low and extremely narrow. Gearhart had to walk sideways with his head bent almost into his chest, the MP5 pointing ahead but riding on his hip. Gearhart hadn't anticipated that the air inside would be so cloudy with dust from the jackhammer; his movements were stop-and-start rather than fluid as rocks poked him on all sides. It was awkward for him, and claustrophobic. He was accustomed to open spaces. After moving several yards into the fissure, the sheriff felt the temperature drop. They must have just passed from under the office building. Gearhart still couldn't hear the water but the air felt thick as well as cool on the exposed skin of his face and neck.

Finally, the air cleared. The sheriff could see the tunnel ahead curving in a gentle S-shape, first to the right and then to the left. The walls were rough, covered with short spikelike rocks, and the passageway was wider at the top than at the bottom. In some places it felt as if there was no bottom, really, just a wedge where the walls came together. The fissure reminded Gearhart of a muffin someone had fork-split but hadn't pulled apart.

The three men walked for several minutes without seeing or hearing anything other than rock and their own footsteps. Then, suddenly, the fissure ended as the walls came together in a V-shaped dead end.

Gearhart shined the light around the wall. There was no way up, down, or to the sides.

Shit.

Gearhart motioned for the men to go back. Rather than trying to turn with the guns and buckets, the men decided to simply sidle back. Suddenly, the officer on the outside stopped. He listened for a moment, then put the bucket down and removed his mouthpiece.

"I heard something," he said quietly.

Gearhart slipped out his own mouthpiece and let it hang under his chin. "Don't move," he said to the others.

There was definitely movement behind them. Scratching sounds, like fingernails on a screen door.

How? Gearhart wondered. The only way in was through the garage. And if the cats had somehow come in that way they would have heard shouts, gunfire, *something.*

And then Gearhart realized what must have happened. There may have been an opening near the hole itself, one that they'd missed because it was hidden by dust. One that the ultrasound hadn't read because it was outside the building. Or maybe the damn cats were clawing through the wall. Grand had said the bastards were smart. The sheriff felt like he did whenever a Hanoi Two-Fuck had been triggered: as if there was nothing to do but wait.

There was no way out and, worse, they had the tar. The cats had to smell it. Because of the way the officers were positioned—one man behind the other—only the outermost officer would be able to fire. If the first tiger didn't go down right away, it could still get one or more of them. Then the others would be able to finish them off.

To hell with this, Gearhart decided.

"Captain!"

"Sheriff?" came the distant reply.

"We're backed into a dead end and the cats are near the opening!" Gearhart shouted.

"Fuck!" McIver shouted. "Sit tight! We're—"

McIver fell silent.

"Captain!" Gearhart yelled.

"Something's going on," McIver shouted down.

Gearhart listened as the scratching came closer. The two officers looked back at him. He wished he could switch places with them, take point. But there wasn't enough room to get around them. He pulled off his gloves. He wanted to feel the metal of the weapon, the gentle kick, if he had to use it.

And then Gearhart heard something he wasn't expecting.

Gunfire. In the garage.

73

A crowd of nearly twenty reporters had run after the LAPD truck. The group was cut off by police and forced away from Wilshire. None of the reporters believed the police when they said they had no idea what the Anti-Terrorist unit was doing in the garage. The situation did not improve when the small National Guard convoy from the Hollywood Hills rolled down Curson.

Of all the press people only the Wall managed to get to the Wilshire Courtyard. He had crossed Curson after the police truck left and hid behind the pedestaled bust of Miracle Mile founder and developer A. W. Ross. While he was there, the Wall phoned Grand and told him exactly where Hannah had gone. Then, as the police were busy moving everyone else back to the museum entrance, the Wall was able to sneak across Wilshire.

The photographer went to the garage entrance. There was a security camera on the left, right beside the electrical closet. As the Wall walked down the ramp to the guard gate in the center of the two-lane road, the security officer stepped out to stop him.

"I'm going to lose my job if I don't get down there," the Wall lied.

"So will I, if you do," the security officer told him.

Just then the National Guard vehicles arrived. The four Jeeps swung through the entranceway and down to the gate.

Mindar was sitting in the back of the first Jeep with Grand. "Open up!" he yelled, rising in the seat. The other Jeeps lined up behind the officer's vehicle, their engines growling.

"Lieutenant, the police captain told me—"

"Now," Mindar said.

The guard ducked back into the booth to raise the black-and-white-striped bar. As he did, Grand yelled over to the Wall.

"There was an electrical closet back at the entrance," Grand said.

"I saw it—"

"Get in there and crank up the emergency lights," Grand said. "Do anything you can to make it bright down there."

"Will do," he said.

As the photographer relayed Grand's instructions to the guard, the convoy charged down the ramp.

Grand was no longer feeling disconnected. He could feel the cats, the sense of danger, the impending confrontation. In the midst of it all, he could also feel Hannah. There was nothing mystical about that. She was brave, she was impetuous, and she was someone he cared about very much. His jaw was locked, his fists were hard, and the muscles of his arm were coiled tight. The Jeep couldn't get down the ramp fast enough.

As the convoy approached P3, they were greeted by a thin fog of dust. When Grand saw Hannah and the other officers crouching behind the flatbed truck, he leaped from the still-moving Jeep and ran over.

"Jim!" Hannah cried in a loud whisper.

He crouched behind her as one of the policemen, a captain, was telling whoever was in the hole to sit tight.

"What's happening?" Grand asked Hannah.

"We think the tigers came in through a side cavern and they may have Gearhart and two men pinned."

Grand didn't wait to hear more. Still squatting, he stepped around Hannah. "Captain, let me have your pistol."

"Who the hell are you?" the officer asked.

There wasn't time to discuss this. Grand reached for the 9-mm pistol, pushing the butt down to release the holster's internal safety catch before pulling up. He ran around the truck to the side facing the hole. There, he quickly emptied the full clip into the two drums that were facing him.

Tar sprayed from the large, raw holes.

"Lieutenant Mindar!"

"Here!"

"Turn the Jeeps sideways on the ramp and then back everyone out!" Grand yelled.

"Jim!" Hannah yelled. "What are you going to do?"

There wasn't time to answer. "Flashlight!" he called back to the police officers.

One of the men tossed him a flashlight. Grand caught it and ran to the hole as the tar pooled and began dripping over the rim.

Grand dropped next to the opening. "Gearhart, can you hear me?"

"I hear you!"

"What's happening?"

"Your tigers are coming!" Gearhart said.

"How many?"

"I can only see the first one," the sheriff said. "A big bastard."

"Bigger than the ones on Monte Arido?"

"Definitely. A seven footer, maybe bigger. It's got a ridge of hair on its back, like a Mohawk. The teeth are longer, more curved."

The cat was a male. Grand wondered if it was the men, the tar, or something else the saber-tooth was after.

"He's coming through an S-turn," Gearhart said. "We don't have a clear shot yet."

"Are you backed as far away as you can go?"

"Yes," Gearhart told him.

"Do you have tar?"

"Two buckets."

"Spill them now," Grand told him, "as far along the floor as you can. The cat may not realize it's only a few inches deep. It might not want to risk crossing."

Grand listened as the men did what he said.

"And keep your lights turned ahead," Grand added. "The saber-tooths don't like the light."

Just then the dusty garage grew much brighter. The emergency spotlights came on in the corners and from several of the support columns. The Wall had done his job. Now Grand had to do his. He had to get the cats out of the fissure and back whichever way they'd come. He stood and looked around. He noticed the equipment locker on the truck, saw the open case marked EMERGENCY AIR SUPPLY. He turned back toward the hole.

"Sheriff," Grand shouted, "do you have air tanks down there?"

"Yes—"

"Put them on." Grand turned to the police officers and yelled, "Someone get me a lighter and someone else get a fire extinguisher. And you better call for backup. If they turn on us, we'll need it."

The idea of fighting the saber-tooths with guns sickened him, but there were over twenty lives at risk. He prayed the cats would retreat, give him time to find a nonlethal solution.

The captain slid a Bic lighter across the floor while one of the police officers grabbed an extinguisher from the back of the truck. Grand went over to the truck, pulled the maps from the back, and went to the hole. The officer gave the extinguisher to Grand. He set it near the hole.

The leaking tar had begun to spill over the edge of the hole. Grand slid inside. The air was still thick with concrete dust and he held his breath. He lay the maps on the tar and removed his jacket. He placed those on top of the maps. Then he ignited the maps beneath the jacket. Neither the garment nor the tar would burn, though the maps would cause the tar to smoke. Grand hoped he was right about fires possibly having chased the cats into the hills. If so, they would vividly remember the smell of burning pulp and hot tar.

Grand squatted beside the jacket. He could hear the scratching of claws, the low breathing of the cats. The saber-tooths weren't far behind. Thick gray smoke began to seep from around the jacket. Grand raised one end slightly and with slow, rhythmic movements began fanning the smoke into the tunnel.

Time had become completely distorted. Millennia had been condensed into days; day and night had run together; and now seconds seemed eternal as he watched the smoke float down the fissure. He shouldn't need a lot of it. Computer reconstructions of their nasal cavities suggested that the saber-tooths had an olfactory sense equivalent to modern-day lions. Like prey, they should smell the smoke almost at once—

"Grand, the cat stopped coming!" Gearhart yelled. "What are you doing back there?"

"Get back on your air!" Grand shouted. "I started a fire! The cats will probably leave the way they came."

Grand listened as the scratching suddenly stopped. He heard low growls, like the sounds Fluffy made whenever he thought he heard someone coming toward the front door. After a moment the scratching resumed.

It was coming toward him.

Grand lifted the jacket so the cats would feel the heat of the fire, smell the smoke more intensely. He stood in the opening. He pulled himself up, lay on his belly, and continued to look down. As the tar smoldered, the smoke became darker and thicker.

"They're leaving!" Gearhart called out.

"Give them some time and stay on your air," Grand said. "There's heavy smoke coming."

The growling stopped and the scraping grew quieter. After a few moments, Grand heard movement—footsteps on loose rock, belts and gear hitting rock. The men were coming out.

Smoke was rising from the hole now. Grand pulled out his handkerchief and put it in front of his mouth. Then he turned and motioned toward the police. Captain McIver ran over with another man. Both squatted beside Grand, their MP5s turned toward the opening.

"Your men are coming," Grand said through the handkerchief. "We're going to have to get them out quickly and then figure out where the saber-tooths are headed."

"You burned the maps," McIver said.

"Hannah has copies," Grand said.

Just then the first of the police officers appeared through the dark gray smoke. They were staggering. Unlike full-face masks used by firefighters, Scott packs don't filter out smoke entirely. Grand grabbed the fire extinguisher and turned the hose down the hole, on the fire. When he was done, he set the extinguisher behind him, by the truck. The policeman with McIver gave the man a hand getting out and then helped him away. McIver helped the second man out and led him back to the truck. Then Gearhart appeared. The sheriff hesitated.

"Come on!" Grand said.

Gearhart pulled out his mouthpiece and let it hang on his chest. He looked up at Grand. "I can't run from them," he said. There was something almost plaintive in the way he used it, in his expression.

"We're not running," Grand said. "We're regrouping."

"No," Gearhart said. "Not me."

He turned back and snuggled the MP5 against his shoulder. The dust, which had mostly settled, was kicked up by the men's return and hung around him like mist. There was still smoke in the air from the fire.

"What do you think you can do?" Grand asked.

"Go back and get them," Gearhart said. "There's a wide fissure low on the floor, about twenty yards in. I missed it because of the dust. If we let those animals get away we're going to lose them."

"No," Grand told him. "There are only so many places the saber-tooths can go."

"It'll take time for backup to get here and we can't police them all," Gearhart said. He took a few steps back the way he'd come. The dust swirled gently and the smoke curled around him more thickly before rolling into the fissure.

"Sheriff, don't."

"It'll be okay," he said. "I'll have an advantage. They'll be facing us ass-backwards."

"You don't know that," Grand said. "They leave sentries—"

"Then the sentries will die." Gearhart started forward, the severed tail still swinging from his belt.

The severed tail.

Grand wondered if the smell of the tail had been what brought the cats to that side of the tunnel, not just the tar.

"Wait, Sheriff! *Don't!*"

Gearhart continued ahead.

With an oath Grand held his breath, swung his legs around, and lowered himself into the dusty opening. He ducked down and looked ahead. Gearhart was a dim figure about four feet ahead of him. Grand stepped over the jacket and reached for him.

Suddenly, Gearhart seemed to rise up and fly toward him, as though he'd been lifted and thrown. His gun bounced off into the darkness. Grand jumped back as Gearhart landed hard on the jacket. He was followed by a saber-tooth, its head held low and bucking like an angry elk, its eyes golden slits in the mist. It had a large ridge of hair down its back and its nose was twitching in a way that exposed a row of long, white upper teeth.

It *was* a male. Grand wondered if the tail had belonged to its mate.

"Help down here!" Grand yelled and bent to get his hands under Gearhart's shoulders, pull him away—

The saber-tooth roared and leaped onto Gearhart. He butted Grand back with his head. Grand struck the stone wall hard. Then, opening his huge jaw ninety degrees, the saber-tooth buried his fangs in the sheriff's belly. Gearhart wailed and pushed desperately at the creature's thickly whiskered muzzle with both hands. The saber-tooth didn't seem to notice. It shook its head from side to side, digging through the sheriff's body and then ripping down.

"No!" Grand screamed.

Pushing himself off the sharp stone, the scientist looked around for something he could use against the animal. He saw a long, pointed shard of concrete that had been broken off by the jackhammer and picked up. Holding it in both hands, Grand ran at the creature, managed to squeeze beside it, and drove the makeshift knife down hard at the back of its neck. The tip struck fat wads of muscle. The creature hissed. It sounded like a car tire spinning on ice. The animal lifted its head, tilted it to the side, and snapped at Grand. The scientist hopped to his left, toward the opening. The fangs missed him by less than an inch. Grand seized the moment to grab the front of Gearhart's vest and try to pull him back.

The cat roared and pounced forward, butting Grand back with a big swipe of its head and pinning Gearhart beneath it. The sheriff put his hands on the ground and tried to push himself from under the cat but the cat wouldn't release him. Bits of flesh hung from the creature's fangs as it raised its head and bit down again, this time higher, just below the rib cage. Gearhart screamed, his body spasming as the fangs tore through muscle and bone. His fingers shaking, Gearhart clawed at air, his hands covered with his own blood.

Grand still had the concrete wedge. He was about to charge again when Captain McIver appeared in the opening.

"Stand clear!" he shouted.

Grand froze, then jerked back as the officer fired his MP5 into the cat's head. The saber-tooth's eyes widened and it rose on its hind legs as though it wanted to charge. Its head struck the roof of the fissure, leaving blood on the stone. Then its powerful hind legs just folded; the cat fell back down at Gearhart's feet, lifeless.

The sheriff wasn't breathing either.

"Come on!" McIver said, extending a hand.

One of the other officers arrived then and covered them. Tar was now pouring over the lip.

Grand threw the concrete aside and dropped beside Gearhart. He slipped his hands under the sheriff's broad shoulders and pulled him back under the opening. He stood, still holding the body. Blood was running down the sheriff's legs, pooling with that of the dead cat.

"Help me," Grand said.

McIver reached in. "Aw, shit," he said. "Shit. Shit."

As Grand was passing the sheriff's body out of the hole, he felt a change in the fissure.

Warmth, coming at him in waves.

The fire was extinguished, and the cats smelled death, he thought. *The death of one of their own.*

They were coming.

74

Hannah ran over and dropped beside Grand. She looked down at the mauled body of Malcolm Gearhart.

The sheriff was dead; there wasn't any doubt about that. But Grand knelt beside him anyway, one knee on the ground, feeling frantically for a heartbeat, then for a pulse, then for a sign of breath.

He finally gave up.

"It's not your fault," Hannah said. She had always hoped to write a farewell to Gearhart, but not this way.

"I told him not to go in."

"I know," Hannah said. "But the sheriff had to do things his way. You couldn't change that."

As they bent over Gearhart, McIver sent two officers to collect the body. Then he called for medical teams to be waiting by on Curson. Meanwhile, Mindar's team moved in. The scratching sounds and long, low hisses rose from somewhere below. It sounded to Hannah like a door to hell had opened and unimaginable demons were crawling forth.

The Wall came over but he didn't take any pictures. He stood there with a shellshocked expression and made the sign of the cross as the two officers ran over with a canvas sheet from the back of the truck. They wrapped it tightly around Gearhart's body.

Grand put his arm around Hannah and stood. "Come on. We'd better get back."

Hannah looked out at the soldiers who were forming a skirmish line beside the truck, men squatting in front and others standing behind them.

"I'm sorry about this," Hannah said to Grand.

Grand nodded and hugged her close. Then they, the Wall, and the two police officers carrying Sheriff Gearhart's remains ran forward. There was blood on Grand's hand and forearm. As soon as they got behind the line, Hannah pulled him down and checked to make sure the blood wasn't his.

It wasn't. Grand had stuffed his handkerchief halfway into his pocket. Hannah pulled it out and began wiping the blood away.

The sounds were getting louder. Or maybe they only seemed louder because everything else was so silent.

Captain McIver was standing between his team, which was on the truck, behind the barrels, and the soldier.

"Pick them off as they come out of the hole," Captain McIver said softly. "We don't want to tag the first one and have him fall on the others.

Grand looked anxiously toward the soldiers' backs. He tried to rise but Hannah was still holding his hand. She pulled him down and gently turned his face toward hers.

"Don't watch," she said.

"Hannah, how can I just let this happen?"

"You did everything you could," she said. "It all happened too fast and people are dying."

There was a sound behind her. Hannah turned. It was coming from the drainage grate. It had been too small and indirect for the men to go through. But tigers were not men.

"Jim?"

He looked back.

"When we were on the truck Gearhart said something about tributaries," Hannah said.

"He was right."

"Do you think this room drains into the underground water system?"

"We'd have to check the building plans—"

Just then the heavy iron grate flew from the opening. It spun through the air like a tossed coin and crashed just feet away from them. A golden-furred head appeared in the bright lights. A moment later saber-tooths began leaping into the garage.

75

The Army National Guardsmen turned. So did the police. Before they could fire, more cats rushed them.

"Watch your backs!" Grand yelled.

Still crouching behind the truck, Grand threw himself on top of Hannah to protect her. He managed to steal a quick look back at the Wall, who had gone over to the Jeeps to take a picture of the garage. The photographer leaped behind them when the cats emerged.

When Grand shouted, McIver turned back toward the original hole in the concrete. He saw two more cats running toward them. He swung his weapon around as the cats leaped the truck in a muscular bound and landed on the other side. McIver drove a flurry of bullets into the cat's underbelly and it landed on the truck, amidst the leaking barrels of tar. The other made it across and came down on McIver. The captain fell back, his ribs cracking audibly. The cat simultaneously turned and leaped at the officer standing next to him; the animal's takeoff crushed McIver's pelvis. The officer tried to turn and fire but the cat's fangs pulled his arm away at the shoulder. The man fell and the cat jumped at Grand, who was behind them. He was still lying on top of Hannah, shielding her from cats and bullets.

Grand didn't have a weapon. The only nearby object he might be able to use was the grate.

"Get under the truck!" he yelled at Hannah.

As gunfire exploded around them, Hannah scrambled toward the truck while Grand crawled in the opposite direction. Standing on his knees, he hoisted the heavy grate chest-high, facing out. He thrust it forward as the cat bore down. The saber-tooth's fang struck the iron bars with a clang.

The cat backed away and Grand stayed with it, pushing hard, focusing his *maat*, crying with fury as the cat hissed its own desperate rage. Grand wanted to work the fangs between the bars and trap the creature, leave it helpless until the police got the situation under control and he could tranquilize the animal, save at least one of the saber-tooths. In the midst of everything he was careful to keep the grate head-on. He was afraid that twisting it to one side or the other might cause the fangs to snap off at the gum line.

Suddenly the cat lowered its head and pushed forward, knocking Grand back. The saber-toothed cat put its front paws on the grate, jerked its head back several times, and pulled free of the bars. With a roar, it charged Grand. The scientist rolled under the truck next to Hannah, sliding under just as the saber-tooth swiped at them from the side.

Hannah screamed and hugged Grand, half in fear, half in relief. Grand held her as he looked past her. There were cats and men on the other side, panic and deafening gunfire on all sides. Grand saw the bloodied bodies of several cats and the mangled bodies of at least seven police and National Guardsmen lying side by side under the glare of the emergency lights.

"Do you see the Wall?" Hannah asked anxiously.

"He was over by the Jeeps," Grand said. "I think he's okay—"

Just then, Grand felt hot pain rip against one of his legs. He looked back and saw a huge set of claws. The saber-tooth was working its way under the truck, its large paw on its side and scratching furiously. He squirreled in a little more; going any farther would put Hannah too close to the other side.

Grand needed to find a weapon, something to keep the cat at bay. He noticed the discarded fire extinguisher several yards out on the opposite side. It was lying on its side near the driver's-side door.

Releasing Hannah, Grand crawled toward it. As he emerged, the cat roared and came around the front of the truck, twisting nimbly between the hood and the wall of the garage. Grand reached the fire extinguisher, rolled onto his back, pointed the nozzle, and discharged a snowy burst at the cat. The animal recoiled and shook its head violently. Grand fired again. As he did, gunfire droned from somewhere behind him. The barrage knocked the cat against the wall, pinning it there for a moment. The cat howled with pain and surprise as its tail slapped roughly from side to side. Then it dropped.

Grand's ears rang with the quiet. The air was heavy with the smell of musk and gunpowder.

The scientist crept back to the truck, stretched a hand to Hannah, and helped her out. Hand-in-hand, Grand and Hannah walked to the back of the truck. There were five National Guardsmen still standing. Lieutenant Mindar was one of them. Everyone else, all the policemen, were dead. So were the cats. Blood was leaking from under the bodies of men and saber-tooths, collecting in larger streams and trickling slowly toward the drain.

Mindar walked over to Grand. The lieutenant looked pale. Perhaps he wasn't; perhaps he only seemed that way because of the bright blood splashed on his cheek and forehead. He called for medical assistance and then told two of his men to stand by the holes and watch for more cats.

"Are you okay?" the officer asked Grand and Hannah.

"Sure," Hannah said.

Grand nodded.

Grand excused himself and took a quick walk around the truck where most of the fighting had been centered. Hannah looked toward the exit ramp and saw the Wall standing between two of the Jeeps. She raised her hand weakly. He waved back and started walking toward her. The rest of the surviving National Guardsmen were hurrying around the garage and checking bodies, looking for any sign of life. Not that there was much they could do. The wounds were savage. Some of them appeared to have been caused by friendly fire.

Grand returned suddenly and was about to say something when Captain McIver's radio came on. Mindar retrieved it. The voice on the other end was hot and screaming.

"Captain, this is Lieutenant Carr! Are you receiving?"

Mindar picked up the radio. "Captain McIver is down. This is Lieutenant Mindar of the National—"

"Lieutenant! We're at the public garage on Ogden. We need backup *now!*"

The raspy pops of gunfire came over the radio and drifted down the ramp a moment later.

"What's wrong?" Mindar asked.

"They're like ghosts! Leaping—vanishing! I don't know if we can hold them—"

The radio went silent.

"Lieutenant Carr?" Mindar repeated.

Silence.

"*Lieutenant Carr?*"

"I'm going over," Grand said.

"What the hell is happening there?"

Grand ran toward the exit ramp. "The pride elite have arrived."

76

The dead cats were all seven-footers and all males. Because there was nothing distinctive about them, Grand had suspected the leader was not among the dead. The police report from the museum seemed to confirm that. And the police lieutenant had said there were cats, plural. The Chumash painting showed twelve and only ten cats had been killed so far. That meant the leader had at least one lieutenant.

A quasi-military structure among animal predators. The leader, the general, remaining somewhere else and watching the fight. Participating only when he had to. Some pack dogs and insects like ants had that kind of organization. But for cats to be operating at this level was unprecedented.

Grand reached the ground level and ran across Wilshire. Lieutenant Mindar and three of his soldiers were close behind with Hannah and the Wall running after them. Squads of police were arriving now from Beverly Hills along with deputies from the West Hollywood District Sheriff's Station. They were sealing off the streets and setting up skirmish lines along several blocks on all sides of the tar pits and its surrounding buildings.

Several of them intercepted Hannah and the Wall and kept them from going through. Grand was happy about that, and ignored her shouts for him to get her through. He didn't want to have to worry about her. There was only one thing he wanted to focus on: saving the last of these creatures. He didn't know how, but there had to be a way.

The scientist ran past the Page Museum and then past the Los Angeles County Art Museum. The three-level, concrete parking garage was across the street from the art museum. Grand saw police officers along the lighted sides on all levels, firing into them.

On all levels, he thought. There were more than two cats.

The men were firing into the center of each level, shouting instructions to one another and moving here and there to pin what were obviously very fast-moving creatures. There were columns and parked cars, which were obviously making it difficult for them to hit the creatures.

Grand arrived at the bottom level. Halfway across the garage a chain-link fence had been torn from the concrete wall and crumpled.

"What the hell was there?" Mindar asked.

"A blowpit," Grand said. "I should have thought of that."

"I don't understand—"

"The tar ebbs and flows through underground channels," Grand said. "When the pressure builds, the tar has to vent in a controlled place or it'll come through the street or basements."

"And this is one of those places," Mindar said.

Grand moved closer. The iron lid had been pushed off and the heavy bolts that held the fence to the wall had been ripped out. He was angry at himself not only because he hadn't thought of the blowpits but because the cats always moved in divided, flanking patterns.

As Grand and Mindar reached the northwestern side of the garage they saw a police officer tending to two fallen comrades by the ticket booth, which was forty yards to the west. To the north, in the garage, two other officers were stalking a golden cat that was behind a vintage Wildcat convertible. Grand could just see the animal's forequarters. The cat was larger than the ones they'd seen, with high, powerful shoulders and a low-slung head. The nearest of its fangs was broken off toward the point.

The two officers were moving forward slowly. They were apparently looking to approach the cat from either side of the car.

They never got the chance.

The cat withdrew behind the car. The men continued forward. They were about three yards from the car and three feet apart. A moment later the cat jumped onto the roof and then launched itself onto the officer to the left. Man and cat hit the asphalt and then the saber-tooth twisted and bounded toward the other officer. As the officer turned to fire, the cat tilted its head sideways, the top toward Grand. It bit the officer through the back and his gun fired wild, the bullet ricocheting off the floor and striking one of the cone-shaped support columns. Dragging the howling man forward, the cat swept back toward the first officer. The saber-tooth reared up and landed on the grounded man, crushing his chest. Then it dropped the other man on top of him. The officer writhed for a moment and then was still. The action lasted less than five seconds.

Mindar was still holding his MP5. He raised it to fire but the saber-tooth did not remain where he was. Grand wasn't surprised. If lone predators killed something, they usually left quickly. Scavengers and other predators tended to respond quickly to the scent of blood.

The cat turned to its left and raced toward the low wall that stood between the garage and Ogden. Grand ran with it. The creature leaped the wall easily. With another bound it cleared the chain-link fence outside the garage by vaulting into an overhanging branch of an adjoining tree and then jumping to the street. As the cat landed, Grand looked up. Two other cats were jumping off the second level of the garage, which was fifteen feet from the ground. They landed cleanly on the other side of the fence. For the moment that they were under a streetlight, Grand saw that one of the saber-tooths was the same size as the cat from the ground level. The third was behind the other two and not all of it was visible. But what Grand could see was surprising. The cat towered over the others.

A moment later all three cats ran toward the ten-foot-high fence outside the art museum. The fence was made of thick, green metal bars with nothing to link them on top. If the saber-tooths didn't clear the bars they'd be impaled. Without breaking stride they gracefully leaped the fence and landed on the other side, in the Cantor Sculpture Garden West.

Mindar came up behind Grand. "It's like they've got goddamn wings!" he shouted as he raised his weapon. The metal slats were too close together to allow him to fire. Grand was already running back down Wilshire, alongside the fence, and Mindar ran after him.

The scientist looked to his left as he ran. The saber-tooths had become one with the darkness, maneuvering carefully through the life-size bronzes. They reached the Director's Roundtable Garden, slipped under and around the abstract by Calder, then pressed on to the outer rim of the tar pits. The surrounding fence was six feet high with metal mesh between dark iron bars.

Police were moving in on the east side of the fence. Suddenly, two of the cats leaped the fence in the rear. They raced across the dark lawn toward the museum itself. The third cat seemed to have disappeared. Mindar was looking ahead; Grand didn't think he noticed.

Grand suddenly stopped.

"What are you doing?" Mindar asked.

"There's something I want to check," Grand said. "You go ahead."

Mindar ran to join the police. Grand turned to the fence. He put both hands on top of one of the iron supports and swung his legs over the mesh. He landed on the other side, crouched, and looked around. He heard crashing glass in the distance.

That was probably the atrium, he thought. The saber-tooths may have been heading for the other pits and perhaps saw the familiar foliage. They'd have no idea what glass is. *Or maybe the cats are being decoys again.*

There were roars, gunfire, and shouts. They were followed by screams and more crashing glass. The police moved in en masse. Realizing that the wind was moving toward the east, he moved in that direction so his spoor would blow away from the pit. There were life-size recreations of a family of mastodons on that side of the pit. One of them was "stuck" in the pit and moving slowly from side to side. Its huge tusks were upturned and its trunk was upraised and curled as though it was trumpeting in despair. Two other mastodons were standing on the shore, an adult and a baby.

Two years before—the last time Grand had been to the museum—this pit had been surrounded by small, thick palms. Now it was mostly sun-dried grass and open space, probably someone's idea of making the pit viewer-friendly. There were only two palms near the elephants, roughly twenty and forty feet tall. They had rough bark, like a pineapple.

Grand was still crouching. He got up slowly and walked behind the elephants. There was a rowboat on the shore tied to one of the trees. When the water levels were high enough at the pit, workers used it to fish soda cans and plastic water bottles from the tar. Grand stopped and untied the rope. It was a half-inch thick and about fifteen feet long. There were two oars in the rowboat. He tied the rope to the ends of the oars and draped it over his shoulder. Then he peeled off a large section of bark. All the while he peered into the darkness on the other side of the tar, watching for any sign of the saber-tooth that had stayed behind.

The smell of tar was strong as Grand moved around the edge of the pit. Puddles of water had collected in the center and around the edges of the tar, reflecting the streetlights. Small bubbles of tar popped just offshore while a larger bubble held its dome before bursting in what seemed like slow motion. As Grand rounded the mastodon, spotlights along the perimeter of the park itself began winking out briefly as something passed in front of them. It was large and moving toward him. He stopped beside the taller of the two trees and bent his knees so he'd be ready to move if it attacked. He began breaking the bark into smaller pieces and also used the action to focus his *maat.*

"They're in the atrium!" an officer yelled in the distance. "One of them's in the rafters. We need reinforcements *now!*"

The rafters were a design element, a network of metal struts that crisscrossed the top of the atrium. Police ran up the walk. Grand had known he wouldn't be able to save the other two saber-tooths. But if there was a chance to save this last one, he would.

As the saber-tooth neared Grand, it also came closer to the street. It began picking up hints of streetlight. This was indeed the leader of the pride, at least ten feet in length and just over five feet at the shoulder. Its fur appeared to be silver and there was a long, high ridge of hair running along its back. Like the other cats it held its head low. The saber-tooth also had thick, white whiskers that drooped beside its striated fangs.

The last time Grand faced one of the saber-tooths the cat had a companion. The scientist stole a quick look behind him, just to make sure there was nothing there.

They were alone. That was fitting for Grand, and maybe for the leader of the pride.

Grand turned back to the cat. It was about ten feet away and undistracted by the mastodons. Their unfamiliar odor and inanimacy obviously told him that they were not prey. He put his hands together and began crushing the pieces of bark. He needed to be the resolute hunter, but it was difficult. Grand was still a scientist. This was probably the largest cat that ever lived, a magnificent animal by any standard and something no living human had seen for thousands of years.

What was it thinking? he wondered. *Was it confused, scared?*

The cat certainly didn't show fear. Grand wondered if this pit had been his home, the saber-tooth's private feeding area. Perhaps the leader itself no longer hunted. Perhaps the other cats had gone to fetch prey for it. Offerings for the saber-tooth king.

The gunfire stopped. There was an eerie calm behind the pit. Then, in the distance Grand heard car engines starting, orders being shouted. A moment later the scientist saw a large police recovery van drive up on the walkway and stop between the flagpoles in front of the museum. Police medics ran out carrying stretchers and emergency medical kits. It wouldn't be long before Mindar, the police, or Hannah found him here.

The struggle was over and somehow the giant cat seemed to sense that. The saber-tooth stopped moving. Grand looked into the animal's dark, golden eyes. They seemed to lack the anger, the fire he'd seen in the eyes of the cat at the Juncal campsite.

The cat resumed creeping forward. Perhaps it wanted one last confrontation, to die in battle. Or simply to die. It was both sad and ironic that Grand and the saber-tooth both had the same thing in mind, the cat's survival, and that they have to fight one another to ensure it.

"I want to help you," Grand said softly.

The cat began to growl. There was something hollow, almost mournful in its cry. Grand finished crumbling the bark. His fist was filled with fine, spiky particles. If necessary he'd throw them in the cat's eyes, blind him and get behind him, use the rope and oars to create a tourniquet. Ancient peoples used to use them to tie people to sacrificial altars, twisting the sticks one around the other to make the bonds tighter. If he could get it around the cat's neck and tie it to one of the trees, he might be able to hold it there until it could be sedated—

Suddenly, police officers moved in from the west on foot. They were coming from the direction of the Ogden Street garage, which they'd probably just secured. The police were followed by a phalanx of squad cars, their red and blue roof lights flashing. Each officer was wearing a helmet and body armor and carrying a powerful Mini-14 rifle. Headlights and spotlights from the cars illuminated the street ahead and on both sides.

The northernmost car suddenly stopped. A moment later, so did the others. The squad leader of the foot patrol was in the front of the dozen-or-so officers. She called for the others to stop.

The car crept ahead. The rim of its spotlight had picked out the saber-tooth. As the car moved forward, more and more of the cat fell into the brilliant glow of the light. The saber-tooth's shaggy silver-white fur seemed to shine in the light. Grand, who was standing behind the palm tree and the mastodon replicas, was not visible to the police.

The saber-tooth turned and pawed at the light, roared at the intruders. The long, fierce cry was different from the one it had uttered moments before. This one made the water on the tar pit ripple.

"Shut off the light!" Grand yelled.

Through the two trees the scientist saw the police step back and lower their rifles. He couldn't hear what they were saying but he didn't have to. The rifles were aimed through the mesh of the fence.

Grand ran back along the curving side of the dark pit. "Dammit, *don't shoot!*"

The squad leader saw the scientist. "Hold fire!" she shouted.

The saber-tooth roared again.

"The light!" Grand shouted. "Kill it!"

The leader told the drivers to shut off the spotlights but it was too late. The cat suddenly hunkered back on its haunches and leaped onto the plaster elephant in the tar pit. It landed on the elephant's sloping back, just beyond its head. The gray plaster cracked, revealing the mastodon's iron frame. The saber-tooth crouched again.

"Comin' at us!" the squad leader yelled. "Ready!"

The officers turned on the flashlights attached to the barrels of their rifles. The cat bellowed.

There was a wooden footbridge that crossed the southern end of the pit, just before Wilshire Boulevard. The saber-tooth roared and launched itself toward the bridge.

The squad leader gave the order to fire. Over a half-dozen rifles spat at the animal.

"No!" Grand screamed.

The saber-tooth seemed to freeze as it jumped from the elephant. Spots of red appeared on its underbelly and then the giant toppled from the live-size statue. The cat landed with a dull splash on the side of the pit away from the shore. Ripples of tar rolled toward the sides as the cat's head came down near the hindquarters of the mastodon.

It would take a few minutes for the saber-tooth to sink. Dropping the particles of bark, Grand threw one of the oars up between the tusks of the mastodon. With a bit of maneuvering he was able to lock it between the upraised tusks. Grand waded into the tar and pulled himself out. Even here, with the tar just up to his shins, the suction was extraordinary. Grand climbed up to the elephant's head, slid down to its shoulders, and looked down at the cat. The silverback was lying on its side, struggling ferociously. Blood streamed across the surface of the tar. The more the cat pulled, the deeper it went, its hindquarters lowering first.

Grand removed the oar from the tusks. He untied the rope and made a noose, then held onto the exposed metal framework at the top. He tossed one oar back to shore and used the other to break open the side of the mastodon, exposing more of the support structure. Then he dropped the oar and climbed down the frame until his feet were in the tar. Hooking his arm around one of the struts, he held the rope and opened the noose to its fullest extent, a little over a yard across. He lowered it toward the cat. If he could get the rope over the cat's head he felt he could maneuver it over the forelegs and secure the creature. Then they could secure the animal to the elephant and hopefully get a vet here to deal with the wounds.

Hannah and the Wall had gotten through the relaxed police barricade. They stood behind the police onshore.

The saber-tooth swatted at the rope, and then at Grand. The scientist ignored the raking paw as he struggled to work the rope closer. All he needed was to capture the head and one foreleg.

The animal howled and scratched its free left foreleg at the air. As the saber-tooth struggled, its hindquarters suddenly went under, momentarily pulling the cat upright. As it stood there, Grand quickly tugged the noose from the pit and dropped it toward the cat. But the animal ducked and surged forward. It twisted so that it was facing the mastodon. Both forepaws were free of the pit, though one of them was soaked with tar. The cat latched onto the frame and tried to pull itself up. The mastodon began to creak.

"Jim!" Hannah cried.

Using wire cutters, two police officers made a hole in the wire fence surrounding the tar pit. Hannah immediately shouldered around them and rushed through the opening. The Wall stayed protectively close to make sure she didn't wade into the tar to try and reach Grand. Back on Wilshire, a police emergency-services truck had arrived. The officers quickly unloaded a fifty-foot life line and life ring. They also took out a pole-mounted animal noose in case the cat needed to be restrained and a sixteen-foot extension ladder that was long enough to reach from the shore to the mastodon.

The cat was thrashing about the base of the elephant. Grand spoke to the saber-tooth as quietly as possible. But the noose, and his careful maneuvering of it, only seemed to infuriate the cat. Every time he came close to slipping it over the some part of the cat it would swat and howl and sink a little lower.

Grand knew the animal was lost.

The saber-tooth's enormous paws smacked at the plaster skin, forcing Grand to jump higher. The cat roared and threw itself at the frame, furiously trying to latch onto the metal with its front claws and submerged back claws. Any time the saber-tooth managed to get a hold, the tar refused to release it. And as the cat continued to struggle, the elephant began to list. The metal frame bent near the base and the upper struts started to fold inward, outward, and around.

Grand took a last look at the cat, which was hissing and rolling its head, trying to rise. There was nothing Grand could do.

The mastodon shuddered. Quickly reeling in the rope. Grand turned toward the shore and threw the tar-blackened lariat toward the smaller of the two palms. He lassoed one of the lower branches and jumped free of the elephant just as it collapsed. He pulled himself up the rope as he swung across the pit to keep from being caught in the tar. Grand remained on his feet as he reached the shore. Hannah ran over and put her arms around him. He looked back.

The cat clawed at the wreckage but wasn't able to pull itself free. The animal sunk to its forelegs, then to its shoulders. Its struggles slowed. Grand watched, helpless, as the police came in. Two men held the animal noose but it wasn't long enough to reach the saber-tooth; they didn't even try. Then animal shook its head in a last, violent dispute with the tar. It tried to raise its forelegs but there was nothing for it to push from.

In a moment they would be gone again, this time forever.

It was a monstrous joke. He'd always blamed himself for not being with Rebecca when she died. Yet he was here when the cats died and he hadn't been able to save them. Not one. As Tumamait had told him after Rebecca's funeral, "Fate works inconsiderate of our needs and designs."

The police squad leader looked at Grand, who turned his back to the pit. The scientist hugged Hannah.

"I'm so sorry," she said.

The leader gave the order to fire. There was a short volley and then the slashing stopped.

Grand wept into Hannah's neck. She held him tightly.

77

After Grand left the pit with Hannah and the Wall, Lieutenant Mindar sought them out. The officer wanted to thank the scientist for everything he did. Grand didn't say anything about that. All he said was that he was sorry he couldn't save Sheriff Gearhart.

"Don't be sorry." Mindar said. "The sheriff died the way a man like that hopes to die. With his boots on."

"And with his work unfinished," Grand said.

"Yeah. Well, you make your choices."

The sheriff's body was taken away with those of the other victims of the saber-tooth attack. Lieutenant Mindar said he would see to it that Gearhart was brought back to Santa Barbara for burial. Before leaving, Hannah asked if she could use what Mindar had said about Gearhart as her editorial eulogy. A simple quote under a photograph of the sheriff.

Mindar said sure. Hannah felt the sheriff would have appreciated that.

As Grand, Hannah, and the Wall headed back to the car they saw scientists from the Page Museum who had come to claim the cats, while city, county, and state health officials were also at the scene with mobile laboratories to take samples of human and saber-tooth blood, to ascertain whether those who were bitten might be at risk from unknown organisms.

The Wall drove them back.

Grand and Hannah sat in the backseat. Grand didn't speak. He just looked out the open window at the night sky that was rich with stars.

Along certain stretches of the freeway, with the lights in homes and office buildings turned off, the sky barely moving as the car sped home, Hannah almost felt as though time had been rolled back. The sky was clear and the sea air smelled as it probably did millennia ago—the poor cats. They had to have been so confused. If she found herself suddenly transported to their time, Hannah wondered whether she would have wanted to stay alive. Whether she *could* have stayed alive.

Hannah looked at Grand. Yes, she decided. She would go if he were there. She took his hand. He squeezed it but he didn't take his eyes from the window, from the distant hills. Nearly an hour had passed, but he didn't move. She wondered where *he* was.

And then, suddenly, Grand looked at her.

"Do you have the geologic charts?"

"They're in the back. Why?"

"We have to go to Monte Arido."

"Now?"

"Yes," Grand said urgently.

"The National Guardsmen will still be there—"

"I know. That's why we need the charts."

"Why? What's there?"

"Something else the Chumash may have missed," he said.

78

The geologic charts of the Santa Ynez Mountains showed a different cave access. It was an eighth of a mile to the west of where the National Guardsmen were removing the last of the dead saber-tooths. The Wall drove to the foot of the hill; the cave was just twenty feet up, little more than a yard-wide opening in a white stone face.

Grand, Hannah, and the Wall got out of the photographer's Jeep and started climbing.

Grand moved up the gently sloping hillside like a wraith. He seemed to glide over the rocks, focused on a goal only he could see, and it wasn't the cave. Hannah had been around him enough to know when his mind was elsewhere. She wished he would tell her where.

Hannah and the Wall kept up with Grand as best they could. But the pair were exhausted and it was becoming increasingly difficult. Finally, after falling several yards behind Grand, Hannah stopped. So did the Wall.

Grand turned and walked back down.

"Don't," Hannah said.

He came back to her anyway.

"You go ahead," she said.

"No, I'll wait," he said. "Another few minutes won't matter."

Hannah thanked him with a smile. "Why don't you tell us what we're looking for?" she asked as she took long, slow, deep breaths.

"There were more than a dozen saber-tooths," Grand said.

"Which means?"

"The Chumash shaman only painted twelve sets of eyes."

"All right. He missed some of the cats," Hannah said. "Maybe he didn't want to get too close."

"Possibly," Grand said. "But that may not be all he missed."

"I don't follow."

"I've been trying to understand why the pride split into male and female groups," Grand said.

"You said they often hunted separately," Hannah said, "and that the females were drawn by the smell of tar."

"That may not have been the reason they came to this spot," Grand told her. "They may not have smelled asphalt until after they were here."

"Then what attracted them?"

Grand said. "That's what I want to check."

"Okay. You've got me hooked." Hannah reached her hand out to Grand. "Let's go."

Grand helped her up. They continued up the mountainside together, the Wall trudging behind.

Dawn was just beginning to brighten the horizon as they reached the small cave. Grand turned on a penlight he kept for emergencies. The cave was slightly wider than the opening and seemed to snake down. Grand crept along the rock floor and Hannah followed him on very sore knees. The Wall remained outside; even if he had the energy, he wasn't sure he'd fit. Hannah had no idea what he was looking for, though the thought nagged at her: If the Chumash missed one cat, they could easily have missed others. She didn't want to die. But the irony of dying now, when this was supposed to be over, was even worse.

The cave widened the deeper they went, until they were finally able to stand. They continued along the sloping path. When they were about two hundred yards in, Grand motioned for her to stop. She listened.

There were sounds like sobbing.

Grand hurried ahead.

The cave widened. They were finally able to stand. Grand covered the penlight with his hand and the cave was filled with a dull red glow. He moved ahead slowly, cautiously.

Then he stopped. Hannah stopped right behind him. She looked down at a writhing shape in a small nook of the cave. It took her a moment to realize what it was.

"Jim—"

"I know," Grand said. He crouched, being very careful to keep the light shielded.

Huddled in the corner were six small saber-tooths. They were about the size of small bobcats and were all golden-haired save for one, which had a silver coat. It was a male, larger than the rest. Their paws were large, out of proportion with the rest of their bodies, and their fangs were small and sharp.

Hannah crouched beside Grand.

"The cubs probably couldn't make the trip back to the tar pits without resting," Grand said. "The females looked for underground shelter and smelled tar, expecting to find prey. They stayed here to take care of the young while the males went back to La Brea."

The silver-coated cub suddenly broke from the group and walked a few steps toward the intruders. It stood looking at them and then made a sound that was a cross between a purr and a hiss.

"A little tough guy," Hannah said. She looked at Grand. "But he isn't going to stay little."

"No."

"Look at them!" she said. "Why are they here—how did you know? We should call someone at the zoo. They could house and feed the litter until a permanent sanctuary could be established."

"And then what?" Grand asked.

"I don't understand. They survive."

"As what?"

"Jim, you've lost me."

He shuffled closer to the small silver cat. It growled again and didn't back away.

"These cats are hunters," Grand said. "Put them in a zoo and they become an attraction."

"They'll also survive."

"As what?"

"As not-extinct," Hannah said. "Jim, we've been given a second chance. Look what happened to the other cats."

"I know," Grand said. He continued to stare at the bold little cat. "But you can't lock a soldier up."

"What choice do we have?"

Grand looked at her, then started back along the passageway. "There are things we'll need."

"For *what?*" Hannah pressed.

"For doing what nature may have intended when it saved them eleven thousand years ago."

79

The first thing they needed was to come back and feed the animals, which they did. Raw meat and milk. Then Grand and Hannah went back to Santa Barbara and took a short nap. Together, sleeping side by side. When they woke, word of Sheriff Gearhart's death was filtering through the town. According to charter, Chief Deputy Valentine was named Acting Sheriff. He assumed his duties in a somber ceremony outside the closed door of Gearhart's office. Hannah and the Wall were among those present.

As Hannah saw to the morning's business at the newspaper, Grand bought two large cages and padded gloves. Then he returned to the hills. He grabbed the silver-coated male and a female, caged them separately, and returned home. He left the two animals in the garage. Fluffy barked for a minute, then smelled the saber-tooth's spoor and went to the bedroom, the room farthest from the garage. Other dogs in the neighborhood also barked, but not for very long.

Grand called Dr. Honey Solomon at the Santa Barbara Zoo and told her what he'd found. Four baby saber-tooths. He told her where to find them and what she'd need to rescue them. He made her promise that they would remain at the zoo until he returned to Santa Barbara the next day. He didn't tell her where he was going. When Hannah arrived late in the afternoon, they drove to the airport.

Nothing is ever clean or final.

Not a leave-taking, not a decision, not even a death. There are compromises, sacrifices, and complications. There are unrealized hopes and unfulfilled promise. There is risk. And there are always disappointments even in victory or happiness, if only because it cannot last.

Jim Grand had learned that when Rebecca died. When he did what he believed was right and lost the close friendship of Joseph Tumamait. Perhaps that was why the Chumash believed that animals were higher than humans. Because their needs were less complex, their mission on earth clearer and more attainable. For humans, perfection could last a moment but nothing more.

This too was a compromise. But Grand felt it was a good one. The right one. Not just for the saber-tooths but for his own peace.

As Grand and Hannah flew his Piper Super Eagle seaplane north to Ross Lake in the Washington Cascades, the scientist felt renewed. He had the two saber-tooths in the back. He was going to release them into the wild, where fate and nature would care for them.

Divide and survive, just as the adult cats had done.

A special habitat would certainly be created for the animals in the zoo, as much to accommodate them as the tourists who were sure to see them. Grand was not happy about the prospect. On the other hand, he would be there to look after them. In the meantime, as the silver male and his little companion grew to adulthood they would feed on local fauna. It would be difficult for people to find them, let alone capture them. Perhaps in time the cats would create a new environmental niche in the mountains, one that couldn't be taken from them by civilization or climate. A place where an ideal balance could be established.

The seaplane landed on the lake after dusk. Grand taxied to shore, then unloaded the cages. He set the female free first. She wandered off several feet, stopped, and looked back.

He released the silver cub.

The saber-tooth male ran after the other. Without looking back, they bounded into the high grasses.

Standing on the isolated shore, Hannah took Grand's hand. There were tall western red cedars and Douglas firs moving in the warm breeze just a hundred or so yards from where they were standing. The sheer-walled mountains, higher and sharper-peaked than in Southern California, soared with stately power into the darkening sky.

"Maybe I should look into some of those Eastern faiths," Hannah said.

"What do you mean?"

"The ones you were telling me about, where all things are connected."

"Something feels whole here, doesn't it?"

Hannah nodded. "You did the right thing, Jim."

Grand felt tears pressing hard behind his eyes as he looked out at the saber-tooths' new home. He held Hannah's hand gently, caressing the backs of her fingers as he thought of the past. Of the distant past, when these creatures were frozen, and of the recent past when a part of him had died.

The cats were alive and free again.

So was Grand.

Blinking out a tear to the stars and to Rebecca, Grand turned and walked Hannah back to the plane.